PRAISE FOR *SWEET REVENGE*

"Unforgettable...This bold mix of an unlikely romance, a gritty setting, and a page-turning thriller will leave readers craving more."
—*Publishers Weekly* (starred review)

"Revenge can be sweet, smart, sexy, and make for a fast-paced, non-stop read when Archer's the storyteller. Creating heroes to die for and empowered women and bringing them together in powerful action/adventures with depth of emotion and sensuality are her forte. To readers' pleasure, she brings an amazing cast of characters, a strong plot, and romance to the first in her Nemesis, Unlimited series."   —*Romantic Times BOOKreviews*

"*Sweet Revenge* is an intense, fast-paced read. A strong plot, memorable characters, genuine emotions—not to mention plenty of heat. What more can a reader want?"
—Sherry Thomas, author of *Tempting the Bride*

"*Sweet Revenge* is a sexy, action-packed romance with a to-die-for hero and a true love that will make you swoon."
—*New York Times* bestselling author Courtney Milan

"A dark, riveting tale from beginning to end. Zoë Archer's books are not to be missed!"
—*USA Today* bestselling author Alexandra Hawkins

D0954101

WICKED
Temptation

ZOË ARCHER

St. Martin's Paperbacks

WICKED TEMPTATION

Copyright © 2014 by Zoë Archer.

All rights reserved.

For information address St. Martin's Press, 175 Fifth Avenue, New York, NY 10010.

ISBN: 978-1-250-01561-7

Printed in the United States of America

St. Martin's Paperbacks edition / June 2014

St. Martin's Paperbacks are published by St. Martin's Press, 175 Fifth Avenue, New York, NY 10010.

10 9 8 7 6 5 4 3 2 1

To Zack,
aka Nico,
aka the Man Who Can Do It All

ACKNOWLEDGMENTS

Thanks to my agent, Kevan Lyon, for her continued faith. Huge gratitude to my editor Holly Ingraham for loving Nemesis as much as I do, and Amy Goppert for getting the word out. Special thanks to Stephanie Kristen Burns, Maribeth Karns, Lynley McAlpine, and Stacy Gail, for all their knowledge and expertise. Thank you to KB Alan and Vivienne Westlake, at whose dining table much of this book was written. The world of Nemesis, Unlimited couldn't have existed without any of you.

ONE

London, 1887

Bronwyn Parrish haunted her own home. Ironic, given that she was still alive and her husband, Hugh, was chill and alone beneath the earth. It had been eight months since his death, eight lonely months, and yet only now as she drifted from empty room to empty room in her Leinster Square house did she feel the ghostliness of her widowhood. She looked down at her hands, half expecting to be able to see the marble floors through them.

But no—they remained solid. Blue veins threaded beneath the surface of her skin.

Dropping her hands, she looked around at the chamber that had once been the drawing room. It, too, was haunted. By the shadowed forms of servants, who'd at one time silently slipped in and out of the room with glasses of sherry and trays of cakes. By the specters of imported mahogany chaises, and the elegant guests who'd sat upon them and talked of society. She and Hugh had always given lovely dinner parties—everyone had said so. Afterward, she'd retire for the night feeling satisfied with her role as a wife and companion. Before he'd head to his own bedchamber, Hugh would kiss her on the cheek and murmur, "Beautifully done, sparrow."

Her sigh now echoed off bare walls. It was gone. All of it, gone. And soon, she would be gone, too.

Leaving the drawing room, she walked down the stairs that led to the ground floor. The unlit chandelier hung above the echoing foyer and the front door stood wide open. She hadn't bothered closing it after the men had come to remove the last of the furniture that morning, including her bed. She'd slept in it last night—or attempted to sleep—knowing that this was to be the last place of her own. It wasn't even hers now. But the moment she set foot outside the door, she'd have no home ever again.

She went to stand in the room that had served as her private study and practice room, and wanted to hide her eyes from the bookshelves' nudity. They gaped in forlorn dereliction. God, even her books. Nothing had been spared. She ran her hands over the shelves, saying goodbye to the room that had contained her happiest moments. This small chamber, situated at the back of the house, had been given to her by Hugh so he wouldn't have to listen to her working out the strains of Paganini's Caprice No. 24 on her violin. Hugh never objected to her playing once the piece had been mastered—in fact, he loved that his wife had so unusual a talent—but it was the learning of it that always set his nerves on edge.

But Bronwyn hadn't minded the scratches and skips, the juddering stops and wrong notes. She'd enjoyed the process as much as the end result.

In truth, she'd always nursed a secret desire to play professionally. But hadn't told anyone—it would've been a scandal if a woman with her bloodline actually chose to *work* for a living. But she would have never considered playing the violin work. Still, the idea was the same. An aristocratic woman actually earning money was a disgraceful impossibility.

When she'd encouraged Hugh to take her to concerts featuring violin solos, he'd only imagined she went to appreciate the music. He hadn't known that she used to picture herself as the soloist, a throb of envy and joy pulsing beneath her chest when she'd watched the swaying figure. That could have been her. It *should* have been her.

Instead, she'd played for dinner parties. And herself.

Would they let her play her violin? Whoever *they* were. The nameless, faceless woman or girl that she hoped might hire her as a companion.

Bronwyn patted her pocket, feeling the small fold of pound notes and a few coins that constituted the whole of her wealth. It had to be enough to last her until she found herself a situation.

A *situation*. It wasn't the work that she objected to, only that she'd never been asked to do it once in her life, not real work beyond the planning of dinner parties or organizing of charity bazaars. And here she was, lingering for a few minutes longer in her hollowed-out home, with a boardinghouse in Barnsbury waiting for her. She had enough money to last her through the month, plus the expense of taking out an advertisement in the paper, offering her services as a "woman of good breeding to oblige as companion to other women of good breeding."

Bronwyn had seen those companions. Silent, suffering, pinch-faced, and put upon as they chaperoned debutantes or accompanied single or widowed ladies of means on their travels. Not a servant. Not a friend, or equal. Something in between. A nothing. One of those "surplus women" they talked about in periodicals—mainly, wondering what was to be done about them.

That was her now. A surplus woman. Wanted by no one. Not welcome anywhere, including her sister's home.

Frieda's husband was an ass, a bully who thought no one's opinion more important than his own, and he'd made it quite clear that Bronwyn wasn't to warm herself with coal he'd purchased, nor steal roast off his plate. Even if her sister had defended Bronwyn, living with *that man* was an impossibility.

A humorless smile touched Bronwyn's lips. *At least I'd get a roof and two meals if I killed him. Until they hanged me, of course.*

Neither Hugh's father nor brother had offered to take her in. Perhaps they blamed her for his death, though all the doctors had said there had been nothing to be done once the disease had settled in his lungs. She'd been the one at Hugh's bedside when he had died, and for that, it seemed, neither the senior Mr. Parrish nor his son could forgive her.

Quickly, she strode from her former study, back down the hall, across the empty foyer, and into the front parlor, where she stared at the street. Life continued on out there. Carriages rolled by, residents and servants walked back and forth, tradesmen hurried to back entrances. None of them knew or cared about her circumstances. She'd even had to remove the black drapery from the windows and unmuffle the knocker on the front door, so no one would know that death had touched this house with its thieving hand.

Bronwyn pressed her hand to the cold glass. Her wedding band glinted in the pale sun. She'd continue wearing it until . . . at least two years. Until her proper period of mourning was over. But she might always wear it. It would make her seem more respectable. This world was all about respectability.

Though poverty trumped respectability. A widow only eight months into her first mourning would never move, never leave the house. Of course, that presupposed the widow *had* a home. Which she no longer did.

"Damn it," she whispered, allowing herself a small act of defiance by cursing. Though it was still a whisper in an empty room.

She ought to stop putting off the inevitable, and leave. There wasn't anything to be gained by lingering.

She left the parlor then lurched to a sudden stop. Her hand clapped over her mouth to muffle her startled yelp.

A man stood in the foyer. A man who'd appeared out of nowhere and made not a single sound, though her own delicate shoes tapped against the marble floor.

"Get the hell out of my house." In truth, she didn't demand this. Instead, she said stiffly, "I was given to understand by Mr. Moseby that I had until two o'clock this afternoon before I vacated the premises."

The man watched her from beneath heavy-lidded, dark eyes. He held a very fine hat in his gloved hands, and his suit was of far better quality than one might expect from a land agent's hired muscle. The stranger was also, she noted coldly, exotically handsome. Olive skinned and black haired, with a neatly trimmed goatee framing a thin but sensuous mouth.

Despite the elegance of his appearance, an air of calculation and danger clung to him, like a silk cravat wound about the neck in order to strangle someone.

When he spoke, she shivered.

"You misunderstand, Mrs. Parrish." He had a deep, husky voice. Cultured, but sounding as though he were used to speaking in dark places. "I'm not here for the house. I'm here for you."

Bronwyn took an instinctive step backward. Should she scream? All the heavy bric-a-brac in the foyer had been cleared out with the rest of the furnishings. There was nothing to use as a weapon. Nothing but her speed. Back in boarding school, she'd been a champion runner. She glanced at the space between herself and the open front door. Could she make it past this stranger before he caught her?

As if reading her thoughts, he took a step to one side, giving her an unimpeded path to the door. This alone made her pause.

"Who are you?" she demanded. Her heart beat thickly beneath her widow's weeds.

"My name's Marco," the man answered. "I'm here to help you."

She ignored his last statement. "Is Marco your first or last name?"

"First." He offered her a smile, which was perfectly white and straight and even rather coolly charming, but it didn't calm her at all. "Last names are . . . unsafe."

"Yet you know mine," she shot back.

"Naturally. We know quite a bit about you." He didn't fidget or make any extraneous movement, only continued to hold his hat in his gloved hands. "Helping you would be a more complex business if we didn't."

"*We.*" Ice climbed through her at the word. There was more than one of him, whoever this Marco was.

His dark gaze held hers. "Nemesis, Unlimited." A pause followed, as though he expected her to react.

"I've no idea what or who Nemesis, Unlimited, is," she snapped.

His lips gave a slight, rueful twist. "No, I suppose you wouldn't," he murmured half to himself.

"Get out." She pointed to the door, hoping her hand didn't shake too much and betray her.

"Your husband, Hugh Alistair Parrish, died eight months ago from consumption," the stranger Marco said, quickly but in a low voice, as if reciting the result of a parliamentary vote. "He caught it after a trip to inspect a Glasgow cotton mill. It took three months for the doctors to finally reach a diagnosis. You went to the spa at Amélie-les-Bains to get a cure, but nothing worked, and he died with you at his side. The room had white curtains and blue-flowered wallpaper."

Nausea swamped her. These were facts no one but she herself knew.

Yet Marco continued, relentless. "When you finally returned home after burying him, you discovered that your money—including the portion you brought with your marriage—was completely gone. So you approached his financial agent and executor, one Edgar Devere. But Devere told you Hugh had died in arrears."

He quieted for a moment as someone passed by on the sidewalk outside. Once the pedestrian moved on, Marco continued. "Hugh's bank accounts were emptied and all of his liquid assets—including this house—were used to repay his debts. All your finances were tied up with your late husband's. It's been difficult to retrieve your lost fortune because of your widowhood. Everyone you've spoken with, all the attorneys and advisors, have told you the same thing." He drew a slow breath. "You're destitute and no one can get you back your money."

"How . . . how . . ." was all she could manage. Her head spun, and she walked backward, until she collided with the wall. It took all of her strength and lessons in etiquette to keep from sliding to the floor.

She'd tried so hard to keep all these sordid facts from being known. Hugh was the son of a baron's youngest son, and the family name meant everything. Scandal would follow like a relentless hound if anyone learned that her husband had died insolvent, but it was Hugh and his mortification from beyond the grave that had had her work intensely to prevent these details from being made public. To all of their acquaintances, she'd said only that she'd put everything into storage, and planned on staying with her sister in the country for an indefinite time.

"You're a reporter," she accused.

The cursed man had the nerve to chuckle. "I've been called many an insult, but never that one."

"Then how can you know any of that?" Not only the details of her financial disaster, but the color of the flowers on the wallpaper in the hotel room where Hugh had died.

"I'm here to help," he repeated.

"I don't see how or why," she snapped. Fear, exhaustion, and a dozen other emotions shortened her temper.

"There's a tea shop on Edgware Road." He gestured toward the door. "Come with me there, and everything will be explained."

She raised a brow. "Is this what's become of the world, then? Penniless widows are the latest prey. And here I'd thought that white slavery was a myth to keep girls and women from leaving their homes."

Any lingering signs of humor left his face immediately. "Slavery continues to exist. In many forms. But in this instance, Mrs. Parrish, there aren't any plans to spirit you away to some dockside brothel or sell you to an opium lord in China."

"What a blessed relief." Though it was considered crude, she crossed her arms over her chest. "Unless you plan on dragging me bodily out the door, I'm not going anywhere with you, *Marco*."

He had the audacity to give her a slow, deliberate perusal, from the hem of her bombazine gown to the top of her head. Since she was home, she didn't have to wear her widow's bonnet and veil, and she fought the old self-conscious urge to cover her coppery hair with the flat of her hand.

His look wasn't salacious, however, and he didn't seem

to care that she had unfashionably red hair. All he said was, "You'd be a slight burden to carry."

Heat crept into her cheeks. She'd lost weight over the course of Hugh's long battle with consumption, and since returning home, she'd only been able to afford two meals a day, neither of them lavish. "And you are nothing but impudence."

"Waiting for us at the tea shop are an associate of mine, and Miss Lucy Nelson."

Bronwyn pushed away from the wall with a surge of anger. "If you've hurt Lucy—"

"Miss Nelson is as safe as a guinea in the national treasury. She was the one who sent me here."

Confusion thickly clouded Bronwyn's mind. "Why would my former maid contact you?"

The inscrutable man seemed to lose the smallest thread of patience. His jaw tightened. Just a little. "Because, as I've said twice before, I'm here to help."

"Lucy should have come here, herself."

"She wanted to, but the house is being watched, and I didn't want to attract too much attention. Don't go to the windows."

Bronwyn stopped in the act of doing just that. "Moseby's men?"

"The same. They're on the alert that if you make what appears to be an attempt to retain possession of the house, they are authorized to use force."

She swallowed hard. Dear God, what sort of man was this Moseby, that he'd use violence against a woman? "They wouldn't." But her voice didn't sound especially confident.

"I know Moseby," Marco answered, "and he most certainly would."

Pressing a hand to her mouth, she wondered what had become of her life. It had turned bleak and squalid in a matter of months. She was a gentleman's daughter. These kinds of things happened only in periodicals full of exciting, lurid stories. Now here she was, just like one of those women in the stories. Except this was truly happening, not a work of fiction.

Marco turned one palm up. "Come with me. Fifteen minutes of your time simply to listen. And if you don't like what you hear, then I'll be happy to pay for your cab fare to the boardinghouse in Barnsbury."

Of course he'd know her intended destination. But then, he had Lucy to tell him everything. Bronwyn had *trusted* Lucy. Why would her maid—a woman she'd known for six years—betray her like this? Unless Lucy, and these Nemesis people, truly did want to help her. Why? At this point, it didn't much matter. She'd already reached her nadir at the age of twenty-eight. Anything would be an improvement.

"My bags are in my room," she said.

"I'll wait while you fetch them."

Her life truly had altered utterly when a man expected her to retrieve her own luggage. Perhaps that was for the best. She'd played by all the rules of society and good breeding, yet here she was, in an empty house, without a groat, reliant on the word of a handsome but questionable man. Clearly, those rules served no purpose, offered no safety.

Without another word, she turned and walked up the stairs. She felt Marco's gaze on her with every step, and it filled her with a strange, unpleasant awareness.

In her former bedchamber, she collected her baggage: one valise, and her violin case. The instrument, at least, she'd been able to save, and she thanked the Lord for that. If she'd been deprived of her music, her despair would've known no limits.

She returned to the foyer. To her surprise, Marco actually took her valise and case. Testing the weight of the violin case, he asked, "Chanot? A Georges Chanot, I'd wager."

She stared at him. "Lucy must've told you that."

"All violins have their own particular weight and balance, depending on the maker. Easy enough to determine this was a Chanot, once I got a hold of it." He stuck out his arm, offering it to her. "Time to go."

"One moment." After pulling on her cloak, she tugged on a pair of gloves, set her widow's bonnet on her head, and pulled down the veil. The world suddenly misted over, as if loss and grief didn't do that already without a layer of silk covering her face.

She placed her hand lightly in the crook of his arm. Despite her gloves, despite the layers of his clothing, she felt the solidity of him, and the unyielding presence of his muscles.

Heat washed through her.

She cursed herself. What in heaven did she think she was doing? How could she have any feelings of that sort, with Hugh only eight months gone, and this Marco a complete stranger? Disgust clotted in her veins. Disgust with herself.

Glancing up at him, she noticed the slightest compressing of his lips. As if he, too, felt something at her touch.

Saints strike her down for these delusions. Her life was falling down around her like a sinking ship, and she wanted, no, *needed,* to reach a shore. Any shore, no matter how rocky,

"I'm ready," she said.

Marco Black kept his gaze on the street, alert for any sign of suspect movement. The men watching the house shifted from their slouch against a street lamp, but didn't follow them. A bloody relief. He didn't want to have to get into any discreet brawls this early in the game.

His attention wasn't entirely fixed on his surroundings. A small sliver remained for the woman walking beside him.

It was his job—both for Nemesis and for his other work as what was euphemistically termed an intelligence advisor to the British government—to clearly and objectively assess people within moments of meeting them. He'd been able to determine within minutes that a Russian ambassador's wife had been using her considerable beauty to gain information about the latest developments in Chitral.

Thus far, Bronwyn Parrish seemed to be exactly what the dossier they'd compiled had delineated. Her impeccable posture came from years of schooling on the Continent, which also contributed to the sheltered expression on her face. It was a pretty face, to be sure. Smooth skinned, though with a few rose-hued freckles across the bridge of her nose, her lips nearly the same color as her freckles. And eyes the silver green of sage leaves. Eyes that gleamed with a surprising intelligence.

Those eyes were hidden now behind her veil. She kept glancing around the street, gauging it. Mrs. Parrish had potential, but she was a woman born and bred to a class that had little use for females who could think for themselves. He didn't know to what end she'd use that intelligence of hers.

He hadn't wanted to take this job on at all. Nemesis was for the powerless, the poor, not society widows with dead spendthrift husbands. Nemesis wasn't for the upper echelons at all—not if he had any say in it.

Entitlement was a poison, infecting a whole class. Her class. He should know.

But he'd been voted down by the other agents. Worse still, he'd been given the lead on the mission since he was the one operative with enough free time to take on the case.

Yet he was a professional in all capacities. He might not want this job, but once assigned to it, he'd do his damnedest to make sure it succeeded.

They emerged onto Bayswater Road, with the broad green expanse of Hyde Park just on the other side of the street. Beneath a watery early spring sun, nannies pushed their infant charges in expensive prams, and a few impeccably dressed women strolled along the paths. One or two gave him a second glance, but he ignored them.

He liked to break everything down into specific components, goals that needed to be met one at a time. In that way, even the most difficult mission became possible. And right now, he had to escort the Widow Parrish to the Cottage Rose Tea Shop.

He hailed a carriage, but Mrs. Parrish hesitated before stepping into it.

"Easy to see why you're mistrustful," he said, holding the door. "Your husband had the bad manners to die in debt, leaving you to fend for yourself when you haven't done it before. Your finances gutted. Your home taken. And then there's me, a bloke you've never met, claiming to be here to help. Why should you trust me? What's to say that this carriage won't speed you to the docks, or into the clutches of some procurer?"

Though he couldn't be sure, he suspected she raised an eyebrow. "My goodness, you certainly know how to inspire faith."

"Ask yourself this," he continued. "Why would I go out of my way to abduct you, when it's all too easy for women in this city to be preyed upon? Would I really show up at your home and tell you in detail things that no one else knows just to fill a bed in some whore-house?"

She reared back a little at his candid language. *Maledizione,* he was going to have to learn to curb his vocabulary around her. He wasn't used to being around women of her class. Women who found an innocuous word like *whorehouse* offensive, even though London had hundreds, no, thousands of them.

But she didn't run. Instead, she tilted her head as if contemplating what he'd said.

Then she took his offered hand and stepped into the hired carriage.

Damn, that wasn't the first time she'd caught him off guard with her courage. There might be more to the Widow Parrish than he'd initially deduced—an unpleasant thought. Something about her, something he couldn't name or yet understand, took the careful wiring of his brain and rearranged those wires.

There was . . . a need in her. A desire for something other than the emptiness within.

No. People of her station weren't like that. He had too much experience with their vapidity, their casual cruelty, to think that, aside from some superficial differences, she wasn't just like the others. No matter her prettiness or the glint of intelligence in her eyes.

He was a man, yes, but he preferred to think of himself as a mechanism: expertly calibrated, created specifically for its task. In need of occasional lubrication. Always reliable.

He got into the cab and signaled the driver to move on. The ride to Edgware Road was made wordlessly, thank God. She didn't press him with questions, or chatter nervously. Mrs. Parrish seemed to understand the value of silence. Though she did have a pleasant voice, musical but strong. She probably used it only to be heard above the crowd at a party, or to complain to her dressmaker.

As the streets rolled by, he glanced at her violin case. If Lucy Nelson hadn't told him her mistress played, and played well, by all accounts, he wouldn't have anticipated that, either. Most patrician women favored the piano. Violin required a bit more . . . boldness. More passion than gentlemen's daughters cared to show.

When she'd taken his arm, he'd felt it in her—a kind of hollowness, a demand for *something*. As if looking at the world through eyes that truly saw and assessed, rather than existing in a cloud of privilege. And that awareness had drawn on him, pulling him in despite himself.

It had to be an illusion. He'd encountered enough of them in his life. Perpetrated them, too.

The carriage came to a stop, and the driver called down that they'd arrived. After grabbing her valise, Marco stepped out then handed Mrs. Parrish down to the curb. She carried her violin case herself. He watched her take in the storefront, with its inexpensive lace curtains hanging in the windows. "I cannot pay for the cab."

"Taken care of," he answered, handing the driver a coin. Then he opened the door to the Cottage Rose and waved her in. "I know you have questions, and they'll all be answered."

"In fifteen minutes," she said.

"Good memory." One of his most valuable assets was his memory. Pursuing a career in espionage was damned difficult if you didn't possess an unusual ability for recollection. How else would he know the difference between a Chanot and a Cousineau violin, if he hadn't practiced hefting different instruments in their cases? You never knew when such a skill might be needed, either.

If she smiled, he couldn't see it beneath her veil. Instead, she swept past him and into the shop. It smelled of bergamot and sugar inside. Women clustered around slightly battered oak tables, cups of tea held between their fingers, and picked at platters of iced cakes.

The hostess bustled forward. "They're in the back," she said.

"Thank you, Mrs. Akeem."

"Of course, Marco."

As he threaded his way down a narrow corridor rife with china, the widow finally spoke. "I'd figure you for the sort of man who favors public houses rather than tea shops."

"Public houses serve the worst wine," he answered. "When it's libation I want, I've got my own favored establishments. Ones that know the consequence of a good Barolo. And Mrs. Akeem is always welcoming to Nemesis. Ever since we helped her chase off the bigoted idiots who didn't want a woman of her nationality opening a business in this area."

She was silent for a moment. Then, "I prefer Chianti to Barolo."

Another surprise from Mrs. Parrish. He wondered what others were to come.

"Oh, madam!" The moment Mrs. Parrish stepped into the private room at the tea shop, a small, curvaceous woman rushed forward, tears gleaming in her eyes. Lucy Nelson managed to stop herself from embracing her former mistress. Instead, she wrung her hands and cast Mrs. Parrish sorrowful glances.

Marco watched as the widow pulled back her veil, revealing her face like the last act of a play. "What in heaven's name is going on, Lucy? Who are these people?" Her gaze fell on the other occupant of the private room.

"I'm Harriet." Harriet Bradley came forward with her hand outstretched, and Mrs. Parrish was too polite to refuse to shake.

"No last name for you, either, I suppose," Mrs. Parrish said.

"It's an issue of protection," Harriet explained. "Everyone's protection."

"I keep being told that withholding information is a matter of safety," Mrs. Parrish answered. "Yet I always believed that knowing more is the path of greatest security."

Marco moved past her, and offered her a chair—he might not have wanted this assignment, but he still possessed manners. Three other chairs were arranged around a table that held cups and a pot of tea. Fashion prints lined the floral walls, and lamps with painted china bases and frosted glass were also mounted around the room. Given that Marco was the only man in the chamber, he was grateful feminine spaces didn't make him uncomfortable.

"You didn't learn that at your boarding school," he said, offering her a seat.

"French, dancing, music, drawing—though my efforts were appalling." She eyed him and the chair as if certain they were baited traps. Not so easily led, this widow.

"Oh, madam, please do sit," Lucy said imploringly. "I swear on my mother's thimble that these people mean you no harm."

A thimble seemed an insignificant thing to swear upon, but for some reason, it satisfied Mrs. Parrish. She removed her cloak and took the seat Marco offered, though not without sending him one last wary glance over her shoulder.

Eager to do her former mistress more service, Lucy took Mrs. Parrish's cloak and bonnet and set them aside. Once Harriet and Lucy had sat, Marco at last allowed himself to settle into a chair.

Mrs. Parrish immediately poured the tea, her movements practiced and graceful. This was what she'd been born and reared to do: serve as hostess, no matter the time or place. She still looked cagey, but that didn't stop her from inquiring politely as to whether Marco took milk or sugar in his tea.

His half-Italian blood demanded coffee—espresso would have been ambrosia from Jove's cup—but that drink wasn't easy to come by here in England, and when he did get a cup, it tasted more of the river Thames than anything someone would want to drink. But he took the tea Mrs. Parrish offered, noting her tiny flinch when their fingers brushed against each other.

With all the social niceties out of the way, she turned to her maid. "I've spent the last hour in a state of confusion. And I never would have agreed to come to this place if Mr. . . . Marco hadn't told me you were here. Now it's time for you to explain what, exactly, is happening."

"It's about doing a good turn, madam," Lucy answered. "You did one for me, more than once. When you gave my sister Martine a job, even though she'd had a babe, and no father to claim the child."

Mrs. Parrish frowned. "Was I to let her and her baby starve?"

"Most would," Marco said. "A scandal like that, under your own roof."

"There was no scandal," the widow replied heatedly. "Only a woman who'd been used and abandoned, and in need of help."

Harriet glanced at Marco. "I think I rather like her."

He might, as well—a surprise—but he always reserved judgment.

"And Christopher Peele, the footman?" Lucy pressed. "You loaned him some of your allowance so he could open a shop."

"It was a pittance," Mrs. Parrish protested.

"Not to him," her maid countered.

"It seems you're a wellspring of kindness, Mrs. Parrish," Marco drawled, though in truth, he did find her acts of generosity intriguing. On the rough streets of East London or in the slums of Rome, people looked out for one another, especially since the rest of the world had turned its collective backs on them. But as former missionary Eva Dutton, née Warrick, had explained, the wealthy might throw money at a problem, yet when it came to doing actual good, their delicate hands were never truly dirtied.

"You've helped so many," Lucy went on, her eyes full of sympathy, "and now it's time for you to be helped."

A brief flicker of shame crossed Mrs. Parrish's face. Clearly, she didn't care to be pitied. Marco couldn't blame her.

The maid continued. "I knew about Nemesis, and what they did, and so I contacted them to see if anything could be done for you." She looked expectantly at Mrs. Parrish, as if anticipating her to understand what this meant, but she was met only with a puzzled frown.

"She wouldn't know of us," Marco said gently.

"Her kind seldom do," added Harriet.

"My *kind*?" Mrs. Parrish exclaimed.

Marco faced her. "England's favored children. The wealthy. The powerful. Those whose pockets burst with privilege. Nemesis usually finds themselves in opposition to them," he added.

A bitter laugh burst from Mrs. Parrish. "I'm none of those things."

"Once you were." And might be again. "Not Nemesis's typical client." He still didn't like it, but he'd had to yield to the will of the group, and do his job with his usual efficiency.

Marco took a sip of tea. It hadn't magically transformed into coffee. All the while, an invisible, silent clock ticked down the moments before the trail of Mrs. Parrish's fortune went cold.

"You keep speaking of this Nemesis," she said, "but I still don't know a blasted thing about it."

Though he could hold himself perfectly still for hours, Marco found a strange restlessness beneath his skin when he was in the presence of Mrs. Parrish. As if her silver-green gaze held an electrical charge, jolting him into motion. That *wanting* in her. These odd sensations had to be simply a function of the fact that he didn't want this job. There were other missions that could make better use of his abilities.

He pushed back from the table and crossed to the small fireplace at the other side of the room.

He braced his hands on the mantel. "You've had a taste of the cruelty of this world, Mrs. Parrish. It's a bitter and noisome taste, but it's far more predominant than sugar and the metallic flavor of money." Turning, he held her gaze with his own. "Every day, all over this city, all over our majestic nation, men, women, and children are being hurt, abused, or exploited."

"And not one of them can get justice for themselves," Harriet interjected.

"But . . . the law . . ." Mrs. Parrish murmured.

"Favors the wealthy and powerful," Marco said. "Not a miner, or a child forced to make cheap jewelry. People who will not be heard, and have no one to speak for them. Exactly the way the elite want them. That's why Nemesis exists." He planted his hands on his hips. "To give a voice to the voiceless. To get justice for those who need it. By any means necessary."

The widow's eyes went round. "You cannot be serious."

"Observe my hilarity," he answered grimly.

Mrs. Parrish glanced from Harriet to Lucy. "That's . . . that's extraordinary."

"But true," Lucy said. "Nemesis even gets girls off the streets." She swallowed hard. "Girls like me."

If Mrs. Parrish looked astonished before, now she appeared stunned, her mouth hanging open and all the color draining from her face. "Lucy? You were a . . ."

Tears glittered in the maid's eyes. "Not much choice for a girl from Whitechapel, is there?" As she spoke, her accent changed, roughened into the harder tones of the East End. "And me with a sister to support, and my mum dead. But Nemesis found me, got me a decent place to sleep, taught me how to speak proper and dress ladies."

"I had no idea." Though it likely went against all her training, Mrs. Parrish slumped in her chair—as much as her rigid corset would allow. "You never said anything."

"And risk losing my position?" Lucy shook her head. "You'd been kind to me and Martine, but I couldn't trust you to know that I used to be a whore."

Mrs. Parrish flinched at the word. "I wish . . ."

Marco narrowed his eyes. What would she say? Would she be disgusted? Condemning? Everyone in the room seemed to wait for her reaction, not just Lucy, but Harriet and himself, as well.

"I wish," Mrs. Parrish continued, "you'd told me sooner."

"So you could fire her and let all your friends know not to hire her?" Marco asked.

"So I could have done more to help," the widow said angrily. "If there were other girls she'd known back then, and they wanted characters, or at least a place to start. I'm glad, though, that you were able to make a better life for yourself."

Lucy suddenly covered her face with her hands and burst into tears.

Mystified, Mrs. Parrish looked at him.

"As I said," Marco explained, "this is a hard, rough world. It devours girls like Lucy every day. That's why kindness is so hard to accept. It's a word we all know, but almost never experience. And that's how I came to be at your former home today, Mrs. Parrish."

He crossed the room to stand beside her chair. She looked up at him, her lips pursed in a question.

"We've taken down the most powerful men in England," he said. "Fought corporate corruption—and won."

"You sound superhuman," she said.

He'd helped dozens, scores of people before, but no one like her. Certainly not of her social class. And few individuals, regardless of their caste, had her edged awareness. It made him . . . restless. Couldn't she be an empty-headed ninny? Annoying as that might be, it'd make it easier to figure her out.

"We're only people," he said. "But when we have a goal, nothing stops us. And now, Nemesis is going to get you your money back."

TWO

She'd never attended a more bizarre tea party. Certainly not one that involved her former maid—who was once a prostitute—as well as a handsome, middle-aged woman of mixed white and Negro blood, and a man who reminded her of a beautiful knife, all gathered together in the back room of a clean but modest tea shop.

The claims that these three people made were at worst outrageous. At best, they inspired false hope.

"I'm one of the other *kind*," she said. "A society widow. Not a girl on the street, or a laborer. Why would this Nemesis bother with someone like me?"

Marco thankfully stepped away from standing beside her chair and strode back to the fireplace. It was all she could do not to shrink into herself when he was so close. He sent a pointed look in Harriet's direction.

"If *anyone* needs help and has no recourse," the woman said, "Nemesis is there." A corner of her mouth tilted. "And from what Lucy's told us, you aren't typical of your social rank. You're one of the good ones, the ones who take action instead of sitting idle. There are too few like you. You help others, and in turn, those that have benefited from your assistance lend a hand when it's needed. And if we help you, you'll continue with your generosity."

"Assuming that I carry on with my altruistic ways," she noted.

"You might stop," Harriet said. "However, as I said, you aren't like other people of your status."

"I ought to feel insulted on behalf of my class."

"Don't be."

She glanced over at Marco. He rested his hands behind him on the mantel, and the fabric of his coat stretched tight against his shoulders and arms. She was unhappy to discover that the shoulders of his coat were not padded, but instead clung to hard, curved muscles. He wasn't a young man, Marco, nor especially tall, but he moved with an athleticism that most sportsmen would envy.

Hugh had been an avid horseman and even visited a gentlemen's gymnasium in Chelsea, yet he hadn't looked as though his very body was a weapon. Marco's physicality was palpable, intimidating.

"Well, I don't feel flattered," she replied.

"That's not our intention," Marco said.

"Your intention being to retrieve my lost fortune." She shook her head. "If that's so, then I'm sorry to disappoint all of you, but there's nothing to be done. The money's gone, and as of today, so is my house. The task is impossible."

She had the impression that Marco smiled, even as his mouth remained a firm line. "Nemesis thrives on the impossible."

Turning back to Harriet, Bronwyn said, "You seem like a reasonable, rational woman. These claims cannot possibly be true, can they?"

"True as Nelson's Column," the older woman answered.

"But if we're to have any hope of succeeding," Marco

added, "we need to put our plans into motion, and soon. It's been eight months since you lost your money."

"To Hugh's debts," Bronwyn added bitterly.

"Or so Devere says," Marco said.

"Could he be lying about that?"

Marco made a careless shrug, a quintessentially Italian gesture of noncommitment. "No way to know unless we talk to the man himself. What I do know is that each moment that passes, the tougher our job becomes to get your money back."

"We ought to discuss our strategy with the others," Harriet said.

Bronwyn's heart pounded. This couldn't actually be happening—could it? These people, what they proposed. It was all madness. Nothing could come of it but wasted effort. She should just collect her bag and violin, use one of her precious coins to hire a cab to take her to the boardinghouse, and place the advertisement for her services as a hired companion. That would be the safe, wise thing to do.

But she'd been safe and wise. She'd married the man of her father's choosing, and while she'd had little cause for complaint during the marriage itself, when her husband had died, she'd become a pauper. In order to recover her lost fortune, she'd followed the dictates for mourning and communicated with solicitors only through correspondence—and even that was slightly improper. All that had netted her were very polite letters back insisting that there wasn't anything to be done but make the best of an unfortunate situation.

An unfortunate situation. That's what wisdom and safety had netted her. A debt-ridden dead husband, with nothing left for her but a boardinghouse and advertisements in the newspaper.

Becoming a hired companion to a debutante or wealthy widow had no time limit. Such situations would always exist. But if Marco was to be believed, each time the sun set over Notting Hill, she was that much further away from independence. Soon, her fate would be unavoidable, and she'd fade like wallpaper, until there was nothing left of her but an echo of a pattern, sun-bleached and peeling.

"Mrs. Parrish," Marco said to her, "Nemesis is a train that doesn't stop until it reaches its destination. Once we begin, there's no pulling the brake." He stepped away from the mantel. "No disembarkation at stations if the ride becomes too bumpy. Too much is at stake for our agents to start a mission and abandon it halfway."

Harriet nodded in agreement.

"I've got a strong suspicion," he continued, "that there's more to your husband's debts and Devere's involvement with them than what's readily apparent. And whatever that might be, it will come with a substantial danger." He fixed her with his sharp, dark gaze. "This is the moment of your decision. Go forward on this risky path, or not at all."

Her heart now threatened to rip right from her body and leave a dark, wet stain on the front of her weeds. Never did she imagine, when she ate her dry toast and drank her reboiled tea this morning, that by midday, she'd find herself in the midst of a secret society, or that she'd even consider their scandalous, treacherous proposition.

Could she do this? Fear formed a cold vise around her throat. Neither path was exactly what she'd choose for herself. Still, she did have a choice to make, one that was hers alone.

"When do we start?" she asked.

His expression didn't change. Yet something in his weathered, chiseled face seemed to alter. Turning from wariness to . . . a grudging respect. A flare of pleasure spread through her. He appeared to be a man who doled out his esteem with a parsimonious hand. But she had earned some of it just now.

"Immediately," he answered.

Nothing could be accomplished without first speaking with Devere, or so Marco insisted. But all of Bronwyn's letters to him had gone unanswered, and in her widowed state, it was impossible for her to actually go to his offices.

"We'll find a way in." Marco's tone was utterly confident. "First, we've got to get you situated."

"The boardinghouse . . ."

He shook his head. "Too far, and no respectable boardinghouse keeper is going to approve of what we'll be doing."

Bronwyn didn't care for the sound of that.

"Take her from here"—Harriet glanced around at the tea shop's private room—"to headquarters?"

"The safest option," he answered.

"Haven't I got a say in this?" Bronwyn interjected.

"Of course," he replied. "But if you're intelligent, you'll do what we say, when we say it."

"Sounds rather like being married," she muttered, and both Harriet and Lucy snickered.

He crossed his arms over his lean chest. "Consider it as a marriage of convenience. Close your eyes and think of England. Better yet, think of your money."

"This isn't about my fortune," she objected, standing.

He raised a brow.

"Well, it *is* about my fortune," she said. "But I swear to you, my motives aren't mercenary. I just . . ." She glanced around the room, barely seeing its tidy but worn furnishings. "I've been dependent on others my entire life. My father. Then Hugh. And without my money, I'll be dependent again—this time on people I don't know, people who truly don't care what happens to me. I'll be a . . . a thing to them."

"You're not a thing, madam!" Lucy insisted.

"That's exactly what I am. Something that's useful, until I'm not." She struggled to sort through her thoughts, like picking out notes from a cacophony to make a melody. "Then what? My boarding school was the best on the Continent. For all that . . . what did I learn? Not a blessed thing about making my way in the world. But having some coin in my coffers . . . then I'd have some say in my future, in my life. I could . . . I could be in command of myself. For the first time."

She gulped for breath, shocked at the words that had spilled forth—an untapped spring, bubbling to the surface. How long had they been trapped, needing to come out, until this very moment? In front of two strangers and her former maid?

It felt odd to speak so freely, when all her life she'd never even thought she'd have the right. *No one wants to hear your opinions,* her deportment teacher had instructed. *It's vulgar to speak your thoughts.*

Bronwyn had taken those lessons to heart, and since then had carefully erased her ideas from her mind, so she'd never be tempted to say them aloud. Things like her desire to play violin professionally rather than become someone's decorative wife. Yet in this shop, with these people, she hadn't tried to stop herself.

She waited. Any moment now, shock or revulsion would appear on the others' faces.

But none came. Only nods of approval from Harriet and Lucy. Marco remained impassive. He and Harriet exchanged glances. The older woman slowly smiled. Turning back to Bronwyn, she said, "You don't know me, nor

I you. But we're both women, and women who aren't given the consideration we deserve. Trust me right now. Going to headquarters is the best choice for you."

"Do I *have* a choice?"

"Of course," she answered. "But this isn't our first mission. You'd be wise to benefit from our experience."

Beyond Bronwyn's world of afternoon teas, charity bazaars, and balls, she herself had very little experience with the world. She'd nursed her husband through a fatal illness, but that consisted mainly of reading to him and catching his coughed-up blood in a handkerchief or basin. The doctors had dismissed her suggestions immediately. She hadn't even left the grounds of the spa because she'd been warned that pickpockets preyed upon travelers.

God, what kind of world birthed generations of women who could do almost nothing for themselves but make sure they could plan and dress for a dinner party?

This was her choice. Her first step on her own.

"If time is short," she said, "then we ought to leave immediately."

Lucy stood and, in what looked like an impulsive move, took Bronwyn's hands in hers. "I'm so glad, madam."

"Thank you, Lucy. For everything. I hope your new situation is good."

Her former maid beamed. "I'm dressing an earl's daughter!"

"Quite a rise in station," Bronwyn said wryly.

The smile fell away from Lucy's face. "My new mistress is kind, but . . . she isn't you."

For the first time since Hugh's death, tears pricked Bronwyn's eyes. "Thank you."

Suddenly, Marco was beside her. He carried her valise and her violin case. She blinked in surprise, not having heard or seen him move. She ought to expect that from him. He was a man, solid and real, but there was a part of him made up of secrets and shadowed corners holding unknown dangers.

"We need to move quickly," he said.

In moments, Bronwyn was bustled outside and into a waiting cab. Harriet and Marco climbed in after her, and Lucy stood on the curb, waving them off.

They traveled in silence, rolling through the streets of London, into decidedly working-class neighborhoods. The buildings stood close and were streaked by soot. The avenues themselves teemed with people and carts, all of them hurrying to unknown but clearly important destinations.

She'd never been to these parts of the city. They were rather . . . grim. Ugly. But then she saw a woman carrying a basket of bread. A man played with a child on the front stoop of his house, tossing a ball back and forth. For all that they weren't the prettiest parts of London, there was life in them.

Astonishing, the size and variety of this city. Her repulsion slowly fell away, in crumbling pieces, until she had to fight the urge to press her face to the window and stare, taking everything in.

The cab pulled up outside a chemist's in Clerkenwell, and Harriet and Marco stepped down from the carriage and waited for her.

"Is someone ill?" she asked.

Marco scowled. "Society." With that, he entered the chemist's shop. Clearly, Bronwyn was expected to follow.

Inside, a man in the apron of his profession waited on a customer, filling the woman's order for toothache powder. There were no other patrons in the shop.

"It'll be just a moment, sir," the chemist called to Marco.

Baffled, Bronwyn wandered around the shop, looking

at the numerous bottles of medicine and health tonics displayed on the shelves and in glass cases. They promised every sort of cure, from dyspepsia to catarrh to nervous despondency. She was well familiar with chemists' shops, having frequented several when Hugh first became ill. The brass fittings in this one didn't shine as brightly, and the wooden cabinets were worn and in need of polishing, but it didn't seem to matter whether the patrons were wealthy or working-class—everyone's bodies were fragile and subject to the whims of sickness.

Finally, the woman with the aching tooth left the shop. But instead of assisting Marco, the chemist glanced around the store as if ensuring it was empty. His hand drifted beneath the counter. There was a click, and Bronwyn watched with silent amazement as one of the cabinets swung open, revealing a narrow staircase.

"*Grazie,* Mr. Byrne," Marco murmured.

Harriet climbed the stairs, but Bronwyn hesitated. What was she supposed to do?

"This way, Mrs. Parrish." Marco waved her toward the staircase.

She sent a curious glance toward the chemist, who regarded her with an equal measure of curiosity, his gaze lingering on her weeds. Given the nature of the neighborhood, the quality of her clothing—even in mourning—stood out. But the dress she wore was the only one she had left. Everything else had been sold. The woman with the toothache likely had more clothing than Bronwyn.

She ascended the narrow, dark stairs. She felt Marco's presence behind her. Instinct told her not to look over her shoulder, but to just keep climbing.

A battered door stood at the top of the stairwell. Harriet rapped her fist against it in a pattern of knocks.

At her knock, the door swung open, and the burly form of a man blocked most of the light behind him.

"This her, then?" he asked in a slightly rough accent.

"And a very good afternoon to you, Lazarus," Harriet answered crisply. "Your manners haven't improved since we've been gone."

"This isn't a salon, is it, Harridan?" the man retorted.

"If it was, you'd be thrown out by the footmen."

Marco rumbled, "Lazarus, let us in, damn it."

The burly man stepped aside, muttering, and Bronwyn followed Harriet into a very ordinary walk-up flat. The door opened to a parlor, at the center of which was a large, worn wooden table. Beyond the parlor lay a small kitchen. Leading off the parlor was a flight of stairs. Curtained windows that fronted the street let in gray afternoon light. Aside from the mass of dossiers and papers on the parlor table, it was a singularly unimpressive room.

She took a few steps inside and turned a slow circle, taking in her surroundings. "For all Lucy's talk, I would've thought Nemesis's headquarters would have boasted marble columns and war rooms to rival the cabinet."

"Nemesis operates in a pro bono capacity," Harriet explained.

"This isn't a moneymaking operation," growled Lazarus around the stem of a clay pipe. He had a salt-and-pepper beard, and carried himself like an old soldier. "Otherwise, we'd be damned foolish businessmen."

For some reason, Bronwyn found herself turning to Marco for confirmation. "But I thought, when you said you didn't take up causes for people like me, it meant . . ." Her cheeks heated.

"That this time we're doing it for a percentage because you'd have the cash to cover it." He set her bags down. "Wouldn't be very fair of us if we treated you differently than our other clients." He said this almost grudgingly.

"Fairness never entered my mind," she answered.

"Why should it," Harriet said, "when you haven't been treated fairly?"

"But all this grandeur"—Marco waved at the modest chamber—"is financed out of Nemesis agents' own pockets."

She stared at him, shocked. These people couldn't possibly be real, bankrolling justice for its own sake. "There can't be very many of you, then."

He chuckled, a sound like the pouring of a rich, dark wine into fine crystal, then cut his laughter short. "Never enough."

"Some are on assignment right now," Harriet said. "Desmond and Riza just came back from a mission that took them to the United States—you'll meet them later."

Her mind whirled. This world was so new, so hidden. How could she have ever known of it? And yet, like a receding tide, it became revealed.

"Your work is pro bono," she said, "yet I can't imagine what kind of outside employment you'd have to keep the Nemesis coffers full. Perhaps you're bank robbers."

Lazarus chortled. "We stay on the side of the law. Usually."

"Usually?"

"It's true that we all have jobs beyond Nemesis," Harriet said, ignoring Bronwyn's alarmed demand. "Jobs where no one knows anything about this."

"None of you sit behind a desk," Bronwyn said. "It seems so mundane."

"Few of us do," Marco replied.

What did he do outside of Nemesis? Of the three agents she'd met, he seemed the least likely to lead a quotidian existence. Would he go to some offices, remove his hat and coat and put them on hooks, then go through number-filled ledgers, go out to a chophouse for luncheon, then return back to work and yawn through the afternoon? The idea felt so ludicrous, she dismissed it at once.

However Marco lined his pockets when not helping penniless widows, it certainly couldn't entail anything so commonplace. What might suit him? What did he *do*?

An urge pressed upon her, demanding to know. Who he was—really. She'd never met anyone so opaque, so intriguing, so full of hidden depths. So terrifying.

"The issue of Nemesis's bank accounts doesn't matter," he continued. "When going to war, first the troops settle into their encampment." Opening his arms, he said, "Welcome to your new home."

"She's staying here?" Lazarus demanded when Bronwyn fell into stunned silence.

"We need the good widow close at hand," Marco explained. "She'd rile up too much scandal if any of us went trooping through a hotel room or boardinghouse. Scandal can be the enemy of subtlety."

The flat wasn't that far in quality from the boardinghouse, but she still needed a moment to adjust herself to the idea of *sleeping* here. At least temporarily.

"If it's scandal you're avoiding," Lazarus interjected, "then she can't stay here. On account of the fact that it's where *I* live. An old soldier like me won't be in *Debrett's*, but even I know that an unmarried woman can't share a roof with an unmarried man. And pretty unmarried women aren't an exception."

"You won't be staying here, you ass," snapped Harriet. "I will."

Was that jealousy Bronwyn heard in the other woman's voice?

"And where the bloody hell am I supposed to go?" Lazarus demanded.

"You'll be at my place," Marco said wearily. "But you're

keeping your boots on the whole time. I don't want my rooms smelling of your feet."

"Like roses, they are," the soldier answered with a grin. "Roses with bunions."

Harriet made a face, and Marco shook his head, yet all Bronwyn could do was watch the interplay between these strangers. A wave of loneliness washed through her. She'd been so isolated and for so long, even before Hugh had died. But these Nemesis people were friends of a sort, united by a common purpose. She was the outsider suddenly thrust into their midst.

"Can you show me to my room?" she asked Harriet as she picked up her luggage. She needed to get away from the reminders of what she'd lost.

To her surprise, Marco plucked the valise and violin case from her hand, and headed for the staircase. *That* certainly couldn't be proper. But the world had gone so topsy-turvy, she couldn't hold anything to the standards of what she'd known. So she followed him as he silently climbed the stairs.

"How do you do that?" she asked his back. She wasn't a big woman by any stretch, but the steps creaked beneath her feet.

He seemed to know to what she was referring, because he answered without looking back, "A combination of talent and training."

She wondered what sort of work required a man to train in the art of moving noiselessly. Was he a thief? It made sense, given the shadows in his eyes and the sleekness of his movement. But the Nemesis operatives claimed to be lawful. Or somewhat lawful.

At the top of the stairs stood a hallway, covered by a battered carpet. A handful of doors lined the corridor. Marco pushed one open and gestured her in. It was a narrow chamber with an equally narrow bed. The window looked out onto a drab yard where someone had attempted to grow a garden and failed.

Aside from a washstand, the other piece of furniture was a small writing desk. Idly, she opened the drawer, and pulled out a copy of Hardy's *Return of the Native*. She opened the cover.

THIS BOOK IS BOLLOCKS—JD, someone had scrawled.

Whoever JD was, they shared the same opinion of the book.

"I prefer Haggard, myself," Marco offered, setting down her valise and violin case.

She returned the volume to its drawer. "Gaskell for me, even though she's not *au courant*." She traced her fingers over the worn surface of the desk, its top gouged from countless pens. "I had to sell all of my books when Devere took everything." Even *North and South,* despite her fervent wish that her own Mr. Thornton might appear to beat the men taking her books.

Turning back, she saw that Marco's face had gone expressionless. "There's water in the ewer. Freshen yourself up—we're going out."

"Where?"

"To Devere's offices."

She gaped at him. All she wanted was to hide from the uncertainty her life had become. "Us? Now? There?"

"You and me," he answered. "If I go alone, Devere might not allow me in to see him. We don't have much time, so, yes, now. Nowhere better to start than with the man who knows the most about Hugh's debts."

Bronwyn herself had never been to Devere's place of business. Hugh had always gone. Without her, of course. But she knew that his offices were located on Cannon

Street in the City, and so, in short order, she found herself in a cab with Marco.

She looked out the window as they wound deeper into the financial heart of the capital. She felt raw, exposed. "For eight months, I've been trapped inside my home. It's all changed—in just a day. It's like . . ." She struggled to name the sensation. "I'm a baby bird that's fallen out of its nest."

"Whether you fly or perish is up to you," he answered.

"That's not especially encouraging," she said tartly.

He shrugged. "As little as you know me, I know only slightly more about you. No way to foretell how you'll manage the tasks ahead."

"Surely Lucy told you everything about me. I'm certain one of those dossiers on the table is mine."

" 'Words, words, words,' to quote Will Shakespeare. It's in the doing that someone shows who they really are."

"If you have so little faith in me," she said, her temper rising, "why bring me to Devere's? Surely a man as clever as yourself could find out what he needs to know without me."

"In less than a minute," he agreed easily. "But there's more I need to learn than how Hugh came into such debt. There's learning you, too."

"Then we're both strangers to each other," she fired back.

"So we are." Should she be insulted by his plain speaking? Pleased? All the *politesse* that had shrouded her had left her here, without a cent, reliant on the benevolence of a group of vigilantes. Precarious didn't begin to describe her circumstances.

At the least, she wished Harriet had accompanied them to Devere's. Being alone with Marco felt like having a cold blade pressed to her spine. With Harriet around, the blade felt swathed in batting—acting as buffer between herself and this unpredictable, cunning man.

"Ever met Devere?" Marco asked.

"He came to a dinner I gave once. A very agreeable man—or at least he was to me."

"Age? Height? Hair and eye color?"

"You sound like one of those Scotland Yard men in the penny dreadfuls. Is he a suspect in any crime?"

"That's to be determined," he answered enigmatically. "But I need to know his manner and appearance."

She sifted through the debris littering her memory. So many people came and went at her dinner parties, people she'd meet once and then never again. Of course, she had her regular guests—friends of Hugh's from Oxford, the usual people in their set, bishops and journalists. But her husband's financial agent had appeared at her table once and once only.

A face materialized in her mind. "Middle forties, if I were to guess. Light brown hair. Full mustache and sideburns. Blue-brown eyes, like water full of silt. Rather small nose for a man. He'd laugh into his fist, as if he were coughing."

Marco nodded. "Perhaps you missed your calling as a Scotland Yard detective."

She laughed at the outrageousness of his suggestion. As if women could ever be police investigators. As if *she* could ever be a investigator. That was even more ludicrous than her wish to be a professional violinist.

The hired carriage at last pulled up in front of a sober brick building. Men in dark, serious clothing teemed on the streets, hurrying to keep the great machine of England's businesses running, or else get ground up between its massive cogs. No women were on the curb. Dread curled in her stomach. She shouldn't be here, in this province of men.

Marco got out of the carriage and offered her a hand to help her down. Even though she was dressed as darkly as the businessmen, her veil and weeds would stand out like an electric light among candles.

She remembered what Marco said in the carriage. He didn't seem to trust her, or her capability.

She took his hand and stepped onto the curb. As she expected, men stared at her, some of them even stumbling as they passed, as she openly violated the rules of decent society.

"Don't retreat," Marco murmured as she started to pull back. "If you do, this all ends. Take a step back and it's over. Choose."

She swallowed hard. Straightened her spine. And pressed forward.

"Bella," he said in a low voice. The Italian sounded lovely but out of place in this world of square buildings and sober men.

Together, they ascended the steps leading inside the building. Just before they entered, Marco's shoulders rounded and he seemed to actually shrink by several inches. Reaching into an inside coat pocket, he produced a pair of spectacles and a cloth, which he used to clean the glasses with short, nervous gestures. Slipping the spectacles on, his chin weakened.

It was an amazing metamorphosis.

Her own confidence wavered. What had happened to him? She had to rely on this man, yet he seemed to fade before her eyes.

Inside the building, they stood at the periphery of a large, open room filled with desks. Clerks rushed back and forth with sheaves of papers in their hands, and while some wrote with pen and ink, the clack of newfangled typing machines punctuated the air like scores of tiny firing squads. Many of the clerks looked up as Bronwyn and

Marco drifted farther into the chamber, and the clerks exchanged puzzled glances with each other. Women must seldom come to this sanctum of finance, and widows in full mourning were likely as common—and welcome—as ash in blancmange.

Without Marco's strength, her own faltered.

One of the clerks managed to shake himself enough from his shock to approach her and Marco.

"May I help you, sir?"

But instead of speaking, Marco waved toward Bronwyn, as though she were the person the clerk was to do business with. This was a surprise to both the young man and herself.

She cleared her throat. "Ah. Mr. Devere, please."

"Pardon me, madam," the clerk stammered. "You are?"

"Mrs. Parrish. My late husband was one of Mr. Devere's clients."

"Oh . . . I see . . ." The ink-stained young man threw an anxious glance over his shoulder at his colleagues, all of whom were watching with appalled interest. His gaze then shot to one of the glass-fronted doors lining the back wall. The blinds within the chamber were drawn.

"How long has Devere been missing?" Marco asked suddenly in a thin voice.

The clerk went white. "I . . . that is . . . I'm not at liberty . . ."

Marco turned to Bronwyn and muttered, "He doesn't know anything."

Still recovering from the shock of Devere's absence, she murmured, "Perhaps someone else would be better informed."

"Doubtful." Marco flashed the clerk an apologetic smile.

In their short acquaintance, Bronwyn would never describe anything Marco did as apologetic.

"A shame that is," he said in that unusual, reedy voice, "a deuced shame. We've come all the way from the home office to speak with Mr. Devere, and he's not about."

"Home office?" echoed the clerk.

"Taxation bureau. We've been in touch with Mrs. Parrish with regard to her late husband's estate, or what's become of it, but naturally she couldn't tell us anything." He gave a nasal, reedy laugh.

The clerk laughed, as well, looking at Bronwyn indulgently. She'd seen that look on her father's face, and Hugh's, too, whenever she asked them a question about a topic they felt was beyond her woman's intellect—things about the current political climate, or education reform. Though she'd always borne their patronizing glances with a smile. But this was a different world from the one she'd known. She didn't have to bear the condescending looks anymore.

Something strange stirred to life within her. She didn't recognize it at first. It felt hot and seething.

Anger.

Suddenly, she wanted to kick both the clerk and Marco in very precious places.

"Thing is," Marco continued in a confiding tone, "my superiors have been twisting my cravat about Mr. Devere and his clientele, including Mrs. Parrish, here. They'll be sure to sack me if I don't come back with something. But can I help it if the chap's up and vanished?" A feeble whine crept into Marco's voice. "Isn't that always the way, with our bosses blaming us for things we don't have control over?"

The clerk nodded vigorously. "Mr. Galbraith is forever barking at me, threatening me with getting the ax, and all because *he's* the one who misfiles the paperwork. He needs to relearn the alphabet, is what he needs."

Marco laughed as if this were the cleverest thing uttered by anyone in the course of human history, and the clerk joined him. But then a stout man in an expensive waistcoat walked by, glaring at the clerk, and the laughter abruptly stopped.

"Mr. Galbraith, I presume," Bronwyn murmured dryly.

The young man gave a less vigorous nod. "I ought to get back to work."

Marco heaved a sigh. "Ah, well." He cast a longing glance toward what presumably was Devere's office. "If only I could have had a poke through Mr. Devere's files. Didn't need to talk to the man himself, just check a few numbers." He glanced at the clerk. "If I manage this assignment, I could get an advancement. There'd be a vacancy—and some enterprising young clerk might get that position, especially if I put in a good word with the brass."

The clerk looked thoughtful for a moment, then stepped closer. He cast a shifty glance around the room. "Five minutes. That's all I can give you in Devere's office. Then you'll have to disappear like he did."

"Five minutes is more than enough," Marco answered quickly. "My thanks. And how long did you say he'd been gone?"

"Three months," the clerk replied, without realizing that he hadn't said anything of the sort earlier. "Working chaps like you and me have to stick together." He walked hastily to a desk, pulled a key out of a drawer, then returned and pressed the key into Marco's hand, along with a scrap of paper that had his name and address. "If that vacancy opens up," he explained.

Marco gave the clerk a small salute. Bronwyn followed him as he crossed the room and unlocked the door to Devere's office. They both stepped inside, and he shut the door. He didn't bother turning on the gas lamp. Shadows clung thickly to the paper-strewn room. A heavy, musty smell hung in the air.

"An actor," Bronwyn whispered as Marco sifted through the mounds of papers. "That must be your other profession when you aren't working for Nemesis."

He'd dropped his invisible disguise the moment they'd entered Devere's office, and now moved confidently through the room, his gaze sharp and precise behind his spectacles. Rifling through a folder of more documents, he said, "There are more important mysteries than how I earn my bread. For example, where is Devere and what the hell does this mean?"

She peered through the gloom at the papers he held up. Symbols and numbers covered the documents, as arcane as a dead language.

Contemplating the papers again, he muttered, "Codes are a child's game, but it'll take more than five minutes for me to crack this one. Devere's better than I thought."

"The man vanished with the answers about Hugh's debt," she said brusquely. "There's nothing *better* about that."

"We've got different value scales, you and I," Marco answered.

Not wanting to just stand around uselessly, she began combing through the folders and folios scattered across every surface. "Either he left in a hurry, or someone's been through here," she speculated.

"Or a little of both."

Her limbs tingled with the oddness of this experience. "What am I looking for?"

"Anything with your name on it, or that might have something to do with Devere's own financial accounting."

With one eye on the clock—clearly wound daily by a clerk hopeful of Devere's return—Bronwyn did as Marco directed, examining what seemed like an endless array of documents with columns of numbers upon them. "Either Devere or the clerk he employed to transcribe the numbers must have been in some kind of trouble."

Marco looked up sharply. "Explain."

She bristled slightly at his commanding tone, but said, "The handwriting starts off neat, but over the course of months begins to get messier and messier. As if the person writing were growing agitated. Something was bothering them. And see here." She held out a sheaf of newspaper clippings.

INVESTMENT OPPORTUNITY—MILLIONS OF POUNDS GUARANTEED! proclaimed one.

UNTOLD WEALTH TO BE FOUND IN THE MINES OF SOUTH AMERICA! another blared.

"Devere seemed quite interested in this sort of chancy financial possibility," she noted.

A small smile tilted Marco's lips. "Well done, Mrs. Parrish."

Why did those few words from him give her a spark of gratification?

He held up another folder. *"Eccolo."*

"Something about Hugh?"

"Devere's personal banking records." Moving around the desk, he stood shoulder to shoulder with Bronwyn. She fought the urge to edge away, as if putting distance between herself and a loaded weapon. Instead, she followed his blunt-tipped finger as it slid down a column of numbers. "Curioser and curioser. There's no swell in Devere's accounts. Even after he claimed your fortune."

It seemed an odd leap of logic. "If Hugh was in debt," she posited, "the money wouldn't have gone into Devere's own account. It would have gone to his creditors."

Marco's gaze met hers. "Did your husband spend lavishly? Was he the kind of man who made impulsive purchases?"

She shook her head. "If anything, he was slow to buy. I had to remind him over and over again to have his valet purchase new cuffs and collars for his shirts. His frugality always baffled his parents, who'd spoiled him terribly as a child."

None of this seemed to shock Marco. "Devere wasn't paying off your husband's creditors because Hugh Parrish didn't *have* creditors."

"Devere took the money for himself?"

"Apparently not, because there's not a ha'penny extra in his bank account." He narrowed his eyes. "So then where's the sodding money?"

A very good question. She started to speak, then stopped.

"Go on," he urged.

"It seems to me that if somebody takes money, but there's no sign of the money, that it probably wound up somewhere other than their own pockets."

"Creditors' pockets." Marco scratched absently at his goatee. "Or maybe he was a speculator, and owed business partners."

Bronwyn jumped when there was a sharp rap on the glass outside. "Time's up," the clerk hissed through the door.

Marco tucked the banking folder as well as the one containing the coded documents inside his coat. "Are you a betting woman?"

"I've earned my share at euchre," she answered.

"Good." He crossed to the door and placed his hand on the knob, but didn't turn it. His grin flashed white in the gloom of the office. "Because tonight, you and I are going gambling."

THREE

Taking Mrs. Parrish to Bethnal Green was itself a gamble for Marco. Society ladies didn't frequent this grim part of town. He didn't know if she'd scream or faint or be stunned into horrified silence. But she could identify Devere. While Marco might find the man based on her description alone, it was always better to have someone actually familiar with the target close at hand, lest he make a dangerous mistake. If he nabbed the wrong bloke, Devere would find out about it, and then there'd be no chance of getting Nemesis's hands on him.

"I'm not entirely certain what we're doing here," Mrs. Parrish said, glancing out the cab's window. Streetlights weren't plentiful in this run-down part of the city, and between the hood of her cloak—he'd had her remove her veil, though she'd objected—and the shadows, he could barely make out her features. But he didn't need to see them now to remember everything, such as the tiny dip in her lower lip, or the straight line of her reddish-gold eyebrows, or how she'd set her chin whenever she was trying to be brave. Her chin often formed that firm shape, pushed slightly forward. It was a struggle, he saw, for her to keep her determination.

Marco had them swing by Nemesis headquarters and pick up Desmond for the trip to Bethnal Green—this wasn't an assignment Marco wanted for himself, and it would be better tonight to have another agent accompanying them. Introductions had been made quickly between Desmond, his sister Riza, and the Widow Parrish. Night had fallen, which meant that they had a limited amount of time. If Mrs. Parrish had been surprised by Desmond and Riza's half-Indian parentage—clearly evident in the color of their skin and hair—she made no mention of it. She'd paused briefly, but then shaken their hands and been swept up in the mission.

A scalpel, Eva had called Marco once. *A suave scalpel,* the Nemesis agent had said, more specifically.

He almost grinned to himself. Nothing by half measures. He might not want to be on this case, but when he was the lead on a mission, he moved with speed and precision. An old habit ingrained by training. When the lives of thousands of soldiers or civilians were at risk, he couldn't proceed slowly. Even when it came to gathering intelligence, he had a surgical precision. No lingering, not when the anesthetized patient could wake at any moment and begin screaming.

He'd snatched a folio of papers off a diplomat's desk in the beat of a fly's wings. He'd broken into a French arms manufacturer's safe box in less than two minutes. Though the Widow Parrish was genteel, he'd rather spend his time seeing to the needs of the poor—over the course of his work with British Intelligence, he'd seen far too much poverty and privation, both at home and abroad.

He'd never been a member of the elite—and didn't want to be. He'd endured enough at their hands to ever want anything to do with them. It was one of the main reasons why he'd become an intelligence agent, and why he helped form Nemesis six years ago. Their targets were often from the highest ranks of society, which gave him a cold, brutal satisfaction when the bastards were brought down.

She was of them, the Widow Parrish.

Still, he'd been strong-armed into this job, and now that he'd committed to it, he wouldn't doze his way through.

"Back at Devere's offices," he said as the carriage rocked over the rough pavement, "you said something that made me think."

"A rare occurrence," Desmond offered.

Marco in turn offered the agent one of his favorite Italian hand gestures.

"I can't imagine I have anything to add to your elaborate thought process," Mrs. Parrish said.

"You said that if Devere didn't take the money for himself," Marco explained, "that it wound up in someone else's pockets."

"Yes, and then you asked if I was a betting woman."

"Which you apparently are," he said.

"There's a small thrill in taking a chance," she admitted, though uncertainty edged her voice. Then she tipped up her chin, and though the charcoal light within the carriage mostly hid her face, his imagination filled in the details. With the fairness of her redhead's complexion, doubtless she wore a warm pink hue.

He forced his thoughts to something other than the color and temperature of the pretty widow's skin. "Devere thinks there's more than a small thrill in gambling. We saw those newspaper clippings in his offices. If he's the sort who's interested in reckless investments, likely he's a gambler, too. And not at euchre."

"London's thick with gaming hells," Desmond said, "all over the city." He glanced at the increasingly tumble-down buildings as the cab threaded its way along the

slum's streets. "A man of some means, even small as Devere's might be, wouldn't come to this shithole. Beg your
pardon, Mrs. Parrish," he added when Marco kicked him.

"None . . . ah . . . taken."

"We're a coarse lot," Marco noted. "Except Simon,
who's smooth as buttered satin."

"Toff bastard," Desmond said good-naturedly.

Mrs. Parrish continued to stare out the window. Barefoot children in rags chased after the cab, and people
huddled on curbs and in doorways, some cradling bottles
of gin. "I've never . . . I didn't know it was like this."

"Never went slumming?" Desmond asked snidely.
"Ow! You sodding kicked me again."

"I repent nothing," Marco answered, "especially when
you're being a rude ass." He might not have any love for
the higher ranks, but he still knew the value of courtesy.

The widow looked appalled at the suggestion that she
would ever go on one of the guided tours of London's
slums.

"Come and visit this like a tourist?" she demanded.
"Why?"

"With the exposés in sundry newspapers," Marco said,
"and the zeal for reform, genteel men and women like
you venture into Whitechapel and Bethnal Green to shake
their heads at the occupants' misery. They pretend that
somehow, the poverty-trapped men and women are to
blame for their wretchedness. An easier thought than to
acknowledge the truth."

A square of weak light fell across her face, revealing
the look of illness on her face. "People used to tour Bed-
lam, too, and throw garbage at the patients. But that was
nearly a hundred years ago. I'd never revel in the misfor-
tune of others, or congratulate myself on my privilege."

"Others do," Desmond said.

"It's only . . ." Her gaze lit upon a young girl leading a

naked toddler down the muddy lane. "Missionaries would come to my house, asking for donations for places like this. I gave them money. Of course I did. Whatever you think of genteel women like me," she fired at Marco, "we're always taught to be charitable. It's our duty. But I never saw this place before. I never knew . . . how bad it truly was."

Genuine shock and horror edged her voice.

Had he been too quick to judge her based on her class?

"It wasn't enough," she murmured. "The money I gave the missionaries, or the funds we raised at our little charity bazaars. How could it be? A few dozen pounds can't fix this." She waved at the plight just outside the cab.

"No, it can't," he answered. From London to Toulouse to Moscow, he'd seen poverty. It was a constant, no matter where he traveled. Which made him all the more determined to make a change.

Turning her gaze to him, she said, "And here I am, pursuing my fortune when so many others have nothing."

"You don't have much, either," he felt obliged to point out.

"Yet I'm not so far gone that I sleep beneath rags and get my dinner out of a bottle," she countered.

He stretched out his legs. "Guilt's a powerful motivator. Just ask my mother."

"Don't make fun of me," Mrs. Parrish snapped.

"I'm not. Once you have your fortune back, you can use it to help people. *Truly* help."

"Perhaps I'll surprise you and actually do that."

He was beginning to wonder if she really might, and was alarmed that he believed she would.

"Nothing's going to happen until we get your money back, and to do that, we need to find Devere," Marco continued. "There's one person in the whole of London who knows everything about the city's gamblers: Charlie."

"And this Charlie resides here?"

Marco shrugged. "Don't know if Charlie lives here, but she does work here."

"Charlie is a she?" Mrs. Parrish sucked in a breath. "You're taking me to a brothel?"

"God, no. I'm taking you to an underground bare-knuckle brawling match."

"I thought you were jesting," Mrs. Parrish shouted above the din, "when you mentioned the brawl."

"I never joke about boxing," he yelled back. "It's a beautiful, ancient art."

The boxer in the makeshift ring took a punch straight to his nose, sending blood spraying in an arc that spattered on the shirts and jackets of the nearest bystanders. The match itself was held in a former slaughterhouse, huge holes in the walls and ceiling, and the massive space teemed with sweaty, shouting men—and a few women— all of them there to bet on the fates of burly, cold-eyed brawlers. The scent of coppery blood and rank sweat hung thickly in the air.

"I can see the aesthetic majesty," Mrs. Parrish muttered.

He scanned her face beneath the hood of her cloak. She was pale, and looked a little ill. Despite this, her wide eyes seemed to try to take everything in at once.

Desmond pushed through the crowd to join Marco and Mrs. Parrish. His black hair was plastered to his spice-hued skin, and he looked cross. "Where the hell is this Charlie?"

"Working," Marco answered. "But she'll join us just as soon as she collects after the match."

The crowd roared as one of the bruisers went down hard, and four blokes were required to drag the unconscious fighter out of the ring. Men clustered in a group as money changed hands, all of them gathered around one central figure that wasn't quite visible amid the chaos. Finally, the bettors dispersed, revealing Charlie at the center of the madness, pocketing a huge wad of cash.

As they stood waiting, a red-faced man staggered toward Marco. *Ah, hell.*

"You," the man slurred, pointing a finger at Marco.

"Me," he answered.

"You were the bloke that done took my kids away," the bloke snarled.

"Seeing as how you beat them every morning and night," Marco answered, "I didn't think you'd miss them very much." The three children in question had been placed in an orphanage, and were later adopted by a childless couple in Greenwich. Last Marco had heard, the eldest son was apprenticed to a printer.

"How'm I supposed to get any money if my kids ain't working?"

"I suggest getting a job."

When the bloke swung at Marco, he was prepared, taking a short sidestep and avoiding the blow. The bully stumbled forward, and Marco kicked the back of his knees, sending the bloke sprawling to the dirt. But the fool didn't stay down. He lurched to his feet and threw another punch. Marco struck fast, a direct hit to the bully's jaw.

The man sank to the ground, bloody and unconscious.

Marco shook out his fist. He caught Mrs. Parrish's stunned look, and only stared coolly back. A moment later, Charlie caught sight of Marco and gave a small wave, then crossed through the throng. The crowd parted for Charlie, her natural authority like a ship's prow, cutting through the waves of humanity.

Recovering herself, Mrs. Parrish said under her breath, "Now I feel especially dowdy."

"Ah, don't compare yourself to Charlie," Marco answered. "There's no one like her."

The woman in question stopped in front of them. She tipped back her bowler hat and plucked the stub of a cigar from her mouth, then planted her hands on her hips. In all of Marco's travels, he'd never encountered a woman—a *person*—as singular as the bookmaker. She seemed somewhere in her early forties, though she wore her age with a triumphant glow of beauty, defiant in her lack of youth. Charlie favored shirtwaists and well-tailored waistcoats, as well as the finest in neckcloths. Though she wore masculine trappings on her top half, she preferred skirts, as if to remind everyone that she was indeed a woman.

"Nemesis comes a-calling," she said. "Here I haven't asked for my favor yet."

"Charlie did us a kindness some time ago," Marco explained to Mrs. Parrish. He wouldn't go into the details of how Charlie had helped them obtain a corpse as part of a mission to ruin a corrupt nobleman, since that tale might make the widow finally pass out, or else storm off in horror.

And one of their best agents had once boxed in this very place. A right brute of a man, that Jack Dutton, as he called himself now, married to Eva and running a school in Manchester. But that didn't keep Jack or Eva from taking on their own Nemesis cases in their new location.

"And my kindnesses always come with a price," Charlie added with a not particularly friendly grin. She glanced at Mrs. Parrish. "She ain't one of yours. Not with those pretty little hands."

The widow tucked her hands into the folds of her cloak. "Charming establishment you have here."

Charlie threw back her head and laughed. "I wouldn't

keep pigs in here, love, but thanks for the sentiment."
Then her gaze fell on Desmond, and a feral gleam lit her
eyes. "But *this* one is yours."

"How can you tell?" Desmond asked, placing his own
hands on his hips.

"It's in the eyes, love," Charlie purred. "I knew a bloke
who was a sniper for the army. Could shoot an enemy
right in the heart at two hundred yards in dense jungle. You
Nemesis lot have the same look in your eyes." She pointed
a finger at Desmond. "Dangerous, you are." She grinned.
"Almost as dangerous as me."

"We'll just have to test that theory," Desmond answered.

"Maybe *you'll* be the favor I call in," she murmured.

Marco stepped between them. "We're actually here for
a reason."

The Widow Parrish looked ashen, swaying on her feet.
She had to be roasting beneath her heavy mourning clothes
and woolen cloak. The crude boxing arena couldn't be an
easy place for her to be, either, with blood staining the dirt
that comprised the ring and the ongoing racket of men
bellowing at one another.

Yet she didn't voice a word of complaint.

And bugger him if that didn't appeal.

He wanted to pull her close and have her lean on him,
give her support. No. Her case fell to him, but he wasn't
her protector. It'd been her choice to get involved with
Nemesis. Either she'd flow with the current or be dragged
under—depending on whether or not she was a strong
swimmer. He wasn't her raft.

But, damn it, what were these compulsions? She was
sheltered. Delicate. That had to be it.

Not qualities he cared for. And though Mrs. Parrish
had been shielded from the outside world, she'd already
shown that she wasn't actually frail.

"Let's move this conversation to a more salubrious location," he said.

"An abattoir would be more salubrious," Mrs. Parrish murmured.

"This building was, once," he noted.

She grimaced. "It must have been much more pleasant back then."

Charlie gave another raffish grin. "And right cesspit it is. But I'm the gem floating on the top."

"That's a mental image I'll always treasure," Mrs. Parrish said.

The bookmaker laughed. "I like you, your ladyship. There's more than steel and whalebone holding up your spine." She glanced around the boxing arena. "It's going to be a few minutes before the next match is announced. We can take this to my pub."

"You own a pub?" Mrs. Parrish asked.

Charlie smirked. "There isn't a piece of this filthy city I don't own, in one way or another."

The Two Cats pub wasn't much of an improvement on the boxing ring. Tucked into a rotting corner of a nameless street, choked with coal and tobacco smoke and crammed with furniture that had barely survived countless scuffles between patrons, the pub could safely be called a hovel. Marco had seen his share of run-down taverns and hostelries from here to Constantinople. The Two Cats impressed even him with its shabbiness.

None of which he voiced to Mrs. Parrish. He made sure she was tucked close beside him in the settle, away from the searching eyes and groping hands of the patrons. *Patrons* being an elegant term in this case for *shambling drunkards*. Of course, if anyone did make a play for her,

Marco had more than his share of weapons tucked away to defend her. His fists being two of them.

He felt her warm presence beside him. Not her actual heat, but something else, a searching quality that made him aware of her every movement, every breath. It drew on him. Intrigued him.

Across the table sat Charlie, with Desmond wedged against her in the small booth. Their gazes kept catching on each other, then breaking apart. Desmond drummed his fingers on the table, as he always did when unsettled. The agent had faced down gun-toting gangs and drug-addled madmen without a bead of sweat, but Charlie seemed to put him on edge.

A barmaid thumped down four glasses of dubious beer. She scuttled off when Charlie jerked her head, dismissing the server.

Mrs. Parrish picked up her glass. Gently, Marco laid his hand on her wrist and pushed the glass back down onto the table.

"You don't want any part of that," he said sotto voce. "Unless you fancy spending half the night in the privy."

After giving him a grateful look, she carefully pushed the glass away from her.

Charlie, however, had no concerns about the beer. She threw hers back and finished the entire contents in two swallows. Likely she'd developed some immunity to whatever lived in the beverage.

Charlie wiped her mouth on her sleeve. "If it's another favor you want . . ."

"Not a favor," Desmond said. "Information."

"Information *is* a favor," the bookmaker corrected. "Nothing more powerful or dangerous."

"Then add it to our bill," Marco said. "No one else in London's got the knowledge that you do."

"Damn right," Charlie said. "The British Museum ain't nothing compared to me."

"We're looking for someone," Desmond said.

Mrs. Parrish continued, "A financial advisor named Edgar Devere." She then gave the bookmaker the same description of Devere that she'd given Marco earlier.

Charlie snarled. "I know him. Owes me thirty pounds. Worst bloke to count on to come through with blunt."

Raising a brow, Marco prompted, "Bad investment?"

"A money-thieving bastard is what he is," snapped Charlie.

Mrs. Parrish said nothing at this foul language, though her hands tightened into fists as they rested on the table-top. "Does he owe other people money?" she asked.

"No bookmaker in London will take his bets anymore," Charlie answered, "on account of he doesn't pay anyone back."

"Maybe he did come through for some of them," Desmond said, "and you didn't hear about it."

"There isn't a bloody thing that happens in this town without me knowing about it," Charlie countered. "Especially when it comes to welching." She glanced at Brownyn, then at Bronwyn's drink.

Bronwyn waved at it, silently giving the other woman permission.

Charlie grabbed Bronwyn's glass and downed her drink in only a few gulps. Desmond stared like one trans-fixed.

"When was the last time anyone's seen Devere?" Marco pressed. The man might not have been at his of-fices for three months, but that didn't mean he kept away from London's gaming action.

Charlie shrugged. "It's got to be months now." She peered at Mrs. Parrish. "Did he take a bet from you?"

"He took everything from me," the widow answered.

Charlie whistled. "Bad investment, love."

"It wasn't mine, but the result was the same."

Charlie pulled a pocket watch from her waistcoat. The case was engraved and set all over with rubies—a risky item to own in this part of town, but it was a measure of her stature that she could carry such a precious object without concern that she'd be a pickpocket's victim. No doubt someone found out the very hard way not to steal from Charlie.

"Delightful as this little chat's been," she said, rising to her feet, "I've got beer money to earn. Consider this another favor Nemesis owes me." She winked at Desmond. "Come and see me if you want to see how the bad people play."

Before Desmond could answer, Charlie was gone. The other Nemesis agent leaned back, looking stunned.

"Seems I've missed a lot since I've been in America," he muttered. Then, with a "what the hell" shrug, he drank down his beer.

Mrs. Parrish looked almost as stunned as Desmond. "That was . . . an interesting woman."

"A London original," Marco answered. "But she taught us one thing tonight. Your money isn't anywhere in the city. And neither is Devere."

"Somewhere else in England, then?" Mrs. Parrish asked.

"We've got one good place to find out," Marco said. "Devere's lodgings. It's time for a break-in."

"My God," the widow said on an exhalation, a look of trepidation on her face. "There's more?"

His look was pitiless. "It never lets up, not from one moment to the next, until the job is done."

Mrs. Parrish looked gray with exhaustion, and still stunned at the new world she'd seen and her immersion within it, so after parting ways with Desmond—who had his own agenda for the rest of the night—Marco found them a cab and headed back toward headquarters.

He sat opposite her, watching as she fought to stay awake. But at last her tiredness won, and she leaned against the threadbare squabs and fell into a light doze. Yet her hands were still curled into fists, protecting her even as she slept.

Did she miss her husband? His presence in her life, in her bed? Society proscribed strict rules for the means and how long a woman was supposed to mourn the loss of a spouse. If left to her own devices, would she cast off her weeds already, or would she be like the queen, and cling to her sorrow for the rest of her life?

Why should it matter to him?

He wished for a glass of good *vino nobile*. He'd be sure to pour himself one when he returned home—though, damn it, Lazarus would be there and demand a glass of his own, and Marco's cache of imported wine was a private hoard he didn't like to share with anyone. He was far more jealous of his wine than his women. When his lovers demanded more devotion from him, and he was unable to give it to them, he let them move on to other men without a word of objection.

Spies didn't form commitments. They couldn't. Neither did Nemesis operatives—usually. Though Eva had with Jack, and Simon with Alyce. Even Michael with Ada. But Marco was different from all of them because he alone worked as a spy.

When he'd taken the job with British Intelligence, it was the same as a vow of celibacy. Not literal celibacy, because he'd go mad if he couldn't give and receive pleasure. But another kind of celibacy. He'd never know what it was like to court a woman. To speak with her father. To see her waiting for him at the end of the church aisle, or waiting for him at the window of their home. And while part of him mourned that loss, he knew he'd never be content with that life.

He'd picked espionage for a reason. Those in power were usually of the elite, and it gave him no small amount of gratification to dismantle their plans. Stability, however, wasn't one of the reasons why he'd chosen spying as his profession.

But here was Mrs. Parrish, wearing the very symbols of her commitment to another. He didn't care for the late Mr. Parrish. That man was dead, leaving behind a woman unprotected. And maybe Hugh Parrish hadn't had any control over whether he lived or died, yet there was a petty, mean part of Marco that thought it damned selfish for Parrish to die without ensuring his wife's safety.

Diavolo. Maybe Mrs. Parrish *did* deserve help from Nemesis.

She stirred, her eyes blinking open. Looked at the carriage. Then him. She started.

"It's not a dream," he said.

She sat up straighter, tugging on her cloak. "I couldn't decide if it was a fulfilled wish or a nightmare."

"A bit of both." He watched her rub at her face, then asked, "Still want to move forward with this?"

"Yes," she said after a moment. "I want my fortune back—and, as you said, there's so much I could do with that money. Some real good. Maybe I won't live as lavishly as before, but I don't need six bedrooms to be happy."

What did he need to be happy? He usually considered himself a contented man. He had his work for the government, but more importantly, his missions for Nemesis. Both shaped and changed the world. Perhaps in small ways, but enough to give him a sense of accomplishment. Not many could say the same, including his father, who manufactured vulcanized rubber gaskets, which brought him wealth but didn't erase the lines of worry from his forehead. Or gain him entry into the realm of high society. For the titled, Marco, his father, and his grandfather would never be more than tradesmen, more fit to enter through the servants' entrance than the front door of the houses of the aristocracy.

A sharp memory jabbed him. His first year at university, and though his father had also attended the same university, Marco had still been the object of the titled students' scorn. They'd locked him out of his room several times. Left boot black, shoes, and rags on his bed. As though he were their servant.

Instead of returning home, as they'd hoped, Marco had made sure to excel at every endeavor. Including captaining the rugby team, earning trophies in boxing, and taking top prizes in his courses.

And for Prescott Black, the only thing that had real power wasn't a thing at all, but a person, Marco's mother, Lucia. Her smiles made his father smile, and her raucous laugh made him laugh.

And if he envied what his parents shared, he knew it to be an anomaly. In his work, he'd seen too many unhappy marriages, too many people tied together for the wrong reasons. His preferred lovers were widows, and hardly any of them had good things to say about their dead husbands.

Mrs. Parrish was a widow.

He kicked that notion out of his head like an errant football. All his thoughts needed to be on the mission. As much as he enjoyed making love, he could always put his desires on hold until the time was right. And the time—and the person—were definitely not right when it came to Mrs. Parrish. Pretty as she was, and admirably fighting hard against her own fears.

The widow frowned as she looked down at her hands,

clasped in her lap. "Strange. I've never thought about . . . what I needed to be happy."

"Happiness isn't a promise when we come into this world."

"Duty, responsibility," she murmured. "Those were the things I'd been taught. To be a good daughter, a wife. A mother."

Interesting that, though she was childless, there was no wistful longing in her voice at this last word. "How long were you married to Mr. Parrish?"

"Doubtless Lucy told you."

"It might've escaped my notice."

She looked up, her lips curling into a wry smile. "I have a difficult time believing anything escapes your notice. So I can only imagine that your question is a circuitous way of asking me why I have no children, despite the six years I was married." She gave a short laugh. "Your roundabout question would have shocked me only yesterday."

"And today?"

"Perhaps I'm just exhausted, and can't summon enough energy to be scandalized." She rubbed her face. "But in answer to your question-yet-not-a-question, Hugh wanted a family."

"You didn't."

"Not yet. I needed . . ." A frown creased between her straight brows. "Time as myself, before someone called me mama."

"Mr. Parrish supported this idea?" If so, the dead man was far more progressive than others of his sort. While Marco was raised among the sons of self-made men and had two sisters, Simon came from the ranks of the elite and possessed many, many siblings. From what he'd described, and Marco's own observations, genteel women were treated like prized hunting bitches, whelping one pup after another to ensure the family line. The queen herself had birthed nine children, though two were no longer living.

Mrs. Parrish picked at the seam of her cloak. "My husband believed something wasn't quite right with my . . ." She cleared her throat. "He thought it a biological issue. Made me visit several doctors, all of whom declared me of sound health and perfectly able to . . . breed. Yet to everyone's bafflement, I never did."

Scratching at his goatee, Marco said, "A vinegar-soaked sponge."

The widow did look shocked now, her gaze flying to his. "How did you know?"

"Unless he was remarkably unobservant," Marco said, "your husband would've noticed if you put a prophylactic on him." God above—Marco would have been aware if her slim hands rolled one of the lambskin or rubber devices over his *uccello*. "Same with rinsing after coitus. If my wife leaped up right after we'd made love"—odd how his voice grew deeper at those words—"to clean herself, I might get a little suspicious."

"Do you have a wife?" she asked.

"I am and will always be a bachelor," he answered.

"You cannot say *always*," she said. "Unless you've got the gift of prophecy, too, no one can know the future."

"I might not be able to read tarot cards or tea leaves, but I know that I'll never marry." He continued before she could press him further. "Getting a cap would have required you seeing a doctor for a fitting, which was risky, since it might lead to Mr. Parrish finding out. He was likely the sort of man to announce his intention of visiting your bedchamber ahead of time. After dinner, say, when you were both in the drawing room, and you were reading a novel while he perused the evening paper. Giving you plenty of time to prepare for his marital attentions."

Mrs. Parrish was silent.

What a dull and passionless way to conduct a marriage. And entirely typical for the English. Marco had memories that he'd like to forget, of his mother stalking up to his father and dragging him by the neckcloth out of the study, and then they'd reappear several hours later, flushed and languorous. At the time, he'd been repulsed. Even now, he didn't relish the thought of his parents' sex life, but it set a standard that he'd rarely seen replicated.

He never thought about what kind of husband he'd be—that was a path he'd deliberately gated and locked. But if *he'd* been married to Mrs. Parrish . . .

Basta. An unprofitable thought to pursue.

She spoke stiffly. "I expect you'll call me unnatural. One of those awful progressive women subverting God and the law."

"You might've noticed, Mrs. Parrish, that I'm not really the man to accuse anyone of subverting anything." He leaned forward and braced his forearms on his thighs. "Every Nemesis agent chose their work because they don't believe that anyone should have a say in how others lead their lives. Especially when it comes to the powerful dictating the choices—or lack of choices—for those without power. So if you decided you didn't want to swell up with child every nine months, I'm not going to pass judgment on you."

She stared at him. "You're not?" she said, disbelief plain in her voice.

He shook his head. "I applaud your guile. For years, you were able to trick your husband and several doctors. That takes bravery and cunning. Two things Nemesis always appreciates."

"And you?" she asked. "Do you appreciate a woman with cunning?"

He found himself smiling. "What do you think?"

She actually smiled back. "I think you're the oddest man I've ever met."

"But you've admitted to being somewhat sheltered."

"Yet instinct tells me that there aren't many men like you roaming this earth. And I do believe that's for the best."

He laughed. "I'm deciding whether or not to be insulted."

"I'm deciding whether or not I tried to insult you," she answered.

Unexpected heat pulsed through him, rattling him. Though he moved quickly when it came to missions, he liked knowing all the variables ahead of time, understanding exactly how every component worked, and what to anticipate. It made him nimble, fast to react, and completely confident in his actions.

Yet here was this little widow, sheltered but struggling against the bonds of her insulated life, carrying a small yet bright torch of rebellion. Consistently unbalancing him. He didn't like questioning his own judgment. It made everything dangerous. Including himself.

He was grateful when the cab pulled up outside headquarters. After paying the driver, Marco let him and Mrs. Parrish into the chemist's shop. Together, they went through the secret entrance, and within a minute, both stood in the parlor, where they were met by Harriet and Lazarus. Their voices abruptly stopped the moment Marco and Mrs. Parrish set foot in the parlor, but judging from the dark stain on Harriet's cheeks and the way Lazarus tugged on his beard, yet another argument had been interrupted.

"Now what?" Marco asked.

Harriet pointed an accusing finger at Lazarus. "Please tell Colonel Numskull that if you can't get to the groin, the best way to incapacitate a man is to slam the side of your hand into your opponent's throat."

"A good, solid punch to the solar plexus," Lazarus retorted. "*That's* the way to take a bloke down. He can't prepare for it, and you can shock the hell out of him. Or knock the wind out of 'im. Maybe even stop his heart."

"A hit to the throat is always going to hurt," Harriet argued. "And it cuts off any way of breathing. No better means of disabling your enemy."

"*Madonna,* is there nothing you two won't fight about?" Marco said with a sigh.

"No," they said in unison.

"Well, that's an agreement about something," Mrs. Parrish offered.

They both looked appalled at the idea.

"What did you learn?" Harriet asked, as if trying to distract herself from the notion that she and Lazarus might be in accord about anything.

Striding to the rickety sideboard, Marco poured himself a few fingers of whisky. He threw the drink back, letting its heat singe away thoughts of the spirited Widow Parrish. But alcohol wasn't entirely successful, and he felt himself all too aware of her dark, still presence in the room.

He quickly briefed Lazarus and Harriet on everything the evening had revealed, including Devere's citywide debts and sudden disappearance.

"Maybe someone caught up with him," Lazarus offered. "Didn't like the bloke's habit of holding on to his money instead of paying up. Then gave him what for." Lazarus mimed sticking a knife into someone's gut.

"Charlie would've heard about it," Marco countered.

"Perhaps she knew and didn't tell us," Mrs. Parrish said. "She did say that information was powerful. She didn't want to give us that power."

The widow was thinking more and more like a devious Nemesis agent. Did that mean she was being strengthened, or corrupted? "She's got nothing to gain by withholding the possibility of Devere's death from us," Marco said. "It'd serve her better to tell us everything she knew so we could find him and she'd get her thirty pounds."

"What's it to be, then?" Lazarus asked. "Got everything you could from his offices."

"His lodgings next, I'd wager," Harriet suggested.

"He wouldn't leave anything important there," the old soldier countered. "Not if he owes half the city blunt. It'd be the first place the chaps wanting him would look."

Harriet opened her mouth in a retort, but Marco cut her off. "Unless they're looking for the wrong things."

Despite the fact that Harriet had just made the suggestion, now Lazarus nodded sagely at Marco's wisdom. Harriet crossed her arms over her chest and kicked the leg of the table.

The widow covered her mouth with her hand, but as though she were holding back a smile. She'd only been working with Nemesis for a day, and already she was falling into the rhythms of the place and people.

As if that searching self he'd felt in her had been searching for . . . this.

But that wasn't possible. Not her. Not this.

"Tomorrow," Marco went on, "I'll break into Devere's lodgings and conduct my own search."

Lacing his fingers together, Lazarus gave his knuckles a solid crack, making both Harriet and Mrs. Parrish wince. "Right, then. Haven't done a proper bit of second-story work in a while."

"Mi dispiace, amico." Marco placed his hand on Lazarus's shoulder. "You'll have to wait a little longer."

"You'll take Desmond with you?" Harriet asked. "I'd join you myself, but I've got to be at my regular employment tomorrow."

"Not you, nor Desmond." He turned and gave a slow

smile to the widow. "My partner for this particular job will be Mrs. Parrish."

She took a step backward. "Me? I don't know anything about breaking into anyplace."

"Leave the technicalities to me," he answered. "But with Harriet unavailable, I need a nice, respectable woman with me to make *me* look nice and respectable."

"While burglarizing a man's home," Mrs. Parrish added. She gripped her hands tightly. Would she refuse? He'd wager this would be the first time she'd actually broken the law. He could find a way into Devere's lodgings without her, but having her along would certainly help. Yet he wanted her near him.

Just to keep her safe.

After a moment, Mrs. Parrish sighed. "Just don't ask me to hit anyone. Don't burglars hit people?"

"Not the good ones." He'd broken into countless places—from heavily guarded palaces to shacks in slums—yet he found himself oddly looking forward to this experience, much as the impulse troubled him.

FOUR

Exhausted as she'd been last night, Bronwyn had found sleep elusive. Perhaps it was because of the unfamiliar bed—much more narrow than the one she'd been used to, and the mattress was stuffed with what felt like straw and rusty tacks. Her mind had played and replayed all the strange scenes she'd witnessed over the course of the day. Questions about her missing fortune and the evasive Devere kept tumbling through her thoughts like thrown dice, with no way to know if the pieces would land in her favor or cause her ruination.

She'd seen blood before—basins of it—but never spilled so violently as she'd witnessed last night. The whole boxing arena had stunk of sweat and the copper tang of blood, and the smell still lingered in her nostrils. It kept her awake enough to hear the sounds of a strange house creaking all around her like bones.

And there had been the fights themselves—including Marco's fast, brutal brawl with the awful man. Seeing him in action had been . . . shocking. Terrible. Slightly . . . arousing. The images had followed her to bed. Whenever she did manage to doze off, her dreams were rich with a voice like wine, and the gleam in a pair of wickedly clever dark eyes.

She woke feeling unrested, and disloyal to Hugh's memory.

Now she sat at the table in the Nemesis headquarters parlor, nursing a cup of tea and nibbling on dry toast, only half listening to Harriet as the other woman talked generally of her work at an accountancy firm.

"And that's why our most prestigious client is an emperor penguin who pays in sardines," Harriet said.

"Mm, very interesting," Bronwyn murmured. When Harriet laughed, Bronwyn realized just what the other woman had been saying, and her cheeks heated . "I am so sorry!"

But Harriet waved off her apology. "You're forgiven if you don't attend to every fascinating pearl of information from my lips." Her gaze turned sympathetic. "How strange all this must be for you."

"*Strange* is too mild a term. *Outlandish,* perhaps. Or *fantastical.*"

The other woman's look grew sober. "Sadly, there's nothing of fantasy about the work Nemesis does. The things I've seen since I've joined, the knowledge I've gained . . ." She rubbed her arms. "I'd say I wish I could unsee and unlearn it all, but I'd rather have full understanding and make a difference, rather than bury my head in the sand and do nothing."

Bronwyn studied the woman across the table. With her skin color, Harriet likely experienced a difficult existence, yet she chose to make her life even harder. Humbling, that kind of courage.

"How does a woman get into the business of vengeance?" she asked.

Harriet spread her hands. "How can she not? This is a

world run by men. Everything belongs to them—including women. We're always the ones to suffer, to be treated like children or animals." Anger heated her gaze. "The gifts my father regularly bestowed upon my mother were bruises and blackened eyes. She tried to leave him. Many times, but he threatened to take me and my brother away from her if she stayed away. The damn courts gave him that right. It didn't help that she was black and he was white. So she stayed. And went to an early death, courtesy of his fists and our glorious nation's law."

"I'm . . ." Offering an apology seemed so paltry. "I can understand why you'd want to help others."

"If only Nemesis had existed back then," Harriet said, her voice hard. "But it does now, and now I do my part to make certain no woman is hurt by any man's cruelty."

"Did your father . . . he didn't . . ."

Harriet smiled mirthlessly. "Oh, he tried to hit me once after my mother died." She pointed to a series of crescent-shaped scars on her knuckles. "His teeth made these when I broke his jaw. Left me alone after that."

Memories from last night flashed through Bronwyn's mind—the thud of fist meeting flesh, the tang of blood, men's shouts. And Harriet's mother, the victim of another man's brutality . . .

A whole realm of viciousness Bronwyn had never known.

"It doesn't amount for much," she said slowly, "but . . . for whatever it's worth . . . I'm sorry."

The other woman made a small nod. "I learned how to protect myself. I just wish more women were given the same tools, so they'd never have to suffer as my mother did."

"Can you show me?" Bronwyn asked after a moment. "How to use my fists as weapons?" This was a cruel world.

She was beginning to understand that fully. And she couldn't pretend anymore that she wasn't part of it.

Which was why, when Marco entered the flat fifteen minutes later, Bronwyn was hitting a pillow that Harriet held, with the older woman shouting, "That's right! Give it to him good!"

"Are you tenderizing your pillow?" Marco asked, closing the door behind him, and setting his hat down on a chair. "We could get you a softer one, if you prefer."

Bronwyn whirled to face him. She panted with exertion. Her hands already throbbed, and the effort of using just her fists dragged on the rest of her body. "Harriet's teaching me how to use my fists."

"I don't envy whoever is at the other end of those punches, be they pillow or man."

She turned away protectively. "Show me more, please?"

Harriet glanced at the mantel and set down the pillow. "Much as I'd relish the privilege, I have to make my omnibus, or I'll be late for work. But there's a women's gymnasium in Brompton, and they offer lessons in fisticuffs, target shooting, and judo. I used to go there with Eva. I'll take you there sometime. In the meanwhile," she added, buttoning her coat and pinning on her hat, "Marco can give you some more guidance. He won trophies at Cambridge."

Bronwyn's brows lifted. Here was a small piece of the puzzle that was Marco. A Cambridge man, and champion pugilist, as well. Both facts were expected surprises.

At the door, Harriet said, "Enjoy your foray into burglary." She waved, and then left, her footsteps light on the creaking stairs leading to the chemist's shop.

With Harriet gone, leaving Bronwyn alone with Marco, the parlor became immediately smaller. He was a lean man, not very tall, yet his dark, edged presence filled the room. She put her breakfast dishes away, conscious of his gaze on her. Could he sense with that uncanny awareness of his that she'd dreamed of him?

"Devere keeps his lodgings in Highbury," Marco said as she made unnecessary trips back and forth from the kitchen.

"It seems it would make more sense to go at night." She finally returned to the parlor. "Safer."

But he shook his head. "The front door to the building is unlocked during the day, and usually only the landlord is around. All the other lodgers are working bachelors."

"Leaving the place essentially empty," she deduced. "And we'll look less suspicious, too. A gentleman and widow calling on a friend."

He eyed her gown. "Those weeds are like a sign lit by electric bulbs. WOMAN IN FIRST MOURNING OUT ON THE STREET. You stand out wherever you go—and it's not just because you're pretty."

Her heart thumped at his admission. It shouldn't matter if he considered her homely or the most beautiful woman in the world—they were working together, and she was, as he'd pointed out, mourning her husband. It shouldn't matter. Yet it did.

Was he being honest? He didn't seem like the sort of man who doled out compliments readily, but one who would use them like weapons.

"These clothes are all I have," she answered, "and I *am* in first mourning. There's nothing I can do about that."

He cursed quietly in Italian. Either she was entranced by the language or the man speaking it, because even his swearing sounded musical.

"You still have Harriet's cloak from last night?" At her nod, he pressed, "Then put that on, and wear the hood up again. Leave that frightful bonnet behind."

She should object to not wearing her veil, but she hated

the blasted thing, clinging to her face and fogging her vision. So she hurried up the stairs and donned the cloak. At least it was chilly out, as evidenced by the leaden sky, or else she'd suffocate beneath the heavy wool.

"This has to do," she said, coming back down to the parlor.

She resisted the impulse to step backward when Marco reached for her. His fingers brushed her cheek as he pulled up the cloak's hood, and though his hand was gloved, his brief touch shot warmth through her, recalling her dream. Stunned, she could only stand there, staring up at him.

His pupils dilated within the darkness of his eyes, and he gave one quick, rough inhale.

"It'll do very well," he said in a low voice.

From the exterior, Devere's lodgings on Aberdeen Road appeared perfectly respectable. Potted plants flanked the doorway of the terraced house, and the brick façade looked regularly scrubbed of the city's ubiquitous coal smoke. Though bachelors lived within, curtains hung in most of the clean windows, revealing that the men might be single, but they still took pride in their home. Or the lodgers paid a charwoman to come in and tidy everything up on a regular basis.

The building was respectable, but Bronwyn and Marco's purpose wasn't. She kept glancing over her shoulder as they climbed the front steps, certain that the passing pedestrians could see their criminal intent hanging over them like a dark miasma.

"The more suspicious you look, the more people have a reason to suspect you," Marco muttered as he escorted her up the stairs.

"I can't help it," she hissed under her breath. "I've

never"—she shot a quick glance behind her—"let myself into someone's home uninvited."

As Marco had predicted, the front door to the lodging house was unlocked, and he opened it confidently. They stepped into a carpeted foyer, with a hallway just beyond it, and doors presumably leading to flats off the hallway. The carpet showed wear from the tread of numerous men over the years, the banisters on the staircase rubbed to a shine from countless hands, but like the front of the building, everything seemed neat and cared for.

"Devere invited us when he took your money," Marco said. He gazed up the stairs. "Third floor."

She allowed him to lead her up the steps, even as her heart beat in her throat. She wasn't certain what she'd say if anyone caught them there. The landlord could throw them out, or, worse, summon the constabulary.

"Is that how you justify it?" she asked.

"I don't need justification to do my job."

They didn't pass anyone in the stairwell, the whole building resonant with the silence of men away at their offices. Finally, they reached the third floor, and Marco walked directly to one of the two doors off the landing.

He tried the doorknob. Locked.

"And now?" she whispered.

"Now we go inside." From within his coat, he slipped a slim leather case and flipped it open.

She started when she saw the line of thin metal picks neatly arranged within the case. "Those are—"

"Carpenters work with hammers," he answered, bending down and sliding one of the picks into the lock. "Masons have their trowels."

"And you have a thief's lock picks."

"I never steal anything," he replied without looking at her. He carefully inserted another tiny metal tool into the lock. "I liberate important information."

He manipulated words to absolve himself of wrongdoing, sending a tremor of unease up her spine. Just *what* did he do when he wasn't working for Nemesis? Likely he had to pick more than a few locks for the organization's missions. Still, something about the ease and artistry of him at the lock . . . he had a skill that went beyond Nemesis's needs.

She'd read the sensationalized tales in periodicals about blackguards, scoundrels, even highwaymen from long ago, and found those stories . . . interesting. Faintly titillating.

The sight of Marco now gently easing picks in and out of the lock made her heart beat harder—and not with fear.

Heaven help me, I've turned into a reprobate, aroused by the sight of a man breaking into another man's home.

Her reverie broke when she heard the front door downstairs open. "Oh, hurry," she whispered urgently.

Yet before the last syllable left her mouth, Marco had turned the knob to Devere's flat, revealing the rooms within. They stepped inside quickly, with Marco shutting the door noiselessly behind them. For a moment, they paused, waiting. But there were no hasty footsteps on the stair. No calls for them to quit the premises immediately.

She exhaled. They were safe. And she'd just participated in her very first criminal act.

"There's a chair by the table," he offered, "if you need to sit down."

"My feet can hold me, thank you." She exhaled.

He seemed to fight a smile. "We'll make a burglar out of you yet."

"I thought you said you didn't steal."

He shrugged. "Definitions are slippery things."

"But not as slippery as you."

He appeared entirely unperturbed as he gazed with

perceptive eyes around Devere's rooms. Bronwyn tried to see what he saw. There was a front parlor with a small stove in one corner, and beyond that, a bedroom. The furnishings were of decent but not extravagant quality. Though the curtains were open, a heaviness lingered in the air.

"No one's been here for some time." She wrinkled her nose at the musty atmosphere.

"A month at least," Marco said. "Maybe more." He moved through the rooms, quietly opening cupboards and poking behind furniture.

Trying to make herself useful, she did the same. "Tell me what we're looking for."

"Documents, notebooks." He pulled open the top drawer of a writing desk, removing a sheaf of paper. This he set on the parlor table, and continued to prowl through the room.

Bronwyn moved past him and into the bedroom. Her skin tightened to be in a stranger's bedchamber, and a man's, at that. But there was more at stake than propriety. The bed itself was unmade, and when Bronwyn opened a chest of drawers, she found only a few shirtfronts. Everything else had been cleared out.

"Moldy cheese and spoiled milk in the pantry," Marco said, just loud enough for her to hear from the other room. "He left in a hurry."

"What if he took what we're looking for with him?"

"He's sloppy enough to owe money to the most dangerous people in London," Marco answered. "If he bolted, he'd do it without thinking clearly. Whatever we need is still here."

He spoke with such assurance, she couldn't doubt him.

There was another, smaller desk in the bedroom. She discovered a notepad, but the paper inside was blank. Still, she tucked it into a pocket in her cloak. It might prove useful somehow—though she doubted it.

Sudden inspiration struck her, and she knelt beside the bed. She lifted up the mattress, and gave a little cry of excitement when she uncovered a portfolio. Grabbing the folder, she took it out to the parlor.

"Look what I found!"

Marco stepped close as she undid the portfolio's cloth tape fastening, then opened it.

He started to laugh, and she fervently wished the myth of self-immolation was true, because she'd never been more mortified in her whole life, and that included the time she appeared at a debutante ball with her skirt tucked into her bustle.

The portfolio held postcards. More specifically, pornographic postcards.

Men and women tangled in numerous configurations, some of them downright gymnastic. She wanted to slap her hands over her eyes, or turn away, but she couldn't. Her gaze remained fastened to the pictures.

"These postcards must be doctored," she heard herself exclaim. There were knots of limbs intertwined, mouths open, hands upon bare flesh. "People can't really do those things."

"Can't they?" he murmured. He picked up one particularly appalling/intriguing picture where a man held a woman up against a wall, her legs wrapped around his waist, the couple enthusiastically . . . coupling, if the blurriness of the postcard was any indicator. "This one's always been quite fun." He dropped it back into the stack and moved on in his search of the room.

She tore her gaze from the pictures to stare at him. "You've *done* this?"

"I might've," he said over his shoulder as he rifled through another drawer.

Now she was absolutely certain she would burst into flames. It was impossible to look at him now and not imagine him doing those filthy, *wonderful* things in the pictures. And he was so clever, he could come up with many more variations. Intelligent men had always intimidated and intrigued her—but this added a whole new dimension to what a quick-witted man might be capable of.

As he continued to sort through the drawer's contents, he asked, "You never did any of that with your husband?"

Considering he wasn't part snake, no, she thought. "Of course not," she said aloud. The very idea that Hugh might even suggest such positions was ludicrous.

"My apologies, Mrs. Parrish. I didn't mean to offend."

"Apology accepted." She gathered up the photographs. "Clearly, this has nothing to do with my fortune or Devere's whereabouts."

He returned the drawer to its place in the cabinet. "But we *did* learn he likes a wank before bed."

She shot him a glance that said such comments were not appreciated.

"While you were busy looking at those pictures," he continued, turning back to her, "I found this tucked inside an empty marmalade jar at the back of a cupboard." He brandished a sheet of thin, almost transparent paper that was covered with strange symbols as well as letters.

"Those are the same symbols we found on documents at his offices yesterday," she noted.

From within his coat, he pulled out those same documents and spread them on the table. "Very kind of Devere, to leave me a means of cracking his code."

She glanced back and forth between the papers. It was an impossible task to take those arcane pictographs and turn them into something comprehensible, but Marco braced his hands on the table and studied the documents. He overlaid the new paper onto the ones from the office. The images on the papers suddenly formed completed letters.

"That *stronzo,*" he muttered.

"What?" she demanded. "What did he do?"

Marco's hands clenched into fists. "Devere was a gambler, all right, except he didn't gamble with his own money."

Her eyes widened. "He used *Hugh's* money."

"His, and other clients.' " He pointed to pieces of the paperwork. "See here. Details of some garden-variety gambling. Boxing matches, card games, horse races. But the bigger losses came with investments in business schemes. Like those newspaper clippings we found. Railway lines and housing developments, none of which were ever built. Just stole cash from fools like Devere."

"I cannot believe that Hugh would ever condone those kinds of *investments.*"

"He didn't. None of Devere's clients knew."

"But if he lost all that cash," she pressed, "why is it that none of those other clients have come forward demanding their lost money?"

"Because he paid them all back."

"Not me," she countered.

"He didn't have to." Marco looked grim. "A widow with no living male relatives—who would you complain to? What recourse would you have to get your fortune back? If someone was going to be stuck with the bill, it was going to be you."

Rage clouded her vision. "He got away with it because I'm a woman. How . . . unfair." A paltry word to describe what had happened.

Marco tucked all the papers inside his coat. "A fair world for women, it's not. Never has been."

There was Harriet's mother, and all the women who'd suffered at the hands of men, with barely any legal recourse. All her own property had become Hugh's upon their marriage. In truth, she'd become his property.

"So long as I had books and a room in which to practice

my violin," she said bitterly, "I didn't care." She shook her
head. "I hadn't known. If I'd made myself pay attention, I
could've done something. For myself. For other women."

"You're doing something now."

"But what?" She spread her hands wide. "Devere took
my money and ran off. There isn't a sodding lot to do
about it now." She was too angry to care about her crude
language.

"Not true." He folded his arms across his chest. "This
isn't the end of the search."

"He could be anywhere," she pointed out. "Japan or
Peru or Norway."

"Then we go to Japan or Peru or Norway and wring
that money out of him." Again, Marco sounded so in control, so self-assured, but she couldn't share in his cer-
tainty. "If he bolted in a hurry, then he left something
behind that will tell us where he's gone. He did leave behind this key to his code," he added, nodding at the sheet
of thin paper. "Need to keep looking."

He sorted through the other documents on the table,
but after several minutes, he'd offered no answers.

Frustrated, she stuck her hands into the pockets of her
cloak. Her fingers brushed against the edges of the notepad she'd taken. Her temper frayed, and she tossed the
notepad onto the table.

Marco's focus sharpened. "Where did you find that?"

"In the bedroom desk. You needn't bother. There's
nothing written on it."

"Not now. But there was." With that cryptic remark, he
flipped open the pad and stared at the blank paper. From
his endless supply of inner coat pockets, he produced a
small piece of charcoal. He used it to lightly rub back and
forth across the surface of the paper.

Figures appeared on the sheet, figures pressed into the
paper by a pen nib. The original writing was gone, but it

had left behind a series of ghostly lines. A few words, but mostly numbers. *My God.*

She read it aloud. " 'Dov. 12:45, 1:50, 6:32. Cal. 3:25, 5:15. 9:41.' These are times," she deduced.

"A train schedule," Marco said. "Ships, too. Steamer ships. *Dov.* is Dover."

"Which would make *Cal.* Calais," she realized.

"Our man fled to France." He tore off the sheet of charcoal-rubbed paper and pocketed it. "It's a good place for people fleeing financial misdeeds. Other misdeeds, too. But we're not concerned with that."

She recalled stories of people like Beau Brummel and Byron who'd run to France to hide from their creditors. If Devere owed money to Charlie, and others, he'd likely do the same. "He won't come back."

Marco's expression was grim. "To break even, he had to steal, and I doubt there isn't a single bridge he hasn't burned in England. France gives him the chance to start over. We'll find him there."

"My understanding of geography isn't particularly vast," she said, "but France is a fairly large country, with many places for someone who doesn't want to be found to disappear."

"Two hundred and sixty thousand square miles, more or less."

"More or less." His knowledge felt like a barrier, keeping her at a distance, even as she felt herself drawn closer as their minds worked together.

Stalking to the window, Marco peered out at the street, his gaze always in motion. "Devere's proven he isn't the wisest philosopher in the agora. He won't think of places like Lyon or Marseille. But he'll want to find himself new work. A tiny mind like his will consider only one city— the biggest and most dangerous city in France."

The answer leaped forward in her mind. "Paris."

"Paris," he concurred.

Goodness, the more time she spent with him, the more her brain worked, like an unused muscle finally exercising. Would she be sore from the activity, the way her hands ached from her boxing lesson with Harriet?

Her taxed mind recalled something he'd said moments earlier. "*We'll* find him?"

Light fell across his face in sharp angles as he turned from the window. "You've met Devere. If Nemesis has a chance of finding him, it's because you'll be able to identify him."

He spoke in such a matter-of-fact way about it, as though every week she took a train to Dover, hopped on a steam packet to Calais, and then ventured into Paris to track down a thief. Fear tightened along the back of her neck. What Marco proposed went far beyond even breaking into a man's lodgings. This was . . .

Adventure.

Part of her reared back in fright at the word. It meant unpredictability, walking off the well-trod paths she knew, leaving the role she'd been playing all her life.

Precisely why it intrigued her.

But this sort of adventure would be far different from the sort she read about. This was *real,* with all the sweat, blood, and danger to go with it.

Marco suddenly tensed. What had him so on guard? All she heard were the sounds of carriages and a few voices on the street outside. But then she caught it: someone's tread on the stairs.

Grabbing her wrist, Marco started to pull her toward the bedroom. But before they made it into the other chamber, the door to Devere's rooms opened.

A man stood on the threshold. He wore a decent but loud checked suit and a bowler hat. It wasn't Devere. Seeing Marco and Bronwyn standing in the flat, the stranger's eyes widened, then narrowed.

"What the hell are you doing here?" he challenged.

"Who are you?" Marco's voice changed, his accent much less refined.

"A friend of the bloke that rents this place," the man fired back. "He asked me to look in sometimes while he's away."

"Where's my rent?" Marco demanded.

The man glanced at Bronwyn.

"It's been three months," she said, striving to make her own accent more common, though she wasn't as successful as Marco. "And not a cent."

Her attempt at a Cockney tone must have been decent enough, because the man snapped, "Check your ruddy ledgers, because everything's been paid. My friend took care of that before he left."

"You heard from him since he went?" Marco demanded.

The stranger's face closed up like a vermin trap. "I ain't telling nobody nothing, especially not some rent collector who can't read a sodding account book." He pointed at the door. "Get moving."

"I'll give it another look," Marco vowed, "but if I read my numbers right, then you'll be seeing us again." He strode toward the door, and Bronwyn trotted quickly after him. They slipped past the glowering man, and though she wanted to run down the stairs, she made herself keep with Marco's slower pace. She also resisted the impulse to look back over her shoulder, like a burglar fleeing a crime.

Which is exactly what she was.

They reached the street, and though the danger was behind them, her heart still knocked painfully from their encounter with the stranger in Devere's room. It had all been so terrifyingly visceral and real.

"A bunch of tripe," Marco said suddenly.

"What?"

"We weren't the only ones playing parts back there. That bloke was a thug looking for his employer's money. Devere wouldn't have paid for his room for months, not if he skipped out that quickly. He wouldn't be coming back, so nobody would check on his flat."

"Oh," she said softly. None of that had occurred to her.

"It's just a matter of time before the debt collectors ransack the place," Marco continued, glancing up and down the street. "We were lucky we found the clues when we did."

He hailed a cab, and soon they were heading back to headquarters. Marco sat with that same watchful elegance he always displayed.

Looking out the window, he muttered something.

"I beg your pardon?" she asked.

"I said, 'You did well back there,'" he admitted.

"Believe me," she answered, "I'm just as surprised as you are." She hadn't even thought about how to best play along with Marco's rent-collector ruse. Only slipped into the part, though with less finesse than he'd shown.

"Not just the gambit with that poorly dressed oaf." He glanced at her. "Finding that notepad. Figuring out Devere was heading to Calais and Paris."

She picked at the stitching of her cloak. "You would've found the notepad and figured it out without me."

"Yes," he answered easily. "But you deciphered a good deal, too. I'm trained. You aren't."

Perhaps she was being as suspicious as Nemesis wanted her to be, but his praise sounded . . . grudging. As if he didn't want to admit to himself, let alone her, that she could actually manage the situation, or even thrive within it.

Annoyance heated her cheeks. "Why shouldn't I be able to do those things? Because I'm a woman?"

He lowered his eyelids. "Perhaps you've noticed that both Harriet and Riza are Nemesis agents, and female."

"My social class, then?"

He gave another Italian shrug. She was beginning to hate those shrugs. They communicated so much while also remaining perfectly opaque. If only there was an English equivalent.

"You may think me nothing but a silly society lady," she said. "But I've seen things. More than most."

His brows rose in disbelief.

"Consumption isn't a pretty disease," she continued.

"I've seen it," he replied, his gaze shuttered.

"And I nursed my husband through the illness. I watched him die. Slowly. Awfully. My life hasn't been all tea parties and regattas."

He bowed his head slightly. "Again, I have to offer you my apologies. Your maid didn't tell us the extent of your involvement with Mr. Parrish's illness."

"It was considerable," she said tightly. "He took his last, labored breath in my arms."

"It's not an easy thing," he murmured. "To see death, to touch it, even, and be unable to stop it."

What had he seen to give him this shared, bitter knowledge? She'd been terrified when it had become clear that Hugh wouldn't get better. And some of her fear wasn't just for him, but for herself. If a young man like him could die, couldn't she, too? Did Marco think of his own death when confronted with its specter?

Instead, she asked, "When do we leave for Paris?"

"Tonight."

She braced herself as the carriage rocked with a turn. "He's been out of the country for three months. Surely we can wait until tomorrow."

"Doesn't matter if he's been gone an hour or a year," Marco answered. "All time is valuable, and every moment we spend on this side of the Channel is a moment less for us to get your money back."

Arguing with him would be ridiculous. Clearly, Marco knew what he was about. This wasn't his first assignment—anyone could see that. He'd already advised her to do precisely what he directed. So she had to trust him, though every part of her shouted that trusting him was almost as dangerous as whatever threat they faced abroad.

Marco couldn't tally the number of times he'd made the voyage from England to France. He now preferred his intelligence assignments to keep him in Britain and had enough seniority so that his choices were usually honored. But when he'd been a young agent, he spent so many hours ferrying back and forth on the English Channel—on steam packets, fishing boats, cargo ships—he almost qualified as a sailor. Thank God he didn't get seasick.

Mrs. Parrish might. The Channel was notorious for its rough crossing. Even now, the *Pauline Ann* rocked its way over the water. Most of the passengers had taken to their cabins—if they could afford cabins. The unlucky souls without private accommodation leaned over the rails, denied solitude in their illness.

Earlier, he'd knocked on Mrs. Parrish's cabin door, but there'd been no sound within. Either she'd been too ill to speak, or she was outside for fresh air. After a quick turn around the ship with no sign of her, he assumed she was sick in her berth. Meanwhile, his own stomach rumbled, but with hunger, not seasickness.

So he found himself a seat in the dining room. Most of the tables were empty, the waiters staggering between the few hardy passengers with plates of roast beef and mashed potatoes, as the chandeliers swung overhead. Just as he was about to cut into his overcooked, gray meat, he glanced up to see Mrs. Parrish standing in front of his table. Immediately, he got to his feet and offered her a chair. She took it, looking not at all green. In fact, her cheeks held a pretty pink color, and he smelled cool air and mist on her skin.

After she sat, he resumed his own place, and motioned for the waiter. She gave her order in perfect French.

"I looked for you," Marco said once the server had gone. "You weren't in your cabin and you weren't on the promenade deck."

"There's a way onto the bow." She sipped a glass of wine, glancing at the mostly deserted dining room. "We've got the place to ourselves."

"Like you had the bow to yourself," he noted.

He guessed that she modeled her shrug on the one he often made, the one he'd learned from his mother. It often had the consequence of maddening the other Nemesis agents, and his father. Poor English. They never learned the benefit of a proper body gesture. But the Widow Parrish seemed to be on her way.

"Is there a strategy when we reach Paris?" she asked. The waiter appeared with a plate of actually edible-looking chicken and asparagus. He bowed and smiled at her thanks, but disappeared before Marco could demand the same food.

Seeing as how the dining room was nearly empty, there wasn't any harm in speaking of the plans. "Two Nemesis agents are going to meet us there. You haven't met them yet—Simon and Alyce."

"A brother and sister, like Desmond and Riza?" She cut herself a dainty piece of chicken, her table manners faultless even in the middle of a rough evening crossing.

"Husband and wife."

She raised her brows. "I didn't know Nemesis agents could marry."

"No rules to say they can't." He swallowed some depressing wine.

Frowning, she said, "But the way you talked, I thought that meant . . . it wasn't possible to wed if one was in Nemesis."

"I used to think so. The work isn't conducive to happy marital unions," he conceded, "given that we're on assignment half the time or working at our other employment the other half. Not many spouses would tolerate that kind of neglect. Yet somehow, there have been exceptions."

"So some spouses do endure the work."

"Most wouldn't." Was there a Nemesis operative that had caught her eye? Desmond?

His heart unexpectedly pitched. It had to be because of the ship's movements. What else would cause that sensation?

Not her, or her possible choice. If she wanted Desmond, it didn't matter to him. It couldn't. He was on an assignment he didn't want, and all he had to do was complete it. Whether or not he felt a growing attraction to a spirited, redheaded widow was irrelevant.

Do the job and move on. That had ever been his axiom, whether working for the British government or Nemesis. *Always forward.*

"Simon and Alyce met on an assignment," he noted. "He was working to oust the corrupt management of a copper mine, and she worked at the mine itself. It wasn't a likely match. His family title dates to the Tudor period, and she broke rocks for a living. Somehow, *amore* found them."

He shook his head. Even having attended their wedding a month earlier, Marco still couldn't quite believe that Simon had become a married man, or found a woman brave—or foolish—enough to take him as her husband.

"He's got connections to circles we'll need," Marco continued. "And as his wife, Alyce can learn things, too."

"And then?" Mrs. Parrish pressed.

"Then . . . we figure out the rest of our plan. An assignment is fluid, like the ocean. It hits unexpected squalls, or doldrums, and we adapt. But there is something I know for certain we've got to do once we arrive in France."

"That being?"

Oh, she wasn't going to like this. "We get rid of your widow's weeds."

FIVE

Marco expected his announcement would be greeted with resistance at best. At worst, she'd throw her glass of wine in his face and storm off in a rage.

Neither happened.

Instead, Mrs. Parrish rolled the stem of her glass between her fingers, contemplating it, while a small frown creased between her brows.

"Why?" she asked simply. She didn't look at him, reminding him of one of those Renaissance paintings of shy, vicious nymphs in attendance on Diana—beautiful, serene, and capable of killing an unwary man.

"The French might not be quite as obsessed with mourning as the English," he explained, "but they know a widow's dark clothing when they see it."

"Surely France is filled with widows," she murmured. "Unless French men have somehow created a patent medicine that grants them eternal life."

"Bordeaux is the closest they've come to that."

"It doesn't make them immortal."

"Fortunately, no. Men die there just as they do everywhere else." He, himself, had escaped death more times than his considerable memory could recall. That especially persistent, talented German assassin and their deadly encounter on the rooftops of Constantinople came to mind, though. But only because Marco had a scar just below his kidney to remind him of how near he'd come to the afterlife.

Thank God he had no woman waiting at home for him, worried that he might not return from an assignment. How could he put anyone through that kind of hell?

"Widows in France are common enough," he continued. "Noticeable, though. Easier to remember a woman dressed in weeds than one out of mourning."

"And whatever it is we're going to do in France, we aren't supposed to be memorable," she deduced.

"The best way to collect information is through subtlety."

She did look at him then, her gray-green eyes narrowed. Shadows from the swinging overhead lights drifted back and forth across her face, adding to the illusion that she was some cunning forest creature lying in wait among the trees.

"A spy," she said abruptly.

He didn't move. Not a blink or twitch.

"I've been trying and trying to figure out what it is you do for employment when you aren't working for Nemesis," she said. "The way you took on different personae made me think at first you were an actor. Then a thief, with the skill you had picking locks. But now I see it. You're a spy." She shook her head. "Those words didn't really leave my mouth, did they?"

"They did." Mrs. Parrish might be somewhat sheltered, but she wasn't stupid. "I can also deny it, but we're partners in this mission. It won't succeed unless we trust each other."

Her expression barely changed, but he could read her, and the slight parting of her lips, the dilation of her pupils.

His lack of denial shocked her, yet she was learning the game, learning how to keep herself opaque. Adaptable, this widow. He liked that.

Softly, she said, "You realize, of course, the chance you've taken by admitting your . . . activities." Setting her glass down, she spread her hands. "What's to prevent me from going to some foreign agency—the Russians, for example—and telling them all about you in exchange for a substantial amount of money? More money than Hugh's missing fortune."

"Nothing's stopping you." He smiled. "Except for me."

His smile seemed to alarm her. She collected herself. "I could slip away, out of your clutches."

"Mrs. Parrish," he said, "I'm thirty-eight years old. Do you honestly think that I would've made it to this advanced age if I wasn't very good at my job? One mostly ingenuous widow presents little challenge, no matter how clever that widow might happen to be."

Color drained from her cheeks. "That sounds suspiciously like a threat."

"No more a threat than you suggesting you'd sell me out to the Russians." He took a bite of his tired roast beef and attempted to chew it.

"Which I'd never do."

He swallowed, though it took effort, and chased it with the last swallows of his wine. "There you go. We've reached detente simply on the basis of mutual distrust."

"I thought this was about trusting each other."

"Two sides of the same coin." He waved the waiter over to refill his wine glass. Once the server had come and gone, staggering, Marco continued. "Besides, I'm already known to the major intelligence bureaus across the Continent and Asia, so exposure isn't much of a threat."

"Yet you hold my life in your hands."

"The man driving a wagon could easily run down people in the street. A ship's captain could run the vessel into the shoals and drown the passengers. But most don't. Every day is a delicate balance between our darker impulses and the need to keep the world safe and sane."

A stunned little laugh burst from her. "Now I know for certain you're a spy. Words come so glibly to you."

"I'm half Italian," he answered. "Either we talk with our hands or with our mouths. But either way, we talk. However"—he lowered his voice—"it would serve us both better if you didn't make a habit of calling me that word, especially in public."

Instead of speaking it aloud, she mouthed it silently. *Spy*. It made her lips form intriguing shapes. Shapes that gave him unwonted ideas.

"There," she said. "That's the last I'll say it in public. It's only . . . as you said, I'm not exactly conversant in the world outside what I already know. The fact that you are . . . what you are . . . it must be very exciting."

His mouth twisted. He'd thought so at first. Then learned the truth of it. "Sometimes. Mostly it's ugly, gritty, and dangerous." He held her gaze as he spoke. She flinched slightly.

He usually worked under cover of darkness, but that didn't make blood any less sticky, or flow less freely. And he'd spent more than one night awake, thinking of the soldiers he'd sent to their deaths just because he'd passed a piece of paper into someone's hands.

He saved more lives than ended them, even if he could never receive thanks or commendation for his work. Simon had medals and a soldier's bragging rights—though he never exercised them. Marco could only try to sleep easier, contemplating the Russian missionaries he'd saved from execution—a ruse the Russian government had itself attempted to perpetrate in order to blame England and thus spark more war.

"Now that you've successfully guessed my other occupation," he continued, "you can understand why we'll need you out of those weeds and into something less memorable."

She rubbed between her brows, her expression more thoughtful than pained. "Half mourning?"

"Just as noticeable. The intent is to keep us both as forgettable as possible."

"I doubt anyone can forget you," she said, then looked abashed at her own admission.

Ah, so he was mistaken. The widow had something of an interest in him, not Desmond. Something that went beyond the mission. That he felt a tug of interest in her, too, didn't help matters. Her looks, yes, but her intelligence, as well, her willingness to push past her uncertainty and fear. These things pulled on him, intrigued him. He should only be interested in completing the job, and then going on to the next. There wasn't time or room in his life for dalliances with women like her. He had a feeling she wouldn't be content with a few weeks, which was as much as he could give any lover before moving on to an assignment. Temporary—that's what he was, in everything but his chosen professions.

"Invisibility is a skill that takes years to master, but it can be done." Concentrating, he made himself feel small, shabby. Someone hardly worth anyone's attention. He drew into himself, as if disappearing into his own skin.

Then he called for the waiter.

The server was only twenty feet away, but it was as if Marco hadn't said a word. The waiter glanced around the dining room, a pitcher of sloshing water in his hands, looking for someone who might need his services.

"Waiter," Marco called again, and with some volume. *"Garçon."*

Nothing. The server didn't move.

As if releasing a breath, Marco inhabited himself again. He grew bigger on the inside, worthwhile.

"Waiter," he said again.

The server immediately came to his side.

"I'm done battling my dinner," Marco said. "Take it away."

"Of course, sir." Bowing, the waiter removed Marco's plate, and scurried out of the dining room.

Turning back to Mrs. Parrish, he was gratified to see the astonishment on her face.

"I knew you could playact," she breathed, "but that was . . . some kind of sorcery."

"No magic, only the will to make myself unseen." Then he surprised himself by adding, "I can teach you how."

A corner of her mouth turned up. "I've had enough of being invisible, thank you."

That was something he often considered, especially after his years working with Nemesis. He could choose when to make himself disappear, when he wasn't important or worth attention. Not many had that option.

"You'll have to abandon your weeds," he said. "Until the mission is over. Then you can wear bombazine for the rest of your life, if that's your desire." Though he thought it a damn waste. All that black crape did her creamy complexion no favors. "Will you do it?"

She didn't speak, her gaze fixed on the dark windows and the occasional spray of seawater hitting the glass. For one of the first times, he couldn't quite read her. But he wouldn't bully her into making a decision. Either she came to this choice on her own, or not at all. A reluctant or resentful partner made for a rocky job.

And he wanted to know what decision she'd make, with no one but her own mind telling her what to do.

At last, she exhaled.

"All right," she said, more to herself than him. "This might not be an adventure story with a guaranteed happy ending, but . . . I'll try to do my part to get us one."

He felt it then. A small filament, a thread of danger that he wasn't as indifferent to Mrs. Parrish as he'd like to be. One of the rare moments in his adult life that he didn't feel himself in perfect control.

The last time Bronwyn had visited a modiste, she was arranging her mourning wardrobe. In truth, the seamstress had visited Bronwyn at her home, since she wasn't permitted to leave the house. Some of her clothing had been dyed—the more budget-conscious option—but other gowns had been specially made to accommodate her new status as a widow.

Mired as she'd been in sadness, leafing through fashion prints of women in dull, somber clothing hadn't lifted her spirits. If anything, sorrow had weighed even more heavily on her chest, crushing her, the bolts of crape and bombazine forming dark shrouds around her.

This is my life, she'd thought. *For the next two years, this is who I'm to be. A shade. A living reminder that everything dies.*

Now she stood in front of the mirror at a Calais modiste's shop, trying not to feel too much pleasure in her new clothing.

"Are you sure Madame would not prefer the emerald jacquard?" the large but elegantly dressed woman asked in French. "The color, it would set off Madame's skin and hair."

"This will do well enough," Bronwyn answered in French as well. She smoothed her hand down the skirt of the pale slate gown. Her other choices had been similarly muted: a fawn merino day dress, a wool sateen walking dress the hue of a bay leaf, and, because Marco had insisted on a gown for evening, a pearl-gray lutestring silk with minimal embellishment. The modiste had all these dresses premade, requiring a minimal amount of alteration to make them fit.

The dresses weren't the lively, bright hues that the seamstress—and Bronwyn's own color-loving heart— wanted for her. But Bronwyn wouldn't be swayed.

She stepped from the fitting room. Though the hour was early, Marco was all alertness as he paced the shop. After docking last night, they'd taken rooms at one of Calais's many hotels. A door had adjoined their room, and though she knew it was a useless gesture, she'd locked her side. Again, given the long and strenuous day, she should have fallen instantly asleep. Instead, she'd lain awake, listening to Marco moving quietly in his room. Hugh's bedroom had been separated from hers by a bathroom and closet, so she'd never grown familiar with the sounds of a man readying for bed.

Yet either the walls of the hotel had been exceptionally thin, or she'd been too attuned to Marco. He had a soft, careful tread, yet she'd felt his every step. The tap running as he washed before bed. This morning, too, she'd heard the splash in the basin as he'd shaved, and heat and curiosity had pulsed through her sleep-fogged body, as though it—and her imagination—were out of her control.

They'd breakfasted in near silence. When they'd finished and they'd checked out of the hotel, he'd taken her immediately to this small shop a cab ride away. Then installed himself in the front room while she'd sequestered herself with the seamstress. Typical of her countrymen, the Frenchwoman hadn't looked askance at Bronwyn being accompanied by Marco, without the chaperoning presence of a maid, nor the fact that Bronwyn wasn't moving from mourning to second or even half mourning. No, it didn't seem to matter to the modiste what Bronwyn's intentions were, only that the money for the gowns would be paid.

Morality had a different price across the Channel.

The shop itself brimmed with beautiful gowns made of luxurious fabrics, though most of them showed signs of slight wear. Their original owners must have had to part with them, needing to raise money for one reason or another. Perhaps their protectors had cast them off. Or maybe the women had had to see one of those secret, special doctors. The kind that ushered away unwanted pregnancy. Bronwyn herself hadn't needed such a doctor, using her own preventive measures, but the whispers she'd heard from some of society's faster set told her that those men existed, and, for the right amount, could rid a woman of a unwelcome baby.

She'd also heard that some women didn't survive the procedure. What a brutal world this was, if only one looked past the pretty surfaces and elegant gowns.

Her own dresses were probably for sale somewhere in the London equivalent of this shop. The thought was even more sobering.

Marco turned at her approach. She waited for a breathless moment as he boldly looked at her, up and down, a slight frown creasing his brow.

"Did you care for him very much?" he asked.

She blinked at the unexpected question. He seemed just as surprised that he'd asked.

Her immediate reaction was to snap that it was no blasted business of his how she felt about Hugh. Yet she'd been holding herself in for an eternity. All her thoughts, her feelings about marriage, and marriage to Hugh in particular; she'd been unable to speak to anyone about them. Her role had been that of attentive wife, then nursemaid. And then, ultimately, widow.

Words and emotions built within her, like one of those pressurized valves used in steam engines. Marco was the perfect person to speak to—a spy, a man who dealt in secrets. Who lived on the outside of society. What did it matter if he knew her thoughts?

She walked to the counter, where an array of paste jewelry shimmered in the gaslight. Picking up one brooch in the shape of a beetle, she said, "I was happy to have the offer. I wasn't one of the poorest girls on the market, but I wasn't wealthy, either. My father was a second son's son, and we got by on the income of a small estate with a decently performing tin mine on the property. Hugh was the best offer I received. It didn't hurt that he was good-looking and sometimes made me laugh."

Marco kept silent as she continued to sort through the jewelry. She pictured the butterfly and leaf pins adorning the bosoms of the same women who'd sold their gowns. Did they know that the jewels their protectors had given them weren't real, or did it come as a bitter surprise when they'd sold the jewelry, only to learn they were cheap baubles?

If those women didn't know how little they meant to the men who kept them, they'd learned soon.

"We were . . . happy enough," she murmured, more to herself than Marco. "He called me 'sparrow' and liked the dinner parties I'd host. That was sufficient, I suppose. It wasn't . . . a passionate marriage." She couldn't look at him when she spoke, and her face heated like a furnace, but it felt right and freeing to speak this way. Was it because he was an outsider, a spy? Perhaps because she truly didn't know Marco, she could tell him things she'd never said to anyone.

"And when he got sick?" Marco asked quietly.

She held a ruby-colored earring between her fingers, watching the light play across its glassy surface. "Our

doctor in England suggested we go abroad to a spa. I
learned what I could tolerate." The basins full of phlegm
and blood. Seeing her husband's once hale body wither
into a white, bony husk. "I just wanted him to get better,
but he wasn't improving."

"Got angry, too," Marco noted.

She whirled to face him, but didn't quite pay attention
to the fact that she held a bee-shaped pin, because she
stuck her finger. A drop of crimson welled. He stepped
forward at once with a handkerchief, dabbing at her tiny
wound.

"I . . ." she stammered. No one knew about those feelings of hers. She wouldn't even admit them to herself.

"It's natural," he said. "Here you marry a young, healthy
man, and then suddenly you've got an invalid to tend to.
Like a child with no hope of ever getting older, or becoming independent." He carefully bandaged her finger with
a strip of fine cotton torn from the handkerchief. "It's
worse," he went on, "because your husband will only get
sicker. Now you aren't a wife anymore, but a nurse. Doing
some rather ugly jobs, I'd wager. What woman in her prime
would want that for herself? Who wouldn't be angry?"

It took her a moment to catch her breath. "No wonder
you are . . . what you are. You've got an elegant brutality."

"Not trying to be brutal," he answered.

"Then why say such things?"

He held her gaze. "Because you want me to."

Was it retreat or self-protection that had her hurrying
back to the dressing room? She tugged off the dress,
while the modiste clucked and warned her not to pull too
hard or the pins would pop out.

She didn't want to meet her own eyes in the mirror,
afraid of what she might see. A cold-blooded widow glad
for her husband's passing, or a bereft wife who longed for
her deceased spouse?

It took all her strength to lift her chin and stare at her reflection.

Both, she realized. She was both. Guilt assailed her like thrown grenades that she should be glad that Hugh had died. At the end, he hadn't been himself at all. Even his brief periods of high spirits had been more mania than happiness, leaving him exhausted and weakened. It had been a beautiful summer day, hot and clear, when he breathed his last. As if the world hadn't immersed itself in permanent winter when he got sick. As if other people continued to lead their lives.

"Madame, please," the seamstress murmured. "You will tear the gown."

Bronwyn's fingers stilled. She'd been moving in a daze, trying to rip the dress off herself. But then, she'd been in a daze for months. Years. Perhaps not until Marco crossed the threshold of her erstwhile home had she awakened. Even then, she barely understood what was happening around her, as if slowly peeling away the layers of dreams to face the cold light of morning.

"I'm sorry," she whispered, but she didn't know who those words were for: the modiste, or Hugh. Or even herself.

She did miss him. That was no delusion. He'd been part of her life for many years, and his absence left a void within her, slick and icy. But only here, in this little dressing room, staring into her own eyes, could she face the truth: she'd cared for him. But love? Love had been missing. Yet she'd never expected it. Marriages arranged on the basis of fortune didn't have the luxury of love, only the hope of cordiality and respect.

Carefully, she peeled herself from the gown, letting the seamstress assist her in removing it. When she was stripped down to her underthings, she put on her weeds, and they felt heavy as iron.

"I shall have these gowns ready for you by tomorrow evening," the modiste said.

"Tomorrow morning," Marco called from the front of the shop. "There's an extra fifty francs in it for you."

"Of course, sir!" The seamstress snapped for her assistant, and a skinny girl of around fourteen scurried out from behind some curtains and gathered up the heaps of clothing before retreating.

"Matching hats, parasols, and gloves, too," Marco added.

Bronwyn stepped from the dressing room. "I can't afford any of that."

Disappointment flickered in his gaze as he took in her weeds, but the expression was gone almost as soon as it appeared. "Consider it operating expenses," he answered. "Everything will be settled when your fortune is restored to you."

"What if it isn't? I'll have to work in a mill for years to pay Nemesis back."

"Then we'd better be successful." His smile was an elusive thing. "I'd hate to think of you breathing in cotton fluff in Manchester."

"You are all solicitous concern," she muttered.

Her breath caught when he reached for her, his fingers light against her cheek as he lowered her veil. "Can't have you causing a scandal in the streets of Calais."

She gave a small, wry laugh. "It's too late for that. Scandal has become my constant companion."

The remainder of the day was spent in a sham of tourism as she and Marco took in the attractions and sights of Calais. A sham because she had no interest in the bustling market at Place d'Armes, or the heavy towers of Église Notre-Dame. Her thoughts were scattered like startled doves, flying in as many directions as the sky could hold. Marco did her the favor of speaking little, though it was obvious he knew his way around Calais and could, if she asked, tell her in depth about the history of the Tour de Guet, or the wonders of the electrified lighthouse.

He had an instinct for knowing what she needed, and that, too, disturbed her.

But she wasn't easy in his company. She felt too aware of him as a stranger, a man embroiled in the dark work of espionage, and, worse still, a *man*.

Eight months since Hugh had died, and before that, it had been nearly a year of celibacy as he battled the disease. At this point, spending extended periods of time in the company of an obese fishmonger might intrigue her.

No—it was him. Marco. A shadowed mystery of a man who tempted her with his black eyes and worldliness. Who seemed to know her in a way that was both frightening and alluring.

She was grateful when the day came to a close. Grateful, too, that they'd walked enough around the crowded port city that she fell into a deep, dreamless sleep the moment she lay down in bed. If she dreamed of him, she was blessed with a poor memory of it, and woke to the illusion of a blameless conscience. She also woke to the sound of steady knocking at her door.

Pulling on her wrapper, she answered the door, and found several of the hotel maids waiting with boxes. The boxes bore the name of the modiste, and Bronwyn directed them to place her new wardrobe onto the bed. Two more maids appeared, carrying valises—she assumed they were there to hold her new clothing.

Bronwyn opened a box and studied the fawn-colored dress. At least it wasn't black. She craved color, just the same. Still, even in disguise, she couldn't bring herself to wear the vivid blues and greens she once adored. Not yet. No one would pay particular attention to a woman in dull hues. They'd simply think her dowdy, not in mourning.

And that was something her ethics could tolerate.

One of the maids helped her dress and pack. She examined herself in the pier glass over the mantel. The dark brown hat the modiste had selected was actually a rather jaunty number, with a handsome curl of pheasant feathers curving down to bob cheerfully with each turn of Bronwyn's head.

"Monsieur wants you to meet him in the lobby as soon as you are ready," the maid said in French.

Wants, not requests.

She didn't know much about spies. In fact, she knew nothing at all, but she could deduce. And they likely didn't work often with others. Or, if they did, they wouldn't be the epitome of social graciousness. Unless it suited their needs.

Bronwyn carried her violin case while two porters took her valises. She wouldn't get a chance to play for God knew how long, but she'd refused to leave it at Nemesis headquarters. It gave her some comfort, knowing that her old friend might be mute, but at least it came with her on this wild journey, her secret dream came with her like an invisible shadow.

She descended the stairs into the lobby, and Marco rose from his chair at her approach. If she'd been hoping for a look of frank masculine approval in his face now that she'd doffed her weeds, she was sorely disappointed. He only nodded, brief and clipped, and waved her toward the front door.

As she stepped out onto the curb, the sun felt especially harsh and cutting. The traffic on the street seemed sharp, too present.

"This is the first time I've seen the world without my veil in months," she murmured to Marco.

"How does it look?"

"Brighter. Dirtier." Mud and debris collected in gutters, and soot streaked the buildings' façades. The veil had hidden all this from her, yet now she could see.

She could also see how good-looking Marco was in the sunlight. The planes of his face were harder, more angled, the shadows beneath his brow deeper. It didn't give her any solace to realize that her companion on this escapade was handsome. Dangerous and handsome—one adding an edge to the other.

Her own appearance in the daylight must have caught him off guard, too, for he stared at her for several moments, frowning. Something was happening behind his opaque eyes, and whether he liked what he saw or not, she couldn't tell. But she had his attention, and secret gratification welled.

Even with his attention, her heart pounded with a strange fear. People in the street might stop and glare at her. A widow too soon out of mourning. A disgrace, even here in France. Such scandal wouldn't be tolerated.

Yet nobody noticed. No one stopped and pointed, or shouted. She was only one woman out of dozens on this street, hardly worth attention.

Did her widow's weeds weigh more than this gown? She felt . . . lighter. As if her next step would liberate her from the earth's gravity, and she'd go soaring up into the sky, and disappear forever. But she wasn't afraid.

Guilt once again threatened to drag her back down. She oughtn't to feel glad to be out of mourning.

"Take on whatever role you have to," Marco said in a low voice. "However you survive, you do it. Each morning, each breath. Survive, and move forward."

"Is that how you get through every day?"

He spread his palms, indicating that he did, indeed, stand before her.

"I don't know if I can ever learn the ways of Nemesis," she said.

"You already have," he answered. "And you're managing."

It astonished her to realize that he was right.

Marco watched her the entire train ride from Calais to Paris. She had a book spread on her lap—Stevenson's *Treasure Island,* which Harriet must have loaned her, since it was one of her favorites—but her gaze was fixed on the window and the passing landscape. Small villages, large towns, and the countryside of farmhouses and the brown fields of early spring.

She didn't seem unfamiliar with France, and spoke the language well enough, but still she kept looking out the window, as if the rather ordinary and dull scenery held more interest than the swashbuckling deeds of cutthroat pirates. It was as though, despite her trepidation, she ate up everything she could see, every experience she could have. Eight months of seclusion—and the long tending of a husband's illness before that—surely would make anyone long for a life beyond the pages of a book.

But it was more than her widowhood or previous duties as a nurse that made her stare at the French scenery. That want, that hunger he'd felt many times . . . that was the origin of her limitless curiosity, regardless of her fear. And he watched her with the same avid curiosity. What was going on behind those sage-leaf-green eyes of hers? Damn it—why should he care?

Without her veil in the daylight, she was both prettier and more unusual looking than he'd realized. The sun showed the minuscule hollow in her chin, the angularity of her nose. Yet together, these flaws made her striking, unforgettable, even when he closed his eyes. She burned there like the afterimage from staring directly at the tungsten filament of an electric light.

He'd known many lovely women in his life. Taken more than his share to his bed. She was not the most beautiful, but she kept drawing his gaze, his thoughts.

She's your latest mission. Of course she interests you, even if you don't want to be here.

Though when he searched for it, that reluctance at taking the job to recover her fortune had started to dissolve in infinitesimal fragments. Nemesis was dedicated to the poor, the helpless. She was and wasn't these things. Yet at the thought of her burying herself as a paid companion, forever a nonentity, something cold and slippery congealed in his stomach.

He started at the unexpected sensation. Just a small twitch, yet she had to have been as aware of him as he was of her, because she finally turned from the window and asked, "Is everything all right?"

"Thinking of what our next step is," he said. They sat alone in a first-class carriage, so he could speak freely. "As I said on the ship, we're meeting two Nemesis agents in Paris to help us find Devere."

She smiled, making his insides clench. "Here I thought there was nothing you couldn't do on your own."

"There's not much point of having a team if you don't make use of it," he answered. "It's not always about being a lone wolf."

Her smile widened. "I see you as more of a tiger or panther. Hunting alone in the jungle."

"A solitary business, hunting."

"But necessary," she noted. "One has to eat."

"Or eliminate a threat," he added.

"Not everyone in the jungle is a meal or a threat," she

countered. "Maybe there are innocent creatures you leave alone."

"No such thing as innocent. Especially in a jungle."

"What about when it's time to mate?" she asked. "Do you hide yourself away then, too?"

Heat shot through him like an injection of morphine. Except instead of lethargy in his veins, he felt sharply, potently aware.

"Some things are worth leaving the safety of isolation," he rumbled. *The hell are you doing, Black? Don't flirt with her, for God's sake.* But he couldn't seem to stop himself.

"Not enough to get married," she pointed out.

"Spies make for bad husbands," he said.

"A decidedly poor matrimonial candidate."

He bowed. "You have described me to the atom, Mrs. Parrish."

"Oh," she said with an enigmatic smile, "I'm certain there's more to you than that."

The widow grew bolder by the moment. Though he couldn't quite think of her as a widow anymore, now that she'd cast off her weeds. Even though she hadn't selected brighter gowns, there was a new confidence in her since she'd left mourning behind—even if it was only temporary. When they finally returned to England, doubtless she'd take up her crape and bombazine again. A shame, that. Black didn't complement redheads' complexions, and it seemed a crime to cover her striking face with a veil, or hide those intelligent eyes of hers.

The train pulled into a small village station, and a passenger entered the carriage. He gave them both a bow before settling down with a newspaper, the headline blaring the latest about the end of the triple alliance between France, Germany, and Austria-Hungary. No doubt the boys at the home office would be neck-deep in investigating what this meant for Britain.

It surprised Marco that he didn't itch to involve himself in it. He'd been content with his work at home—running an East End tavern that catered to Russian anarchist exiles. By operating the tavern, he could collect information casually, without any of the patrons aware of his activities. The police might think of those men and women as dangerous criminals, but to British Intelligence, the Russian émigrés provided valuable information about what transpired back in their home country. Besides, they weren't half as risky to England as they were to Russia. It wasn't Britain the anarchists wanted to dismantle, but their own tyrannical government.

But the damn police had raided the tavern a few weeks ago, shutting it down. He'd be able to reopen in a month or two, but it left him with time on his hands. Which was why, out of all the Nemesis agents, he'd been the one picked to handle Mrs. Parrish's case. At first, he'd cursed his luck, being stuck with a job he didn't want, helping a woman from a class he didn't respect. But now . . . something had changed.

She wasn't like the others. He saw that now. She possessed an unexpected depth. And a willingness to give, to help others. Damn it if that didn't intrigue him. He was beginning to *like* her, beyond her obvious physical charms.

With the passenger's presence, Marco decided it would be best to keep silent until their arrival in Paris. He and Mrs. Parrish could speak in English, but there was always the possibility that their companion spoke that language, especially if he was the kind of man who could afford a first-class ticket.

Within a short while, they arrived at the massive Gare

du Nord station in Paris. Steam from the engines curled up to the soaring ceilings, and it seemed the entire mass of humanity had decided to gather on the platforms. After paying a porter to tote their baggage—though Mrs. Parrish insisted again on carrying her violin case herself—Marco tucked her hand into the crook of his arm and led her through the seething crowds. The air was full of the hiss and chug of trains and French voices shouting at top volume to be heard above the vehicles.

Outside, cabs lined up, waiting for fares. He ushered her into one of the carriages and called up to the driver, "Hôtel Cluzet."

"Oui, monsieur."

As the cab rolled through the teeming, lively, filthy streets of Paris, Mrs. Parrish asked, "Is there anything I need to know about the agents we're meeting, besides what you've told me?"

"Simon's been with Nemesis since the beginning."

"And how long ago was that?"

"Nearly six years now. Back then, it was just me, Simon, and Lazarus."

"Good to see you've been ambitious," she said, "and added new people."

"We're not an army," he pointed out. "Only a collection of fools who think they can make a difference."

"As one of the beneficiaries of your mad foolishness, I'm glad you exist."

Maledizione, he might actually be enjoying her company.

"I've been wondering about Simon and Alyce," she said. "A man of society and a woman who worked at a mine. I can't imagine his family was much pleased by the marriage."

"They weren't," he said flatly. "Things were strained before between Simon and his family. This wasn't much help to ease that strain. But there wasn't any talking Simon out of it. He was in love."

A thoughtful look crossed her face. "You think you can just talk someone out of love?"

"I've got no ruddy idea what love is," he answered truthfully.

She sighed, and watched as the carriage drove past one of Paris's innumerable, tiny parks. "Neither do I."

The cab at last pulled up outside a small hotel near the Place de l'Opéra. After getting down from the carriage and paying the fare, Marco paid several porters to take their bags up to their rooms. Mrs. Parrish at last surrendered her violin case, though she watched it with longing eyes as it was carried off by a uniformed porter.

The hotel itself was of a decent quality—not the Crillon, but certainly not one of Paris's innumerable cockroach-breeding facilities masquerading as lodgings for hire. It had an open and airy foyer, full of brass and potted palms, and well-dressed guests were gathered around small tables or perusing guides to the city. The hotel even boasted a clanking elevator. After checking in with a glossy front desk clerk, Marco escorted Mrs. Parrish toward the hotel's café.

In the fine French tradition, many of the tables were positioned in curtained alcoves, allowing for a measure of seclusion without the expense of a private room. A few men and women were having a *casse-croûte* of coffee and pastries. He inhaled deeply. Here, at last, was a culture that truly appreciated a fine cup of coffee. It could almost make a man weep.

He spotted Simon and Alyce at once. Difficult to miss Simon, since he was the epitome of blond English aristocratic good looks. Thank God Marco had a decent amount of female company, or else he'd resent the bastard. Well, he couldn't fault Simon for his looks anymore, since he was clearly, obnoxiously in love with Alyce, his wife, a woman of angular handsomeness and shrewd eyes.

The couple sat together in one of the alcoves, engaged in conversation. Though Simon's attention was riveted to Alyce, he seemed to know the moment Marco and Mrs. Parrish entered the room. Simon and Alyce stood at the same time.

Marco brought Mrs. Parrish forward. "Mrs. Parrish, this is Simon—"

"Addison-Shawe," she finished. Her gaze was fixed on Simon, and not, it seemed, because of his handsomeness. "We've already met."

SIX

What surprised Marco the most was not the fact that Mrs. Parrish already knew Simon, but the throb of melancholy that greeted this news.

Simon smiled and shook Mrs. Parrish's hand.

"Agents don't use last names," Simon gently reminded her.

Mrs. Parrish blushed slightly. "I was caught off guard. Of all the people to belong to Nemesis, I never expected someone like you."

"Like him?" Alyce asked pointedly. Her working-class Cornish accent was noticeable, especially in comparison to Simon's smooth, elegant tones that came from generational breeding and punitive educational reinforcement.

"Anything I say is going to sound horribly snobbish," Mrs. Parrish said, "and I'm hardly in the position to judge anybody." She offered her hand to Alyce. "I'm Bronwyn. Since we're going by first names only, it seems only fair for me to forgo my last name, as well." She sent Marco an edged glance.

Point taken.

As she shook Bronwyn's hand and introduced herself, Alyce's prickly demeanor lessened. Slightly. But she was in almost all ways a sharp woman—mind, appearance, attitude. Her only softness was reserved for her husband.

"You know Simon, how?" Alyce asked as they all took their seats.

"They moved in the same social circles," Marco surmised. Stupid of him not to have thought of it sooner. London's elite was a small, closed set, one to which both Simon and Bronwyn—odd to call her that after thinking of her as Mrs. Parrish for so long—belonged.

And when this was over, she might cross Simon's path again. But she'd likely not cross Marco's. Thus the brief sensation of loss.

"The Mayhews' ball," Simon said.

"And the tea at the Baggets'," Bronwyn added.

Did Marco and Alyce wear the same expression? Because she reached out and took Simon's hand in her own, staking her ownership. Marco didn't have the same option. Besides, he had no claim on Bronwyn. Still, it was all he could do to keep from glowering. There wasn't anything to be done with his unwelcome interest in her. He was here to do a job—one he hadn't even wanted in the first place—and nothing more.

Yet there was an ember growing brighter inside him. He usually favored widows as bed partners. It was always casual and transitory. When this mission was over, he could look her up in London. See if this ember grew into something hotter. Temporarily, of course.

"I was sorry to hear about Hugh," Simon murmured. "He always boasted of your skill as a hostess." He glanced at Bronwyn's gown, which was assuredly not appropriate for a widow in first mourning.

"Widow's weeds stand out," Marco said.

Simon and Alyce nodded, though a blush continued to stain Bronwyn's cheeks.

"You've dragged us across the Channel for a purpose," Simon noted. "Other than the pleasure of seeing Bronwyn again."

Quickly, Marco recounted everything that had transpired since he first set foot inside Bronwyn's door, and all their discoveries. Including Devere's disappearance into Paris.

"Why involve us?" Alyce asked.

"I wondered the same thing," Bronwyn added. "If someone like Charlie knows about Devere, he likely doesn't move in the same echelons as Simon."

"But Devere didn't always slum," Marco pointed out. He smiled his gratitude when a female server came and poured him a cup of coffee. For just a moment, he allowed himself simply to inhale its aroma, heady with the scent of earth and life. He wouldn't shame the coffee by adulterating it with milk or sugar. Instead, he took a small, almost dainty sip, letting it coat the inside of his mouth with its richness.

He hadn't realized that he'd closed his eyes and sighed, until he opened them again to see Simon, Alyce, and Bronwyn staring at him. Unlike her two companions, however, Bronwyn looked dazed, as if she'd caught him in a very private moment—which she had.

"It's a wonder the English ever became a global power," he said, "the way they butcher coffee. If this was Italy, and I had an espresso, ah then . . ." He couldn't hold back his groan.

Bronwyn looked even more stunned. He had a quick vision of that same hazy expression on her face after a bed-breaking orgasm.

His plan of seeking her out after the mission was completed now seemed even more appealing.

"Our friend Devere," he continued, "isn't addicted to coffee. It's gambling that makes his pulse race."

"He wouldn't be so stupid," Bronwyn interjected. "Not after having to flee England for the same reason."

"There were men in my village," Alyce said. "Barely paid enough scrip to keep a roof over their families' heads and bread in their bellies. But every night, they'd be down at the tavern, playing cards, until they owed each man in Trewyn more scrip than they could earn in a lifetime. A sickness, it was. I'm guessing Devere's got the same disease."

Marco continued, "So he'll frequent any spot that will have him."

"Isn't gaming illegal in France?" Bronwyn asked.

"They outlawed it in Paris in '37, and public gaming was made illegal in '57," Simon answered. "Everyone goes to the casinos in Monaco or on the Côte d'Azur."

"Then where would he gamble in Paris?" she pressed.

"Underground gambling hells," Marco said. "Floating games that change locations from night to night. That's where Simon and Alyce will play their roles. They may be underground, but the gaming halls run the gamut from elegant to shabby. Simon can go to the higher-end gaming halls and suss out where a bloke might go to win a bit of dirty money."

"And me?" Alyce asked.

"Wives understand a hell of a lot more than their husbands," Marco explained. "If there's more information about where the men and women of Paris go to secretly lose their cash, the wives will be the ones to know of it. At the least, they'll be more willing to share their wisdom."

"So I get to needle the highborn ladies." Alyce grinned. "Damn fine job you've given me."

"What about us?" Bronwyn pressed. "Much as I enjoy Paris, I doubt I could spend much time watching them build that new tower by Eiffel, or visit the Louvre, not while Simon and Alyce are out working."

She wasn't content to sit idle. She wanted to be useful. The ember of attraction glowed brighter within him.

"We'll be collecting information on the ground level," Marco said. "Asking a few discreet questions. Nosing around a few *arrondissements* and *quartiers* to see if anyone matching Devere's description has been popping up."

"And when we do find him?" she asked. "What then?"

Marco smiled. "Then we finally get some answers."

"Good," Bronwyn said, but she rubbed her arms, as if warding off a chill.

She had good reason to be cold. The closer they got to Devere, the greater the danger. All the more reason to keep her near.

When it came time to do reconnaissance, Marco didn't leave Bronwyn alone at the hotel. He'd brought her to Paris for a reason, too. She was his best chance at identifying Devere.

After parting company with Simon and Alyce, and settling into their rooms, Marco and Bronwyn set out to ground themselves in the city. He'd spent time in Paris gathering intelligence back in the tumultuous Seventies to keep an eye on the always shifting French government, but hadn't yet had the unique privilege of searching for a habitual gambler on the run from English creditors.

"What do you know of Paris?" he asked Bronwyn as they rode in a hired carriage.

"I know its train stations," she answered. "Hugh and I passed through here several times. Once on the way to our honeymoon in Italy, and then when we were en route to Amélie-les-Bains."

His interest was piqued. "Italy?"

"Rome, Venice. Florence." A warm glow suffused her

face. "Every step felt imbued with history and beauty. I didn't want to leave."

"My mother did," he said. "Met my father, who was sourcing materials for his factories, and decided she'd rather have him than history and beauty." Where the hell did that come from? She didn't need to know anything about him—and yet the words had leaped from his mouth, as if they had a will of their own. He knew so much of her—though there was a part of him that craved more—it felt right to give something of himself back. Who he was. Beyond the Nemesis agent. Beyond the spy.

"That must have been difficult for her," Bronwyn said. "Leaving her family and friends behind."

Marco hesitated to speak. He'd seldom talked to anyone about his family. But perhaps because he knew so much about Bronwyn, he felt he could grant her a small piece of himself. "She claimed to miss the Tuscan weather more than her overbearing mother," he answered, "but she lit up whenever a letter arrived from home. That's what she called Lucca, the town where she grew up. Always *home*."

"Did she ever return for a visit?"

He shook his head. "The thought of dragging three children all the way across the Mediterranean sent her to bed with skull-splitting headaches. But she wouldn't leave us behind. A conundrum she hasn't resolved, even though her children are all grown." He wondered, now, what kept her from returning. Fear of confronting what might have been, had she stayed? Regret terrified her.

Vivi senza rimpianti, she would always tell him. *Live without regrets.* Such a philosophy created in her son and daughters a need to always move forward, always look ahead. Regardless of the consequences. Alessia had moved to the United States to become a writer, and Francesca lived with an artist in Brompton, creating her own paintings, as well as serving as muse. And he—the spy, the secret righter of wrongs. An unconventional trio, the Black siblings.

None of them had married. Odd, given the happiness of his parents' marriage. Or maybe it made perfect sense. There wasn't any hope of re-creating that matrimonial satisfaction.

Bronwyn hadn't been content in her marriage. Like many of her class. A damned waste—especially for her.

His mind kept going toward places he didn't want it, eroding the control he so prized.

He brought his thoughts back as the cab climbed a hill. "But Italy is a fair distance from Paris, and hardly our concern. We've got another destination right now. Rue Saint-Denis."

She frowned, clearly unfamiliar with the name. "Is there something particular located there?"

"It's the sort of place Devere might frequent. That's my hope."

"I didn't think you needed hope," she replied. "Whatever you want, you simply will into being."

"I'm not a magician," he noted.

"Thank heavens for that. Nothing and no one would be safe if you could truly make yourself appear and disappear."

"What matters now is that *you* don't disappear. From now on, you stay right beside me."

"For my protection, or yours?"

He cast her a glance that said he wouldn't bother replying.

The cab rolled to a stop on rue Saint-Denis. No gentleman would ever bring a lady to such a place, but despite the circumstances of his birth, he was no gentleman, and never made claims to be one.

At least Bronwyn seemed to understand this. She

stepped down from the cab and managed—barely—to hide her shock at what she saw.

Women in various states of dress and undress stood in doorways or leaned out of windows, calling to the men passing by in the street. Difficult to tell beneath the layers of cosmetics how old the prostitutes were, though they seemed to range in age from girls just out of childhood to older, worn women. Though no matter how old the prostitutes were, they all had the same tired, disinterested glaze in their eyes, having seen too much of the world and its ugliness. Yet they smiled and beckoned, offering a moment's pleasure, companionship, the illusion of love or its absence. Whatever a man desired.

Marco only nodded politely when the whores threw their gaudy solicitations at him. He could never bring himself to pay for sex. Better to be alone than know that it was his coin that gave him entrance to a woman's bed and body. Besides, he was here in this neighborhood to work, not sample its human wares.

"Only fifty francs, monsieur," one teenaged prostitute cooed.

"Just one hundred, and I'll let the pretty mademoiselle watch," another whore trilled. "Unless the mademoiselle wants to do more than watch."

A bright red stain rose on Bronwyn's cheeks. She pressed closer to him as they walked. He didn't want to feel Bronwyn's slim curves snug against him, tempting him with what he couldn't have. For now, at any rate. Perhaps later. For a brief time.

He ducked into a doorway with a sign advertising, cheekily, CONFISERIES ET FRIANDISES—confectionery and sweets—pulling aside the curtain to reveal the darkened interior.

More women were here. Most of them in their underwear and negligees, some idly strolling back and forth across a shabby parlor, and others lounging on tattered chaises, reading periodicals or else staring into the air. One of the young women had her head in another's lap, dozing lightly as her friend picked through her hair, pulling out lice and crushing the tiny insects between her fingernails.

Three men sat in the parlor, one with a girl beside him idly stroking her fingers beneath his open shirt, and the other two were busy playing cards with a couple of whores.

A man in a bright waistcoat and several layers of macassar oil on his hair approached. He glanced at Bronwyn curiously, but directed his question to Marco. "What pleasures would you like, monsieur?" he asked in French. "The confectionery caters to all appetites."

"No pleasure but to find that rotten brother-in-law of mine," Marco said stiffly, also in French. He let himself visibly tremble with outrage. "He isn't my brother-in-law yet, not with the way he carries on at places like this."

"August doesn't know any better," Bronwyn immediately said, speaking the same language. "You mustn't be too harsh with him, Philippe."

Brava ragazza. She didn't miss a moment.

"That's why we're in this blasted mess—because no one in your family ever took that brat in hand." He turned a put-upon gaze toward the pimp. "Her father insists we cannot marry"—he gave the word aggrieved emphasis—"until her brother is found and cleaned of his addiction to . . . to . . ." As if too ashamed to say the word, he only glanced at the bored prostitutes. A few of the women watched the scene unfolding with slight interest, since it was clear ladies like Bronwyn made infrequent appearances at Rue Saint-Denis brothels.

"To my beautiful girls?" the pimp asked with a smirk.

"Poor fallen souls," Bronwyn murmured piously, almost

making Marco smile. "Perhaps August merely wants to guide them in the path of righteousness."

The pimp and some of the prostitutes laughed. Bronwyn looked mystified at their snide laughter, playing her part so well Marco would've thought her born to deceive.

"If this paragon of morality does spread his gospel here," the procurer said, "why should I tell you? He could be one of my best customers."

A hundred-franc coin suddenly appeared between Marco's fingers. The pimp's eyes rounded with greed.

"What does honorable August look like?" he asked, pocketing the coin quickly.

Bronwyn described Devere. The procurer sighed in a sham of sadness.

"Alas, mademoiselle, that chaste man hasn't been shepherding my girls along the way of righteous living."

"You aren't protecting him, are you?" Marco demanded. "Pocket the money I gave you then tell that whoremongering cub we're looking for him so he goes underground."

Bronwyn gasped at his coarse language, as she was supposed to, but Marco assumed a man suffering from a case of swollen bollocks would be near his breaking point, and unable to stop himself from swearing.

"Let me think . . ." The pimp stroked his mustache, then stopped when another one-hundred-franc coin appeared between Marco's fingers. He reached for the money, but Marco held it out of his grasp. "No, monsieur, I haven't seen him."

"Has he been in Rue Saint-Denis at all?" Bronwyn pressed.

"If he has," the procurer said, "I haven't seen him. Girls? Anyone see the gent the lady described?"

A tired chorus of "No" rose up from the prostitutes. Their pimp turned back to Marco and Bronwyn with a shrug.

"So sorry," he said without any sincerity.

Marco tossed him the coin, which the procurer caught the way a snake would catch a rat. "There's more if you do find him. Send a telegraph to the station at Boulevard des Capucines, and if your claim's substantiated, I can promise you three times what I've paid you today."

"More," Bronwyn added. She sent Marco a melting glance that was so full of heat and promise, his groin actually tightened, though his brain knew it was all part of the role she played. "This waiting is intolerable."

"I understand the burning urges of young love." The pimp gave another mournful sigh that surprised Marco with its sincerity.

"What would you know of the purity of our feelings?" Bronwyn sniffed.

A cynical smile twisted the procurer's mouth. "Nothing pure about anyone's feelings, mademoiselle. Here's a surprise for you—once, I wasn't the old panderer you see before you. No, I was a young man with ambitions, dreams of love. That bitch called the world sends all bright plans to hell."

"I . . ." The mask fell away from Bronwyn's face for a moment, showing true regret. "I'm sorry."

The pimp laughed again, brittle as frost. "Tears aren't for me, mademoiselle. I may have lost my love, but I'm surrounded every day by beautiful, adoring women. Isn't that so, girls?" The last question was given with an edge of threat.

"Yes," and "Without a doubt," the prostitutes answered.

"Remember, send a telegraph to Philippe Durant at Boulevard des Capucines if you see my future brother-in-law," Marco said.

The procurer bowed. "Of course, monsieur. And if you need a place to ease some of the pressure until the wedding . . ."

With a huff of outrage, Marco stormed from the brothel, Bronwyn at his side. They emerged onto the street, where still more prostitutes called out their offers.

"At least we know he hasn't spent my money on . . . that." Bronwyn nodded toward the brothel. "If I knew I'd lost everything just so Devere could disport himself the way they did in those French postcards, I'd find him and use my new pugilism skills on his bland, moronic face."

Her passion and fire grew from moment to moment. They were just as perilous as the mission was certain to become. More so. He could predict and plan the job.

Ushering Bronwyn into a cab, Marco called up to the driver, "Montmartre."

She glanced over her shoulder, a pulse of shock moving through her. "Even *I've* heard of that place. Rather bohemian, isn't it?"

"If by *bohemian*," he said, "you mean it's populated by writers, artists, prostitutes, dancers, thieves, addicts, and sundry riffraff, then yes, it's that."

By the time the cab reached the construction site of the new Sacré Coeur basilica, dusk had fallen over Montmartre, and gas lamps glimmered to life. The steeply canted streets were thronged with people the likes of which Bronwyn had never seen. Artists had proudly paint-stained fingers and shoes, and wore bright but shabby waistcoats and deliberately careless cravats. The painters wore their hair in long waves that brushed their shoulders, and draped themselves over café chairs to argue things that had to be very important, the way they waved their hands and pounded the tiny tables.

As Marco led her through the winding avenues, she

soaked in the atmosphere of this wild place, so removed from the strictures and tight vises of society's expectations. If anything, the *citoyens* of Montmartre reveled in their outlandishness, laughing wildly, walking arm in arm with friends, and gesturing with bottles of wine.

"Is he drunk?" she asked as they passed a staggering man wearing a wide-sleeved shirt and hazy expression.

"Opium," Marco answered. "The substance of choice for poets."

"I wonder if his poetry is any good," she murmured.

"Doubtful, if he needs opium to access his muse."

A corner of her mouth turned up. "A literary critic, too!"

He made a rather rude noise. "Don't know an iamb from a dactyl, but I know people. Everyone's got their *diavoli,* chasing them, and everyone's got a different way to keep those devils at bay. Our poetic friend loves the idea of being a poet, but he hasn't got the talent he desperately wants, so a few draws on the pipe and he's the next Baudelaire."

She studied Marco, not the poet, since he was far more fascinating than the other. "It frightens me a little, how much you can see."

He shrugged his shoulders, causing the fabric to pull across his lean muscles in an intriguing way. There really was nothing quite so pleasurable as a well-tailored suit on an able-bodied, fit man. And one who was so astute fascinated her even more.

"Always been in my nature," he said. "It wasn't Nemesis or my intelligence work that made me this way. All I have to do is look at someone, and it's like they turn into a book. Sometimes the book is in another language, but soon enough I can translate it."

She gave a shudder. "I'd hate to think of what you read

in me." She could already guess—naïve, unsophisticated, privileged.

But the look he gave her was far from dismissive. Something that came perilously close to respect shone in his dark eyes. "Your book keeps changing. It's being written with every step you take, every procurer you fool."

Shock still reverberated through her at what she'd seen. She knew such places existed, even in London, but it was a far different thing to actually be in one, and see the women who worked there. "People dream of traveling to Paris, and one of the first attractions you take me to isn't Notre-Dame or the Tuileries, but a brothel."

"Devere's not the sort who's interested in sightseeing," he answered. "A man like him cares about three things: money, gambling, and women."

They turned down another narrow street, and were confronted with a set of precipitous stairs. Marco seemed to know where they were headed, and she let him hold her a little more firmly as they made their way down the steps. His grip was warm and strong, steady.

She felt a stab of gratitude that the flight of stairs was so long and steep, giving him a reason to touch her firmly. Guilt, like an oily slick on a puddle, followed immediately after. She was still in mourning. Even if her marriage to Hugh hadn't been ripe with physical passion, she ought to remain true to his memory.

But the tendrils of desire for Marco uncurled through her, like the tenderest shoots following a long winter. She was a young woman, healthy and in her prime. He was, as well. And with each passing moment, he revealed more of himself to her, drawing them closer together. It was only natural that she might want more than Marco's hand on her.

She misjudged the next step, and pitched forward. Bracing herself for a long and painful tumble down the stairs, she blinked when she barely moved. Marco had moved fast as a cat, and now stood on the step in front of her, holding her steady in his arms. The position not only made her potently aware of the strength in his tight, sinewy body, and the feel of his muscles beneath his clothing, but it brought their faces close together. This close, she saw the slight bristle on his cheeks, and the curves of his lips.

If she were to lean forward only a few inches, she could put her mouth on his.

They balanced like that for a few moments, in the glare of a street lamp, suspended in a breathless point in time. She could only stare at him, her hands gripping his forearms. He stared back, his eyes hooded, expression taut.

Do it. Cross these inches between us and kiss me.

Instead, he set her carefully upright and moved with deliberate precision back to her side. He still held on to her arm, but it wasn't quite the same. The disturbing mix of guilt and desire swirled through her.

At last they reached the bottom of the stairs, and turned right down a café-lined street. After the sudden intimacy and heightened senses during the moment on the steps, the noise tumbling from the cafés blared painfully, and she shrank back from them.

But he pulled her relentlessly onward, until they reached one establishment called Le Perroquet Bleu. Tables spilled out onto the sidewalk, with a striped awning overhead. Colored lanterns hung from the awning, casting bright spots onto the patrons and the pavement. Banquettes lined the interior walls with bentwood tables and chairs arranged in front of them. Longer tables had been arranged in the center of the bright room. Mirrors hung on the walls, making the crowded space seem both bigger and also more thronged with men and, to her shock, women. And these women did not have the look of the prostitutes in Rue Saint-Denis. They were fairly respectably dressed, but drank and laughed just as freely as the men. As if they deserved their freedom. As if it were their right to be out in the world, rather than confined in the approved, narrow spaces designated by society.

It looked terrifying. It looked wonderful.

In the midst of this bohemian chaos, Marco managed to find them a table against the banquette. A waiter in a white apron and harried expression came over.

"Two absinthes," Marco said.

Bronwyn raised her brows as the waiter hastened off to get their drinks. "Trying to drive me mad?"

"It's not half as dangerous as people believe." He stretched out his arm along the back of the banquette. "Besides, you've never had absinthe before. Today's a good day to try. Your first brothel. Your first absinthe."

She wasn't surprised that he knew she'd never tried the drink, rumored to make people have strange and ornate visions.

He continued, "The widow I met in London isn't the same woman who sits in front of me now."

"Because I'm out of my weeds," she noted.

"Partly. But some of the fear's left your eyes, too. The set of your shoulders is straighter. So it seemed the right time to try something different from what you've known."

He wanted her to explore. Encouraged it. How . . . unexpected . . . that he should care, given how confined she'd been for . . . her whole life.

"Aside from sampling the fabled drink," she said, "what are we doing here?"

"Devere doesn't visit brothels because he probably can't afford all but the cheapest ones, which a man of his station would probably avoid. Even a dunce like him knows those prostitutes are likely to pick his pocket when he's sleeping afterward."

Would there ever be a point when she could talk about things of a carnal nature as candidly as Marco? They came from such separate worlds.

"Those women are likely rather . . . unhealthy," she added.

"They get blamed for spreading disease," he said, "but it's their customers who bring the sickness to the women, then take it home and give syphilis to their wives. And their unborn children."

Had Hugh been one of those men? Was she even now carrying the disease within her and didn't know it?

"You'd realize by now if you were sick," Marco said, as if reading her thoughts. Uncanny, this man. But it was a relief to know that, even if Hugh had visited a prostitute—the idea making her feel truly unwell—she was safe from illness.

"But Devere won't go to that class of brothel," Marco continued. "So he'd come to a place like this." He gestured toward the lively café around them. "There's female company available, and it's not of the commercial variety."

Turning in her seat, she surveyed the café. True to Marco's words, women sitting alone or with groups of friends smiled and flirted with men. They touched the men's arms, or stroked coquettish fingers along men's faces and down their chests. For their part, the gentlemen leaned close and whispered things in the women's ears that made them giggle. And if Bronwyn's eyes didn't deceive her, there was a gingery man in the corner sliding his hand along a blond woman's thigh.

Sensual possibility hung ripe in the air, making the café warm and sultry, despite the cool evening.

She glanced back at Marco. He wasn't watching the

room as much as he watched her, focused intently on her face, her mouth. The moment on the stairs flashed through her mind. Was he thinking the same thing? Had he wanted to kiss her as much as she'd wanted him to?

The waiter appeared, breaking the spell. He set two glasses holding measures of green liquid in front of them, along with two slotted spoons, a bowl of sugar cubes, and a carafe of what appeared to be plain ice water. The waiter hurried off again.

"It seems rather complicated," she murmured, examining all the paraphernalia on their table.

"If a painter can do it, anyone can. First, take the spoon and lay it across the top of your glass. Make sure the slotted part is over the absinthe," he cautioned, as she followed his instructions. "Put a sugar cube on the spoon. Good. Now pour the water over the sugar cube. You're looking for three to five parts water to one part absinthe. Excellent," he commended as she continued the process.

"Oh, my," she exclaimed. The green liquid turned white and cloudy.

"That's called *louche*."

"Shady," she translated. "Like the people who drink it."

"Including us." He followed the same procedure with the sugar cube and the water, and soon they both had glasses of milky, anise-scented liquid in front of them. Lifting his glass, he said, *"Salute."*

"To your very good health." She clinked her glass against his, their gazes holding, then took a sip. She expected the drink to taste strong and bitter, but the surprisingly pleasant herbaceous flavor coated her tongue and warmed her throat.

She started to take another drink—a bigger one this time.

"Slowly, my good widow," he said. "It might not be the

madness-inducing danger everyone claims it to be, but it's still alcohol, and I need your wits sharp."

She set her glass down. "Perhaps I should just have a lemonade."

"I think you can handle your absinthe. Only pace yourself."

At least he had some faith in her ability to know her limitations. So she slowly measured out the time between sips. In the meanwhile, she continued to watch the activity in the café and on its open terrace. Life in the café wasn't all about the possibility of a tryst—there were people playing chess, others arguing about art or politics or both, and one young man even had a sketch pad out and drew the scene. Perhaps Bronwyn herself might make it into one of his paintings.

Yet all she saw were the pairings of men and women. The feminine invitation through veiled glances, the masculine swagger as the invitation was answered. Some of the would-be swains had their advances rebuffed and had to slink back to their seats, where their companions laughed and knocked them on the back in a strange male gesture of consolation. Other men were more successful, and sidled up close to women, where soon fingers began to brush against each other, or more bold caresses were attempted.

Taking a sip of her drink, Bronwyn tried to picture herself as one of these women of Montmartre. She'd stroll into a café, feeling the gazes of men upon her and drawing power from it. A table would be waiting for her, and a glass of absinthe. Perhaps she'd chat with some female friends, or maybe she'd enjoy the pleasure of being alone, answerable only to herself. As she'd sit, men would try to catch her eye, but she decided she'd be selective. Much as her body craved release, she wouldn't take just anyone to her bed. She'd want a man of refinement, intelligent and perceptive, but who also possessed a raw masculinity that fine tailoring couldn't quite hide.

She drank from her glass again, tasting the different herbs of the absinthe. A man would come into the café— she decided she'd want him dark, not too tall, with a compact muscularity. The moment he entered, he'd see no one but her. She would give him her boldest glance, the one that said she wanted him, and he was lucky to have won her favor. He'd stalk toward her, gleaming like an unsheathed blade. He'd call her *chérie*. He'd chat with her for a while, their touches turning bold, until neither could take the wait any further. They'd go back to her rooms. And then they'd do the things she'd seen in those photographs she'd found beneath Devere's bed. She hadn't known that someone could put their mouth anywhere but on another person's mouth. Now she understood differently, and wanted that with her dark stranger.

"Time to switch to lemonade," a husky voice said, interrupting her reverie. Oddly, it was the same voice as the man in her daydream.

Or not so odd. The man she'd pictured in her fantasy had been Marco.

Blushing, she looked at her glass of absinthe. It was empty. The room itself swam a little. Fine sophisticate she made, getting tipsy—all right, drunk—from a single serving of absinthe. And then entertaining lustful thoughts about the man who was there to help her recover her fortune. There was nothing in Nemesis's pledge to her about providing her with a lover.

"I wish you weren't so handsome," she blurted, then wanted to crawl under the table and never emerge.

"I don't," he answered.

"Conceit!" She pointed a finger at him.

He lifted his dark brows. "Not conceit. Truth. There's a certain way people—women especially—react to me when they look at me. All I can deduce is that either I'm handsome or ugly, and most women don't favor ugly men in their beds."

She thought she might go up in absinthe-doused flames. "Perhaps they do like ugly men," she countered. "Maybe ugly men make better lovers because they have to work harder." There! She could be as bold as him.

"I don't have any experience with ugly men as lovers," he answered. "Or handsome ones."

Well, he'd managed to shock her despite her resolve to be more bold.

"I don't see Devere," she said abruptly.

He sipped at his absinthe and flicked his gaze around the café. "It's early yet. We'll give him a few hours."

"Why this café in particular? It seems like there are dozens of them in Montmartre."

"Englishmen are known to frequent this one."

Now that he mentioned it, she did hear the harder tones of her native language knocking against the soft lyricism of French. Those who did speak French rather than English had a more flat, nasal quality than the natives. Some of the men had a certain *Englishness* about their appearance and dress, despite their attempts to imitate the locals' raffish elegance. She'd missed all this when they'd first come in, and in the distraction of her erotic daydream.

"He wouldn't go by his real name," she speculated. "We can't ask anyone about him."

"And we wouldn't even if we knew his alias," Marco said. "Getting the word out that we're looking for him is a surefire way to force him back into hiding. No," he said, stretching out his long legs, "we'll try to wait him out. I can think of worse ways to spend the evening than sitting in a Parisian café with a beautiful woman."

Her pulse raced and the heat suffusing her didn't come from the absinthe. "We'll need to do something with our time here."

"Your Englishness is showing." He gave another lazy smile. "Time has different significance in France and Italy. Each minute doesn't have to be packed with meaningful activity. There's simply the pleasure of *being*."

"This is something you have experience with? The man who's both a Nemesis agent and a"—she lowered her voice to a whisper—"spy."

He laughed. A genuine, deep laugh that found the hidden places in her body. "Touché."

"Perhaps this pleasure of being is something we can learn to do together."

"Perhaps," he agreed. "What's your favorite piece to play on your violin?"

"Difficult to pick a favorite," she said, "but I've always been partial to Bach's Partita No. 1 in B minor."

"I'm not familiar with it."

"The first movement has this wonderful chaotic darkness to it." She closed her eyes, hearing the piece play silently in her mind. Her fingers twitched, moving across invisible strings. "As if walking through a strange, shadowy city, and you don't know what's around the next corner. A girl with a basket of flowers, or a caped thief. And you can't decide which you'd rather meet."

A silence followed, and when she opened her eyes, she found him staring at her with an intensity that warmed her skin and caught her breath.

"More." His voice was low and rasping.

"More what?"

"More talk of music," he said.

"I . . . I don't know what to say."

"Anything. The first piece you learned to play, the one you hate the most. It doesn't matter. Just talk to me of music."

So she did. It was awkward at first, and she stumbled, searching for words. How could she speak about something so personal, something that defied language, and to *him,* this man who unbalanced her at every step? But gradually, she became more comfortable, and he prompted her with questions. Questions that showed he truly listened when she spoke, and cared about what she said. No one had ever taken such an interest in her violin playing before. It intoxicated her far more than any absinthe or wine ever could.

It was only when her throat began to grow sore that she realized how much she'd talked.

"My goodness," she said, after a soothing drink of lemonade, "I've been prattling on for hours. You should have stopped me."

"But I didn't want to. And it wasn't prattle. It was . . ." He seemed, for the first time, lost for words. "Inspiring."

"It is to me," she answered. "Ever since I was given my first violin when I was twelve I—" She laughed ruefully. "There I go again. Talking about myself and my hobbies."

"It's art, not a hobby," he said with more heat than she would've anticipated.

"You haven't heard me play. I could be terrible."

"Not the way you talk about music. I can hear it in your voice. What you make with your violin goes beyond mere dilettantism into the realm of art."

She oughtn't revel in his praise, but gratification rose up in her like a tide. He was the first to ever recognize what her playing meant, and her pride in it.

"Perhaps I'll play for you someday," she said.

"Yes."

"Can I tell you a secret?" she whispered.

"I can't think of anyone more qualified to hear your secrets."

She glanced around the café, as though someone might be listening in. But no one was. "I've always dreamed of being a professional violinist."

She waited for his expression of scorn, or, worse, disgust. Yet he only nodded at her.

"A worthwhile dream," he said.

Her eyes narrowed. "You don't think it appalling that a woman should desire to earn money? And as a *performer*?"

"Nothing appalling about it," he answered. "What's bloody appalling is that people put it into women's heads—into *your* head—that being financially compensated for your art is something that should be beneath you."

She frowned. "And you don't think it degrading that I'd seek to parade myself in front of strangers?"

"If they're paying for the privilege, there's nothing degrading about it. The audience are the ones who should feel honored to have you play for them."

For a long while, she could only stare at him. "I . . . Thank you."

Now he frowned. "For what?"

"For listening. For understanding. I don't think anyone else would have."

"You entrusted me with a secret," he said solemnly. "It's I who should be thanking you."

Though she merely sat at a table, her heart pounded. She couldn't believe how he'd responded to her most closely kept secret, and not only had he not shamed her about it, he'd shown remarkable understanding. Surprising sensitivity.

Oh, goodness—he was a very dangerous man. A woman could easily find herself hopelessly enamored.

"Tell me something of yourself," she pressed.

His expression instantly became opaque, and he leaned back. "Not much to tell."

She laughed. "I find that difficult to believe, especially of a man in your line of work."

"I can't talk about any of that," he said flatly.

Though she sensed the divide he put up, like a portcullis clanging down, she'd grown bolder in these past few days. Since meeting him. "Then tell me something that has nothing to do with Nemesis or your other line of work. Something about you as a child."

He rubbed at his goatee. For a few moments, she believed he wasn't going to answer her. Then, "I was a sickly child," he said flatly.

"You?" She couldn't keep the astonishment from her tone. "But you seem so . . ." *Virile,* her body whispered. "Strong."

"Malignant scarlet fever," he said. "Took me years to recover. I couldn't play. Couldn't go to school. I thought it would keep me at home as my mother's *bambino* my whole damn life." He frowned as if caught off guard by his vehemence.

"You aren't sick now," she noted.

"Eventually, I recovered. "

She never would have guessed he'd been anything but capable from the moment of his birth.

"All those years indoors," she said. "Did you ever learn an instrument?"

He continued to scan the room. "My mother tried to press piano lessons on me. But I tricked the instructor to play for the duration of the sessions, so that when it was time for him to go, I hadn't played a note."

Naturally, he'd been devious, even as an ill child. What a trial for his mother. And a source of pride.

So many discoveries in one night. In a day. And none was more astounding than the discovery of him. And herself.

SEVEN

Dawn pinkened the sky, and most of the café's patrons had either staggered home or else passed out at the tables. The waiters grabbed these men and dragged them out to the curb. The servers sent dagger-filled glares at Marco and a sleepy Bronwyn. Closing time.

She rubbed her eyes as she and Marco got to their feet. "Tonight was a waste."

"We know he doesn't come to this café," Marco said. "But that doesn't mean our trail's gone cold."

They walked out onto the street.

"Easy," he murmured, when Bronwyn stiffened as he placed his arm around her waist. "Just giving you a little support. You're dead on your feet."

Instead of pulling away, she leaned on him. Hunger tore through him at the feel of her. He'd learned tonight of her true passion beneath the genteel surface. She was far more than a society widow. She possessed fierce intelligence and a hidden drive, known only to him. Her secret burned within him like a coal.

He'd planned on suggesting a brief liaison once the mission was over, but those plans couldn't hold back his body's needs now. They refused to be denied.

* * *

Bronwyn watched, mystified, as Marco released her to duck into a narrow alley. For a moment, she stood on the sidewalk, debating. Was this part of the plan to find Devere? Or did he have something else in mind?

"Bronwyn." His voice, lower and huskier than ever, curled from the darkness.

An invitation. She'd felt the need in him when he'd held her a moment ago. Need that rang through her own body like the low chiming toll of a bell. She felt poised on the cusp of something, something huge and terrifying and possibly wonderful.

She could refuse the invitation. He left the choice to her.

She stepped into the alley.

The moment she did, predawn shadows enveloped her. And the solid heat of his body, pressed snug to hers, as one of his hands cupped the back of her head. The fingers of his other hand splayed low on her back, pulling her even closer. She couldn't see him, but she felt him. The hard width of his chest. His firm, sculpted arms. His breath fanning warmly over her face. He felt strong and dangerous, capable of anything.

And still, in the tightness of his embrace, she could sense it. He would let her go, if she wanted.

Instead, she gripped his forearms, rose up on her toes, and brushed her lips over his.

His mouth took possession of hers. He didn't waste time on soft, coaxing preliminaries. He hungered. For her. His kisses were openmouthed, his tongue finding hers and stroking it boldly. This didn't feel like practiced seduction. It was need and want, unfettered, and it poured through her like music, striking every nerve and filling her with sensation.

She'd never had a kiss like this. As though it were lovemaking itself. As though the meeting of lips could be enough. And she kissed him back, with all the hunger that had been building within her for what felt like years. He tasted of wine. Her head spun as she allowed herself to fall into intoxication. His hands were broad and warm and unapologetic in their hold of her.

The alley fell away. Paris disappeared. Everything vanished in a haze, leaving only her and Marco, and the fires they stoked within each other. Fires that could burn everything to the ground, leaving only ashes.

A moan curled up from the back of her throat, answered by his growl. He held her tighter, and even through her clothing, her corset, and all the garments between them, she felt the power of his body. The things this man must be capable of . . .

God, she'd never known it could be like this. Only in her fantasies. Certainly not in her real life.

At the thought, she tore her mouth away, turning her head to the side. His hold of her immediately loosened, and she found herself leaning back against the brick wall behind her, seeking balance. Her eyes adjusted to the darkness, and she could just make out his shadowy form, standing like a boxer. Arms at his sides, feet planted wide. Panting as if he'd emerged from a bout. But who was the victor?

"He's here," he rumbled. "Standing between us."

Hugh, she thought. "Not him. Me." She pressed her hand to her pounding heart. Was it real? Was this too soon?

"You want this. Us." There was no question, only statement.

She rubbed at her forehead. "I'm a damned muddle."

He swore under his breath in Italian. "*Culo di Cristo,* I want you." The admission seemed to shake him.

"I . . ." She struggled to speak the words. "I want you, too," she confessed.

He cursed again. "Have to stay focused on finishing the job." He seemed to be speaking more to himself than to her.

"You're right." She was glad. And angry. With herself. With him. Though she'd stopped wearing her weeds, she was in mourning. No matter how much desire burned within her, long held at bay, she couldn't give in to it. She couldn't be untrue. Not to Hugh, but herself. To the faith in herself that she could feel loss without needing to fill that chasm with sensation.

But, oh, did Marco tempt her.

"It's nearly dawn," he said. "We need to move on."

Yes, she thought, as they left the alley and returned to the street. *Need to move on from the frivolous desire I feel for him.*

Yet it would be far simpler to tell herself that than to actually make it happen.

Italians were remarkable in their ability to curse. It was a prized national art form, as much as frescoes or sculpture or pasta.

Marco used that ability to call himself every foul name he could think of. English was far too limited, so he turned to his other native tongue. Because he'd been a goddamn fool to touch Bronwyn, to kiss her. Giving him a taste of what he couldn't have right now. But the small taste only whetted his appetite for more.

The widow burned. And he wanted to be immolated in her fire.

Do the job, he repeated to himself. *When it's over, you can indulge yourself.* It's how he'd always worked, how he managed to stay alive and sane through nearly two decades of spying and work for Nemesis. His system had never failed him, and he'd be a *testa di cazzo* to stray from a methodology that had kept him breathing, when other men he'd known were in the grave.

Both of them had made the right choice by stopping when they had. It didn't make falling asleep any easier, though. After tossing around restlessly on his bed, he relieved some of his tension with a fast, hard wank. He'd tried not to think of her as he'd touched himself, yet his damn resolve broke, and it was her hand he imagined around his cock when he came. It didn't feel quite . . . right. Though they had kissed, she hadn't given him permission for anything else. But he'd used her as he'd pleasured himself. And he wasn't certain how he could look at her without feeling, for the first time, a stab of conscience.

The rows of booksellers lining the Seine looked like a reader's paradise to Bronwyn. She admired the clever design of the wooden stalls, that opened and unfolded much like books themselves. There had to be dozens of stalls, some selling illustrations or photographs in addition to the countless books, titles on their spines in French, English, Spanish, Italian, and even Latin, for the students across the river.

As she and Marco walked past the booksellers, it was all she could do to keep from stopping and browsing through the stalls' wares for hours. Much as she loved music, books were doorways leading to worlds she'd never know.

But things were tense between her and Marco, dimming her enjoyment of the books. He and Bronwyn hadn't spoken much to each other all day. There was almost remorse in his gaze. Did he regret kissing her? And did she feel the same? He was the first man she'd kissed since Hugh's death—and she was still theoretically in mourning.

Yet she wanted to grab Marco and kiss him again. What was wrong with her?

How was she supposed to feel?

She tried to distract herself with the books. "I almost wish we weren't meeting Simon and Alyce." Her voice sounded strained, thin. "It would be wonderful to find a copy of *The Count of Monte Cristo* in its original language." Though she hadn't any money to buy the book, even if she found it.

"Monsieur Verne holds more appeal for me," Marco said.

She raised her brows. "Seems awfully fantastical for a pragmatist like you."

His mouth tilted in a slight smile. "Yet even pragmatists like to believe in impossible things."

She seized on the topic, grateful for the distraction from her thoughts. "Do you think it will ever happen? Ships that fly all the way to the moon? Electrically powered submersibles? It seems so outlandish."

He gave one of his shrugs. "It may be as commonplace in the future as a Channel crossing. A man alive a hundred years ago would scarcely believe he could travel from London to Edinburgh in only a matter of hours."

"Perhaps they'll invent a potion that makes us live twice as long," she said. "How amazing it would be to see such miracles come to pass."

Despite the circumstances for her being in Paris, she wanted to revel in this moment, with the timeless Seine and limitless books. But between their search for Devere, and her confusing feelings about Marco, she couldn't.

She caught a glimpse of Simon and Alyce up ahead, both looking at a book Alyce held. Their heads were bent together, and they exchanged small, intimate smiles.

Longing pierced Bronwyn. She'd never had that kind

of closeness with Hugh. They'd been content to share a house, a table, and sometimes a bed. At the time, she hadn't felt deprived or lonely. All marriages she knew were conducted in the same way.

But here was a glimpse of something she'd never truly witnessed: genuine love and respect between a husband and a wife. It glowed in Simon's eyes and shone in Alyce's smile, and the way they unfashionably found excuses to touch one another. A hand brushed against a sleeve. How Alyce sometimes bumped her shoulder against her husband's in a gesture of affectionate teasing.

As she and Marco approached the couple, she glanced at him from the corner of her eye. Hoping to see a similar look of longing on his face. But he was as opaque as ever. An expert in hiding what he truly thought. One might imagine nothing affected him at all.

But she knew differently after last night.

Simon glanced up as they neared. He was a well-trained operative, because he didn't wave or call out, or any of the things ordinary people might do when spotting friends on the street. He only gave them a clipped nod.

"Productive night?" he asked when Bronwyn and Marco reached him.

"Devere can't afford whores," Marco reported bluntly, "and he's not looking for company in the cafés, either. At least he wasn't last night."

"A bloke of single-minded purpose," Alyce said.

"So it seems," Bronwyn answered. Barges floated up and down the Seine, and pedestrians strolled along the stone quays and beneath the bridges spanning the river. Rubbish floated on the surface of the water and boatmen shouted curses at each other. How would she remember this moment later? Therein lay the beauty of remembrance. One could select things to recall and draw a veil over the rest. Years later, when she thought back to this time, she'd remember the darkly handsome, purposeful man beside her, the books, and the ancient river.

"And you?" Marco picked up a volume and idly thumbed through its pages. It appeared to be about tropical plants. "Have you uncovered where we can run our gambling friend to ground?"

Simon stuffed his hands into his overcoat pockets, yet somehow he still looked elegant. "Alyce and I learned some things as we suffered through the world's most excruciating dinner party."

The Cornishwoman rolled her eyes. "They spoke English for my benefit, but they kept saying they suffered from *ennui*, which, close as I can figure, means 'having too much money and not enough brains to find something to do.' For God's sake, they live in palaces and eat foods I can't even figure out, but they say they're just so *bored*." She shook her head in disbelief.

"Parisians seem to have perfected artful agony," Marco agreed. He slipped the book back onto its shelf and pulled out another, this one about architecture. "What of the gaming?"

"The high-level games seem to concentrate around Place Vendôme," Simon answered. "But there are about three regular floating games of the lower level you can find in Clignancourt."

"That's where we'll find Devere," Bronwyn guessed.

"If I were the sort of belly-crawling vermin that he seems to be," Simon answered, "then yes, you'll find him there." To Marco, he said, "I'll give you the addresses where the games are usually held."

As the two men talked, Alyce's stomach gave a sudden loud growl. The woman covered her belly with her hand and chuckled with embarrassment. She whispered to Bronwyn, "We haven't had breakfast, and I'm so hungry.

I barely ate anything last night on account of not knowing what the blazes they were serving me. Things they called *escargots* and *cervelles*."

"Better avoid that," Bronwyn whispered back. "It's snails and brains."

Alyce's complexion took on a distinctly green hue. "We didn't have much to eat in Trewyn, but Lord preserve me from eating garden pests and cow brains."

"If a server offers you *boeuf* or *poulet*," Bronwyn said, "you're safe."

The other woman nodded. "Cheers. Everyone talks about how la-di-da the food is over here, but I thought I was going to starve."

"Worst comes to worst," Bronwyn advised, "keep a cooked sausage in your reticule and slip it onto your plate when no one's watching."

Alyce laughed—a husky, full laugh—causing Simon to gaze at her with undisguised adoration. Something flashed in Marco's eyes, too, but he wasn't looking at Alyce. He looked at Bronwyn.

Her heart thudded. Ever since last night, hot tension had been growing between them, barely checked by the kiss.

"The first game's tonight at eleven," Simon noted. "Runs until dawn, so I'd suggest you rest up beforehand."

She could use it, too. Absinthe and Marco had played havoc with her dreams.

"And those are the only games worth investigating in Paris?" he pressed Simon.

The gentleman looked offended. "Six years of friendship, but where's the faith in my abilities?"

"Right up your—"

"All right, lads." Alyce held up her hands. "We're all tired and *hungry,* so we'll keep the schoolyard taunts in our pockets. And yes," she added, "these three games were the best options. There aren't heaps of underground gaming hells, not with fear of the law."

"I didn't think the citizens of Paris were so law-abiding," Bronwyn said.

Simon looked wry. "They're mostly afraid of raids and having to pay off the police. Otherwise, there's a long and storied tradition of Parisian disobedience."

"Then I think England calls you home again," Marco said, "or wherever else your next assignment is."

Drawing his wife close, Simon said, "We haven't had our honeymoon yet and I promised Alyce to show her my favorite café in the Cap d'Antibes. It's too early for the high season, so we should have the town to ourselves."

His tone was perfectly polite, but given the way Alyce turned pink, Bronwyn had a very good idea how they'd make use of their solitude.

Bronwyn stuck out her hand. "Thank you both for all the work you've done on my behalf. I'm afraid words are rather tiny things when it comes to expressing gratitude."

In turn, Simon and Alyce shook her hand. Bronwyn had to resist the need to shake her hand out after Alyce's impressively strong grip.

"All in a day's work, et cetera," Simon said.

"A night's work, rather," Alyce amended.

After Marco shook hands with the other Nemesis agents, they parted company. The last Bronwyn saw of the couple, they were strolling hand in hand along the banks of the Seine, Alyce marveling at the scenery while Simon watched the look of wonderment on her face with a fond smile.

Another ache of longing spread through Bronwyn. She'd come to Paris to find her missing fortune, yet what she discovered was how much else was missing in her life.

* * *

She found it on her bed, later that day. A small, brown-paper-wrapped parcel, with no writing on the paper and nothing else to indicate what it was or where it had come from.

Tearing off the paper, she discovered it was a book. *Le Comte de Monte-Cristo.* She flipped open the cover and saw someone had written something on the flyleaf.

Enjoy the adventure.—M.

It surprised her to realize she already was.

It would be hours before the gaming club opened, leaving Bronwyn and Marco ample time to dine. They sat at one of the numerous restaurants lining the street, a bottle of red wine standing sentry at their small table, and a succession of *plats* placed in front of them. No *escargots* or *cervelles,* but roasted chicken and potatoes suffused with herbs and garlic, almost austere but rendered down to its purest form of gastronomic pleasure.

The pleasure of the food felt distant, though, with the strain still hanging between her and Marco.

She searched for an innocuous topic. "This bistro's food reminds me of someplace."

"Amélie-les-Bains?" he asked.

She made a face. "God, no. The spa served boiled beef to its healthiest patients, and the others ate barley gruel. I swore off boiled anything after that."

"They should be tried for crimes against cooking. My mother would never stand for food treated as an afterthought."

Did he know that he spoke of himself and his family? She didn't want to point it out. Instead, she held this small piece of information, the way a diver would cradle a pearl pried from the depths of the ocean. There was warmth and affection in his voice when he talked of his mother.

Strange to think that he even had parents, rather than emerging fully formed from the world's secrets.

She wanted to ask him dozens, hundreds of questions about his past and his family, yet he had to be approached carefully, like a wild animal, in gradual sideways steps, hoping that he wouldn't bolt. Or at least not retreat into silence.

After taking another bite of her chicken, she mulled the taste. "The Lake District," she said at last. "When I was a little girl, we took a holiday in the Lake District. The first time I'd ever been out of London. I couldn't understand where all the buildings had gone. It scared me. I thought a monster had come and eaten them up."

He smiled a little.

"My mother said that out in the country," she said, "the buildings were like dandelion puffs, and blew away, leaving the green hills behind. I wasn't scared after that. And that first night at our inn by Ullswater, they served us plain roast chicken. It tasted so . . . real. Like how a chicken was supposed to taste. Until now, it was the most delicious thing I'd ever eaten."

"Italian cooking is always best. This comes a close second." He gestured at his plate with his knife and fork. "Peasant food. Meant to nourish more than just the stomach." Before she could respond to this, he asked softly, "What happened to your parents?"

"Lucy didn't say?"

"She mentioned you were orphaned, but no details."

Bronwyn pushed the food around on her plate. "An accident after I'd been married—train derailment. You probably read about it in the papers. The Bulhouse Bridge tragedy." She took a long sip of wine. "It's one of the reasons why you find me dependent on the munificence of Nemesis. Had my mother and father still been alive, they would've welcomed me home. And you already know I haven't got any siblings besides my sister and her oaf of a husband." Then, because it seemed opportune, she pressed her luck. "You?"

He surprised her by actually answering. "Mother and father both alive. Two sisters. Both unconventional."

"And they come from *your* family?" she couldn't help but tease.

He actually laughed, warming her more than the wine.

Perhaps now would be a good time to ask him other questions. Learn about where he'd gone to school, what he studied there, how he'd become a spy. She hungered for any crumb of information about him. Something that helped her solve the unfolding enigma that was Marco.

The tension between them loosened, yet as they continued to eat, and while the wine and food and man opposite her cast warmth over her, she was at all times aware that later that night, they'd be hunting the miserable fellow who'd stolen her fortune. It seemed that since her widow's veil had been lifted, the world was always edged with darkness.

Marco glanced over at Bronwyn. She sat beside him on a hard wooden bench in one of Clignancourt's seedy cafés, positioned across from the shabby private home that hosted tonight's gaming hell. Her lips pressed thin and her hands knotted together in her lap. Should he tell her to make herself more at ease? Her tense posture stood out in this place of slovenly, listing drunkards and bleary addicts, but no one seemed to pay her much attention, mired as they were in their own demons.

The smell of cheap wine and liquor hung over the garishly lit café. Unlike the cafés of Montmartre, the ones of Clignancourt held no intellectual debate or artistic ambition. He recalled how she talked of music, the passion she felt for it, her secret wish to become a professional violinist. Her passion had inflamed his own. But there was none of that among the people of Clignancourt. Only the desire to escape the grim world.

"We should have gone into the gambling hell," Bronwyn murmured.

"Safer out here."

She gazed at the café with disbelief. Two men scuffled in the corner while a whore shrieked at them. "Hard to believe."

"Even legal gaming hells don't have much access to doors or windows," he said. "No fast exits. The crowds are thick, too, and noisy."

She raised a brow. "A seasoned agent like you shouldn't be fazed by such conditions."

"I'm not. But usually I go into scenarios like that alone, or with a trained partner."

"Does that make me a liability?" she asked flatly.

"Not at all. I need you to help me identify Devere if he shows, but I can do my job better if I know you're safe. This place might be a rattrap, but it's more secure than there." He nodded toward the house across the street, where men and the occasional woman slouched in, ready to throw away their money on crooked games of chance.

"Harriet taught me how to fight," Bronwyn countered.

"A fist can't protect you from a knife in the back."

"But you can."

"When you're with me," he said, "nothing will happen to you."

He always looked after the safety of his clients. That had to be the only explanation for the overwhelming sense of protectiveness he felt toward her. Just part of the job.

It was his coolness—and outstanding language skills— that had attracted the attention of a government recruiter at Cambridge. In addition to his boxing, he'd been captain of the rugby team, and known for doing whatever was necessary to obtain a victory, including inventing plays that had never been used before. The agent who'd approached him had said that his skills would go to waste if he followed in his father's line of work. Marco had been younger then, almost naïve, and hadn't been able to fathom how this stranger knew so much about him.

But the offer of government work that made a true difference—not some useless sinecure or dull work behind a desk—had intrigued him. That, the possibility of traveling to the distant corners of the empire to defeat Britain's enemies, and striving to erode the power of the elite.

Before he'd been approached by the government recruiter, he hadn't known exactly what to do with himself. Oh, he excelled at all his studies, but to what end, he hadn't known. Going into the family business didn't interest him. Neither had soldiering.

But the secret work of espionage had. Quietly, deliberately altering the course of . . . everything. Including the dismantling of power by those of the old guard. It was a new world, where intelligence, ambition, and drive shaped destiny—not the good fortune of birth. The old guard had made him, his father, and his father's father feel insignificant . . . he would be the one to tunnel beneath the castle's foundations, until the whole structure came plummeting down.

It had been the same with Nemesis. Creating change through assiduous planning and organized mischief. Even better, because he worked directly to undermine the elite and their entrenched power.

Yet he never spoke to anyone of his early years with British Intelligence. Though he'd picked up the work quickly, he'd still made his share of mistakes, and he'd no intention of reliving those.

Just as it would be a mistake to pursue his interest in Bronwyn while in the middle of a mission.

When the waiter came by with grease-smeared glasses for wine, Marco ordered coffee instead. Likely the coffee would taste as bad as they made it in England, but it was already midnight and Devere hadn't shown. He and Bronwyn would have a long night of waiting ahead of them. And it was growing more and more difficult to remind himself why he needed to keep his distance from her right now.

For the moment, he couldn't have her. And even after the job was done, he could only give her a few weeks, maybe a month. That was the most he'd ever been able to offer his lovers.

Maybe she wouldn't want that arrangement. She was a good, decent woman and he was . . . himself. The kind of man who was poison to good, decent women.

Not that he'd tried—because he knew himself. He lived and worked in the shadowy, nasty corners of life. Hardly the sort of man who could ever be allowed honorable intentions toward a woman. Especially someone like Bronwyn.

But knowing that, during the job, they shouldn't share a bed or anything else besides the mission only frustrated him. And when something frustrated him, he always found a way to get around the obstacle.

But this would be his first retreat. A strategic one, but a retreat just the same.

They hadn't had any success. Devere hadn't shown for the whole of the night.

So the following evening, he and Bronwyn stood in the shadows opposite a defunct fabric warehouse in an industrial part of the city, the site of tonight's game. There weren't any cafés in which they could wait, leaving them on the street. He kept them well away from the light cast by a lone gas street lamp. Pedestrians in this part of town were few, and those who did appear all hurried furtively into the gaming hell, paying him and Bronwyn no attention. A few stray dogs nosed through the garbage. The infrequent rat also made an appearance, scrounging for dinner. Bronwyn saw the vermin, but didn't shriek or gasp. Though she did shudder.

Marco and she waited in silence. A function of not wanting to attract notice, and also the strain between them that had lasted for days.

The bell of Notre-Dame de Clignancourt struck one o'clock. Another man hurried toward the gaming hell, this one glancing around with more caution than anyone else. He looked gaunt, as if he'd been on the run for a long while, his hair wild, and his shoulders were hunched in defense.

Bronwyn gripped Marco's wrist. "That's him," she whispered. "Devere."

"Stay close," he muttered. With long strides, he crossed the street, and heard her lighter tread behind him on the pavement.

"Good evening, Mr. Devere," Marco said in English, stepping in front of his prey.

The man drew up short, his bloodshot eyes wide. Judging by the way his shabby suit draped his body, he hadn't eaten a decent meal in weeks, if not months. His skin hung in sallow folds from his cheeks.

"I don't know you," Devere said tightly.

"But we're old friends." Bronwyn stepped out from behind Marco, crossing her arms over her chest. "You, me, and my late husband, Hugh Parrish."

"Don't," Marco growled when he saw Devere tense, preparing to run. "Unless you want to give me an excuse to knock you down."

"You already have a reason," Bronwyn said angrily. She stepped close to Devere, her face rigid with anger. "*I'll* thrash him if you don't."

Their target looked back and forth between Marco and Bronwyn, trying to decide who was a bigger threat. Seeing the fury on Bronwyn's face, and the coldness in Marco's, Devere finally seemed to realize that he'd find no ally or easy way out with either of them.

"What do you want?" he shrilled.

"My money," she retorted. "You stole it from me, and I want it back."

Devere's mouth folded. "Impossible."

Marco stepped between Bronwyn and Devere, and knotted his hand in the other man's neck cloth. He dragged him into an alley, and Bronwyn followed. "You're going to answer that question again, and this time, I advise you think a little harder." For emphasis, he knocked Devere into the wall, then grabbed the man's hand and twisted it.

"I can't get you the money!" the man whined. "It's not mine anymore!"

"Whose is it?" Bronwyn pressed.

"These . . . men," Devere finally admitted after Marco strained the thumb joint of his hand. "They loaned me money, and I had to pay them back."

Marco snorted. Of course. A hardened gambler like Devere would go to loan sharks to help finance his expensive habit. And such men weren't particularly forgiving when it came to repayments.

"Give me their names," Marco demanded.

But despite Devere's obvious fear, he wildly shook his head. "I can't tell you."

"I think you can," Marco said through his teeth.

"You don't understand. If I say I'll—" The rest of his words were cut off by a muffled scream. He screamed because Marco had dragged a small, claw-shaped blade down his cheek, and the sound had been muffled because Marco had clapped a hand over Devere's mouth.

"Don't!" Bronwyn cried.

Marco didn't take his eyes from Devere's, nor did he remove the blade from where it rested against the other man's cheek. "My companion here, she's tough but tenderhearted. Myself . . . I wonder sometimes if I even have a heart. The chances aren't good. For me, or for you. Given that I'm bigger than Mrs. Parrish, what I decide to do is the prevailing law. And the law isn't on your side. So," he continued, digging the small blade into Devere's flesh, "I advise that you reconsider your silence."

Devere said something into Marco's hand, so Marco took his palm off the man's mouth.

"Les Grillons," Devere finally confessed. "I borrowed money from Les Grillons." He looked terrified at his admission.

Fuck.

Marco removed his grip on Devere's hand, but kept him pressed up against the wall.

"The Crickets?" Bronwyn translated. She sounded dazed. "Not a very dangerous name."

"The name's something of a joke," Marco answered. "Crickets can be harmless little creatures, or they can be a pestilence. Same with Les Grillons."

"So you know of them?" she asked.

He nodded grimly. "The oldest and most dangerous crime syndicate in France."

Marco's use of violence was . . . shocking. It felt like lead in Bronwyn's stomach, seeing him unleash that brutal part of him. Her own threats had been minuscule compared to what he'd been capable of. But this was a new world. One where violence was the common currency.

By this point in her dealings with Nemesis she should be past being shocked. But between Marco's cruelty and the revelation of an actual *crime syndicate* she was stunned. She'd read of such organizations in the British papers, but even so she could hardly believe they existed. The grim expression on Marco's face, and the terrified one Devere wore, proved not only that the syndicate existed—it flourished.

"Everything," Marco growled, still clutching Devere's neck cloth in his fist. "Tell us."

"The investments were supposed to pay off," Devere piped. "They told me they couldn't fail. I'd make my money back threefold. I'd be wealthier than my richest client, and retire on the profits they'd made for me."

"But the investments did fail," Bronwyn said. "And you had gaping holes where your clients' fortunes used to be."

Devere's face twisted in anger. "Tried to gamble in London to earn that cash back, but I was bloody unlucky there, too. Damn luck's always against me." He started to spit, but must've thought better of it with Marco looming over him, so he gulped down his saliva. "Les Grillons loaned me money to fill up my clients' accounts. The ones I'd used to make the investments in the first place."

Nausea clogged her throat. This man played recklessly with money that didn't belong to him.

"You didn't pay me back," she pointed out.

"Someone had to reimburse Les Grillons," the man answered. "I took the money, but I knew you wouldn't be without resources. The world you come from . . . your kind always sees to its own."

"Not always," she answered tightly.

"Don't you understand?" he said piteously. "I have no one. And all I needed was some cash. I wasn't out to ruin you, but you were the easiest source of money. You've got family to look after you."

"If it wasn't for him," she said, tilting her head toward Marco, "I'd be on the street."

Devere's disbelieving laugh turned into a choking sound as Marco's grip tightened. Glancing down, she saw Devere's feet actually leave the pavement as Marco hauled him higher in a choking hold.

"Who . . . are . . . you?" Devere gasped.

"Someone who can make your life either safe or very unsafe."

The cuts on Devere's face proved this. Bronwyn still didn't know where Marco's clawlike knife had come from. God, what other weapons did he carry? He himself was a weapon. Terrifying to contemplate.

"I'm already . . . buggered," the other man wheezed. "Couldn't pay . . . Les Grillons the . . . full amount. Still . . . owe them."

"And now they want your head on a spike," Marco said thoughtfully, as if talking about the price of apples at the market instead of a crime syndicate wanting a man dead for unpaid debts.

"Let me . . . down . . ." Devere managed to gulp.

Marco seemed to debate this. "One condition."

"Anything."

"You do. Not. Run." He held Devere up so that he and the other man were eye to eye. "We'll be going after her money, and Les Grillons has it. And you'll help us."

"I can't!" He glanced up the street, and yelped.

Several blocks away, a figure stood, outlined by the weak streetlights. Menace radiated out from the figure.

"It's them," Devere gulped. "Les Grillons."

"Stay by my side," Marco said, "and I'll protect you."

Devere seemed to consider this. "Promise you'll . . . keep me . . . alive."

"No promises," Marco answered. "But your chances of surviving go up if you remain with me."

Devere's gaze strayed to Bronwyn, as if she'd actually consider protecting him. She only stared back at him.

Seeing that he wasn't going to be the recipient of her feminine sympathies, Devere turned his wide gaze back to Marco. "All . . . right. I won't . . . run. I'll . . . help."

Marco still looked dubious, but Bronwyn said, "We can't hold him in this alley forever. Or keep cutting him," she added.

Slowly, Marco lowered Devere back down to the ground, and gradually released his hold on the man's neck cloth. Devere bent over, coughing.

Suddenly, his hand lashed out, grabbing her ankle. He pulled, and she went toppling over, landing hard on her back. Marco immediately was at her side.

Devere's running footsteps echoed on the street. Followed by the Grillons man's steps.

"Dio cane," Marco swore, helping her to her feet. He glanced back and forth between the place where Devere had disappeared and Bronwyn.

"Go after him," she urged.

"Not leaving you in Clignancourt alone," he rumbled.

She lifted the hem of her skirt to reveal the sturdy boots she'd secretly purchased at the modiste's. "I championed in running at my boarding school."

He muttered another curse, then dashed off in pursuit. Bronwyn took a deep breath—thank God she'd thought to lace her corset a little looser tonight—hiked up her skirts, and joined in the hunt.

EIGHT

The night city streaked past her as she kept Marco's shadowed form in sight ahead. He was like a bullet racing through the twisting streets and alleys of Paris. She'd suspected he was in excellent physical condition. Now she had proof as he ran swiftly and with purpose in pursuit of his target. But always Devere and the Grillons man were in the distance. She'd turn a corner just in time to see them disappear down another street. Something glinted in the Grillons man's hand. A gun.

Her breath was hot and rough in her throat, her lungs. Despite what she'd said to Marco, it had been years since she'd run, and even longer since she'd done so at this pace. But anger and desperation and fear pushed her, far more than any timed sprint or race, and so she ran. She still couldn't believe what Marco had done in that alley. His savagery, and how very good he was at it.

She ignored the solicitations and jeers from men she passed. Only kept on running, her gaze always fixed ahead on Marco.

Bronwyn tried to keep up as best she could. She wanted to shout to Marco that the man from Les Grillons was armed, but to do so would put everyone in danger. Where would this mad chase end?

Up ahead, she glimpsed Devere push open the heavy doors of a large, elaborately adorned building. The man from Les Grillons was next. Marco immediately followed. It took her several moments to catch up, and as she neared the structure, she read the words COLLÈGE SAINTE-BARBE carved beneath an ornate stone clock above the doorway. A school. She could only hope that the students didn't board there, lest they be caught in the middle of the danger.

Shouldering open the door as it started to swing shut, she stepped forward to find herself in a stone arcade surrounding a dark courtyard. The pillars of the arcade formed long, sinister shadows. Bare-branched trees made skeletal shapes in the courtyard. For a moment, there wasn't a sound, not a hint of movement, and she stood beneath the colonnade, wondering what to do.

A gaunt shape that could only be Devere darted out from the shadow of a pillar.

He shouted toward the Les Grillons operative. "I don't know them! I didn't go to them for help!"

The Grillons man spoke from the shadows. "It's too late for you, *ami*. No one can help you now."

Devere scuttled across the walkway surrounding the courtyard and prepared to vault down into it. Just as the man's hand touched the stone balustrade, a shot rang out.

Devere fell to the ground.

"Marco!" Bronwyn called out.

"Take cover, damn it," he growled at her. Marco found shelter behind one of the stone benches in the courtyard, and Bronwyn covered her mouth as she saw the gleam of a gun in Marco's hand.

A shape emerged from the darkness—the Grillons man. He stopped twenty feet away from where Devere, wheezing in pain, lay splayed upon the stone. In the vestiges of moonlight, the assassin's face was revealed. It was surprisingly mild, despite the man's cold eyes.

"He isn't worth protecting," the Grillons assassin said in French toward where Marco crouched.

"Maybe not," Marco answered, also in French, "but you'll get no more money from him."

The killer only shrugged. "Everything comes with a price. But if you meet our terms, we can be very agreeable."

Marco moved out from his cover, positioning himself between Devere and the assassin.

"Step aside so he can pay," the man said.

Marco didn't lower his gun. "The bank is closed, and I'm the guard."

Bronwyn's heart climbed into her throat as Marco and the assassin continued to aim their weapons at each other. Neither man moved or blinked. The only sound came from Devere, groaning in agony.

She felt ready to scream. Who would shoot first? Or would they fire their guns at the same time, and both wind up dead? Surely, there had to be something she could do. But if she took a step toward either Marco or the assassin, she risked having their guns turned on her—on purpose or by accident.

Noise sounded above—the students and faculty waking.

Finally, the Grillons man lowered his weapon. "This won't be forgotten. We have spies and informers all over Paris, all over France. We know you now. And your time will come soon. *Bonsoir.*"

With that, the assassin melted back into the darkness. Bronwyn scurried away from the door, but the killer never passed her. He'd found another way out.

She hurried over to Marco.

"You hurt?" he demanded. "He didn't touch you, did he?"

"No." Something black pooled beneath Devere's prone form. Blood. She was no stranger to it, but not spilled upon unfeeling stone. "We need to get him to a doctor."

Marco dispassionately studied Devere. "Only saints can perform miracles."

Stumbling back, she looked down and saw that Devere's bloodstained chest was still, his eyes open and staring at the cold night sky.

My God. A man was murdered tonight. His life just . . . gone. And I witnessed it.

Bile rose in her throat.

Marco tucked his gun into his coat. "We've got to get out of here." He glanced up as lights came on in the second-story windows, and confused, panicked murmurs about a gunshot floated down into the courtyard.

Before she could say anything, he grabbed hold of her hand and pulled her away. In seconds, they were outside and striding quickly away from the school.

Behind them came the shrill of a gendarme's whistle.

"Cold?" Marco asked in a low voice.

She realized she was shaking. "I can't believe . . . I didn't think it would go this far. As far as murder." She stumbled over the last word, barely believing it was leaving her lips.

"A little killing is nothing to Les Grillons," he answered grimly. He turned them down a street and then another, leading her through twisting lanes and deserted boulevards. She barely noticed where she was, or indeed, could feel anything but a numb sickness.

Her mind whirled, trying to make sense of everything. She needed a distraction. "That group—Les Grillons— how . . . how do you know them?"

"Heard about them when I was doing intelligence work abroad," he answered, remarkably calm considering a man had just been shot to death. "Never crossed paths, but I knew all about their work. They'd been around for decades but truly came into their own in the ashes of '71 and the fall of the Commune. Made a killing—sometimes literally—through loans to rebuild businesses and the city itself. Then the spirit of entrepreneurship overtook them. It's not just loans at exorbitant interest rates that fill their pockets, but demanding protection money from shops and businesses, importing opium, keeping brothels. Name a corrupt enterprise, and Les Grillons has their fork in the pie."

Despite Marco's strong hand gripping hers, she shuddered. "This has to stop. We'll take the next packet back to England—"

He didn't slow his steps, but stared at her. "We're not giving up. Not now."

"A man's dead, for God's sake!"

"He is." He finally stopped walking and faced her. "Because he ran. If he'd stayed with me, he'd still be alive."

"So it's over." She verged on desperation.

"Les Grillons can't get what they want with a bullet." He placed his hands on her shoulders, and she didn't know whether to lean into his touch or shy away from it. "Devere was killed, but I'm alive, and I don't stop a job until it's finished."

"I'm the client," she insisted, "and I say it's not worth it."

"I'm from Nemesis, and I won't quit till we get your fortune back."

Anger washed through her. "Kill yourself, then. I'm going back to England." She started to turn away, but his grip on her tightened, holding her in place.

"You heard him. They know us now. Including my name."

Her heart pitched—that had been her mistake.

"Even when we get your money back, the danger isn't going to go away," he continued. "Not here and not in England. The only way to take the heat off us is to wound them, destabilize their organization." He gazed off into the distance, his brow furrowed. "This is much bigger than I'd planned for," he growled.

The knowledge chilled her. He planned for *everything*. But Les Grillons fell outside of even his carefully articulated schemes. *My God.*

He shook his head. "If I could, I'd send you home, but you're not safe on your own. You'd be vulnerable, even in Britain. He saw your face, and learning your identity would be a child's game to him. I've got to keep us both alive, so you're staying at my side."

Again, she was poised on the edge of something deep and cavernous. Now blood had been spilled. Where would it all end? In more death?

But he wouldn't stop. And neither would Les Grillons. Everything felt wild, spinning out of control, and she was caught up in the middle of the maelstrom.

"What if I stayed in the hotel until everything was settled?" she asked.

"This could take months, and we don't have the funds to keep you here."

"If I returned to England, I could go to my sister's in the country. Or stay with Harriet."

"I can't go back to England now, and I don't trust putting you on a ship with no one to protect you."

Frustration welled. She was trapped, no matter which way she turned.

"Tell me where to start," she said at last.

"We start," he said, "in Italy."

* * *

She would've expected Devere's murder to make the front page of the newspaper, but as Marco perused it the next morning over breakfast at the hotel, all he found was a small paragraph buried behind political scandals and reviews of art exhibitions. An unknown man's body had been discovered at the college, and in the absence of a positive identification and witnesses to the crime, the police chalked it up to yet more examples of the city's chaos. The victim would be buried in a mass grave within a week's time, unless someone came forward in the interim to claim the body.

"Life comes so cheaply," she murmured. Her toast lay uneaten and cold, and even drinking her tea seemed an impossible task. How could the ending of someone's life be reduced to cold, anonymous words in a newspaper? She'd heard the gunshot, smelled the cordite and blood. Seen his lifeless body in the wake of brutal violence.

How could she ever look at anyone again without imagining them with a hole in their chest?

"The only thing less valuable than a human life is dust," he answered, still scanning the paper.

Tension made her nerves and temper snap. "Do you have an answer for everything?"

His dark eyes met hers. "Not everything."

She picked her toast apart into little pieces, scattering crumbs. "You said last night that we have to go to Italy."

"A man I know lives in Florence." He set the paper aside and crossed his legs, wicked and elegant. She remembered the knife in his hand, and how familiar he was with using it, and how comfortable he looked holding a gun. Yet heat continued to spread through her whenever she looked at him or heard his voice. Which only proved that she'd completely misjudged herself. Far from enjoying a quiet life, some part of her strangely liked this danger. This uncompromising, grim world.

Yet he was more than just danger. He'd shown her understanding—more than anyone else ever had. There was respect in his eyes when he looked at her. She wasn't a thing to him, a decorative object. She was . . . real. And he helped her recognize that for the first time in her life.

"An Italian spy," Marco continued. "Giovanni helped a member of Les Grillons go into hiding. If anyone's going to know the key to retrieving your fortune, it's the one man who got out of their grip alive."

"That information your friend Giovanni has sounds sensitive," she noted. "Not the sort of thing he'd go telling just anyone."

Marco smiled, and her stomach clenched at the flash of white teeth surrounded by his dark goatee. "I'm not just anyone."

How could she feel anything other than horror at what was happening around her? Yet when she was with him, that awfulness receded.

"Giovanni owes me a debt, too," he went on. "He'll tell us what we need to know."

"A telegram is just as effective as a train ride all the way to Italy."

"But not as discreet. As our friend said last night, Les Grillons has spies all over the city. For now, the hotel is secure. It's run by money older than Les Grillons. But as soon as we're outside the doors, there are few places they can't touch. Including telegraph offices."

She took a sip of her cold tea. "If Les Grillons knows about us," she mused, pushing past her continuing shock, "then we won't be able to go straight to Giovanni. Not without risking ourselves and him. We'll have to do some evasion."

A corner of Marco's mouth turned up. "You've changed since first we met. More observant. Aware."

Was she? When she'd come into the hotel café that morning, she'd quickly scanned the room, looking for exits, assessing people and whether or not they might pose a threat. Not the kind of behavior a socialite usually indulged in.

She *had* changed. Continued to evolve, even now. She might not ever be a Nemesis agent, but there was something within her, an awareness that maybe had always been there, being brought to the fore.

Even if she retrieved all of her money, she wouldn't be the same woman she'd been just a few weeks ago. The metamorphosis was irreversible.

The Gare de l'Est station was a veritable hive, with people, porters, shoe blacks, and newspaper vendors swarming over the platforms. Though Bronwyn carried her violin case, a porter followed them with the remainder of their luggage. While Marco strode with his usual upright, alert pace, she could sense an even greater sharpness within him than before. He didn't glance around or behind him, yet she felt tension in him as her hand rested lightly in the crook of his arm.

He walked to the ticket booth. "Two tickets to Vienna," he said to the clerk, "and two more to Marseille."

"Are more Nemesis agents joining us?" Bronwyn asked in English as the clerk totaled up the amount.

"It's just us."

"Then why—" She lowered her voice to a whisper. "Does this have to do with . . . the crickets?"

"They're watching us now," he answered in a low voice. In French, he thanked the clerk when four tickets slid across the counter.

Her blood chilled. She fought the urge to look around and see if she could spot the men from Les Grillons. So she kept her gaze on Marco, calm and steady as he pocketed the tickets.

He turned to the porter. "We left our trunk outside," Marco said in French. "It's gray with brown straps."

The porter rolled his eyes. "Of course, sir." Leaving their bags, he ambled off.

They didn't have a trunk. But everything Marco did was for a reason, so she didn't question him.

She followed his gaze toward a cart full of bags of various sizes and colors. Another porter stood beside it. With his eyes still on the cart, he said to her, "I need you to ask that porter whether those bags are headed to Vienna. If they are, give me a signal. Something small enough that our Grillons friends on a bench over there don't see it."

It was a struggle not to look toward the row of benches to try to pick out which of the people seated upon them were from Les Grillons. "And then?" she asked.

"Then keep the porter busy for a few minutes," Marco answered. "You'll think of a way to distract him."

She wasn't certain she had his faith in her abilities, but, drawing a breath, she headed toward the baggage cart. As she walked, she felt conscious of someone watching her. With a surreptitious glance, she caught sight of two large, muscular men sitting with apparent ease on a bench. One read a newspaper, while the other gazed at his fingernails—the picture of boredom. Yet she *knew* they followed her progress as she walked toward the cart.

Ice crystallized along her spine. Marco had spoken the truth. They were being followed by Les Grillons.

"Excuse me, monsieur," she said to the porter in deliberately accented French. "Are these bags headed to Vienna?"

"Oui, mademoiselle," the man answered with as little interest as he could muster.

She shifted slightly, and tugged on the cuff of her glove. She hoped Marco recognized the signal for what it was.

And he must have, because when she glanced over to where he'd been standing, he was gone—along with their suitcases.

But her responsibilities weren't over.

"Are you *sure* these are going to Vienna?" she pressed the porter. "Because I would hate very much for my luggage to wind up in Berlin, when I absolutely have no intention of going to Berlin, and I would be very cross, indeed, if I were to wind up in Vienna with entirely nothing to wear but the clothes on my back."

"I'm certain, mademoiselle." The porter sighed.

In the very edge of her vision, she espied Marco doing something with their baggage and another set of cases that were heading to Vienna, but she couldn't be quite certain, since he crouched behind the cart, invisible to both the porter and the Grillons men on the bench, as well as the rest of the station.

Whatever it was, he was still doing it, so she had to keep up her distraction.

"I'm visiting my brother in Vienna, you see," she chattered on. "We all thought he was mad to move so far away from London, but he fell in love with a Viennese woman and insisted he'd follow her to the ends of the earth." She heaved a dramatic sigh. "It sent my mother into an absolute nervous frenzy, I can tell you. She wouldn't leave her bed for weeks. We had to call a physician. Even so, it wouldn't dissuade my brother from moving away to the very edge of the civilized world."

"Oui, mademoiselle," the porter said, desperately bored.

She almost felt sorry for the poor man. Marco suddenly appeared beside the porter, and set their bags upon the cart.

"Don't forget these," Marco said loudly to the porter. He handed the man a coin.

The porter looked grateful for the interruption. "I won't, monsieur."

Offering Bronwyn his arm, Marco led her away from the cart. And when the porter wheeled it away, one of the two Grillons men rose from the bench and followed it.

Speaking low in her ear, Marco said, "They know we're aware of them, and that we'll try some way of evading them. But our luggage can be followed, so that bloke will be sticking close to what he thinks are our bags. Once he sees the bags being loaded onto the Vienna-bound train, he'll be Vienna-bound, too."

"What he thinks are our bags?" she whispered.

"While you effectively distracted the porter, I did a bit of sleight of hand. Switched the contents with another set of luggage. These." From behind a pillar he pulled out two suitcases—gray with brown straps.

Before she could respond to his sleight of hand—and thievery—the first porter returned, looking cross. "Didn't see any gray trunk with brown straps, monsieur."

Marco gave a rueful chuckle. "That's right. We left it at home for this voyage."

It appeared that the porter barely kept himself from troweling a thick layer of curses over Marco. Instead, he said through clenched teeth, "Where are you heading, monsieur? I'll load your baggage."

"It's all right." Marco handed him a coin. "We've inconvenienced you quite enough for one day."

After snatching the coin, the porter trundled off, grumbling to himself.

"I cannot believe you *stole* those bags," Bronwyn muttered.

"I didn't leave the previous owners with nothing," he answered. "They've got perfectly decent replacement luggage. And the switch helped us lose one of our Grillons companions."

"Leaving us with one more. Unless you have plans for these bags, too." She nodded to their new cases.

"Only that they're accompanying us." He picked up the two bags and, motioning for her to follow, began to stride toward one of the platforms. Sadly, she'd had to leave behind some of her new clothing, but she'd wear nothing but rags if it meant getting away from danger.

The sign proclaimed the train steaming at the platform as heading for Amsterdam. Marco climbed aboard a second-class carriage, and she followed without question. In this realm of subterfuge, he was the reigning king, while she barely ranked as a courtier.

They continued on down the aisle between the second-class seats. Behind her, she heard the door to the carriage open and close. Pretending to examine the brass racks overhead, she threw a quick glance over her shoulder and saw the second Grillons man trailing after them.

More fear clambered along her neck, digging in with chilled claws. She wanted to turn to the seated passengers and beg for their help—but it was a futile hope. What could any of these people do against a force as powerful and terrifying as Les Grillons?

Marco gestured to two seats near the back of the carriage. "Here we are, my dear," he said loudly enough for anyone in the car to hear.

She took a seat, forcing herself into silence when she wanted to demand of Marco just what in heaven's name he was planning. He sat beside her, though he kept their bags with them instead of sliding them into the overhead racks.

"Tickets to Marseille aren't very effective for getting us to Amsterdam," she whispered.

"We're not going to Amsterdam. But our *ami* in the

next train car is. When I say so, follow me as fast and quietly as you can." He adjusted the cuff of his trousers. Then, suddenly growled low, *"Now."*

At once he was on his feet and out the door at the back of the carriage, carrying their bags. She wasted no time in following, all the while her heart pounding painfully.

They found themselves in a freight car, stacked high with cages full of dogs, cats, and even a goat. The animals kept up a steady stream of barks, meows, and bleats as Marco strode to the other end of the carriage, where another door stood. He tried the door, only to rattle the handle. It was locked.

Instantly, he knelt in front of the lock and had produced his picks. As he worked the picks, Bronwyn kept one eye on the other door—waiting to see if the man from Les Grillons would follow—and the other on an orange tabby cat, reclining in what had to be the most plush cage she'd ever seen. It had Sèvres porcelain bowls full of food and water, and a velvet cushion, on which the cat lolled, utterly indifferent to the chaos around it.

"Lucky beast," she murmured.

The door at the back of the freight car swung open, and Marco was on his feet, their bags in hand. She trailed after him onto a small open structure between train cars, shutting the door behind them. Still no sign of Les Grillons.

Marco lightly tossed the baggage onto the tracks below, then leaped down nimbly. He helped her descend, and then up onto the platform. They walked briskly away from the Amsterdam-headed train.

Glancing over her shoulder, she saw no evidence that the Grillons man pursued.

"We're safe," she said.

"No such thing as safe," he reminded her. "Only saf*er*."

"Thanks to your diabolical mind, we're definitely saf*er*."

He nodded, as if this were his due. But he had no need for false modesty. Not where subterfuge and skill were concerned.

"That blade you used on Devere last night," she continued. "I . . . where in God's name do you carry it?"

He tapped the lapel of his coat. "Special pocket sewn here. In case I can't get to the knife strapped to my calf."

"What about getting . . . blood . . . on your clothes?"

"There's a reason why I wear dark suits."

God. Good thing he was on her side.

Within moments, she and Marco were settled in a first-class carriage on a train marked as bound for Marseille. There continued to be no sign of the men from Les Grillons.

The storm of the past few minutes was over, but she still shook from its whirlwinds. Had all that really happened? It had transpired so quickly. But her hands continued to tremble.

Seeking comfort, she cradled her violin case close as the train steamed and idled, waiting for more passengers. Even here, no one cared that a man was murdered last night, and that she'd seen it happen. Or that she and Marco had just eluded two men who wouldn't hesitate to kill them. "What is this world? I don't . . . recognize it. It's so much more . . . brutal . . . than I thought."

A brief image flashed through her mind: Marco, not Devere, lay sprawled upon the ground in the school's courtyard, and it was his blood turning the stone black, and those were his eyes staring emptily at the stars. Fear and sorrow stabbed through her.

"As I said, I thought about sending you back to England,"

he murmured. "Finishing up the case on my own, now that Devere's dead."

A shiver danced between her shoulder blades. "Yet here I am. Bound for Marseille."

"Because they spotted you," he answered, "and I don't trust your security to anyone but me."

The coldness that had gathered in her bones slowly dissolved. Strange how he could touch her with these off-hand comments.

The train's whistle shrilled. A well-dressed couple with a small child entered the carriage and took their seats, with a nanny busy supplying the child with entertaining distraction by producing a steady parade of toys. Meanwhile, a barefoot little girl sold posies outside on the train platform as passengers buffeted her like a dandelion seed on the wind.

"That's why there's Nemesis," Marco said in English as he followed her gaze.

"I don't think your work will ever be finished," she replied.

The train gave another whistle, then chugged away, leaving behind not just the men from Les Grillons, but the tiny flower seller, as well, who disappeared into the vast crowds.

"It won't," Marco answered.

When traveling from Paris to Amélie-les-Bains, Bronwyn had been more concerned with saving Hugh's life than her own. English doctors had proven all but useless, except for a few recommendations to get Hugh to one of the spas on the Continent. So they'd gone, with the bright hope that he could cleanse his body of the disease. But gradually, between vile treatments of arsenic, iodine, and creosote, and enforced bed rest, that hope had dimmed.

Bronwyn now sat with a book in her lap—*Le Comte de Monte-Cristo*—journeying to Marseille, but she didn't see the words arranged in orderly lines, and she paid little attention to the forests and valleys of France. Instead, she saw the fading look in Hugh's eyes as he'd realized that he would never again return to England—he'd weakened far too much to make the return trip—and that his hold on life loosened with each cough, each fleck of blood Bronwyn caught in a linen handkerchief.

And through it all, she had to keep smiling gently, assuring him that he was healing, and soon they'd be home again, even though they both knew she fed him kind lies. The last weeks had been the worst, as the disease ravaged him, and the blood could no longer be contained in just a little handkerchief. He'd died with his eyes wide open, staring with fear at death.

After he'd died, she'd taken the train back to Paris, the packet back to Dover, and another train to London. Seeing nothing but her own blank interiority, and the realization that she'd never again hear Hugh's voice, feel the brush of his mustache as he kissed her good night, or anticipate his return home from an afternoon at his club. There was . . . nothing.

Nothing but the anticipation of two years of emptiness. As though she would go into her own form of death—alive, but not truly. Invisible to the world. Forcibly shut away to show her sorrow over the loss of a man who'd never actually loved her.

Now she watched the elegantly dressed family that shared the sitting compartment. While the nanny amused the child, the husband and wife read—he a newspaper, she a novel. They didn't speak much to each other, but their hands would brush against each other from time to time, as if assuring themselves that the other was still there, that they needed the assurance of touch. And every now and again, they would look at each other and smile. Small smiles, private and intimate. The looks born from true and comfortable desire.

What would it be like to feel that? What would it be like to feel any heat at all, other than mild pleasure?

Her gaze strayed to Marco, studying a sheaf of documents. A frown formed a small crease between his dark brows. He was honed and severe, handsome and intense as the depths of night. A man who carried tiny knives in his clothing, who had overcome childhood illness to become the frighteningly competent man he was today.

But for all that, he'd never treated her with contempt. He'd trusted her to distract the porter. Relied on her to keep her head as they'd fled Les Grillons at the train station. He'd given her that book. Listened to her dreams without sneering in contempt. Even encouraged her. Over and over he'd seen to her safety.

And then there had been that kiss . . .

If she'd ever thought him cold, the kiss had proved otherwise. There was a heat within him. As pressurized as a volcano, and when it finally erupted, it devastated everything in its path. Including her.

Her face heated at the memory, as did other parts of her body. There was the passion she'd never experienced in her marriage. In the most unlikely place and person.

Insane to have these thoughts *now,* when an actual crime syndicate hunted them, and this journey to Italy was not taken for pleasure—at great risk to her and Marco's lives. Yet she couldn't stop the steam engine of her mind, a machine with no brakes, only the force to keep barreling forward.

Hugh wasn't alive, but she was. And each step forward on this mad journey with Marco and Nemesis only proved this. Proved that she wanted more for herself than the nullity of widowhood, or life as a paid companion. She needed more than that.

Evening fell in a violet cloak, spreading over the French countryside. The lamps inside the train were turned on, and the family left the sitting compartment to seek out their supper in the dining car.

"I've seen you eat," she said in the sudden quiet, "so I know you have to do it. Unless you just need coal, like an engine."

He set aside his papers. "I'm not a sodding train."

"You hardly blinked when Devere was murdered."

"We've both seen death," he pointed out.

"Never like that, for me. Not violent and brutal."

A shadow passed briefly across his gaze. "I hope that's the last you'll see of it. I might not be pulling at my hair, but that doesn't mean I don't feel it every time I watch a man die."

She swallowed hard. "Have you witnessed many deaths?" *Or caused them?*

"I don't keep a tally," he replied, which wasn't an answer, and yet it told her everything she needed to know. No wonder his default expression was removed and coolly cynical. It kept him secure, like an ironclad battleship.

"And I also happen to be hungry," he added. Standing, he held out his arm. "Shall we?"

They ventured to the dining car, where waiters bearing silver-domed dishes moved as effortlessly as weathered sailors between the cloth-covered tables. She and Marco were escorted to an empty table. Almost as soon as they were seated, a server set down a plate of oysters nestled in ice.

Marco pried the glistening oyster from its shell and smoothly swallowed it down. His eyes briefly closed, and the tiniest smile formed at the edge of his mouth. She'd heard the legends, the ribald jokes about oysters, and what it meant when a man liked eating them. Clearly, Marco enjoyed the sea creatures.

His eyes opened, and his gaze fixed on hers. Daring her.

She picked up an oyster and used her tiny fork to pull the meat from the shell. Then, holding his gaze, she tilted her head back and let the briny oyster slide down her throat.

Her smile matched his as she set down the shell.

They consumed the rest of the platter in silence, but with each swallow, her whole body felt alight with readiness. Perhaps the legends about oysters were true.

Or maybe you want him. He had a way of eating that showed a profound sensuality. Watching him swallow fleshy, quivering oysters only proved what she already knew. He might shield himself with toughened cynicism, but possessed a unique sensitivity. He'd be an excellent lover. Hands in all the right places. Lips, too. And his body, hard with muscle, profoundly capable . . .

She wanted that. Wanted to experience it for herself.

But she could hardly drag him off to a sleeping compartment and tear his clothing off—appealing as that idea was. She needed more from him than just his body. She craved knowledge of the man beneath the armor.

The waiter came with more dome-covered plates. He uncovered two beautifully cooked steaks, pepper-crusted and sizzling, and jewel-like miniature vegetables glossed in butter. Two hungers lived side by side within her. At least she could eat the steak.

As she cut into her meat with an ebony-handled knife, she asked, "If you couldn't work for Nemesis, or follow . . . your other line of employment . . . what would you do?"

His movements with his own knife were deft and precise. He took a bite and chewed. "This for your dossier about me?"

"The most dangerous crime syndicate is hot on our heels. If I'm on the run with someone, I like knowing about them. You weren't so circumspect when you kissed me." She was proud of herself for not blushing.

But his own cheeks darkened. "I did. And stopped. This thing between us can't go any further. Not while we're on the mission."

An interesting distinction. One she wanted to explore further. But later. Right now, she was beginning to have other plans. Things shifted inside her. Fear continued in edged angles, but there was something else, a sense of her own capability—she'd helped get them out of Paris. She could use her skills for something that she wanted.

Horrific as Devere's death had been, it showed her how quickly a life could be snuffed out, and how she had to seize experience wherever she could.

He wasn't the only one with guile.

She ate a gilded coin of carrot. "You've been evading my question. What would you do with yourself if not this?" She gestured with her wine glass at the dining car, encompassing the whole of everything that had happened to them.

"Impressive persistence."

"Thank you, but you're still evading."

Instead of trying to dismiss her, or come up with another distraction, he actually seemed to think over her question, his gaze turned to the mirror of the train window that, in the darkness, reflected back the dining car more than revealed the passing countryside.

"I used to think about being an engineer," he said at last, turning his gaze back to her. "Or an architect."

She mulled this. "Makes sense. You obviously enjoy crafting intricate plans. Taking diverse pieces and fitting them together into a unified whole. Start with a small element—a cornerstone, a support beam—and build from there. Until it all comes together."

He lifted his brows. "You'll be after my job, next."

"I don't want your job," she replied. "I want to know you."

Frowning, he asked, "Why?"

"Because I've never met a man who carried a knife in his lapel. Because you murmur beautiful curses in Italian. Because you fascinate me." Her own candor came as a surprise.

"I'm just a means to an end."

She stared at him. "Not to me, you aren't." The words sprang from her, and she only realized after she'd spoken them how true they were.

"Is that how you see yourself?" she pressed.

He gave the tiniest of rueful smiles. "*Dio,* you could teach the boys at headquarters a few things about interrogation. None of them have big eyes and long lashes that turn a man to melted wax."

"I'm not even batting my eyelashes. But if it makes you feel better, here—" She fluttered her lashes in her best imitation of a coquette.

Shockingly, his cheeks darkened even more. It actually worked.

"You're right," he said gruffly. "It's appealing—the idea of putting something together. A bridge, a building. Takes just a single brick or a rivet to start. Then, months later, the river can be crossed. Sick people have a new hospital to help cure them."

She took a fortifying drink of wine. "I was correct. You could've been an actor. The way you pretend that you've got ice in your veins. 'I'm just a means to an end.' You know your way around a disguise; that much I know."

He scowled. "Don't pretend I'm something I'm not."

"Don't pretend you're less than you are," she fired back. "If there's anything this whole misadventure has taught me, it's that very few things are what they appear." She felt the angles and contours of a different identity forming within her. "Including me."

"Bronwyn?" a woman's voice asked. "Bronwyn Parrish?"

She glanced up in alarm as a man and a woman approached their table. The man wore a brown tweed suit, and the woman had on a blue wool traveling costume—both indisputably English in their tailoring.

"Merde," Bronwyn muttered under her breath.

"You know them?" Marco asked lowly.

"Friends of Hugh's," she said quietly, then, more loudly as the two newcomers came to stand beside the table. "Charles, Lydia. What a surprise."

"I should say," Lydia answered, glancing at Bronwyn's decided lack of weeds. She shot an even more censorious look at Marco. "And this is . . . ?"

"Paolo," he answered, his voice now heavily accented with Italian. He rose up from his seat and shook an astonished Charles's hand, then took Lydia's in his own and pressed a kiss to her knuckles with an unctuous solicitousness. "I am . . . *come si chiamo*? I am friend of Signora Parrish." The emphasis he gave to the word *friend* left no doubt in anyone's mind what kind of friendship he offered.

For half a moment, Bronwyn thought to deny Marco's scandalous assertion. But a voice inside her whispered, *You're already in it. Nothing to do but go along.* She'd cast off her widow's weeds, traveled across the Channel, been to a brothel and the bohemian cafés of Montmartre, where women lived almost as freely as men. She'd seen a man murdered.

What difference did scandal make? Charles and Lydia

might carry stories of her misbehavior back to England, but Bronwyn wasn't entirely certain that, if she should retrieve her lost fortune, she wanted to stay in London. Even if she did, she'd learned things about the world. There were far worse things than the censure of London society.

The world around her spun like a globe whirling on its axis, but she could find her footing.

This time is yours, that voice whispered. *Revel in it.*

NINE

"Paolo," she drawled, pulling out several centimes from her reticule, "do be a dear and get us more wine."

"Si, mi amore." With a sleek bow, Marco took the coins and ambled over to the bar situated at the end of the dining car, then gave her the most outrageous wink. Bronwyn was surprised the train didn't derail.

"Won't you join us?" she asked Charles and Lydia.

Perhaps it was the English sense of politeness, but Charles stammered, "If . . . if you like."

"Please." She waved at two empty chairs nearby.

Charles pulled the chairs close to their table, and he and Lydia perched awkwardly in them as they waited for Marco to return.

When he did, he poured them all glasses of wine. "My *dolce amore,* she is generous, *no*? With more than just her *denaro*." He took her gloveless hand between his and pressed kisses across her fingers. His lips were firm, warm, the whiskers of his goatee both soft and bristly against her skin. Then he turned her hand over and kissed her palm. His tongue darted out briefly to touch the delicate webbing between her fingers.

She fought the urge to close her eyes. Heat washed

through her like a flood in a summer storm. Heaven help her, if this was how he kissed her *hand,* imagine what it must be like if he did the same to her lips, her mouth. And other parts, just like in those postcards.

"Paolo, please," she said breathlessly. "You'll shock our English friends." Yet she didn't tug her hand away.

"We're not shocked," said Lydia weakly.

"It's just so . . . unexpected," Charles said, tugging on his collar, "running into you here."

"I must admit," Bronwyn answered, "coming to France wasn't part of my plans. But Paolo was so persuasive."

"I tell her," Marco said, " '*Cara mia,* you *must* go to France. This English air cannot breathe. We go to France and breathe.' " He traced patterns on her wrist with his blunt-tipped fingers, patterns of heat echoing through her in elaborate arabesques.

"I always breathe well when Paolo is around," she said with a slow smile.

"Because of the exertions." He turned to the English couple. "So good, she is, at the exertions. I think, she is so good, she cannot be just made widow. A bit of a *putana,* aren't you, *cara*?" Then he gave Charles one of those magnificently vulgar winks. "Good to have a *principessa* in the street but a *putana* in the bed, no?"

Lydia gasped. "Don't *dare* answer him, Charles!"

"Ah," Marco said sadly. "Your woman, she is no *putana.*"

Lydia pushed back from the table, and both her husband and Marco got to their feet. "I won't sit here and listen to this . . . this filth." She marched away from the table, with Charles rushing to keep up.

Once they had gone, Bronwyn forced out a laugh. Yet Marco still didn't let go of her hand, and she didn't try to snatch it back.

"If your other careers don't prove fulfilling enough,"

she said on a strained chuckle, "you can always try being a genuine gigolo."

Slowly, as though with great reluctance, he released her hand. His olive complexion had darkened, and he took a long swallow of wine.

"Money and making love are poor colleagues," he said. Then, "I, ah, apologize. It seemed the wisest strategy."

"We both participated in the ruse," she answered.

"And excelled in it, too."

No judgment edged his words. More than admiration gleamed in his eyes. She wasn't a girl. She knew desire when she saw it. Doubtless it shone in her gaze, as well.

Too late, Marco realized he'd trapped himself. He'd booked only one sleeping compartment, instead of two. It had been his idea to play the part of Bronwyn's gigolo—and now he paid for both choices. Just as he'd paid the price after kissing her.

Why her gigolo? Couldn't he have been her Italian cousin? No—he'd wanted it, wanted her. He kept discovering more and more about her, beyond easy categorization. She was much more than he'd first supposed. Now he needed to taste a desire that already burned him, though he tried to smother that flame. And here he'd gone and thrown further kindling on the fire.

Even before Charles and Lydia had shown up, dinner had been an exercise in exquisite torture. The oysters, of course, had been a mistake. He ought to have refused them or claimed an allergy. Instead, like a ruddy idiot, he'd swallowed the slick, sea-tinged morsels, all the while watching Bronwyn and thinking of that slick place between her legs. A place he wanted to savor much more than the oysters.

The rest of the meal had been by turns a delight and a

torment. She was changing before his very eyes. He'd once thought her sheltered. Kinder than the other women of her class, but one of them, just the same. But he saw her evolving into a woman of boldness, who tested the measure of her own strength. She'd been shocked by both his violence against Devere, and the man's murder. Yet despite her shock, she hadn't collapsed into a swooning, useless heap. She'd gathered herself up. Moved on.

And she'd cut into him deeply with that clever mind, seeing things about him that no other Nemesis agent had ever discovered. She was far more dangerous than Les Grillons. She was capable of doing him a much greater injury. A knife wound or bullet hole could heal within weeks or months. Bronwyn could hurt him in a far more vulnerable place—a place he'd always kept well guarded. Until her.

As they now made their way from the dining carriage to the sleeping compartment, he watched her sway gently with the motion of the train, and every now and then, her hand reach out to lightly brace herself against the wall.

He tensed when someone opened a door to a private room. He could have his knife in his hand in less than a second, ready to protect her. But the threat wasn't a threat—only a man ambling to the dining car.

Something was stirring to life inside him, something more than desire. What the hell was this feeling? He'd protected other Nemesis clients before, yet the idea of anything happening to Bronwyn filled him with ice-edged rage.

His hands clenched into fists. Anyone tried to *touch* her, let alone hurt her, and they'd meet a very ugly death.

"This is us." He stopped outside one of the sleeping compartments and fished the key from his waistcoat pocket. *Maledizione,* his hands were actually shaking a little.

Bronwyn watched him with heavy-lidded eyes as he unlocked the door. The same look she'd been giving him all through their meal after the English man and woman had stormed off. The look that had left him hard and aching, barely able to eat for wanting her.

He'd thought the job would be too complicated if they became lovers. Now . . . now being near her felt impossible. Not without knowing the feel of her around him.

She stepped into the compartment, and he followed, locking the door behind them. For the first time since they'd boarded the train, they were now truly alone.

The compartment wasn't large, despite the fact that it was first class. Wood and brass fixtures gleamed richly in the lamplight. A rather narrow bed was bolted to one wall, and an even more narrow chair sat in one corner, making the whole space somewhat cramped. A porter had already been through and turned the sheets down, and thoughtfully pulled the blinds.

She stood in front of the window, and, as he watched, reached up to slowly pull the pins from her hair. They dropped to the carpet, and with each one, more of her hair uncurled around her shoulders, until it was loose.

Was he supposed to stop her? Was he to play the honorable gentleman and sleep in the armchair nestled in the corner? He'd no desire to do either.

Words felt cumbersome and unnecessary. They both knew what they wanted, all moments—from the kiss to the ruse in the dining car—leading to this one.

He crossed the small compartment with a single stride, until he stood only inches from her. Her breath came shallowly as she stared up at him. He wasn't feeling particularly calm, either.

And then they were both pressed tightly together, her arms around his shoulders, his hands cradling her head, as they kissed with a deep hunger. She tasted sweet and spicy, and her mouth was bold. When her tongue lapped against his, the sensation shot directly to his cock, and he was hard as iron.

He cupped her breast. Even through the layers of her clothing, she formed a perfect, small weight in his hand, and she moaned into his mouth.

"*Tutto*," he muttered. He spun her around and quickly undid the fastenings of her dress. When this loosened enough, it slid down her shoulders, and she brought her hands up quickly to hold it in place.

"No, *cara*," he murmured. "Let me see you."

Slowly, she lowered her hands, and her slackened gown slid until it pooled at her waist. For a moment, she kept her chin lowered, a bright blush high on her cheeks. The lamplight revealed the soft paleness of her arms, her neck, as she stood with her corset and the top of her combination showing.

"Ah, *bella*," he said on an exhale.

She peered up at him through her lashes. Then her chest rose and fell as she drew in a deep breath, as if readying herself. And then, slowly, slowly, she shimmied out of the gown. Took her time carefully folding it and tucking it into one of the suitcases. Delaying.

Until she couldn't delay any more. She stood before him in her corset, combination, stockings, and boots. Tiny strawberry-hued freckles dotted her flesh.

How many other men had seen her this way? Was he only the second? How goddamn brave she was. So brave that it made him feel humble and thankful and even a little afraid. All at once. He couldn't remember the last woman he'd taken to bed who'd shown so much trust. Who'd given so much of herself. Far easier to think of sex as just an exchange between two bodies, a mutual satisfying of animal need. But this held so much more. She'd been so fearful when he'd first met her, so full of trepidation. Yet here she was now, more courageous than she'd ever been.

He'd half a mind to pull the blanket from the bed and cover her. Shielding them both. But his need was too strong, and he looked and looked.

Drawing herself up even more, she worked at her corset, until at last the constricting garment peeled away. Through the fine lawn of her combination, her nipples made large, rosy circles, pointed and tempting. She drew in another strengthening breath, then unbuttoned her combination and shoved it down over her hips and to the floor.

Now she was naked, save for her stockings and boots. And the sight of her in partial nudity nearly made him tear the train apart. The fine silk of her stockings framed the red-gold curls at the apex of her thighs. Her small breasts were delicious and high, crowned with those beautiful nipples. Yet she couldn't meet his gaze, looking everywhere but at him.

"Dio mio, sei bellissima," he growled.

She glanced up. The uncertainty on her face flickered, her expression turning bolder. "I don't speak Italian," she said in a husky murmur, "but if it means what I think it does, you'd better kiss me. Now."

He pulled her close, reveling in the feel of her body against him, kissing her, tracing every curve—from the dip of her waist to the flare of her hips and the softness of her belly. He took one breast in his hand, thumbing the nipple to an even firmer point. When he lightly pinched it, she melted against him, pressing her hips tight to his. The feel of his clothing against her bare skin must have aroused her, because she moaned again when his wool suit rasped over her flesh.

The train continued to rock as his other hand slid down her stomach, then lower, until he dipped a finger between her folds. Now it was his turn to moan as he found her soaking. He stroked her, first with one finger, then two, his thumb circling the taut bud of her clit. She gasped into his mouth. Then, hesitantly, her hand slid down his chest, then lower. He groaned roughly when her hand caressed down the front of his trousers and cupped his straining, aching cock, uncertainly at first, then with more boldness.

"Sei bellissima," she breathed, and he didn't care if she spoke the words properly. All that mattered was the way she touched him, tentatively, then with audacity.

But he didn't want this to be over before it had had a proper start. Having nursed a husband through a long illness, and then eight months of widowhood, she was due some pleasure.

So he led her to the narrow little chair and eased her to sitting. He pulled off his jacket and threw it aside. Then he knelt in front of her.

"You remember that postcard we found," he said.

Eyes wide, she nodded.

"Did it arouse you?"

Another nod, this one a little more hesitant.

"You saw that woman with that man between her legs. Licking her. Tasting her. And you wanted to be her. Wanted to feel a man's tongue on your pussy."

She inhaled at his crude language, but didn't reprimand him. If anything, the flush on her skin deepened.

"Now it's your turn, *fragola.*"

"Fragola?"

"Strawberry." Gently, he lifted her legs and rested her thighs on his shoulders. Baring her gorgeous pussy.

She slid her hands down, covering herself.

"No, *cara,*" he said softly, "don't hide. Not with me. You and I, we can be whoever we want together. In this compartment. In this flicker of time. You want to be the woman in the postcard, and I want to be the man. Let's be them. Let's be *us*."

For a moment, she continued to shield herself. Then, gradually, she leaned back, her hands gripping the back of the chair so her breasts were thrust upward.

He'd never seen anything more beautiful, more erotic. More courageous. And after sending up a silent prayer of thanks to all the gods of love, he bent his mouth to her.

She gasped at the first stroke of his tongue. And the second, and the one that followed that. Damn him, but she tasted delicious and felt like living silk, wet and eager for his attentions. His tongue caressed her. His mouth devoured her. She was a feast, and so responsive, he nearly came just from tasting her. It was almost a mistake to look up at her, see the flush spread over her skin and her eyes closed, mouth open in ecstasy. A mistake because he wanted nothing more than to tear open the buttons on his trousers and plunge his cock into her. But she would have as much pleasure as he could give before he even considered pursuing his own release.

He slid a finger into her as he sucked her clit. Moved his finger in and out of her, feeling her tightness around him and the bud of her clit between his lips. Her teeth clamped against her bottom lip, holding in her sounds of pleasure. He found the swollen spot inside her and stroked against it.

She barely managed to clap a hand over her mouth as she bowed up with a scream. Her body was tense and exquisite in her climax, and she gave herself to her orgasm completely.

With a groan, she collapsed back against the chair. She was quiet for a long time, save for her gasps.

Eventually, she stirred. "How do you say 'now you' in Italian?"

"*Ora tu.*"

"Ora tu," she repeated.

"Non ancora, fragola. Not yet." He bent back down between her legs. Made her come again. And once more. For all the years of suffering she'd endured, for all the uncertainty she'd faced since her husband's death, he wanted to give and give sensation. Only when she lay draped bonelessly in the chair, panting and glassy-eyed, did he relent.

"Marco," she sighed, when he finally sat back on his heels, "I want everything."

"Sì, cara." He stood and shucked his clothing with unseemly haste. He couldn't remember wanting—*needing*—a woman more.

As he disrobed, she removed her boots and slowly, maddeningly rolled down her stockings, revealing long ivory legs. Her hungry gaze went straight to his cock, which stood up even higher beneath her scrutiny.

"I'm flattered," she murmured.

"And I can't wait for you anymore." With one movement, he scooped her up into his arms and carried her the short distance to the bed. There, he draped her across the linens, and she made a symphony of delicately flushed skin, along with the blaze of her hair spread upon the pillows. When she opened her arms to him, it took all his strength not to throw himself upon her and take her like an animal.

Instead, he forced himself to move slowly. He knelt at the foot of the bed and prowled toward her. The blush on her flesh deepened when she sensed his predatory intent, and she moved slightly in retreat. Then she touched his arm and pulled him toward her. Welcoming him.

He stretched out over her, bracing his hands on either side of her head. He barely had to nudge her knees apart—her legs were already open to accept him. Slowly, slowly, he lowered his head for a kiss. She met him halfway, as if too eager to dally, and she made a little erotic hum when they kissed.

He lowered his hips, allowing himself the gradual, unfolding pleasure of feeling her bare skin against his. Her softness to his solidity. And there, ah there, the tip of his cock met her flesh, so wet and ready. He teased her a bit, rubbing the head along her folds and opening. Impatient, she lifted her hips higher, but he managed to find the strength to hold himself back.

But not for long. It seemed like an eternity that he'd wanted this woman. And slowly, he slid into her.

She cried out, and he growled.

The sound of the train's wheels and its rocking motion set the pace as he stroked in and out, surrounding himself with her tightness. She gripped him, taking all of him, her legs wrapping around his waist. Bracing himself on his elbows, he fought the urge to close his eyes and revel in sensation. Instead, he watched her face and the play of pleasure across her features. There was no false modesty, no holding back. She finally gave herself to sensation, and to him, completely.

He felt his release building, fiery and unstoppable. So he shifted his hips, moving up slightly so that with each thrust, he rubbed against her clit.

Her orgasm hit her almost at once, and his own followed immediately after. He'd just enough presence of mind to pull out, his seed scattering across her stomach. It went on and on, his climax, until he was wrung dry, and collapsed beside her. They lay gasping for many moments.

Cristo santo, it had never been like that before. Where he'd given so much and received a bounty in return.

He staggered to the lavatory and retrieved a damp cloth, which he used to clean her. She watched his ministrations, a curious, soft expression on her face.

He made his way back to the bed and sank down. Something in him was pierced when she snuggled close. God, she gave so much. He had so much less to give. His body only. The years had carved him out, leaving him hollow, and nothing and no one could ever fill that chasm.

Marco was awake, washed and dressed, an hour before the sun rose. An old habit. He couldn't remember the last time he'd woken past daybreak, and it was impossible for him to lie abed—even with the delicious form of Bronwyn pressed close and soft limbed beside him. So he spent the time sitting in the chair, reviewing Devere's coded documents and becoming more and more glad that the blasted fool was dead.

Devere had been playing far too easily with his clients' money. Worse still, he'd kept digging himself in deeper and deeper, until he'd made that moronic decision to get into bed with Les Grillons. The loan he'd taken from the syndicate must have been astronomical, and Marco had to wonder if Les Grillons had agreed to the loan with the knowledge that Devere would never be able to pay them back. Perhaps the organization had gone along with the scheme just for the sadistic pleasure of watching Devere twist, knowing that no matter how much he recompensed them, it wouldn't ever be enough, and the ultimate price would be the idiot Englishman's life.

Bronwyn sighed in her sleep, and Marco glanced up from his documents to watch her drowsily stretch, then fall back into slumber. Something ached in the center of his chest. He dug his knuckles there to soothe it, though it provided little relief.

He could use his fists. Been trained in all varieties of hand-to-hand combat.

Before anything could happen to her, he'd kill. Or give

up his own life. He always acted in the best interest of the mission—but he moved in perilous territory now where she was concerned.

He wasn't a stranger to working with female agents, both in his work for British Intelligence and for Nemesis. They were tough, capable women. And while Bronwyn had proven that she had all those qualities, she was untrained. He ought to teach her some defensive techniques. And a few offensive maneuvers, too.

Nothing would befall her. He swore this to himself.

Bronwyn woke by the time the sun turned the Provençal hills purple and gold. She stretched again and smiled at him. A tentative smile. And she tucked the sheets close around her. Ah, so she was feeling hints of uncertainty and guilt.

"Sleep well?" he asked mildly. Seemed a likely beginning to a conversation after tempestuous sex.

"Dreams." A small frown appeared between her brows.

"Your late husband," he deduced. "He was angry."

"Not angry, but . . . mystified. We were back in our home in London, and he was wandering from room to room, looking for my veil. 'I know you just had it,' he kept saying. 'It was here only a moment ago.'" Her frown deepened.

"Last night," he said, setting aside the papers, "doesn't change you. Not the core of you. It doesn't make you a wicked woman."

She sat up, but still kept the sheets close around her. "I *feel* wicked."

"One night," he said. "That's all we'll have. If that's what you want." Though it would be an exercise in agonized restraint to be near her, knowing her fully as he did, and not want more.

Her hair, bright and alive in the early sunlight, tumbled around her shoulders as she shook her head. "It's not what I want. But I feel like . . . like I shouldn't."

"Are you worried about those English people we met in the dining car?"

"It's not their good opinion I'm after." She glanced away. "It's my own."

He moved quickly to sit beside her on the bed, taking her hands in his. She didn't shy away.

"You want absolution?" he asked. "I can't give it. But there's a woman I know—her name's Bronwyn. She's wicked in the best of ways."

"And her heart?" she pressed. "Is that wicked, too?"

He considered it. "It's a heart that seeks comfort and pleasure." Philosophy classes at school hadn't taught him much, but experience had. "Everyone's does."

"Including you?"

He looked down at their joined hands. "When I can get them. But that's all I can ask for. I've got nothing else to give."

"What do you want?"

"What do *you* want?" he asked.

She gave a mirthless smile. "A good evasive technique, answering a question with a question."

"In this case, I really do want to know what it is you want."

She shook her head. "I wish I knew."

"Maybe I can tell you what I'd been thinking," he offered, "and if the plan—"

"You and your plans," she interrupted.

"I'm never without them. As I was saying, I'd been mulling it over. I knew since Paris that I wanted you, but I told myself I'd wait until after the mission was over. And then we'd come to . . . an arrangement."

"Arrangement," she echoed, brows lifted.

"Become lovers," he said bluntly. "If that was something you wanted to pursue."

"Oh," she said, "I do."

"But," he cautioned, "I never stay with a lover for long. A month at most. And then we both move on."

"Surely you've made exceptions."

"I can't make exceptions," he answered flatly. "This"—he nodded toward the bed—"is all I can offer. And sooner or later, my lover wants more. Better to be honest at the beginning. No misunderstandings."

She gave a strained laugh. "More plans. What if someone won't fit into those neat schemes of yours?"

Like her. His plans to wait until after the mission had shattered apart. There was no reassembling them. The best he could do was salvage what he could.

"It's always been this way. It's all I can give."

"But in your plan," she noted, tracing invisible patterns on the linens, "we wouldn't become lovers until after the mission. That clearly didn't happen."

"The choice of what happens next is up to you. We can stop—"

"I don't want to," she said with flattering haste.

"Or we can continue on with our affair. Once the job's over, we might even stay lovers. But our time together *will* end."

She frowned. "Have I no say in any of this?"

"Of course you do. But I cannot change who or what I am. To try would be a fruitless, and painful, exercise. So," he said, "what is it that you want?"

She was silent for a long time, and his heart knocked like a boxing bell in his chest as he waited. If he had to, he could keep his hands from her—but last night had shown him so much of what they could be together. Still, he wouldn't force her into any decision, no matter what he wanted.

Finally, she gazed at him. "I want us," she said quietly. "For as long as we have together."

* * *

Shortly after breakfast, the train finally pulled in to the station in Marseille. A porter met Marco and Bronwyn on the platform with their new baggage.

"Where are the freight trains?" Marco asked the porter.

Looking puzzled, the man pointed toward some distant platform. "Past there, down some steps, then to the left to the freight yard."

"Any heading to Italy?"

"One going to Venice, monsieur. Another to Rome. And a train to Milan."

Marco thanked him with a coin, took the bags, then left the porter on the platform.

The freight yard was a mass of intersecting tracks like a madman's scrawl, and hulking train cars. A few of the workers watched with curiosity as two finely dressed people picked their way through the maze of modern industry.

As she and Marco walked across the tracks, he explained quietly to her, "It won't be half as luxurious as our accommodations to Marseille, but if we take a freight into Italy, no one on Les Grillons' payroll will check our papers and get word back to them. They've got my first name, and they know what we look like. So they'll know to look out for an English man and woman matching our descriptions, traveling together. Especially once they realize we never crossed the border from France to Switzerland."

She gave a wry laugh. "I'll never doubt your skills at subterfuge."

"Those who have," he answered truthfully, "have paid a high price."

Marco found them space in the freight car headed for Milan. After securing their luggage and then climbing into the car, he helped Bronwyn up into the carriage. Large crates filled the space, and he pried back one of the slats to see with what they'd be sharing their journey into Italy. He snorted.

"What is it?" she asked. "Not commodes, I hope."

"Sofas and beds—though the beds are missing mattresses."

She glanced away. "Were I a different kind of woman, I'd say that there's a good way to pass the long hours into Italy. But, despite our earlier agreement . . . I'm not that sort."

"And what sort is that?"

She gave a melancholy smile. "Free," she murmured. "Seems I can change only so much."

Much as she'd decided to pursue an affair with Marco, she had to wonder if she was making a mistake. Oh, she wanted him, but she already knew that walking away from him was going to be difficult. But it was either that, or nothing at all. And she wouldn't deny herself, not anymore.

They couldn't, of course, uncrate any of the furniture— not without attracting the attention of a freight inspector. But Marco did find some rather musty blankets stuffed into one corner of the car, and spread these out between the large crates once the train was under way. Bronwyn gamely settled herself down on the floor. The slats that made up the sides of the car were spaced decently enough apart to let in light and air.

Rather than spending the lengthy journey making love on a multiplicity of sofas and beds, he and Bronwyn read or talked or did not talk, as the mood suited them. He enjoyed all of these activities with her. The silences between them had lost their strain, and though she'd led something of a sheltered existence, she'd kept herself informed of the latest goings-on in the world.

They'd both read *The Strange Case of Dr. Jekyll and Mr. Hyde,* and talked of the possibility of someone truly transforming into two separate identities. All of the Nemesis agents led split existences, but none suffered from so profound a difference as the fictitious doctor and his mad other self. Still, it made for a lively debate between him and Bronwyn, with her firmly believing that while Dr. Jekyll's case was extreme, men like Devere were proof that people were never quite who you thought they were.

They spoke of music, of course, with her far more knowledgeable about the subject than he could ever hope to be. He knew a bit about the theater, but his work for Nemesis and the government left him with little time for theater-going. They even talked of the possibility of Irish home rule—an idea they both supported.

He'd never engaged in this deep a discussion with a woman who wasn't a Nemesis agent, not for want of trying. But he'd found those talks with other women to be thin and limited. But perhaps he judged those other women unfairly. None of them had experienced what Bronwyn had. None of them had grown and faced such a dramatic metamorphosis in such a short time.

And none of them were her.

This was almost better than sex. He'd never had the chance to know a woman as fully as he was coming to know her and it seemed to wake something inside him. Something he couldn't name.

At Nice, he hopped out and ran to get them provisions. He returned with wine, cheese, *pissaladière* tarts, and pears. And despite the dusty floor of the freight car and its minimal springs, the meal was surprisingly good, made even better by Bronwyn's bold spirit, seeing everything as a new challenge to overcome, even a meal eaten in a freight car as they evaded deadly assassins.

Reaching the border between France and Italy, they

gathered up all their supplies and hid behind a h
just before an inspector entered the carriage. But   as
already past dusk, and the inspector seemed eager to return to his bottle, so there was the most cursory of in-
spections before the man leaped down from the car and
declared it permissible to enter the country.

The train rolled on, and now Marco and Bronwyn
were in Italy. One half of his home—at least in his heart.

He took a deep inhalation. It smelled no different than
it had in France, yet it was different, somehow. "It's my
imagination," he said to Bronwyn as they remade their
pallet, "but there's something about being here that makes
me feel . . . like I'm waking up."

"Awfully fanciful of you." She lay down, propping her
head up in her hand.

He shrugged. "It's the Italian in me."

"Well, I rather like it. Maybe . . ." she said tentatively,
"I could see more of that part of you."

He stretched out beside her, pillowing his head on his
folded-up coat. "When I'm on assignment I'm more like
Machiavelli than Michelangelo."

"It seems as though there's a certain artistry in spy-
craft. Schemes, plans, bringing a grand vision to life."

"Never thought of it that way."

Yet it made a strange kind of sense. She saw creativity
in his work, not just destruction. And now, so did he.

By morning, the train headed north, away from the bril-
liant azure sea and into the mountains. As they journeyed
toward Milan, Marco spent the time trying to teach Bronwyn some basic defensive and offensive maneuvers, all
the while hoping she never needed to use them.

A freight car wasn't the most accommodating of training facilities. Not only had Marco used specially designed

gymnasiums as provided by the government, he and other Nemesis agents would periodically retire to one of Simon's country estates to sharpen what they already knew and learn new techniques. Lately, with the introduction of more female Nemesis operatives, judo and jujutsu had been added to the curriculum.

"The advantage to these arts," he'd explained to Bronwyn, "is that they don't rely on your size or strength to be effective. It's about balance, and knowing how to use your opponent's body and momentum against them."

"Show me," she'd demanded.

So he'd padded the floor of the freight car as best he could with the blankets, then proceeded to show her one jujutsu move. She tried the technique again and again, at first with little success, with him easily breaking from her attempts to grip and twist his arm. The more they worked at the move, the more frustrated she became.

"We'll stop," he said after yet another unsuccessful try.

She pushed the hair from her face. "No. We'll go again."

They kept working at the maneuver, until, finally, she managed to throw him to the ground.

"I surrender," he said breathlessly, the wind knocked from him as he gazed up at her.

She stood over him, looking self-satisfied. "What if I don't accept your surrender?"

In an instant, he lashed out, grabbing her ankle, flipping her onto her back, and covering her body with his as he pinned her wrists to the floor. She tried to kick him off, but he immobilized her legs with the weight of his own. They struggled like that for several minutes, growing even more breathless and heated, until, at last, she lowered her head to the ground and growled in frustration.

If he wasn't already aroused by her strength and fight, that growl hit him stronger than any punch, traveling right to his groin.

"You've proven your point," she muttered. "You'll always be stronger and faster than me."

"I've been at this game for far longer than you," he answered, staring at her mouth. "And you're much more powerful than you realize."

She seemed to sense his gaze on her mouth, because she gave her lips a slow, provocative lick. This time, he was the one who groaned. Only a few inches separated their mouths, and she closed that distance to kiss him savagely.

He met her kiss with equal demand, their tongues tangling. Fire spread through his veins, and his body was tight, primed.

Then the world suddenly spun. He found himself on his back, with Bronwyn kneeling beside him. This time, her hands pinned his. *Madonna putana*—he'd fallen for one of the most ancient tricks: the honey pot.

She smirked. "I see what you mean about my power."

It would've been a simple matter to break her hold, and reverse their positions, but damn him if he didn't feel a hot jolt of even stronger excitement to have her atop him, in control. If they weren't on this bloody freight car, he'd gladly take their tussling to its logical—*essential*—conclusion. But he'd made a promise to himself that she deserved better than a hasty fuck in a train car full of crates and dust.

It would serve her better if he kept his focus. "Here's how to get out of a situation if you're being pinned." Then, gently, he demonstrated the process—using his legs, he bumped her forward, and when her head came close enough, he lightly took hold of her ear. "Then you twist here and make your escape." He released her at once.

"When I get back to London," she said, getting up and dusting off her dress, "I'll definitely seek out that women's gymnasium Harriet recommended. That was a challenge."

He didn't mention that they had literally hundreds of miles to go before they could consider their return to England, and a ruthless syndicate standing between them and London. "Harriet's a fierce one. I'd advise not going up against her until you've practiced more."

"You can be my sparring partner until I'm ready."

"For a time," he said. "But I'm never anyone's sparring partner for long."

She was silent for a moment. "Right."

They awkwardly broke apart, and she wandered over to peer through the slats of the car. The indigo mountains rose up toward a cloud-strewn sky, and cool, evergreen-laden air filled the carriage. It wasn't the ideal way to see this part of Italy, but interest still crossed her face as she watched the scenery roll past.

What could he offer her except his services for Nemesis and the use of his body? Nothing. There wasn't anything else to give. Even so, that ache in his chest returned.

Hours later, they finally reached Milan. He hopped down from the freight car, taking their luggage with him, then helped her down.

She glanced at the car that had been their transportation with a grimace. "Please tell me we'll be traveling to Florence in at least third class."

"There's no need to travel freight anymore now that we're in Italy."

She sighed in relief. "Thank God. I thought my bones would never stop rattling. And I'm more sore from sleeping on the floor than our defensive practice."

He booked them second-class tickets to Florence, and when they reached their seating carriage, they both exhaled as they sank into the upholstered benches. Once the train pulled from the station, she excused herself to wash up, leaving him alone in the carriage.

Only then did he allow himself to scrub his hands over

his face in frustration. He hadn't wanted to take on this job, but he realized that he had another reason for why he shouldn't have been on the case. She appealed to him. He liked her. Cared about her. Far too much. All his vigilant plans were blown to pieces. It was getting too difficult to keep himself only interested in their shared physical pleasure. He was at a loss.

He, who'd faced countless assassins and stared down the barrels of numerous guns, not to mention the knives, poisons, and explosives he'd evaded. There was that cadre of assassins in Vilnius, and the alleyful of knife-wielding toughs in Spitalfields. He'd even been trained in how to avoid the honey pot—and today was the very first time he'd actually fallen for it. By a woman whose family was in *Debrett's*. The irony wasn't lost.

This vulnerability he felt whenever he was with her could burn him down. But he'd only let himself burn once he knew she was safe. And then, when that was done, he'd walk away. As he always did.

The gilded and green hills of Tuscany enfolded them as they traveled south, vineyards forming Dionysian grids that climbed those hills, and rosy farmhouses topped with terracotta tiles looked out agelessly, seemingly without concern that a train bisected these most ancient and revered lands. Bronwyn had loved the place the first time she'd been here, and even the grim nature of her travel now couldn't quite dim her interest in being here again.

Apparently, Marco felt the same.

"*Dio*, but I love being back." He looked out the window, an expression as open as any she'd ever seen on his face. "Almost makes me wonder why I ever bother returning to England."

"You could stay in Italy," she offered.

He snorted. "God knows there's enough injustice in Italy that could necessitate doing Nemesis's work here."

"What about your . . . other work? For the, ah, government?"

"I've put in my time." He studied the cuff of his shirt, surprisingly clean given that they'd spent the night on the floor of a freight car. "Could likely retire on a decent pension, and move to Florence or Rome. No shortage of wrongdoing there."

"Or you could leave the city," she suggested.

He considered this. "It's appealing—a farm of my own. But I'd get restless, and find my way back into the rotten heart of a city. Even the most beautiful towns—with their basilicas and frescoes and bridges—are populated by people, and where people live, so do vice and corruption. Darkness lurks even in sunlit piazzas."

"Then why go back to England?" she wondered.

His brow creased in thought. "For all its incessant, infernal rain, its execrable coffee, its stiff-backed propriety, England's still my home. Where my family is. And my friends," he added.

"I thought I had friends in London," she said wryly. "Funny that when my money disappeared, so did they. But I liked seeing how you and the other Nemesis agents worked together. You'd never turn away from each other."

"The hell we would. Anyone who can't watch the others' backs is kicked out onto their arse."

"They're an assortment of eccentrics, aren't they?" she murmured. "No wonder you fit in so well."

"Good thing my mother insisted on good manners," he answered, "or else I'd treat you to one of the many varieties of obscene Italian hand gestures."

"Please continue my education." When he hesitated, she pressed, "Go on. I'm sure your mother would forgive you—or at least not box your ears as hard—if the recipient of said hand gestures wanted to see them."

He crossed himself. "Forgive me, *madre*." Then he launched into a series of movements with his hands and arms that would make a stevedore blush. She eagerly copied the gestures, as much for the novelty of learning them as to see Marco actually blush.

The lesson came to an abrupt halt when the ticket collector came by and caught them both in the middle of one of the more filthy gesticulations.

With his own shocked curse, the collector slammed the door of the seating compartment, muttering in Italian, but she could guess at the meaning. Something about the utter lack of decency in this modern world. And by a *lady,* too!

Bronwyn began to laugh. A husky, rich laugh that came from deep in her belly. The first time she'd laughed like this in so long.

She almost stopped in astonishment when Marco joined her. And together they chortled like escaped bedlamites.

"They'll likely ban Englishwomen from Italy now," she said breathlessly.

"We've started an international incident," he agreed.

She wiped her eyes. "If they try me, at least I'll know what hand gesture to give to the judge."

"You'd either be thrown into prison for the rest of your life, or receive a dozen proposals of marriage."

She sobered. "Given the choice, I'll take prison."

He went still. "You never said your marriage was as bad as that."

The years telescoped back, until she was a young bride again, full of curiosity and hope. And then the dimming of those feelings as reality set in. "Hugh was a cordial and kind husband. But . . . I don't want cordiality anymore."

She gazed out the window at the timeless Italian country-side. "I don't know what I want . . ." She searched for words for things she herself couldn't quite understand. "Wickedness." The stunned faces of Charles and Lydia flashed through her mind. She shook her head. "Doubtful that I could find that in the confines of marriage."

"You could always take a lover."

"I have," she answered.

"After me," he said.

Disappointment crested like a wave. She couldn't do this. "Oh. Maybe . . . maybe it would be better if we didn't. If I could find someone more . . . reliable."

She waited for him to say something. That not only did he want to be her lover for a long time, but he also hated the idea of her taking another man to her bed.

But he didn't say any of this. He kept silent, and this spoke far louder than any words.

TEN

Florence was an enchantment of a city. They reached it just as the sun had begun to set, casting the winding streets in gold light and purple shadows that painted the multistoried buildings and their window boxes of early flowers. The streets themselves were a confusion, and she readily followed Marco—who moved with purpose and direction.

Every corner they turned they stumbled across either a majestic piazza or church, or statues of gods and angels formed by long-dead masters. Yet even amid the beauty, just as Marco had said, skulked the shade of poverty. Outside magnificent churches, beggars gathered, their faces just as dirty and their clothes just as ragged as the beggars in London. Veterans of wars missing limbs. Women cradling whimpering infants.

Destitution and want were universal, even in this gem-like city of the Medicis.

They passed churches and squares, crossed the gilded storefronts that lined the Ponte Vecchio. Went past the famed palace, and wound their way up into the cypress-lined hills that crowded close to the river Arno.

"Giovanni doesn't live in the city proper," Marco said

over his shoulder as he climbed the sloping road. He'd already taken them on an oblique route around the city, circling some piazzas, doubling back, using alleys almost no one would ever see. "Too dangerous for a man once in his line of work."

"Where might a former"—she lowered her voice to a whisper, even though she spoke in English while everyone they passed only talked in Italian—"*spy* live?"

"There." He nodded toward a medieval tower. "It was once part of the old fortifications. Now it guards Giovanni and his secrets."

The tower was set apart from the other homes, surrounded by more ancient-looking cypresses. A handful of lights shone in the narrow windows. The stone exterior was worn from time, but stood strongly, a testament to the long-ago craftsmen who'd built it. Or the assiduous efforts of the current occupant to keep his home from collapsing around him.

She waited as Marco approached the heavy wooden door and knocked using the heavy iron ring mounted in the center.

The door swung open, and the man who stood there could have been a giant from a fairy tale, were it not for his modern clothing.

"*Sì?*" the massive man intoned. He eyed Marco and the suitcases, and started to shut the door.

Before he could, Marco said something quickly in Italian. The giant held the door a moment, tilting his head to one side as if considering what Marco had said, then closed the door. Leaving Bronwyn and Marco out in the growing darkness.

"We came awfully far to get a door shut in our faces," she noted.

"Too far to get impatient now," he answered.

A moment later, the door swung open again, revealing

the giant. Mutely, he stepped forward and took their bags—though she refused to relinquish her violin case— then gestured with his head for them to climb the winding staircase inside.

She gingerly stepped into the tower, looking up at the stone stairs that twisted over their heads. The entire ground floor of the tower was open, revealing it to be approximately thirty by thirty feet. She was a little disappointed to see no suits of armor, but tapestries did hang on the walls, along with a few modern paintings.

The enormous man and Marco had an exchange, which Bronwyn couldn't follow, but at the conclusion of it, Marco said to her in English, "Giovanni's waiting for us in the third-floor parlor."

"How many floors does this place have?" she wondered as they started up the staircase.

"Seven."

Hopefully that was a good luck sign that their long voyage to Italy hadn't been in vain. They climbed the stairs, with the giant continuing past them—presumably to put their luggage in a bedroom on one of the other six floors. On each landing, they passed heavy medieval furniture mixed in with modern pieces, along with more tapestries and paintings. Oil lamps, not gas, burned on the walls. She half expected torches or candelabras heavily enameled with dripped beeswax.

Reaching the third floor, they found themselves outside a set of elaborately carved double doors. Marco tapped three times before entering, and Bronwyn followed.

The chamber within had roughly circular walls, and the stones that comprised them were pitted with age. But the room itself was fitted elegantly with more of the amalgam between the old and the new. Having spent the last few days rattling around on trains, Bronwyn thought it felt good to be in a space that wasn't moving. If anything, the tower and this chamber looked as though they could outlast time.

But her attention was quickly drawn by the man approaching them. He was middle-aged, fair-haired, and trim and handsome in the way of mature men. He stepped forward and shook Marco's hand, then gave him a kiss on each cheek, all the while speaking quickly in Italian.

"English, please, Giovanni," Marco said. "Mrs. Parrish isn't familiar with the beauty of our mother tongue."

"Forgive me, signora." Giovanni bowed. As he did, he took her hand and kissed it in the manner of an old-fashioned courtier. "I should have known by the flaming beauty of your hair that you were from England's shores."

She blushed at his outrageous flattery. "There is nothing to forgive. Thank you for receiving us."

"Ah, she is as gracious as she is lovely," Giovanni murmured. He turned to Marco, and in that slight movement, she saw the same leashed power in the older man that she witnessed in Marco—though tempered slightly by age. For all his ornate words, this man was just as dangerous as Marco.

"I am thinking," Giovanni continued, waving them over to the sofas, "you have befallen some exceptional luck. Why else should you and this beautiful woman arrive at my home like a knife thrown in the darkness?" As everyone sat, his eyes narrowed, and his voice was slightly edged.

"Les Grillons," Marco answered without preamble.

Giovanni's jaw tightened. "You have brought them to my door?" Despite Marco's request that they speak English, the Italian man used his native language to curse. Extensively.

"We're here and alive," Marco answered, unfazed by the swearing.

"So that means they did not follow you? My body-guard Niccolo is strong, but even he cannot fend off an attack by too many of those Grillons thugs."

Marco explained quickly the ways he used to evade the syndicate, which seemed to slightly mollify Giovanni. But tension still radiated from him.

She wondered if he, too, had knives sewn into his clothing. It was entirely possible. She'd grown to recognize the look of sharp-eyed wariness that spies seemed to possess, even when secure in their homes.

"But Les Grillons keep their business in France," Giovanni noted. "We have our own criminal organizations here in Italy. No need to import more."

Briefly, Marco described everything that had happened since he'd first set foot in her foyer—it seemed so long ago, and also as quick as a bullet. Giovanni made sounds of shock or grim understanding as Marco's tale unfolded. Rather, it was *their* tale, and Bronwyn helped fill in small details as the whole rather sordid history unfolded. Neither she nor Marco thought it fitting to tell Giovanni about making love on the train, but given the speculative look in the Italian man's gaze when he glanced at her, she saw that he already understood she and Marco had been to bed together.

The thought made her heart pound tightly. She'd learned his body, and he hers, but there was still a part of him as protected as this tower, and just as likely to topple. Foolishly, she'd hoped that meeting Giovanni—who'd known Marco far longer than she had—would provide a deeper insight into Marco. But the two men circled each other like wary tigers, revealing nothing of themselves.

At the conclusion of his tale, Marco leaned forward and braced his elbows on his knees, his hands clasped. "So will you help us?"

Giovanni let out a deep sigh. "*Amici,* you have really

put yourselves in the fire. And what you ask of me . . . it could undo all the work I have done to keep the Grillons refugee safe."

"Please, Mister . . . Giovanni," Bronwyn said. "There's no need to fear anything happening to that man. I trust Marco with my life. You should trust the Grillons man's to him, too."

Something flashed in Marco's eyes—surprise, perhaps, at her admission of trust. But he'd shown again and again that he'd never let anything happen to her. Had, in fact, safeguarded her far more than anyone ever had— even her own family.

Before Giovanni could answer, another man came into the room. He was also of middle years, with thinning brown hair and a neatly groomed beard. "Giovanni," he said with a distinctly British accent, "we have guests and neither of them have a drink in their hand."

"My apologies, Thomas," Giovanni answered. "I would hate to besmirch your reputation as a host."

Thomas went to a sideboard and poured out four cordial glasses of what appeared to be sherry. She murmured her thanks as the man handed a glass to her.

"Ah, one of my countrymen!" Thomas exclaimed. "What a pleasure to hear our language again. I'm afraid my Italian accent drives Giovanni quite mad." He handed out the rest of the glasses, then took one for himself and seated himself beside Giovanni.

He placed his hand on Giovanni's knee and gave it an affectionate squeeze. It was not the gesture of friendship, but rather, of love.

Bronwyn struggled to not drop her glass. Instead, she took a shaky sip, trying to steady herself. Of course she'd *heard* of men like Giovanni and Thomas, but never actually met them. To her knowledge.

She glanced over at Marco, looking for signs of shock. But if he was caught off guard by Giovanni and Thomas's relationship, he didn't show it

"I endure your dreadful Italian," Giovanni answered, "for your sake."

"You are all graciousness," Thomas replied.

"Grazie, mi amore."

They didn't seem odd or degenerate at all. In fact, what struck her about the two men was how very ordinary they seemed, just like any middle-aged couple. Though one of the two was, in fact, a former spy.

A spy who held the key to getting her fortune back.

"I must admit my surprise," Thomas said. "We so seldom receive guests, let alone visitors from as far away as England."

"Giovanni and I were colleagues," Marco said.

Thomas took a drink of sherry. "Both in the espionage game, then."

"He told you about that?" Bronwyn asked, amazed.

"How do you think we met, my dear?" Thomas answered. "Giovanni was on a mission in England. I was employed at the Treasury, and was supposed to work with him. And then . . ." His expression turned grim. "There was no place for me in my home country. Not if I wanted to be with Giovanni. So I came here, and he left that work behind. For the most part," he added wryly.

"Hard to leave it all behind," Marco said.

"I do miss it from time to time," Giovanni admitted.

"And I don't miss having you risking your life every day," said Thomas. He turned back to Bronwyn and Marco. "I don't have to worry about that with you two, do I?"

"It is not my life they want me to endanger," Giovanni answered before she or Marco could reply. He shook his head. "I cannot give you what you seek."

Disappointment arrowed through her. "Please—"

"No, I am quite certain of this."

"But you were our only option . . ."

Marco set his glass down on a small table and abruptly stood. "That's your choice," he said to Giovanni coldly. "We'll find some other way. Call your man and have our bags brought down." He reached for Bronwyn, who had also gotten to her feet.

Before Giovanni could speak, Thomas rose. "I can't influence him where his work is concerned, but I refuse to put you out in the cold tonight. You'll stay here."

"Thomas . . ." Giovanni said warningly.

But the Englishman scowled at his lover. "I won't be gainsaid. They'll dine with us and spend the night here. And then they can do whatever they want tomorrow." He glanced at Marco and Bronwyn. "You will stay, won't you? I'm certain all the decent *pensiones* are full, especially by this hour of the night."

Uncertain, Bronwyn glanced at Marco. She detected a hint of reservation in his gaze. But the idea of looking for somewhere else to sleep must have been as unappealing to him as it was to her, because at last he said, "Tonight only. Then we're off."

While Giovanni didn't look entirely pleased by this arrangement, he said, "Dinner is served at nine o'clock."

She had no idea what the next day would bring, let alone how they'd proceed in retrieving her money. There were countless uncertainties when it came to what she and Marco meant to each other. They'd spoken of possibly becoming lovers once the mission was over, but he'd only been able to offer her a very temporary arrangement. Nothing was set. Nothing was sure. Yet, at least for the night, she and Marco would be safe inside this tower.

* * *

Bronwyn and Marco were given a bedchamber on the fifth floor. The room itself took up most of the story, with just enough space outside for a landing. Like the parlor, the walls were curved, and timber beams supported the ceiling. But her attention fixed on the enormous four-poster bed dominating the chamber. It looked as though it dated from centuries earlier, with its heavy wood and ornate carvings. Definitely not Gothic revival, but the era itself. Like the tower, it must have sheltered many. Who knows how many had slept in this bed? How many had given birth, made love?

The thought sent a pulse of heat through her, but she pushed it aside. There were other issues at hand besides the continuous awareness between her and Marco.

Namely—

"Did you know?" she asked.

He checked their bags—presumably to ensure that they hadn't been tampered with or any of the contents removed. "Know what?"

"About Giovanni and Thomas."

Still, he didn't look at her. "Does it matter?"

So he did know. "A little warning would've been appreciated."

Now he did glance at her, his gaze distant. "Again—does it matter?"

She didn't like feeling on the defensive. He'd been the one to withhold information. "I've put my life in your hands. Trust works both ways."

He shut their suitcases, seemingly satisfied that they hadn't been tampered with. "I wouldn't bring you here if I didn't trust you."

"But you left out a crucial bit of information about our hosts." She planted her hands on her hips.

He seemed more distant than ever. "I don't see how it signifies. If you're disgusted by them—"

"I'm a little surprised. But not disgusted."

Some of the coolness left his dark eyes, and his jaw loosened.

"Still," she continued, "I can't help feeling that you were testing me. Deliberately holding it back just to see how I'd react."

He only gave her one of his maddening Italian shrugs.

If this *had* been a test, a way to judge her feelings about Giovanni and Thomas, why should it matter to him how she felt about their hosts? Yet how suspicious that he might care about her reaction to Giovanni and Thomas. As though . . .

As though he cared more than he'd admit to her. Or to himself.

But she couldn't voice this to him. He'd only disappear inside himself, cool and elusive as a shadow. Instead, she dressed for dinner, with Marco serving as her lady's maid.

Then she had the pleasure of watching him undress, then dress. He pulled on a crisp white shirt, and she observed the play of tight muscle beneath the fine cotton. Her hands tingled with the need to feel those muscles, the contrast between the solidity of his flesh and the starched fabric, and then peel off the shirt to touch him skin to skin.

How could she desire him so much, when he seemed determined to hold his true self at bay? Perhaps all she wanted from him was his body. It had been a long time since she'd made love. Now that the dam had broken— she could still feel his lips on her sex, and the way he'd cupped her breast—she was flooded with need.

But it was more than that. She'd spoken true when she'd said he fascinated her. There were layers to this man. Levels that went so deep, she suspected even he didn't know about them. Part of her wanted to tear away those layers and see who he truly was. But it would be an uphill battle, and she had enough battles to contend with now.

"Marco," she murmured, pinning up her hair, "I've been thinking." She stared at him in the mirror. "If all you can give me is physical pleasure, I've decided I'll take it. And, when the work here is completed, I'll take what you offer. Even if it can't last."

"Grazie, fragola," he said, coming up behind her and pressing a kiss to her neck. "You won't regret it."

Oh, she knew she would. But she couldn't stop herself.

Turning, she took in Marco in his evening clothes. "You look dangerous."

"Here I thought I looked elegant."

"That, too." The black jacket clung to his shoulders, just as the trousers defined the length of his sinewy legs. His white waistcoat wrapped snug around his lean torso, and the whiteness of his collar and bow tie set off the olive hue of his skin. He'd slicked back his hair, making him appear sleek as a panther, and just as predatory. Certainly a rapacious gleam shone in his eyes as he took in the sight of her in her satin gown.

Like a possessive caress, she felt his gaze on her, heating the flesh of her exposed chest and the slight curve of her breasts lifted high by the cut of her gown. The gloves that covered her hands and arms were little protection. She felt bare, vulnerable.

Part of her wanted to turn away and shield herself. But he'd already seen her at her most bare. It seemed too late to hide from him, not when he'd had his mouth on her . . .

"We'll have our dinner brought up," he rumbled. "To hell with Giovanni and his hospitality."

"I'd hate to disappoint Thomas," she said breathlessly.

"To hell with Thomas, too."

But they did leave their chamber, and journeyed down

to the second floor to find the dining room, and their hosts.

Thomas seemed far more glad to see them than Giovanni, and complimented them both on their smart appearance. They were seated, and a series of dishes served. The food reminded her painfully of her honeymoon in Italy, each bite recalling her lost youth and hopes for the future. It would have helped had the food Giovanni served been inedible. Easier to just push the offerings around on her plate and pretend to eat. But it was, unfortunately, delicious, and while her palate demanded more, every taste only reinforced how much she'd lost, and how the future hadn't turned out at all as she'd hoped.

She tried to distract herself with conversation. But it was stilted between Marco and Giovanni, casting a pall even on Thomas, so that there was little to do but eat and remember.

"Mrs. Parrish, if I may note," Thomas said, breaking the stillness, "it sounds as though you aren't without recourse if you fail to get your money back."

"I have options for employment waiting for me, yes," she answered. "But I've been thinking of other ways to use my fortune, if I'm lucky enough to retrieve it."

"Such as?"

"A home for widows, perhaps. Somewhere for women like me to go if there is no safe or good option."

Giovanni narrowed his eyes. "Easy to speak of such charity when the money is not in your hands. You might change your tale once the *denaro* is yours again."

"Only one way to find out," she countered.

Finally, after platters of fresh fruit and small sweetmeats had been served, the dinner came to an end. She attempted to breathe a sigh of relief, but the pain of the meal was still laced tightly around her, like a constricting corset.

"Shall we go up to the parlor?" Thomas suggested. An attempt, she supposed, to salvage the rituals of polite society. But there wasn't any such thing as polite society when two spies dined with each other.

To her surprise, Marco agreed.

Thomas offered her his arm, and together, they climbed the stairs to the parlor.

"It isn't easy, my dear," he whispered to her. "They tend to keep themselves locked tight as a vault, these intelligence agents. Training, I suppose."

"Or perhaps a natural predilection for distance," she answered in a low voice.

"Who can say? Some days I consider myself lucky if he reveals the smallest detail about his past. Took me years to learn he grew up in Umbria."

"Why bother trying?" she pressed quietly. "If they're so determined to hold back, why not leave them to their solitude?"

Thomas gave a melancholy sigh. "I ask myself that many times. But I love him, so I take whatever I can and be grateful for it."

They'd reached the parlor, so she couldn't ask Thomas any more regarding the logistics of caring about a spy. Could she be satisfied with crumbs, as Thomas seemed to be?

But the topic wasn't up for debate. It never had been, no matter how much existed between her and Marco. All they could have was this moment. Perhaps the next few moments beyond that. But it was impossible for him to give more.

The massive Niccolo appeared with a tray bearing glasses of herbal liqueur, as well as dried, sugared fruit and nuts. But for all the food and refreshments, the atmosphere in the parlor was far from convivial. Desperate for a topic of conversation, she noted the piano in the corner.

"Do either of you play?" she asked her hosts.

"I was forced to take lessons as a child," Thomas said, "and promptly, deliberately forgot."

"And you?" she pressed Giovanni.

His lips thinned. "I am not feeling very musical tonight."

"I noticed you had a violin case, Mrs. Parrish," Thomas quickly interjected.

"My instrument was one of the few possessions I was able to keep," she answered.

"Would you favor us by playing?" Thomas requested.

Her initial impulse was to refuse. With Marco and Giovanni all but sticking knives into each other's backs, it hardly seemed an appropriate time. But the thought of playing again sent a wave of longing through her, and her fingers twitched as if forming notes on her violin's neck.

If neither Marco nor Giovanni could come to an understanding, if the distance she and Marco had traveled had been for nothing, then shouldn't she get some pleasure out of her time here in Florence? If nothing else, she was learning how to survive dangers and setbacks.

"Of course," she said.

Marco said nothing.

"Niccolo can fetch it for you," Giovanni surprised her by saying.

"No—I mean, no, thank you. I can retrieve it myself." She rose from the sofa—the men all standing as she did so—and left the parlor to climb the stairs to their bedchamber. The violin and its case were just where she'd left them, so after a quick check to make sure the instrument was in good condition, she took them downstairs.

There, the silence was still thick as blood. Standing beside the piano, she pulled the violin from the case and spent several minutes tuning it. Travel across the Channel and the Continent hadn't done much favors to its sound, and she fought to keep from grimacing as she made the most unmusical noises as she tuned the instrument. Finally, she was satisfied, tucked it beneath her chin. Began to play.

Bach's partita, of course.

The first few notes came out awkwardly. She felt acutely conscious of all eyes upon her. There'd been a time when she used to play after dinner parties, but those times were long past. Over the past few years, when she'd played, she played for herself alone, her dream of performing for a paid crowd nothing but a dissolving mist. But now here she was—playing for an audience.

She screeched out a wrong note, and lowered the violin. "I'm sorry. I'm not . . . in form tonight."

"Don't stop," Thomas begged, at the same time that Giovanni said, "Do go on, signora."

But she shook her head, and started to put her violin away.

"Please," Marco said quietly.

Her hands stilled, the violin suspended over its case.

Then she picked up the instrument again and played.

This time, the notes came out true. It took her a few moments to sink into the piece, to feel the embrace of the music around her, how she was bathed in the lambent glow of sound. Those beautiful, dark minor notes. The climbing scales and precipitous descents, as if a night-flying bird rose and fell with evening currents, black against a blacker sky.

In the piece, she rediscovered herself. The young woman she'd been in London, protected, naïve, in contrast to the woman she was now, having immersed herself in a world far more uncompromising and stark than she'd ever experienced or known. She was familiar with death, but now she'd seen its brutal side. With Hugh. And Devere. She'd witnessed the most dire poverty. And she'd made love with a man determined to keep himself a stranger.

A metamorphosis had occurred. Was occurring, even now. Who she would be when everything was over, she'd no idea. All she could do was hold fast to her strength, and survive.

All of this she poured into her playing. She forgot everything but the feel of her beloved violin, the bow as it arced back and forth across the strings, the sway of her body as she gave herself over to the music.

And then, suddenly, it was over. She'd reached the end of the piece.

Her eyes opened—when had she closed them?—to find three pairs of eyes staring at her. Thomas looked delighted. Giovanni appeared thoughtful. And Marco . . . Marco looked stunned.

She lowered the violin as Thomas started clapping. Giovanni and then Marco joined in, at which she gave a small bow.

"I think I rather missed that," she said, which was a terrific understatement akin to saying she missed the ability to breathe.

"Brava," Giovanni murmured.

"Yes, *brava,* indeed," Thomas added. "Do play some more."

Now that the instrument was in her hand, she was loath to part with it. So she played the solo parts of Mozart's Violin Concerto No. 3—lively and bright, full of sunshine and hope. Mozart had been a favorite of hers when she'd been younger, but maturity and experience had brought her to Beethoven and Bach. She hadn't thought she'd ever return to Mozart again. Now she needed him and his ebullience, his childlike complexity.

What was Marco to her? And what was she to him?

Lovers, operative and client? More, or less? Answers kept themselves scarce. But there was this—music. It never withheld itself from her. And she was the agent that made it happen, pulling notes from the air and giving them form through her bow and fingers.

The music drew to an end, and she accepted another round of applause. Thomas beamed at her, while Giovanni continued to look pensive.

But Marco—his gaze was hot upon her, and intent radiated from him like a hunter on the trail of its prey.

Heat washed over her. Surely she blushed. But she'd never seen such ferocity in Marco's eyes, as though he would leap across the room, hike up her skirts, and make love to her against the piano—uncaring whether or not they had an audience.

But that was one public performance she was unwilling to give.

At Thomas's cry for more, she politely demurred, and put away her violin with faintly trembling hands.

"The journey and disappointments of the day have been very fatiguing," she explained. "It's time for me to retire." After bidding her hosts good night, she stepped outside and began to climb the stairs.

"Marco—" she heard Giovanni say.

"A tempo," came the growled response. And then the sounds of Marco's footsteps. In pursuit.

Her heart pounded in double time as she hurried up the stairs, trying to keep from being caught. And hoping that she was.

The moment she entered the bedchamber, she set her violin aside. Then stood in the middle of the room and waited, pulse racing, for Marco to catch up. His tread was steady, deliberate. And with each step, her breathing came faster and faster. Until he appeared in the door, and she all but gasped for breath.

Oh, he was a dangerous one. Without taking his gaze from hers, he stepped into the room and shut and locked the door behind him.

The moment hung ripe as summer, a suspension of time, where neither of them moved, but savored the possibility of what was to be.

She wanted this. Needed it. When nothing else was certain, including the future, there was this desire. It felt as though it would rip through her with gilded claws, and she craved that annihilation.

And he knew what music meant to her—more than anyone else had. He understood what she'd given and gained by her performance tonight. They shared that bond, beyond mere physical need.

But as she and Marco stared at each other, drawing the moment out, it felt as if bright jeweled threads stretched from her body to his. She wanted more than to be taken by desire. She wanted to own it. She wanted to have *him,* fully.

The last time she and Marco had made love, he'd been the one in command. Who'd guided her through the paths of sensation. And she'd been nearly overcome with fear, hiding herself, holding back. Not this time. This time, she would strip away all barriers, so that they were fully themselves.

"I remember another postcard." She swayed toward him, feeling power thrum through her. He stayed exactly where he was, standing in front of the closed door. "Can you think which one?"

"There were many." His voice was a low rasp.

"Yes, but *this* one intrigued me." She stood before him, close enough to see the darkness of his stubbled cheeks, and the widening of his pupils. Though she didn't touch him, his heat radiated into her skin. "A man was standing, just as you are. He was almost fully dressed. I say *almost* because there was one part of him that was bared."

"His cock," Marco rumbled.

Bold as she felt, the word made her burn.

"It was in a woman's mouth as she knelt in front of him," she said breathlessly.

"I remember."

At last, she reached out to touch him. Ran her hand down his starched shirtfront. Lower. Until she found the hard length of his erection through his black wool trousers. He hissed in a breath as she cupped him. It still amazed her that this part of him had been inside her. Filled her completely.

"I remember, too," she whispered. Then sank to her knees.

He said nothing, but his body was tense as a primed gun as she worked at his trouser fastenings. She reached in and wrapped her hand around his rigid penis. Then she drew it out. She imagined a photographer taking a picture of the scene, her looking at the picture. Arousal built higher.

In the lamplight, she got her first real look at him. The thick shaft. The smooth crown. A tiny drop of fluid at the slit. This was part of Marco, too. Mysterious and a little frightening but fascinating, too.

This was carnal, yes, but deeply intimate. Beyond two bodies striving for pleasure. This was them, literally and figuratively exposed. He allowed himself to be vulnerable. Such a rarity—and he shared it with her.

She glanced up. His skin had darkened, his nostrils were flared, and his jaw was clenched into a straight, rigid line. He stared at her through lowered lids. But his chest moved up and down quickly, breath soughing in and out.

At his sides hung his hands, knotted into fists. Oh, he wanted this—she could tell. He wanted it badly. Yet he managed to hold himself back. To keep from frightening her.

There was still a thread of fear in her. More than that, however, was the measure of her strength. Pleasure was hers to bestow and take. Being on her knees made her no less powerful. With the most sensitive part of him in her hand, at this moment he belonged to her. And he wanted to belong to her.

Still, she wasn't experienced. Not in this.

"Tell me," she said. But it wasn't a request. It was a command. "Tell me how to do this."

He swallowed hard. "Grip the shaft . . . yes . . . like that. Lick the head."

She did, swirling her tongue around it and finding the skin silky, with a bit of salt. He groaned, and heat traveled directly between her legs at the sound. She dallied there like that, licking him all around, even the ridge just beneath the head, which made him rumble like a beast.

Her breasts pressed tight against the inside of her bodice, and while she cursed the fabric for keeping her from touching them, there was something impossibly erotic about being completely clothed—in evening dress, no less—while performing this most intimate act.

"Suck . . . ah, God . . . suck me," he growled.

She took more of him into her mouth. Drew on him, as if taking sustenance. And, heaven help her, did he feel wondrous. Hot. Hard. Silky.

Her eyes drifted shut as she lost herself in sensation and strength.

She felt his fingers threading into her hair. Gently pulling her closer. She took him deeper, past the head to the shaft itself. Impossible to fit all of him into her mouth, so she wrapped her hand snug around the base of his penis.

Pumped him in time with her sucking. It took a few moments to find her rhythm, but find it she did.

"Cara, bella, dolce fragola," he said hoarsely. *"È così buono."*

A tide of arousal flooded her at his words, and the tightening of his fingers in her hair. She glanced up again to see his own eyes closed, his head thrown back. This tightly controlled man had given up control. To her.

Suddenly, he pulled from her mouth. She was left on her knees, with his erection in her hand, wet with her saliva.

"Remember that other postcard?" he rumbled, drawing her up to standing. "Where the woman had her skirts hiked up around her waist, her arse in the air as the man bent her over a table, his cock buried deep in her pussy."

"I . . . remember." She glanced over to the vanity. "There weren't any mirrors, though."

He led her toward the small table. "We can do better than those postcards. You'll watch yourself as I put my cock in you. You'll see the look on your face as I fuck you."

Heat flared through her at his words. *Ah, God.*

At the vanity, he placed her hands on the edge of the table. She could already see the stain of desire on her cheeks, how her eyes were heavy, and the loosening of her hair so it formed a wild corona around her face.

She watched as he gathered up her skirts, and felt the slight shaking in his hands as he did so. Cool air touched her through the opening in her drawers. But he didn't seem satisfied. He pulled her drawers down, guided her to step out of them. Aside from her stockings and tiny evening slippers, she was bare now from the waist down. Again she was struck by the erotic feeling of being partly dressed, but also so exposed to him.

Looking in the mirror, she watched hunger carve him

into hard contours as he stared at her behind, and the exposed folds of her sex. Surely he could see how wet she was, how ready, yet he looked his fill. His penis curved up higher, twitching, as he stared at her.

"Marco." She moaned. *"Now."*

"Ora, amore?" He teased her with the head of his penis, rubbing it along her and around her opening.

"Sì," she managed to gasp.

He chuckled darkly. "I like my language on your tongue."

"I like . . . my tongue . . . on you."

His laugh abruptly stopped. And with one thrust, he was inside her. Her gaze locked with her reflection. There she was. With Marco inside her. She looked the picture of unbridled lust. Like one of those erotic postcards. But better—because this was real and now. And him. God above, how she loved it. Loved . . .

No—this was only sensation. Nothing more. Wasn't it?

She continued to watch herself as he slid slowly, almost completely, out. Then back in. Sensation filled her as much as he did. His fingers gripped her hips tightly. Bruisingly. But she didn't care. Wanted that. To be marked by him. Marks that showed he was past control. That they could belong to each other.

His pace increased, his thrusts coming faster. The vanity shook with the force of his strokes—and so did she. She barely managed to tear her gaze away from the reflection of her face to look at him. He grimaced in pleasure, but his gaze was tight on hers. They stared at each other as he . . . fucked her. As she fucked him back, pressing hard into his thrusts, letting sensation build and build.

One of his hands unlocked from around her hip. Curved between her legs. She felt his fingers circle around her bud. Then, with each stroke of his cock, his fingertip lightly tapped against her pearl. With each tap, ecstasy shot through her.

"Ah, God," she moaned. "I—"

The orgasm poured through her. Wave upon wave. A crash of gold and light. She couldn't keep her eyes open, but fell fully into sensation.

Yet even as the pulses of her climax faded, he continued to stroke in and out of her. She watched him in the mirror. Here, together, he was unguarded, unrestrained. A glimpse of his truer, rawer self.

"*Cara,* I—" He pulled out. She felt the heat of his seed upon her bare skin. And though it hadn't been that long since they'd last made love, his climax seemed to go on and on. Until, at last, he bowed over her, his breath hot against her neck.

They stared at each other in the mirror, both panting, and she could see the same expression in his eyes as in hers. Pleasure and satiation. And shock.

They'd held nothing back. Leaving them more open and exposed than either of them had ever been.

ELEVEN

Marco woke with sun in his face and Bronwyn in his arms. For a moment, he could only lie there, shocked. A quick check of the clock on a nearby table revealed the time to be eight o'clock. He couldn't remember the last time he'd slept past five. He couldn't remember waking with a woman. Always, he crept out before she'd awakened, leaving behind cooling sheets and fading memories of a night spent in momentary gratification.

Yet here he was. Waking at an opulent hour, and with the warm, soft form of Bronwyn pressed close, her hand spread over his chest. He marveled at the rise and fall of her hand, in time with his breathing. Deceptive, with its slimness. One might think she had no strength at all with a hand so delicate. But he knew better.

He'd seen her hands last night moving over the neck of her violin, holding the bow as it glided over the strings. And while he'd been to more than his share of concerts in his life—even with female musicians—none of them had fired his blood as she did last night. It was more than seeing her sway like a siren, or imagining how those dexterous fingers might feel on him. It was as if each note she played shot right into him like an arrow dipped in a strength potion. Filling him with her capability. Her resilience. Her passion.

As he glanced down at her, she slept on, peaceful, her hair spread upon the pillow and over his shoulder. What an illusory picture she made, looking like one of those soft-limbed nymphs in a painting. But he knew her to be far more than that.

That ache took up residence in the center of his chest again. But he couldn't move to soothe it, not without disturbing her. So he let the pain fill him. It reminded him of when he'd nearly lost several toes to frostbite outside Moscow. He hadn't felt anything at all in his foot, just a pleasant numbness. And then, slowly, the flesh had started to thaw. The pain had been excruciating as his extremities had come back to life. Despite his high tolerance for discomfort—he'd been trained to withstand torture, after all—he'd almost have preferred losing the toes than suffer as he had. The lack of feeling was better.

Bronwyn stirred. She blinked up at him, seemingly almost as surprised to see him as he was to be there.

Would she turn away? Murmur some distracting inanity? They'd spent most of last night making love, keeping nothing back as they'd laid themselves bare in so many ways. They had done things together—acts he'd more than a passing familiarity with—but now with her . . . They'd become so much more than two bodies selfishly chasing pleasure.

He'd no reason to think she'd give him anything more than her body, when that's all he'd offered her. Yet, fearlessly, she'd cast aside pretense and self-protection. Let him see her totally. And in the way he'd made love to her—telling her over and over again how beautiful she was, how she filled him with need, seeking her pleasure before his own—he'd done the same.

But this morning, in the brightness of an Italian sun,

would she retreat? Maybe he would, out of habitual self-protection.

Instead, she leaned up and kissed him. Her breath was stale from waking, but he didn't care. He kissed her back. Openly. Hungrily.

Thoughts of retreat fled. He wouldn't hide from this. Couldn't.

Already, his body stirred.

"Di distruggere me," he rumbled. Easier to speak of these things in a language she couldn't understand.

"Unfair," she murmured. "When I can't fathom what you're saying."

"I'm not a fair man."

"Not fair at all." She ran her hand over his stubble, and the sensation nearly made him shiver.

They kissed again, hotly. He cupped her breast, tracing his fingers around her tightening nipple. She moaned softly. Pressed herself closer so that his erection was snug and scalding between them.

Suddenly, she was straddling him. The covers fell away from her shoulders, and she was naked in the daylight. Her hair tangled. Her face still slightly puffy from sleep. Real and unafraid. More beautiful than he'd ever seen her.

Bracing her hands on his shoulders, she slid her pussy up and down his cock, wetting him, preparing them both. Then she positioned herself, the head of his penis at her opening, and sank down.

He made an animal sound as he gripped her hips. Neither moved. Allowing themselves this moment to feel and be seen. Doubtless he looked like an unkempt brigand, hardly a sophisticated man who'd make sophisticated love to an elegant woman of society. He didn't care. He only wanted her, as they both were right now.

She lifted her hips slightly. Pleasure tore through him

at this smallest of movements. And when she lowered her hips, taking him deeper in, he groaned.

"Ti senti molto bene."

She couldn't know what he was saying, but she moaned. "Yes."

"Time . . . for an Italian lesson," he growled.

"Now?"

"You'll want to know . . . these words . . ." He lifted her hand. *"Mano."*

"Mano," she repeated breathlessly.

He kissed her hand, his tongue tracing a line on her flesh. *"Bacio."*

"Bacio. I like . . . that one."

"Have another." He leaned up and took her mouth with his. They unfurled together, bare and revealed.

Slowly, she discovered her pace and rhythm. He watched her face as she learned that if she moved her hips just so, they both cried out in pleasure. And when she bent to kiss him as she went faster, they panted into each other's mouths, sharing breath, sharing sensation.

She'd ridden him last night, too, but there was something new about sharing this in the uncompromising light of day, something unrestrained. Her breasts bounced as she moved, and he reached up to stroke them, taking the nipples between his fingers and pinching lightly.

Suddenly, she bowed back, her mouth open, eyes closed. The climax had her. It seemed so strong, she couldn't even make a sound. *Dio e il paradiso,* was she gorgeous.

The moment she curved over him, her orgasm finally releasing her, he flipped their positions. Rolled her onto her back and plunged into her with the ferocity of a lion taking his mate. He was already close to the edge. A few more strokes, and he was gone.

He barely managed to pull out in time. But, God, was it a struggle. He couldn't think of anything he wanted more than to come inside of her, feel her heat as she gripped him through his release. His seed shot from him as if he hadn't made love to her over and over last night. As if he'd been waiting his whole life to have her.

When the last aftershocks faded, he rolled onto his back. Together, they lay side by side, gasping. He stared up at the canopy as more light filled the room.

L'inferno. If he wasn't careful, he'd want this. Every night. Every morning. With her. This racking pleasure that came not only from sensation, but being entirely open, unhidden.

There was a word he hadn't taught her. Could barely utter it in his thoughts. But it whispered to him, and would not be pushed aside.

Amore.

Did he . . . ? Was he even capable of . . . ? He'd never believed it.

Until now.

But he couldn't forget who he was. A spy. An agent for Nemesis. A man stripped clean of everything but purpose. What he and Bronwyn shared wasn't viable. He had to remind himself of that, in case he started to think of the impossible. Things like *amore.*

Men like him didn't dream.

After bathing, Marco and Bronwyn joined their hosts back in the dining room for breakfast. Thomas was all smiles—a genial fellow—but Giovanni was more restrained.

It had been a hell of a setback to learn that the former spy wouldn't help them. But Marco wasn't through yet. He'd other tricks in his arsenal. And while finding the Grillons man without Giovanni's help was a massive obstacle, Marco didn't believe in obstacles that couldn't be overcome. Somehow, he'd locate the former Grillons operative.

He just needed to figure out how.

After he and Bronwyn had been served coffee and rolls by the hulking Niccolo, silence fell over the company. Marco's nerves pulled tight. Yet he only ate his roll and drank his excellent coffee, and quietly schemed.

"Montepulciano," Giovanni said suddenly.

Marco set down his cup. "Just like that?"

"I did some thinking, last night."

"Enough to change your mind," Marco said.

"We seem to be missing part of this conversation," Bronwyn noted. "What are you talking about?"

"The location of Émile Bertrand, the Grillons agent," Marco answered. "Giovanni's decided to tell us our friend's location. And that location is the little town of Montepulciano, which is about seventy miles from here."

"I don't understand." Bronwyn leaned forward in her chair. "Yesterday you were utterly set against giving us this information."

"You changed my mind, Signora Parrish." Pressing his index fingers just beneath his bottom lip, Giovanni looked pensive. "Or it is more accurate to say it was your violin that convinced me. I heard the beauty of your playing and I heard more than music. I heard your heart. While it might have inflamed some of us"—he shot a glance toward Marco—"it made me think. All night, I thought."

"Kept me awake with his tossing and turning," Thomas said in exasperation. "But with good cause."

"I could not, in clear conscience, consign you to the street. That is where you would be without your fortune, no?"

"Perhaps not the literal street," she answered honestly, when she could have just as easily lied. "I thought I might become a paid companion."

Giovanni shuddered. "The drudge of some old woman, or worse, a callow girl trying to ensnare a husband? No, I could not abide the idea that you, the maker of such exquisite music, who have the heart of someone who could play so divinely, would fade like wallpaper and play only in some dreary attic room, all alone."

The image Giovanni painted struck Marco like a fist in the gut. He'd known all along the stakes of this mission. But after last night, failure became impossible.

"There is courage, I think," Giovanni added, "to play as you did in the company of strangers. And I thought, too, about your plans for your money. A home for the poor ladies. I could not refuse, my own mother being once a young widow with many children."

"Though I appreciate your decision," Bronwyn said, "the risk to this Bertrand is still just as high this morning as it was last night, violin or no violin."

Giovanni gave a small smile. "There is no agent for any country better than *amico mio,* Marco. If Les Grillons had followed you from France, we would have all woken up dead this morning. But as we are alive and enjoying this fine *colazione,* clearly he was able to keep them away. I must trust that he will do the same and preserve Bertrand's safety."

Marco merely tipped his head in acknowledgment.

Bronwyn was less restrained. "Thank you so much, Giovanni."

"The thanking is mutual," he answered. "I had an incredible private concert last night, and for the first time, I have met Marco's *donna.*"

Pink spread across her cheeks. "I'm not . . . that is . . . I'm his client, not his woman."

Thomas dabbed at his mouth with his napkin. "Yet, according to Giovanni, not only has he never met one of Marco's lady lights, he's never even met one of his clients. All rather intriguing."

"Isn't it?" She stared at Marco pointedly, and he only stared back with a cool look he'd been cultivating for decades with great success. Yet it didn't seem to affect her. She continued to hold his gaze, until he was actually the one to look away first.

"I imagine you'll want to leave right away," Thomas said sadly.

"We can't move too quickly," Marco answered.

The Englishman sighed. "What a shame. I'd hoped to talk more with Mrs. Parrish, and hear her play again."

"Perhaps if we come through Florence again," Bronwyn suggested.

But Marco had to dash that hope. "Not this trip, *fragola*. From now on, there is a single direction: straight ahead. No looking back."

Giovanni graciously loaned Marco and Bronwyn his carriage to transport them to the train station. And so they found themselves on another platform, waiting for a train to take them away from Florence.

There was no train station at Montepulciano. Even if there had been, Marco would never have taken a direct route. Instead, he booked them tickets first to Pisa. Once they'd arrived at Pisa, their next stop was Lucca. He wished he could spend more time there, to see his mother's family, and bring them news of her. But it was impossible. It gave him a small thrill of gratification, though, to bring Bronwyn to his mother's home city.

From there, they doubled back to Pisa. Finally, they headed on to Siena, the closest station to their endpoint.

It wasn't elegant or fast, but then, neither was most espionage.

Bronwyn dozed several times through their travels. He couldn't blame her after how little sleep either of them had gotten last night. The strangest thing—he'd have thought by now he'd have gotten her well out of his system. He'd seldom gone back to the same woman more than a few times, and never with the enthusiasm he'd shown with Bronwyn. Yet as he watched her lightly slumber, her head leaning against the window of the second-class seating compartment, he sensed a clamoring within himself. A demand for more. More of everything. Sex—yes. But *her,* too.

That word curled through his mind again. The one he couldn't think in English, because it was too real. Too concrete. *Amore.*

Gesú, was this really happening to him?

The station at Siena was just outside the old city. As they disembarked, regret stabbed him. He wished he could show her the wonders of Siena, for it was unlike any other city, and she'd appreciate its labyrinthine marvels. She even cast a longing glance up the hill toward where the medieval town perched. But she didn't ask to see it, and he couldn't indulge her if she did. Time was costly.

A few carriages stood lined up outside the station. Marco walked up to the driver of one, a man with canny eyes and a particularly adept way of holding the reins.

"Got a wife? A family?" Marco asked in Italian.

"Planning on murdering me and stealing my cab?" the driver shot back.

"We've got a long drive ahead of us," Marco answered. "Hate to think of your pasta growing cold at home."

"Signore, if your money's good, that pasta can turn to ice." He glanced over at where Bronwyn waited with the luggage. "Don't much care what happens in my cab during the journey, either."

The idea had occurred to Marco, but like hell would he let the cab man entertain those thoughts about her. "Just drive."

"What was that about?" she asked, once they were in the carriage and en route.

"He wondered if we wanted to see the sights," Marco replied.

The route he gave the driver was just as indirect as their train travel. They left Siena and headed southward, along a rutted road that bounced the carriage like a child's toy. Away from the train tracks, the early spring green hills engulfed them, dotted with vineyards, patches of forests, and farms as timeless as the land itself. Churches roosted like stone birds offering salvation, and minuscule walled villages perched on hillcrests, looking identical to their embroidered tapestry counterparts.

They didn't go straight to Montepulciano, but bounced from village to village like a skipped stone. Marco had the driver circle and pass through one little town three times before moving on. Giovanni had placed his faith in him—that faith wasn't misdirected.

Finally, after hours of travel, they neared Montepulciano. Like the other small towns they'd passed, it sat atop a steep limestone ridge, with a domed church peering up from the base of the hill, and a stately crenellated palace at the very top. Once within the town walls, they passed palazzos and piazzas—all on a miniature scale compared to what they'd seen in Florence. More red-tiled buildings crowded close along the winding streets, with tiny balconies and windows with their shutters thrown open to let in the last of the day's light.

But the carriage could only travel so far before the

streets grew too narrow, and leading the driver straight to Bertrand's door would've been the kind of mistake a junior agent made. So Marco paid the man handsomely before he and Bronwyn disembarked.

The cab trundled away for the long ride back to Siena. But Marco made sure the trip had been worth the driver's while. He paid for his silence, as well.

Taking up their bags, they proceeded along the narrow cobbled streets, passing wine shops, *salumieri,* and curious citizens. Marco followed the instructions Giovanni had verbally given him—nothing could be in writing— heading off the main avenue and down several steep alleys, where a few curious dogs sniffed at their heels but kept a respectful distance.

Finally, they reached an utterly anonymous door that didn't even have a number marking it.

"How to get inside," he murmured. "It'd be a simple matter to pick the lock."

"Assuming the door even *is* locked," Bronwyn pointed out. "Seems as though the crime rate here might be rather low."

"Other citizens of Montepulciano might not lock their doors," Marco noted. "Bertrand certainly does." He stepped back and looked up. "Could climb up to that second-story window. Doubtless I'd find a parlor, and Bertrand in it."

Her eyes widened. "You could climb this?" She patted the wall, which was comprised of golden stone. "It's old and craggy, yes, but hardly the kind of surface that would make for easy scaling."

Well, he wasn't above a little showing off. Especially in front of her. So he set their cases down. Took a few running steps, then jumped up to the opposite wall. He pushed off using the strength of his legs, caroming toward the open window in another home. He gripped the sill for a moment, but didn't linger. Instead, he dropped lightly back down to the ground, landing in an easy crouch.

When he stood, he faced Bronwyn, who wore a wry smile. "Am I supposed to be impressed by that display?"

He shrugged.

She smiled. "It worked. You're the next evolution in mankind. *Felis sapiens.*" But her smile faded. "I don't think any of those options are going to inspire confidence in Bertrand, however."

"Agreed. A man in hiding doesn't take well to having someone pick the lock to his home or suddenly appear in his window. Might wind up with a gunshot to the face."

She shuddered. "Don't make light of that."

"I'm not. This is the best course." He raised his fist and knocked.

Several moments passed. Marco heard a man moving slowly on the stairs. But Bertrand said nothing. Instead, the door unlocked and opened just a crack. The barrel of a pistol edged out, pointing right at Marco.

Bronwyn fought a gasp, but Marco only raised his hands.

"What do you want?" a guttural voice demanded in broken Italian.

"Just to talk," Marco answered in French.

"Who are you?" the man asked, also in French.

"Les Grillons is our mutual enemy," Marco answered calmly. "Giovanni is our mutual friend. He sent us."

The door opened a little more. It would've been too easy to disarm Bertrand and shove into his home—this Grillons man was no trained assassin, but had to have served the syndicate some other way.

"What do you want?" Bertrand pressed.

"Your help," Bronwyn said, stepping forward. "Les Grillons took something from me, and you're my best hope of getting it back. Please, monsieur." She gave him an imploring look.

Marco had to admire her audacity. She'd never once resorted to her feminine wiles to get what she was after, but here she was making a strategic use of them. What man could resist a lovely young woman asking him to play the hero?

God knew, Marco couldn't. Not where she was concerned.

"What's the weather in Paris right now?" Bertrand demanded.

"A hint of mist in the air," Marco answered. "The cold sun comes out in the afternoon."

"And London?" The man was unrelenting.

"Never any sun," Bronwyn said.

A moment passed. Then another. And then, finally, the barrel of the gun lowered and the door opened wider, revealing the man who held the key to Bronwyn's fortune.

He was a soft man, his belly filling out his waistcoat, his eyes small and pale. Despite the Italian sun, his skin remained white, as if he hadn't ventured outside in a good while. But for all his seclusion, he wasn't starving to death.

"Inside," he said in a low voice. "Quickly."

Marco grabbed their bags and stepped in first. The door opened to a stairwell that led to another story. The doorway at the top might conceal a hidden enemy, but Bertrand didn't act like a man with reinforcements.

"Upstairs," Bertrand said once Bronwyn had entered the narrow foyer.

They climbed the stairs to a small set of rooms, each opening on to the other. Visible from the parlor was a little table and cupboard, and a bedroom beyond that. The paint on the walls peeled, and the rooms smelled vinegary, as though wine had been spilled.

"I'm Bronwyn," she said as their reluctant host lowered himself heavily into an upholstered chair—not much of a stickler for the rules of society, this Grillons man. The chair was the only one in the room. He didn't let anyone into his home. "And this is Marco."

They both received a grunt in response.

"Giovanni shouldn't have told you where to find me," Bertrand muttered.

"He wouldn't have done it if he didn't think I'd keep you safe," Marco answered.

"And if the cause wasn't just," Bronwyn added, giving him that same pretty, imploring look. "He knew that only one man could come to my rescue—and that man is you."

What a natural, Marco thought. She was working him like a baker rolling out dough. Making him smooth and elastic, pliable to her will.

Bertrand cast a dubious glance at Marco, and he couldn't quite blame the man for his skepticism. Between the two of them, a casual observer would likely put their faith in Marco long before they entrusted themselves to Bertrand.

"It's true," Marco added. "In this, I'm helpless as a babe."

"I don't know what I can do." Bertrand spread his hands. "Les Grillons think I'm dead, and I aim to keep it that way."

"But you aren't," Bronwyn pointed out. "You're very much alive, and the possessor of knowledge no one has. That must mean you're very clever, to get away as you did, and know what you know."

The Frenchman's cheeks turned ruddy. "Had some help," he said gruffly. "But," he added, "you're right. There are things about Les Grillons only I know. I'm the one who had his hand on their purse strings. Me. The biggest, richest group of crooks looked to me to keep all their pretty francs in a row."

Marco couldn't have planned it better, especially not when Bronwyn crossed the parlor to kneel beside Bertrand's chair. She laid her hands on the armrest and looked up at him beseechingly.

"Then you *are* the man I need," she said. "They took my fortune, leaving me destitute."

Bertrand snorted. "Can't help you. Once they get their talons into someone's money, there's no getting it back."

"But, monsieur, if I don't get even a little of my fortune back, I'll be penniless, cast out into the cold. You don't want that, do you? Me, all alone, without a single friend." Her voice clogged, as if fighting back tears.

He realized that in all the time they'd spent together, she'd never cried because of her circumstances. No, this was for Bertrand, a petty man who needed his pride flattered.

Marco kept silent throughout her performance. Bertrand would only see him as a threat. Yet some of the most successful and capable agents were women, and most of them had never had to use a weapon other than their charm. They didn't even have to take a potential target to bed to get the information they desired. Men were such easily manipulated beasts.

Bertrand proved no exception. "I . . ."

"Yes?" she pressed, rising.

He pushed himself to standing, groaning during the process. Trundling over to a corner of the parlor, he pulled up the rug, revealing the floorboards. Marco spotted the loose boards right away, and it came as no surprise when Bertrand lifted them away to reveal a compartment beneath the floor. He pulled out a small strongbox, which he set on a table. From the cupboard, he retrieved a canister of coffee, then fished out a key from the coffee grounds. He unlocked the strongbox and held up several notebooks.

"My insurance," he said. "If Grillons ever came looking for me."

Though Marco wanted to pull the ledgers out of Bertrand's hands, he forcibly kept himself still.

"See here." Bertrand flipped one of the notebooks open. "Private bank account numbers for two of the Grillons commanders. They keep funds set aside in Switzerland for contingencies. They're separate accounts from the organization. The syndicate can't touch them. You've got access to these, you can funnel money away from them and line your own pockets."

"And if we wanted insurance of our own?" Marco said. "In case they don't look kindly on us liberating some of their francs."

Bertrand's round shoulders rose and fell. "I don't know. You'd be on your own."

"I'd wager there's something in those notebooks that might assist us," Marco noted. He held out his hand.

When Bertrand looked dubious about giving the notebooks over, Bronwyn said, "Those are financial ledgers you kept for Les Grillons, correct?" At his nod, she continued, "You must have been a very thorough record keeper. I can tell you're a man who lets no detail slip past him. Not even the smallest trifle."

The man reddened again at her lavish praise. "I was very attentive. They picked me for the job because of it."

"Doubtless there has to be a word or two in those ledgers that will give us some added protection," she explained. "There must be, if you kept them."

Bertrand handed her, not Marco, the ledgers.

As Bertrand sat in his chair and steadily drank, Marco and Bronwyn ensconced themselves on the floor and pored over the ledgers. Maybe at one time, the Grillons man took better care of himself, for his handwriting was neat and precise, and easy for Marco to read. Columns and columns of numbers and names were arranged carefully, each marking loans and payments from different people.

"Les Grillons is a criminal syndicate," Bronwyn murmured, too low for Bertrand to hear. "Why do they keep books as precisely as Lloyds of London?"

"Not much difference between Lloyds and a crime organization," Marco answered quietly. "They're both businesses. Both rely on income from their clients—or victims—to stay in the black."

She shook her head. "I can't say which appalls me more. The fact that Les Grillons is like the world's most powerful insurer, or that Lloyds is basically a criminal consortium."

"Every business is." He flipped through more pages. "One of the reasons why I never joined the world of commerce. Much to my father's dismay."

She looked up from a notebook. "He's a man of business."

"Vulcanized rubber. I saw a future of board meetings, factory tours, and ledgers just like this one. Couldn't stomach the idea."

She was silent for a long while, but she wasn't studying the book in front of her. Instead, she studied him. "Is he proud of you?"

"Don't know. I never asked."

"He must know the good you do."

Marco snorted. "My father doesn't know about any of it. Not my work for British Intelligence, and sure as hell he doesn't know about Nemesis. He thinks I shuffle papers for some obscure government bureau."

"And your mother?"

"I can't tell her. About any of it. For her safety." He

caught the note of regret in his voice, and it startled him. Then he realized he'd been talking about himself for several minutes. But instead of a sense of panic, he felt . . . not comfortable, exactly, but he liked the idea about this part of him being revealed to her. She had the hands of a violinist—delicate but strong—and she could hold this piece of him as carefully as she held her instrument.

"That must be hard," she said. "You seem close with her."

"Don't see her often, and I don't have time to write much."

Bronwyn smiled sadly. "I miss my mother, too."

They gazed at each other for a moment, each absorbing the connection between them, until Bertrand called out from the other side of the room, "Find anything yet? If not, get out."

"Time," Marco threw over his shoulder. "We need more of it."

"You've got fifteen more minutes," Bertrand grumbled.

"But, monsieur—" Bronwyn pleaded.

"I am sorry, madame," the Grillons man replied. "But I've got my own hide to worry about. Longer you're here, the more I'm sticking my neck out, and I don't want some Grillons blade slitting it."

In this, Bertrand seemed intransigent, so Marco and Bronwyn returned to their study of the ledgers, conscious all the while of the clock ticking, marking the minutes until they were shoved out into the street with their best lead just on the other side of the door. Marco could forcibly take the ledgers from Bertrand, but it might entail a spot of violence—something he didn't want Bronwyn to witness more of. There was always theft, too. Yet that meant consigning Bertrand to a life of even greater fear. The former Grillons bookkeeper might not be Marco's favorite person, but he didn't want to make the man suffer more than he already did.

Besides, Giovanni was taking a risk for Marco and Bronwyn. To steal from or hurt Bertrand would be a betrayal.

So he combed over the notebook, searching for patterns.

"I'm seeing payments from someone named Olivier Maslin," he said to both Bronwyn and Bertrand. "They go on for a long time—from '78 to the end of last year. And then they suddenly stop. Why?"

"Maybe this Maslin paid off his debt," Bronwyn suggested.

But Bertrand, his shirt now stained with spilled wine, shook his head. "Government man, Maslin. Worked in the treasury bureau. High level."

"Not the sort of man who'd need a loan from Les Grillons," Bronwyn said.

"All kinds of people take out loans to pay off their dirty habits," answered Marco. "Like our late friend Devere. Maslin could've had the same gambling problem. Or maybe he had a taste for something else, something expensive, like morphine."

"He had a taste, all right," Bertrand said, his words starting to slur. "For pricey whores. But he'd more than enough to pay for them."

"Then why pay Les Grillons?" asked Bronwyn.

"Because they found out about Maslin's whoring. And that he liked to dress in the whore's clothes and get spanked like a schoolgirl."

"Ah . . ." Bronwyn said faintly.

Marco kept forgetting that, even after everything she'd survived and witnessed, there were still elements of the world with which she was unfamiliar. Including government officials' unusual sexual preferences.

"Les Grillons was able to get some photographs of Maslin playing dress-up," Bertrand continued. "Threatened him. Said they'd take the pictures to his superiors and his wife."

"These are blackmail payments," Marco said.

Bertrand nodded. "Maslin paid. Until he decided to stop. Refused to give Les Grillons another sou."

"So Les Grillons took the . . . pictures . . . to Maslin's superiors," Bronwyn concluded.

But Bertrand smirked. "Nothing to gain by actually carrying through with the threat. When they saw they weren't going to get any more money out of him . . ." He drew his finger across his throat.

"They killed him?" Bronwyn asked, her voice thin and strained.

"Ambushed him when he went to one of those whores. Then threw his body into the river. It made the papers. Hold a moment." Hauling himself up, Bertrand trundled into the bedroom and rifled around inside a wardrobe. He returned with a stack of yellowed newspapers bound with twine, and tossed the bundle toward Marco.

Untying the string, Marco thumbed through the newspapers, until he came to the one with this headline: GOVERNMENT OFFICIAL'S BODY DISCOVERED IN SEINE—ANARCHISTS SUSPECTED.

The article went on to detail how Maslin had been shot at point-blank range, and his disappearance was brought to the police within a day by his adoring wife.

"How . . . sordid." Bronwyn shuddered.

"But exactly what we're looking for," Marco noted. "Our insurance against Les Grillons."

"The police," Bertrand said, lowering himself back into the chair that held the deep impression of his body, "they've been trying to build a case against Les Grillons. But they never have enough. Slippery bastards," he muttered before taking another drink. Presumably he meant Les Grillons, not the police.

Marco turned to Bronwyn. "This ledger links Maslin's death to Les Grillons. It'll put two of their bosses in prison."

"How?"

He pointed to names written in the margins: Reynard and Cluzet. "These names appear again and again, but they aren't listed as payors. They're the ones being paid."

Her eyes narrowed. "If we take this ledger to the French police, it'll be enough to at least imprison Reynard and Cluzet."

At the mention of those names, Bertrand gave another snort. "Those sons of whores. The worst of them. If you can get either of them thrown behind bars, you'll be sodding national heroes."

"Don't want to be a national hero." Marco rose, and offered his hand to Bronwyn. It felt fitting and right, the slide of her palm against his as he helped her to stand. "I just want to get her money back."

But the Nemesis operative in him couldn't help but relish the thought of sending scum like Les Grillons to prison. Striking at these two men could be the key to his and Bronwyn's safety. Provided, of course, that he succeeded.

TWELVE

It didn't surprise Bronwyn that Bertrand was even less likely than Giovanni to be hospitable. Besides, she wasn't certain she *wanted* to stay with that callous drunkard, even if he had more than one bed. So it was with some measure of gratitude that she and Marco left that infernal little set of rooms—ledger in hand, with promises to return it as soon as it had served its purpose—to find a *pensione* somewhere in town.

Once they'd located a small place to stay, they went up to their room. Bronwyn sat down on the bed, sighing. The day had been incredibly long and tiring, and despite her brief nap on the train, she ached with weariness.

"Stay here," Marco directed as he headed toward the door. "Don't open the door for anyone but me."

"Where are you going?"

"Running a quick errand. When I return, we'll find somewhere to dine."

She was too weary to demand more of an answer. Only yawned and nodded. He made it to the door before turning back and striding to her on the bed. He tipped up her chin, but instead of kissing her mouth, he kissed her forehead.

"You played Bertrand almost as well as your violin," he murmured.

"You sound nearly proud of me," she said sleepily.

"Don't believe in feeling pride for someone else's accomplishments," he answered. "It takes away from them, makes their achievements mine, not theirs. But what you did . . . it was damn fine work." In the lamplight, with his morning shave all but a memory, he was the picture of dangerous elegance.

"*Sprezzatura,*" she said. The word leaped into her mind suddenly.

He looked startled. "What?"

"I think that's how you say it." She rubbed at her eyes.

"It is. Why do you say it now?"

"Because"—she stifled another yawn—"it makes me think of you. I read it somewhere, an English translation of an Italian book."

"Castiglione's *Il Cortegiano. The Book of the Courtier.*"

"Yes . . . that's right. The word means, damn, I'm too tired to think of what it means, but it made me think of you."

"Studied carelessness." His voice sounded odd, far away, his expression equally withdrawn.

"Right again." She smiled at him, drunk with weariness. "To work very hard to make it seem as though you aren't working hard at all. What was it that it said in that book? 'To conceal all art and make whatever is done or said appear to be without effort.'" She tapped him in the center of his chest. "Like this. Like everything you do. You think I don't know. But I do know." She waggled her finger at him. "I. See. You. Marco . . . Whoever-You-Are."

He pulled away. "Stay here. I'll be back in a few minutes. And—"

"Don't let anyone in who isn't you. Yes, you said so already."

With an abstracted look on his face, he left the room, locking the door behind him. She stared at the door for a minute, wondering what it was she'd said that had disturbed him so much. A small debate sallied back and forth in her brain as to whether or not she had the wherewithal to stand and splash some water on her face. But the pillows on the bed looked large and fluffy as clouds, and she was just so very tired. Perhaps if she closed her eyes for just one moment . . .

A second later, she opened her eyes. The room was dark now, and she lay in bed. Under the covers and undressed. How . . . ?

A warm, solid form nestled close behind her, one masculine arm wrapped around her waist, the palm spread against her belly.

Marco. He must have come back to the room and found her asleep, then somehow managed to strip Bronwyn without waking her. Then gotten to bed himself and, if his breathing was any indicator, fallen asleep himself.

"Are you hungry?" he rumbled.

Of course he wasn't actually sleeping. Or, if he had been, she'd woken him.

"Not enough to get out of bed," she answered.

"Good. Because the shops are all closed and I'm not in the mood for breaking in anywhere."

She smiled into the darkness. "Glad that I kept a crime wave from erupting in Montepulciano."

"Oh," he said, yawning, "I'd leave money behind."

"Naturally." Heaviness weighted her limbs. He felt so good—his body hot and concrete and lightly dusted with hair. A man's body. Pressed snug against hers. Desire stirred . . . softly. She craved his intimate touch, but this was marvelous, too. It held another kind of intimacy, one she missed. In truth, had never actually known.

After their honeymoon, she and Hugh hadn't shared a bed. When the mood was upon him, he'd visit her bedroom, and they'd make love. But she always fell asleep alone, always awakened alone.

Yet these past days, she'd fallen asleep and woken up with Marco. And while the lovemaking had been passionate and primal, it was these moments that wrapped themselves around her heart as well as her body.

Marco stirred behind her, pulling her closer. He was most definitely naked. And aroused.

Yet he didn't do anything more than brush her hair aside from the nape of her neck and press a kiss there. "Sleep now," he murmured. "We've got more long days ahead of us."

"But you—"

"Sleep."

As if obeying a mesmerist's command, she did exactly that.

"I will be heartily glad not to see another train for a good long while." Bronwyn didn't like to complain, especially about things that couldn't be changed. They'd taken a freight train again over the border from Italy to France, and switched to second-class compartments for the other legs of the voyage.

They didn't speak of it, but they knew—now that they were back in France, the home of Les Grillons, spying eyes would be everywhere. Danger was heading their way, and more to come as she and Marco worked to retrieve her stolen fortune. They would have to tie the two Grillons operatives to the government man's death.

As she and Marco disembarked in a small French town in order to change trains, she was quite ready to never

board another coal-powered vehicle again. Until she had
to return to England.

First, they had to reach Paris. And the train they planned
on taking was due in fifteen minutes. Enough time to
stretch their legs after hours and hours of travel.

"My bones are done with rattling," he agreed. "Don't
plan on taking an assignment out of London for a few
months."

She cradled her violin case against her chest. It was
only natural that he'd think of his next mission, just as she
thought about going back to England. Eventually—soon,
hopefully—all this would be over. She'd have her fortune
back, and she and Marco might have an amorous liaison.
One that would have a limited life span. Then he'd be
gone from her life.

The thought sounded like a requiem, one she had no
desire to play or hear.

This wasn't just desire she felt for him. She . . . cared.
Deeply.

It almost felt like . . .

Like love.

Her mind reared back from the thought. Not love itself. But to love *him,* a man who could shut her out so
easily. Who already had one foot out the door. Could she
allow herself to walk that path that surely led to heartbreak?

Did she have a choice?

"In fact, next time I—" He suddenly took hold of her
arm and led her quickly down the platform. The absolute
stillness of his expression meant only one thing: danger.
Close at hand.

"What is it?" she asked, her voice pitched low.

"Two Les Grillons men. Don't look back. We don't
want them knowing we know they're following us."

Cold fear clasped the back of her neck, but she kept walking. Their bags were still on the train platform, but that didn't matter. To her surprise, Marco walked right past a gendarme.

"We could ask for help . . ."

But Marco shook his head. "They've surely already paid the local law to look the other way. Only thing we can do now is outrun them. Soon as we leave the station, they'll know we're on to them, so move fast."

He hastened them down the steps of the station and led them into the outer edge of the town itself. The pair of footsteps behind them picked up their pace, as well.

"Ready to run?" Marco whispered. He threaded his hand with hers.

She nodded.

"Now."

Then they were off, speeding down the narrow lanes of the town. They threaded their way past carts and pedestrians, men driving wagons and women carrying baskets. She heard cries of outrage behind them as the Grillons men collided with some unlucky passers-by.

A train whistle sounded.

"That's ours," she gasped as they continued to run. "We need to get back."

"This isn't a footrace to our train," he said, leading them down an alley. "The Grillons men will do anything to keep us from getting on. We're running as far as we need until we've got a good spot to turn and fight."

A chill swept down her sweat-slicked back.

"But—"

"No talk. Just run."

To her surprise, he took them through one of the gates of what had been the medieval wall surrounding the town. It opened onto a dirt path, and farmland. Beyond the fields, she could just make out the train track leading north to Paris. Hayrolls were scattered around the field. Marco ran straight for one of them. There was a cart also in the field, but for some reason, Marco seemed to reject that as a place of cover. They had fifty feet of open ground to traverse before reaching the first hayroll.

She gasped but didn't slow when the first shot rang out. The ground just to the side of them exploded in a small hail of dirt.

Dear God, she was being *shot* at.

It seemed an eternity, but she and Marco finally reached the hayroll. At which point, he pushed her into a crouch behind it, then crouched down himself. Her heart thudded even harder when he pulled out his gun and took aim at the pursuing Grillons assassins.

Another whine and small explosion of dirt as one of the Grillons men fired. She winced and pressed close to the tightly packed hay. When a moment had passed, she peered out from behind the hayroll to see that the Grillons assassins had tipped over the cart and were using that as their shelter in between shots.

But Marco didn't shoot back. He seemed to be waiting for something. Then she realized—their bags were back at the train station, and that likely meant that most, if not all, of Marco's ammunition was in his gun. She counted the chambers in the cylinder of his weapon. He had five shots total, if he wasn't carrying any bullets in his pockets.

Every one of his bullets were going to have to count.

He waited until a Grillons thug fired, then Marco shot back. Judging by the curse in French, Marco's aim had been very good—but not quite good enough as two sets of bullets were discharged from the Grillons' guns.

Four bullets left in Marco's weapon.

She didn't have a gun of her own—and wouldn't know how to fire it anyway, never having had any experience with firearms in her life. And she doubted, even in these circumstances, if she could actually shoot at another human being. But there had to be something she could do.

Her gaze fell on an empty bottle lying in the hayroll's shadow. The remains of some farmer's lunch, no doubt. She grabbed the bottle, not entirely certain what she planned to do with it. Impossible to sneak around behind the Grillons thugs and hit them with the bottle—she didn't have enough cover, and would likely be riddled with bullets halfway before she reached the men.

Yet there was some way to use the bottle . . .

She waited for a pause in the assassins' shots, then poked out just enough from behind the hayroll to throw the bottle up into the air.

Just as she'd hoped, one of the killers thought she and Marco were attacking. The man broke cover and shot the bottle as it arced in the air—leaving himself exposed.

Marco fired. His bullet pierced the assassin's chest. The thug went down before the last pieces of broken glass hit the ground.

Both she and Marco retreated behind the hayroll. While illness clogged her throat at seeing another man killed, logically she understood that if the thug hadn't been brought down, he would've killed both her and Marco. It was a difficult rationalization, but she clung to it in the midst of terror.

Marco nodded at her.

Another train whistle sounded. It would be leaving for Paris in just a moment. Yet she and Marco were still pinned down by the other Grillons assassin, who fired now with greater speed.

She looked around for something else to throw at the thug and serve as a distraction. But a handful of hay wasn't going to do much.

Down the slope of the field, the train started to leave the station, slowly at first. Soon, it would pick up speed.

She watched as Marco shot once at the remaining Grillons assassin. And as soon as the man returned fire, Marco let off another round. The man screamed.

"Time to run again," Marco said. He grabbed hold of her hand once more, and together, they ran down the field toward the train tracks leading out of town.

She jumped when more bullets whizzed past. A glance back revealed the Grillons thug kneeling on the ground, one hand clutching his wounded thigh, and the other pointing his gun at them as they fled.

Tucking her violin case under her arm snugly, she ran full out toward the tracks. She tore her hand out of Marco's grasp to pull up her skirts and give herself more freedom of movement. She ran faster over the fields, Marco just steps ahead of her. More gunfire exploded.

None of the enemy's bullets hit. Yet she didn't feel comfortable until they finally reached the low fence between the farm and the tracks. Marco leaped the fence and helped her over just as the train began to gain speed. Marco jumped up onto the small platform between cars, then pulled her up.

She bent over, gasping, but lifted her head enough to see the field vanish, leaving one dead and one wounded Grillons assassin behind.

He guided her into the seating compartment, tucking his gun away. They received some curious looks from the other passengers, what with both she and Marco panting and windblown, and probably smelling of gunpowder. She didn't care. They'd gotten away. For now.

"It isn't going to stop, is it?" she asked once they sat.

He didn't insult her by telling her everything was going to be fine, or feed her some other palliatives. Instead, he said, "Not until the job is done."

The fuse, which had been lit long ago, was burning lower and lower. Until the inevitable explosion. She had to wonder if she and Marco would be safe, or if they'd be caught in the blast.

Odd to be back in Paris again. It felt as though she'd been gone for an eternity, but it couldn't have been more than a few days. Yet while the city was as glamorous and grimy as ever, everything had changed.

The last time she'd arrived in Paris, a powerful crime syndicate hadn't wanted her dead. Now danger crept in every shadow, in each alley, in every sudden movement she caught from the corner of her eye. She'd thought she'd entered a new world with Nemesis, but this was far beyond even that. Her only constants were her violin and Marco.

But he, too, unbalanced her. Now they were more than client and Nemesis agent. They were lovers for now, and perhaps when they returned to London. And they were something else—though *what,* exactly, they were to each other, she couldn't fathom.

And her heart, her traitorous heart, that murmured to her of feelings he couldn't reciprocate.

Oh, God. Did she *love* him?

She . . . did. He knew her better than anyone. Understood her. Accepted her as she was. And he was a man of dark honor and principle. Supremely capable, but with a core of sensitivity he likely didn't show to many. But he had shown her. Making it all the more impossible for her to ignore the growing feelings she had for him.

Nothing could ever come of it. And she would never tell him. It would only serve to push him away faster.

Right now, he was her protector. She wasn't too proud to acknowledge that she needed his protection, more than ever.

Instead of disembarking the train via the platform, he

led her onto the tracks, then through an exit used only by the station employees. They emerged into an alley crowded with cargo-laden drays, and men shouting at one another as goods were taken from freight cars and loaded onto wagons for delivery. The ground was slick and muddy, and the air was thick with the smell of horseflesh and smoke.

She kept her gaze alert for any signs that the working men were disguised Grillons agents. Marco did the same. But no one shot at them, and as they pushed on from the alley onto a main thoroughfare, nobody followed, either.

"Where are we headed?" she asked as Marco walked purposefully away from the station.

"Old safe house," he answered. "Intelligence stopped using it years ago when they thought the location was compromised."

"But it's secure now?"

"Been empty for five years. If French intelligence had been keeping eyes on it, they've long since stopped."

For all the supposed romance of Paris, she didn't like walking its boulevards anymore. Not when every shadow could conceal the means of her or Marco's death. She still couldn't erase from her mind the image of the Grillons assassin's chest, red with fresh blood. Too much like Devere. She wished she'd never seen what happened to the human body when shot. That was knowledge that couldn't be unlearned.

Illness took many lives. But so did violence.

Marco seemed entirely unmoved by the fact that he'd killed someone. He appeared more concerned with keeping her safe. Two sides to the same coin. A complex man— thoughtful, passionate lover, and cool-eyed operative. Which was the real him? Both.

They moved farther from the station, heading into a

suburban neighborhood comprised mainly of homes and small workshops. He turned down a narrow lane—making her nervous, but she had to trust him—then stopped outside the boarded-up door of an old, derelict building. The words L. CAILLARD, FABRICANT DE JOUETS were painted in fading letters onto the brick façade.

Marco glanced up and down the lane. It was empty. Quickly, he pried back the boards covering the door. After testing the door itself and finding it locked, he speedily picked it, then let himself and Bronwyn in. He closed the boards behind them, as well as the door itself.

Inside, light filtered through in dusty bars from the partially covered windows. Bronwyn's footsteps left tracks in the grime that had accumulated on the floor. Shelves lined the room, and on the shelves were dolls in moth-eaten lace dresses, rusted toy soldiers, and cobweb-filmed wooden horses. A toy shop, or so it had once pretended to be. Now it was an abandoned pretend toy shop.

Marco walked to one of the shelves and pulled the head off a slumped puppet. A thin piece of metal stuck out from the bottom of the head, and he inserted it into a piece of decorative molding on the wall. There was a click, and one of the shelves swung open, revealing a darkened hallway.

"Reminds me of Nemesis headquarters," she murmured.

"Not a surprise." He entered the hallway, and she followed him. "Nemesis learned some of its tricks from me, and I learned mine from Intelligence. I, Simon, and Lazarus started the whole Nemesis operation six years ago."

"That wasn't so long past." She was newly wed six years ago, and utterly unaware that there might be a Nemesis, let alone people in need of them.

"Been a long six years." They moved from the hallway into a single room that held a bed, a table, a washstand,

and not much else. The moths had extended their efforts to the curtains that hung in the lone window.

A singularly unimpressive room.

"I was the one who scouted the headquarters' location," he continued, surveying the space, "and I installed the secret door. Acquired my trade from Intelligence. Which gives us such lovely sites as this one." He ran a finger over the table, leaving a trail behind in the dust. "Pretty and luxurious, it isn't, but it's secure. Doubt anyone in Paris even remembers this place exists."

"And thank God for it." She sat down on the bed, and the springs complained. "Being shot at ranks as my new least favorite activity."

In the half-light of the safe-house room, his expression turned grim. "Wish I could go back and kill that second bastard."

"I don't." She rubbed her arms and looked away. "It . . . I don't like it when you're violent."

"Me, either." He crossed the room to crouch down in front of her. "But if I ever had scruples against it, I wouldn't be here now. Neither would you."

"I know. I just wish . . . it didn't have to be so . . . ugly."

"You've seen what the world's like now. It's a damned ugly place."

She finally turned her gaze to him. "Do we have to make it worse?"

"Survival doesn't mean making things worse. It means we live to see another day."

"I wonder if Les Grillons rationalizes it that way, too."

He rose up from his crouch. "Do you want me to apologize for the things I've done? Because I won't."

She also stood. "Not even for cutting Devere's face the way you did? As if you enjoyed it."

"I didn't enjoy it," he said through clenched teeth. "I

was interrogating him. He wouldn't have given us the information we wanted without a little coercion."

"It seemed more like torture than coercion," she fired back.

He spread his hands wide. "The hell is this about? You want me to be something that I'm not. A stainless hero. But I'm not a goddamn hero, I'm doing a job few can stomach but which benefits many."

His jab wounded her with its accuracy. Perhaps she did want him to be more than he was. Perhaps she asked too much of him—but she hated seeing him kill and care nothing about it. It had to hurt him, in a way he couldn't realize or admit.

"So you keep telling me," she said.

"*Dio,*" he muttered, "I didn't even want to take the mission in the first place."

She stiffened. "What?"

"I didn't think it was what Nemesis was for. We're about aiding the poor, the helpless."

"And I didn't fall under either of those categories," she said tightly. "Except that I did. But you didn't think so."

"Not at the beginning." He paced to the window and braced his arms on either side of the glass, peering out at what appeared to be an alley.

"Then why'd you take the case?" She felt brittle as frost. Who knew that heartbreak could happen so quickly?

"The others wanted to, and they knew I was best at dealing with missions involving finance. So I got assigned."

"Fortunate for you."

For a man so astute, it took him a remarkably long time to realize that everything wasn't right with her. He turned away from the window. "You're angry."

She threw up her hands. "Of course I'm bloody angry." It felt good, but not good enough, to curse. "I just found out that the man who's been helping me all this time, who has been *sharing my bed*"—*who's taken my heart*— "doesn't want to be on this assignment."

"Didn't," he corrected. "I've since changed my mind."

Her laugh was breakable like glass, and just as likely to cut someone. Herself, most likely. "That *is* fortunate for me."

"What in God's name do you want?" He took a step toward her. "I'm here. I'm doing everything I'm supposed to."

"Because duty dictates."

He clenched his fists. "I'm a Nemesis agent. Dozens, scores of jobs I've worked besides yours."

"And did you make love to the women involved in those cases? Did you speak to them in Italian, too? Call them pretty names. Maybe not *strawberry*. How about *apple,* or *peach*? I'm sure those both sound lovely in Italian."

His jaw clenched. "Don't."

"Why? Because I'll wound your feelings?" She planted her hands on her hips. "You've done everything in your power to prove that you don't *have* feelings."

She wasn't surprised when he stalked out the door, throwing over his shoulder the command, "Stay here."

And then she was alone. But then again, perhaps she'd been alone all along.

While the abandoned toy shop wasn't the sort of place in which Bronwyn wanted to spend any time, she knew better than to venture out into Paris alone, without Marco's protection. It would be a foolish gesture, one that only put her in danger rather than proved anything to either of them.

Tired, but not weary enough to sleep, she wandered

into the shop itself. There, children's playthings lined shelves, never meant to be actually played with, only serving as a disguise for the shop's real activity. Still, it was a melancholy sight—all those unused toys, waiting for someone to love them but waiting in vain.

She picked up one of the tin soldiers, now almost completely enveloped in rust. A nonexistent boy somewhere would have lain on the floor and put this soldier in command of a whole platoon, facing off against invisible cannon, leading the charge against the enemy. And when the soldier and his platoon emerged victorious from the gallant battle, that boy would've given his soldier a medal made from paper for bravery in the face of terrible odds.

Unlike the boy, unlike the tin soldier, the enemies that faced Bronwyn now were very real. Her hope was for survival, not a paper medal.

She wondered if her heart would survive this, as well.

Setting the tin soldier back upon the shelf, she drifted over to a hoop and rod, both in decent condition since they were wooden and less likely to decay. Taking them down, she held the toys in her hands. How long had it been since she'd played with these?

She rolled the hoop up and down the shop, using the rod to keep it upright. It took several tries before she could master it again. It had been quite a while since she'd been a girl taken to the park by her nanny, and her only concern had been keeping this wooden hoop straight and rolling for as long as possible.

So much easier to do this than think about everything else requiring balance.

Perhaps she did want too much from Marco. He could only offer as much as he could. Or *would*. Despite everything, he was still determined to keep himself as walled off as one of those Italian hilltop towns, ready to fend off any threat.

Or maybe the walls protected nothing. Maybe there was an emptiness within those fortifications, either because the town within never existed, or it had been dismantled, piece by piece, and taken away.

She continued to roll the hoop, looking at the empty space inside it.

There was more to Marco than he'd permit anyone—even himself—to see. She felt it in his touch. Saw it in his eyes. He was more than a Nemesis agent or operative for British Intelligence. But if he'd had to do the things he did, if he was no stranger to ugliness and violence, then he'd have to build a protective barrier. It was either that, or leave himself open to attack, with no means of defending himself.

Still, that didn't lessen the sting of his admission. He hadn't thought her worthy of Nemesis's help. Not because of who she was, but because she'd had the blind luck of being born into the upper classes. And that defined her as worthwhile or not.

Or it had. She wasn't the same woman who'd stood in her empty foyer weeks ago and saw a strange, dark man there. The metamorphosis went deeper than her bones, into the most profound part of her.

Something else had changed, too. She hadn't thought she'd ever know love. And now she did. But it wasn't as she'd dreamed it might be. It was complex and brutal and sometimes beautiful, but it solved no problems, only created more.

The only thing of which she was certain was her own uncertainty.

She froze in the middle of rolling the hoop when she heard the boards covering the door move. The only weapon she had on hand was the rod, and she lifted it in preparation to strike whoever might be coming in. But then the door opened, and Marco entered.

He caught the hoop as it rolled toward him. Looked at her holding the rod like a riding crop. Slowly, she lowered her improvised weapon.

They stared at each other for a moment. Behind him, rain started to patter against the front of the shop.

He carried a hamper filled with what appeared to be wrapped parcels of food.

"Supper," he said.

She nodded. There didn't seem to be much else to say in response.

After setting the hoop aside, he strode into the back room and set the hamper on the table. Then retrieved two overturned chairs and placed them near the table.

The cane backs were shredded, so as she and he took their seats, they had to lean forward. As though things weren't already strained and uncomfortable.

He unwrapped their meal of bread, a covered dish of stew, cheese, wine and—to her mortification—apples. It was almost a domestic scene as they sat and ate. Complete with tense silence. As if they were some long-married couple seething with long-held secrets and resentments.

"This will go on my bill, too, I assume?" she asked between bites.

He didn't answer her.

Well, she wasn't making things any easier. But she didn't *want* to make things easier. Hurt still throbbed through her, unrelenting and indifferent to anything but causing more pain.

From inside his coat, he pulled a slip of paper and slid it toward her. Two addresses were scrawled there.

"The private residences of our Grillons bosses, Reynard and Cluzet," he explained.

She didn't bother asking him how he'd learned the information. No doubt the police would've killed for such knowledge. But he had a way of making the impossible

possible. Except for revealing his true feelings. That truly was an impossibility.

"So we're going to invite ourselves over for dinner," she said.

"No," he answered. He took a drink of wine. "Tonight, we're going to break into their homes."

THIRTEEN

He'd been in a fury—a rarity in and of itself. Some of his earliest training in intelligence had been removing his emotions from his work—long, painful months that forced him to dull his feelings, and were thankfully long behind him. But it had been necessary. Another survival strategy. But each of Bronwyn's words had stabbed him like stilettos. Why?

As he'd stalked the shadowed streets of Paris in search of information, his mind had been uncharacteristically clouded with thoughts beyond his objective. Thoughts of her, and her anger. Shouldn't she have been pleased that he'd changed his mind about her? Did she have to say such brutal things about him? And why should it matter to him what the hell she thought?

Except that it did. Her anger had confused him. Made him want to—God—apologize. Beg for forgiveness. Confess his feelings. Which he could not do. There were few people who trod this earth that he could reveal his emotions to—and they all shared his last name. Family was safe. Everyone else held danger. He'd learned that early as the grandson of a self-made man, and as a spy.

Emotions were weapons, and he was determined not to arm anyone.

So he kept silent, his fist knotted around his heart. As much as that dumb piece of flesh and muscle craved her. Wanted her close. He had to protect himself.

Even so, he'd said too much. Given her the tools to hurt him.

Nemesis had never, until that point, helped any member of the aristocracy. It made sense that he'd be reluctant to do so.

Until he'd learned that she was very different from what he'd expected. That she continued to surprise him. And herself.

Then to throw out the taunt that he'd slept with other clients or women he'd encountered on his Nemesis missions. He'd only done so when it was a matter of furthering the case. What he and Bronwyn shared was . . . different.

But what could he say to her? That she touched places within him no one ever had? That he was feeling the phantom pain of a lost limb—or perhaps that what he experienced was the aches that came with growth, the same he'd felt as a boy as his body had stretched and shaped itself for manhood.

Easier to focus on the demands of the job. He could plan and operate in regard to everything. Except her. So he'd done what he knew best: spied. It hadn't been a simple task, learning where Cluzet and Reynard lived, but the very complexity of the objective had been a relief. At least he knew exactly what needed to be accomplished, and how. He'd gone to the train station and searched until he'd found the Grillons men positioned there. When the men had left in order to be relieved by the next shift of thugs, Marco had followed them to an elegant building in the Marais, which had to serve as the Grillons' headquarters.

Not much of a surprise to see that the building was heavily guarded. It was a measure of Les Grillons' arrogance that they didn't bother hiding the sentries. No pretense that anything other than something nefarious transpired inside.

Marco tensed. Devere's assassin emerged from the building, then walked with purpose toward the train station.

Getting inside to find the addresses of Reynard and Cluzet would be next to impossible. There had to be a softer target, some other way to find out where the two commanders lived.

He spotted an expensive-looking wine shop around the corner. Entering the shop, he was approached by a heavy-set man in a perfectly tailored suit.

"How may I assist you, monsieur?"

"I'd like a case of champagne each sent to Monsieur Reynard and Monsieur Cluzet," Marco answered.

The shopkeeper narrowed his eyes suspiciously. Clearly, he knew the two men and that they were part of Les Grillons. Likely, the shopkeeper paid the syndicate in order to stay in business. "Some occasion you're celebrating?"

"Funny little tradition of mine," Marco replied. "I send my friends gifts on my birthday. Reminds them how important I am."

This lessened the shopkeeper's misgivings—slightly. "Which champagne, monsieur?"

"Veuve Clicquot. Seventy-four." A pricey vintage, but if everything went according to plan, the cost would be covered by Les Grillons themselves.

At this, the wine merchant looked far more pleased. "Of course, monsieur."

Marco paid, and, to ensure lack of suspicion, left the shop. He flagged a cab.

"We'll be following someone," he said to the driver. "Five francs if you keep yourself from being seen."

"We'll be like ghosts, monsieur," the cabman answered.

Eventually, the delivery wagon from the shop pulled out from an alley. True to the cabman's word, he kept a discreet distance, always with several other vehicles or horses between them. Marco kept his gaze sharp for any Grillons operatives on the street. If he was spotted, the plan would come crashing down.

The first delivery was made to an impressive house in Saint-Germain—though whether it was Reynard's home or Cluzet's, Marco couldn't tell. The second delivery was made to a home in the sixteenth arrondissement. Clearly, both Reynard and Cluzet didn't lack for ill-gotten wealth. Both homes were also well guarded.

Now he had his addresses. But it wouldn't be an easy task to get inside them.

After dismissing the cab, and giving the driver an additional franc for services rendered, part of him had wanted to stay out, simply because he could. Because he wanted to prove something to Bronwyn.

But another part of him—louder and more demanding than the first—needed to return to her. He'd had the absurd idea of telling her about how he'd located the homes of Reynard and Cluzet, sharing his techniques for discovering what he'd needed to know. But spies and Nemesis agents didn't talk to each other about the how and why of what they did. It was supposed to be a given that they'd have a task and complete it successfully. No accolades. No admiration. Just confidence in one another's abilities.

Yet he wanted to see the pleasure in her eyes—as he knew he'd see—when he explained how he'd collected the information he wanted. All without resorting to any violence.

Knowing that she'd be hungry after their long voyage, he'd stopped to buy food, and felt matrimonial as hell as he'd carried it back to the toy shop, and to her. She had greeted him with silence when he'd returned. He'd hoped—foolishly—that she'd forgotten their argument, or absolved him of any perceived wrongdoing. But she still remembered that he hadn't wanted to take her case at the beginning.

The rest of the meal had been an exercise in discomfort. Every topic he brought up, she answered monosyllabically, until he stopped talking altogether.

Worst of all, more than anything else, was the hurt in her eyes when she looked at him. That *he'd* put that pain there. And the mistrust he saw in her face. Damn it, he was here to help her—felt things for her that he'd never felt before—yet it seemed as though he needed to beg for forgiveness.

He actually looked forward to breaking into Cluzet's and Reynard's homes tonight. It'd be dangerous, but those perils seemed minor compared to navigating the rocky shoals of a woman's heart.

Once they'd finished their meal, he and Bronwyn waited several tense, silent hours.

Like any men of means, Reynard and Cluzet likely spent their evenings out, enjoying the many pleasures Paris had to offer. Marco hadn't seen any sign that either man had family, which meant it was all the more probable that they wouldn't be home when the clock struck midnight.

He could leave Bronwyn behind. No. She might not be an experienced housebreaker, but she was more secure with him than left alone, even at the abandoned safe house. And she could serve as an extra set of eyes, having become quite perceptive over these past weeks.

"Leave some of your petticoats behind," he said, breaking the silence. "They'll hinder your movement and make too much noise."

Wordlessly, she did as he suggested, though he died a little inside when she reached up her own skirts and shimmied out of two layers of starched cotton.

So, with her movement somewhat silenced, they crept out into the darkened streets of Paris.

It would be a long walk to the home in Saint-Germain, but better that than attract attention by hiring a carriage. The early spring air held a bite to it, and their breath misted as they walked.

God *damn* it, but it felt wrong—this distance between them. Once, he would've welcomed it. He could've gone about the mission without concerning himself with someone else's thoughts, feelings. Unnecessary chatter before a job was an unwelcome distraction. Now . . . now he wanted more, even if was to note the weather.

They finally reached the tall, stylish home. Velvet curtains hung in the window, and the brass fittings all gleamed impressively in the lamplight. On either side of the home stood equally tasteful, expensive houses.

"Crime pays well," Bronwyn murmured. Her first words of the night, and he clutched them tight, like dropped gems.

"Better than honest work," he answered.

He saw her eye the large man standing on the front step. Not even bothering to conceal himself. "We won't be going through the front door."

"Or the back. Someone will be posted there, too."

"Then how do we get in?" she wondered.

"Through there." He pointed to one of the houses two doors down. Still clinging to the shadows, he edged into the mews that ran behind all the fine homes. Bronwyn followed.

Iron fences faced the mews, with thick gates there to keep out unwanted visitors. There was a heavy lock on the gate, but Marco chose the faster option and hopped over the fence. He carried a small phial of lubricant, which he dropped onto the gates' hinges. Then he opened the gate for Bronwyn. It swung open noiselessly.

They stepped into a narrow garden with a dry fountain and espaliered trees. The lights in the house were all dark, even the ones in the kitchen and attic, where the servants might be found. At the back door, he picked the lock, then let them into the house itself.

Bronwyn stuck close to him as they moved up through the town home. He pointed to the floor to indicate that she should step only where he stepped, and she seemed to understand his direction, because the floors kept silent beneath her feet. The house might be elegant and richly furnished, but it was still at least a century old, with the squeaky floors that accompanied a building of its age.

They slipped up from the servants' lower level, up through the public rooms, and the stairs that led to the family's private apartments. But he guided them higher still, moving to the narrow servants' staircase. Here was the greatest danger. Despite the fact that the lights were out, there was always the possibility that one of the family could summon a servant in the middle of the night. But they didn't encounter anyone as they went higher, all the way to the attic itself.

He picked another lock—this one separating the men-servants' rooms from the female servants' chambers. No one was awake doing needlework, as maids sometimes had to do once the family was abed. So Marco paced onward to a narrow door at the end of the corridor. This was unlocked, so it was a simple matter to open it and step through.

Then he and Bronwyn were on the roof. Her fewer petticoats made it much simpler for her to climb out. Paris spread out around them, glittering and shadowed, with the river to the north, and the low hulking form of Notre-Dame squatting on the Ile de la Cité also close by. Though he was no stranger to a rooftop view of Paris, it was a novelty for Bronwyn, so he stood with her for several moments as she took in the panorama. Selfish of him, really, and a torment, because he much preferred the wonderment on her face to any picturesque view, and as she looked around, he watched her—the small smile curving the corners of her lips, the brightness of her eyes.

"Lovely as this is," she whispered, "what are we doing up here? The home you said we want is there." She pointed two houses down.

"Can't get in through the bottom," he answered in a low voice. "So we're going in through the top."

Her eyes widened as she realized what he meant. This was an old part of the city, and the houses crowded close together. The home on which they currently stood shared a wall with its neighbor, which meant that crossing from one roof to the other would be as easy as a stroll. But a distance of about eight feet separated the neighbor's roof from the Grillons operative's home.

"You said you ran in school," he continued. "Did you jump, too?"

"A little, but it's been many years since I've put that skill to the test." Her voice still sounded distant, strained, but whether it was because of the height or him, he couldn't tell.

"Tonight's the night."

He half expected her to protest, or insist that she'd stay on the neighbor's roof while Marco took care of his business inside the Grillons man's house. Instead, she swallowed hard, then nodded.

He took her hand, and she stiffened in his grip. But he

led her across the steeply slanted slate roofs, ensuring as much as he could that they both balanced lightly and carefully.

"What if I slip?" she whispered as they edged along the roofs.

"I'll catch you."

If she understood his deeper meaning, she didn't show it. Instead, she moved very slowly.

He didn't try to urge her to go faster. Haste would only make her more nervous. Still holding her hand, he murmured, "During intelligence training, they'd take us onto rooftops day after day. Most of us—me included—were terrified. I'd never walked on the roof of a five-story building before."

"Yet *I'm* the one shaking now."

"Because you haven't practiced the way I have. They told us on that first day that nerves were the enemies of housebreakers and spies. Fear steals confidence. The more dangerous a situation, the more you need every ounce of confidence."

He kept talking as they walked slowly over the roof. A false step could send either of them plummeting to the ground below. There was always the possibility one could survive a plunge like that, but if one did, the best one could hope for was shattered legs or a broken back, if one's head didn't split open on the pavement.

So they took their time, despite his desire to move faster. She didn't turn back and she didn't stop. Just kept going.

Until, finally, they reached the edge of the roof, with the Grillons operative's just beyond. The houses themselves were actually eight feet apart, but the overhang of the roofs left the distance as five feet.

She hesitated. "I don't know if I can do this." She sidled back, and her hand clasped in his grew damp.

"You wait here," he offered.

"Someone might see me."

"Not at this hour of the night, and not from this angle."

"But if I stay, you'll be alone in there."

Her concern—even if she was still angry with him—touched something raw and unprotected within him.

"I was alone tracking down Reynard's and Cluzet's addresses today," he noted. And he'd broken into countless houses, embassies, and military installations on his own.

Drawing a deep breath, she shook her head. "I'll go with you. You should have someone watching your back."

It was probably the nicest thing anyone had ever said to him. Certainly no woman, other than a Nemesis agent, had ever given his safety so much thought.

"It's easy as hopping puddles," he said. "Use the muscles of your legs to push yourself forward. Watch."

There wasn't room to take a running start, so he crouched low, then sprang, shoving off with the balls of his feet. For a moment, he flew, empty space all around him. Then he landed in another crouch on the opposite roof, gathering his balance in an instant. Rising up, he turned.

She stared at him from across the gap, her eyes as wide as the moon.

"You *are* part feline," she said.

"Just a man."

"More than that."

He shook his head. "No special gifts or magic powers. Perfectly ordinary."

"That's not true, and you know it."

"And you're stalling. Remember what I told you. Use your legs. Push with the balls of your feet. Don't worry about the landing. I'm here." He held out his hands.

She breathed in once. Tucked up her skirt, revealing more of her legs, and crouched. A look of fearful determination on her face.

He'd never admit it to her, but his heart pounded. What if she couldn't make it? She might fall short, and then literally fall. If that happened, he'd dive after her. There was a gutter on the other roof—he could hook his feet into that as he leaped forward, giving him some purchase, as he grabbed for her hands.

And then she jumped. Time stopped as she seemed to hang in the air—both the most terrifying thing he'd ever seen, and the most beautiful. Bronwyn in flight.

But he couldn't be distracted. As soon as she flew toward him, her hands reaching for his, he grabbed her. He braced himself, and her whole body hit him. But he remained standing, keeping them both upright. Her heart beat furiously against his chest as she clung to him.

"There, now," he said, one hand cradling her head, the other pressed against the small of her back. "You flew like a bird. Like a sparrow."

Though she shook, she managed to say, "P-please don't call me that. Say I'm . . . an eagle . . . instead."

"An eagle then. And here we both are, exactly where we want to be." He pressed a kiss to the crown of her head. *"Brava, fragola."*

He thought she might correct him on calling her this, too, but she only said, "Thank you."

He didn't have the heart to tell her that the most dangerous part of the night was still to come.

There was no door that led to the attic on the roof. But there were dormer windows—unlocked—and Marco used one of these to get him and Bronwyn inside. There, they found themselves in a crawl space laced with cobwebs.

On his hands and knees, he led the way to a trapdoor cut into the attic.

Pulling the door ajar, he peered down into a dimly lit hallway. The fine wallpaper and carpet indicated that it wasn't the servants' quarters. Either the help slept in the basement, or else the Grillons man who dwelled here had live-out employees, save perhaps for a valet. But it was good news that he and Bronwyn wouldn't likely encounter any servants roaming the corridors.

Marco closed the trapdoor when a beefy man strolled down the corridor. A guard. Armed, if the bulge in his coat was any indicator.

A moment later, the sentry disappeared, continuing on his patrol. The second the man left, Marco began a silent count in his head. He could feel Bronwyn's fear and impatience, but this was a step that couldn't be skipped or rushed. After ten minutes, the guard reappeared, walking in the other direction.

As soon as the sentry was gone again, Marco signaled to Bronwyn that they had ten minutes to get down from the crawl space and make their way to their destination. She nodded her understanding.

Marco waited thirty more seconds before fully opening the trapdoor and dropping down into the corridor. The guard had moved on. Marco waved at Bronwyn to descend from the crawl space. She looked momentarily dubious, but perhaps her jump from roof to roof had given her more confidence, because she slipped down from the ceiling and into his waiting arms.

She was wise in knowing that they couldn't speak, but signaled to him, *What now?*

He pointed downward. If his instincts were correct— and they almost always were—the place they sought would be on the ground floor. Which left them with several stories to descend without being seen.

Conscious that there had to be more guards, Marco took Bronwyn's hand, and together they slid toward the stairs. Not much of a surprise that the home was fitted with only the best furniture and art, as though the occupant were an aristocrat's younger son or perhaps a prosperous banker. Which he was, of a sort. Les Grillons had made the bulk of their fortune through loans, just like any other bank. Except their interest rates and penalties were much higher. Including murder.

He and Bronwyn reached the second floor without incident, until Marco felt a subtle shift in the atmosphere. A tiny vibration along the floor. He pulled Bronwyn into an unlocked room, easing the door shut just before another sentry passed by. Judging by the sofa and the writing table, it was a small parlor. Marco dragged her behind the sofa seconds before the guard opened the door.

A breathless moment as the sentry surveyed the room. If they were caught, either they'd be killed immediately, or else tortured and *then* killed. Marco could try to fight their way out, which might work, but then the whole plan would be scuppered, and they'd be left with nothing.

Yet all these thoughts he kept well buried. As they waited out the guard, Bronwyn looked with wide eyes at Marco, and he calmly gazed back. No sense in alarming her even more with all the things that could go very wrong. And a spy—or Nemesis operative—who was disconcerted by an obstacle would not only fail at their objective, they'd probably wind up dead.

So he only nodded at her, indicating that everything was fine. Which it was. He had to convince himself of that.

At last, the sentry shut the door and moved on. Marco very slowly exhaled, and Bronwyn let out a shuddering breath.

After another minute, he rose up from behind the sofa, and helped her up. Once he was convinced that everything was clear, he slipped out of the parlor, with Bronwyn close behind.

Descending the stairs, they kept close to the wall and moved quickly but cautiously. There was no place to hide on a staircase. Finally, they reached the ground floor. Marco bypassed all the rooms with open doors—sitting rooms, salons, the dining room. The one he sought would have its door closed. And locked. And so it was, once they reached it. Marco placed her hand on his shoulder and indicated that she should watch the hallway. She would give him a squeeze if she sensed anyone near. After she nodded in understanding, he knelt down to pick the lock, conscious all the while that a guard could pass by at any moment. At last, he picked the lock and let them in, then locked the door behind them.

The study was decorated in the very latest style—a touch ornate for Marco's preferences, but he wasn't sorry his taste differed from a notorious crime lord's. Immediately, he went to the large desk that dominated the chamber. Every drawer was locked. Not much of an impediment. The bigger challenge came from sorting through everything within.

He carefully pulled out stacks of papers and notebooks, and motioned for Bronwyn to start looking through them. He saw the name Reynard written on a book's nameplate.

"What are we looking for?" she asked almost soundlessly.

"Banking ledgers," he answered, just as quietly. "Like the ones our friend Bertrand showed us. Look for a series of numbers starting with 865–03."

She nodded and began to sort through the sheaves of paper. A meticulous record keeper, this Grillons boss, detailing loans, smuggling ventures, profits from brothels, expenses and earnings from the importation of opium. Just like any businessman. But no banking ledger.

Until Bronwyn tapped him on the arm and placed a folder in front of him. Neat columns of numbers showed deposits and withdrawals from a bank. At the very top was a series of numbers: the account code.

From inside his coat, Marco pulled out a square of standard ledger paper. He tore off a tiny piece, and used a solvent he carried to patch the paper over the last three digits of the account number. The solvent made the original ink disappear. With the same pen on Reynard's desk, Marco changed the numbers, matching the handwriting perfectly. He prided himself as Nemesis's expert forger, and this was no exception.

"Remember when I left you alone in Montepulciano?" he whispered as he worked. "I was telegraphing Simon and Alyce. They went to Switzerland and opened an account with the Banque Suisse Nationale, using this number." He pointed to the new account routing code.

"How did you know that's the bank our Grillons friends would use?"

"Those starting numbers are among the exclusive codes the bank uses." Marco blew on the ink to dry it. "Once the pressure starts coming down on Reynard, and Cluzet, they'll both transfer money from their contingency accounts into their Swiss accounts. But they won't know that the cash will actually be going to the new account—*your* new account."

Setting the ledger carefully back where it had come from, he explained, "Les Grillons, they're a distrustful lot. Don't even trust each other. They've all got secret stashes of money and knives behind their backs. All of them have exigency plans should things head south. And they will."

She stared at him. "Nemesis. It runs as intricately as

one of those Swiss clocks. And your cunning mind . . . what's it thinking? I'll never know."

Though she spoke in a neutral tone, he could feel the sadness and anger in her. Despite everything they'd done tonight, it was easier to jump between roofs than close the distance between them.

He glanced toward the door. "Right now I'm thinking the guard's set to come by in minutes."

They stole from the study, with Marco careful to lock the door behind him as they exited. Then they crept back up the long flights of stairs, pressing back into the shadows when a guard passed on the landing above them. He led and she kept watch on their backs, until they returned to the top floor. He wasn't tall enough to reach the trapdoor and shove it open without getting a running start, and that would make too much noise.

"Get on my shoulders," he whispered.

He crouched down, and she climbed up onto him. He stood, bringing her close to the trapdoor, which she pushed open quietly. She pulled herself up into the crawl space. Bronwyn extended a helping hand to him, but he shook his head. He weighed too much for her to support him. Likely, he'd just pull her back down.

But with the trapdoor now open, he could jump from a crouch and haul himself up.

A guard started up the stairs. Marco motioned for Bronwyn to close the trapdoor. She shook her head, gesturing for him to jump up.

The guard was almost there.

Marco ducked into a nearby room and hid behind an armoire. God, he hoped Bronwyn shut the trapdoor.

The door opened and the guard peered into the room. But he only glanced into the chamber for a moment before moving on. After several minutes, Marco emerged from behind the armoire and slipped into the hallway.

The trapdoor, which had been closed, opened, and Bronwyn's relieved face appeared.

He quickly leaped up and hauled himself into the attic. Marco shut the door right before another sentry passed on patrol.

He had them wait a few minutes before creeping through the crawl space to ensure that the guard didn't hear any suspicious noises above. Once he was certain they were in the clear, he waved her toward the open dormer window.

And then they were back on the roof. With its jump to safety. He went first. And this time, when it was her turn, she didn't hesitate. Simply hunkered down and then sprang into a leap. And he welcomed her back into his arms for her landing. It felt . . . too good.

"Bene?" he asked.

She let out a tremulous breath. "That will never be my favorite thing to do."

"Doesn't have to be. Cluzet's home adjoins its neighbor, so it'll be a simple stroll."

Softly, she whimpered. "We have to do this again?"

"It's the best way," he answered. "Set everyone in Les Grillons against each other. Nemesis doesn't do things in half measures."

"I should be grateful for Nemesis's thoroughness." She still hadn't pulled from his arms, and it felt exactly as it should be, that they stood atop a roof high above Paris, wrapped around each other. "But when this is all over, I'll be grateful for some wine."

When it was all over. If everything went according to plan, that wouldn't be much longer. And he and Bronwyn would have their affair, then part ways—forever.

As she extracted herself now from his embrace, he decided he'd welcome some wine-induced oblivion, too.

* * *

They went on to the second home, the one that belonged to Cluzet.

Though they didn't have to jump from roof to roof, they still needed to enter from the attic, since Cluzet kept just as many guards positioned around the perimeter of his house as his nefarious colleague.

Once inside, it was a matter of locating the study. But soon after finishing changing the account numbers, a noise alerted Marco that they were soon to have company. He quickly replaced the ledger, then he and Bronwyn ducked behind some heavy curtains right before the door to the study opened. Someone walked to the desk and sat down.

Ah, damn! Apparently, Cluzet didn't spend his whole night cavorting. The sounds of papers being shuffled indicated that the man was tireless in his devotion to his criminal work.

Bronwyn stared at Marco with wide eyes. They'd never get out of here without being noticed.

"Excuse me, Monsieur Cluzet?" One of the guards. "The supper you ordered is ready."

"Yes, fine." With a sigh, Cluzet stood and left the study. And he didn't shut the door behind him.

Marco took Bronwyn's hand, and they hurried out of the study. They both checked the hallway first for more guards. It was empty. So they rushed down the corridor, all the way to a set of doors that led to a garden.

Stepping out into the garden, she and Marco slid through the shadows of trees and fountains, until they reached the garden's back gate. He hastily picked the lock, and in seconds, they were in the mews, speeding away from the house.

No one within was aware what had transpired. Or that the seeds of Cluzet's and Reynard's ruin had been planted.

Dawn came on in a gray pallor as Bronwyn and Marco made their way back to the toy shop. Her reflection in a window showed she looked equally ashen, weary from the long night's events.

For all its reputation as a city of gaiety, Paris lived on bread and milk, like anywhere else. Marco and Bronwyn now passed the hardworking *citoyens* hurrying through the chill morning, making their deliveries as the rest of the city just began to stir. It was a place of merchants, factory girls, and pickpockets. No different from any of scores of cities across Europe. No one en route to their work paid Bronwyn and Marco any notice. Unsurprising, since she'd noticed that he'd been careful to make himself as inconspicuous as possible. And with her tucked close beside him as they walked, his innocuous appearance seemed to extend to her, as well. They might as well have been crossing sweepers or paupers, people gave them so little attention.

He bought two rolls and coffees from a passing vendor, who barely noticed them. They ate their breakfast on foot, with no time to stop to even lean against a splintered wooden fence to eat.

"More evidence that the life of a Nemesis operative or an intelligence agent is the diametric opposite of glamorous," he said to her between mouthfuls.

At last, they reached the toy shop. They double-checked to make sure the narrow street was empty before prying open the boards covering the door. Once inside, they passed the rows of sightless dolls and moldering game boards, until they reached the living quarters at the back.

Sooty light pressed through the gaps in the boards covering the windows. There hadn't been time or opportunity to clean, so the place was just as dusty and stale as it had been when they'd first come here the other day.

Without a word, she trudged over to the bed, and sat heavily on it. She began to unlace her boots. Neither of them had spoken since Reynard's, and the silence felt as heavy as ore.

"There won't be any apologies," he said into the quiet. "Not from me."

She didn't look up from unfastening her boots. "I didn't ask for one."

"So the fact that you won't talk to me—hell, that you've stopped *looking* at me—means things are right as rain." There was anger in his voice.

She glanced up at him. "Mocking me isn't going to win my favor."

"Damn it," he muttered, "it was easier to break into Reynard's and Cluzet's homes. At least there, I knew what to do." He paced away, then back. "You say there isn't any favor that needs winning."

She kicked aside her boots, one then the other. "All right, you want the truth of it? I'm disappointed."

He tensed. "I've done everything—"

"Not in you. In myself." She rubbed at her face. "I thought myself a realist when it came to the world. That I could see things as they were rather than how I wanted them to be. But it was just a trick I played on myself. I still believed . . ." She sighed. "I believed in dragons. And knights to slay those dragons."

"I'm no knight." His voice sounded rusty, unused.

"I know. And I also know that I don't want to be rescued. What I truly need are lessons in holding the lance, so that any time another dragon crosses my path, I can slay it on my own."

He crossed to her, and crouched down. "You're already halfway there. More than halfway."

"I had a good teacher."

He shook his head. "What did I teach you, except not to trust me?"

"I should have. Who you truly are or aren't is none of my concern. But everywhere that it counts, you've shown yourself to be honorable—"

He snorted.

"Honorable," she persisted. "Loyal. Dedicated to your cause. Even if you don't think the cause deserves it." The very traits that made her love him. And kept her at arm's length.

He winced. "That was . . . badly done of me. The others were right. I was being . . . a snob. Thinking that someone who came from your background didn't merit helping. But even an old cur like me can learn." He glanced toward the window. "This is a barbarous, cruel world. To women, especially. That doesn't change just because you happen to have genteel parents."

"No," she said softly, bringing his attention back. "It doesn't change." Her lips pressed tightly together. "I shouldn't have said what I did. I can't fault you for doing exactly what you said you would. Or being exactly who you claimed to be."

For Marco, there was some relief in that. But not much. Damn it, he *wanted* to be the sort of hero she'd imagined. But heroism and survival didn't go hand in hand. Besides, he didn't think himself capable of that kind of golden, selfless altruism. He took, and he was ruthless, and he was empty.

But what was this pain that filled him, the way water filled its vessel? Why was it that when she finally understood the kind of man he was, a scraping sort of agony tore through him? He wished . . . he wished for things that could never be. That she could want him truly for all that he was. But it would never happen. And if, by some miracle, it did, could he accept it? Could he let her love him?

What did he know of love, except that he'd denied it to himself for most of his life. Impossible to unlearn that self-denial. To dismantle the fortifications he'd built around himself, even if he wanted them gone.

Now, all he did was nod. In acceptance.

"The account numbers have been changed," she said abruptly. "What happens now?"

"First, we sleep for a few hours, get our strength back"— though he referred more to her than himself—"then we go to the police and let them know about the connection between Les Grillons and the murder of Olivier Maslin."

A moment passed. She exhaled. "All right. But we can do all that later. I'm too weary to think." She presented him with her back. "Get me out of this dress."

With remarkably steady hands, he undid the fastenings of her gown, until it parted and revealed the smooth flesh of her upper back. His hands hurt with wanting to touch her there, but instead he curled them into fists as she got to her feet and continued to disrobe—impersonally, not looking at him once. Her dress came off first, then her remaining petticoats, and her corset. Until she stood in just her chemise and drawers, pale and weary in the morning light.

He forced his gaze away. For all the words they'd exchanged, and the acknowledged fact that he couldn't be what she wanted, he still wanted her.

He rose from the bed and strode to a corner of the room. Taking off his coat, he rolled it into a ball and set it on the floor.

"What are you doing?" she asked, pulling the covers back from the bed.

"Getting ready to sleep."

"Not on the floor, you're not." She pointed to the bed. "Get in. It's big enough for both of us."

Which was worse—sleeping on the floor with the spiders and the dust, or sharing a bed with Bronwyn and being unable to touch her? As if drawn like metal to a magnet, he couldn't resist her. His feet took him toward the bed. He'd be close to her, however he could. And if that meant hours of aching and needing with no release or relief, he'd endure that. Because he had to.

FOURTEEN

I'm making a bloody mistake, she thought.

You can't let him sleep on the floor like a dog, her mind argued back.

And if you and he share a bed, what do you think is going to happen?

Nothing. We'll sleep.

Don't be stupid. You can't really be that naïve. Not anymore.

She shook her head, as if to dislodge the fight she was having with herself. But she'd made her decision. She couldn't, in good conscience, sleep in the bed while Marco took the floor. He'd managed in truly desperate and dangerous situations during this journey—chasing Devere through the streets, fending off a Grillons assassin, and all the other Grillons thugs chasing them. Yet nobody could get any good rest on a filthy, hard floor, and so she climbed into bed and waited for him to join her.

First, she endured the trial of watching him undress. Tonight, she'd seen him in action. He'd made a sleek, dangerous picture leaping from rooftop to rooftop, gliding through the shadows like he was part of them. Now he stripped off his waistcoat and shirt, until he was bare-chested. He toed off his boots.

His hand hovered over the fastenings of his trousers, and the rigid line of his erection was the reason why. He didn't wear drawers. So he'd be naked and aroused as they tried to sleep.

Did she breathe a sigh of relief or disappointment when he left his trousers on? She had to look away as he climbed into bed, the morning light carving the hard contours of his arms and chest.

Then they were in bed together. A distance of inches separated them, since the bed wasn't especially wide. His heat radiated out, soaking into her skin. And when he shifted slightly, readjusting his position, his arm brushed against hers, sending her nerves sparking.

She closed her eyes, gritted her teeth. Exhausted as she was, her body felt awake, alive. A shiver worked its way through her.

It didn't seem to matter what her brain understood. She hungered for him. Irrefutably. His touch, his mind. His heart—what little of it he could give her.

She couldn't deny herself any longer. Opening her eyes, she rolled onto her side, facing him. Only to find him gazing at her, his eyes dark, nostrils flared, jaw tight.

She reached out and lightly caressed along his face, feeling the rasp of stubble beneath her fingertips. He leaned into her touch, his eyes still open, and pressed her hand closer to him. He cupped the side of her cheek with his hand, and for a moment, they did nothing but look at each other, the moment stretching out in slow, irrefutable pulses.

They leaned toward each other. His lips brushed against hers. Once. Twice. Lightly. Something in her heart cracked at the gentleness in his touch. It would've been easier to lose herself in something fast and explosive, without feeling. But *this* undid her. When he pressed his lips more firmly to hers, she met the kiss readily. They sank into each other, testing, delving deeper, relearning this thing between them that had its own bright life.

He trailed his lips down her neck, she felt a pang of mixed pleasure and sorrow. Nothing would come of their trysts but sensation, one that would leave her more empty than ever, mourning her shattered heart. But she couldn't stop herself. And it seemed neither could he. They craved each other, even as they knew they could have only this.

Their limbs tangled together. She reveled in the feel of his legs against hers, the wool of his trousers abrading her softer skin. He reached down between them, cradling her breast through the muslin of her chemise like she was something precious but strong. She arched up into his touch.

He peeled away her chemise, baring her to the waist. Still holding her breast, he lowered his head. She gasped as his lips found her nipple, drawing on it, circling his tongue around the sensitive tip. He gave the same attention to her other breast, and she writhed beneath him.

He had an instinct for how to touch her, how to set her afire. His hands roamed over her body, and in his touch, she sensed everything they couldn't speak. *I want you. I need you. This can't ever last.*

Impatiently, he tugged off her drawers. She was nude, fully exposed, and let him look his fill as she stretched out on the bed. His face grew tight and sharp, his breathing ragged. She gasped at the sensation of the rough skin of his palm skimming over her belly, then lower. He cupped her sex—only that, held her in his hand in a gesture of tender possessiveness.

But she wanted even more than this, and pushed her hips up, demanding. He obliged, kissing her as he stroked between her folds. He rumbled his approval at finding her wet and ready. And when he slid one, and then two fingers inside her, she cried out into his mouth.

She was pinned with desire—his mouth on hers, one hand stroking her breast, the other hand between her legs. Lost. She was lost to this. To him.

How does he know me so well and yet we can't bridge this distance between us?

She gripped his shoulders, the muscles tensing and shifting beneath her touch.

Freeing herself, she opened her legs wider, sensation building. His strokes became faster, deeper, as his thumb pressed against her bud. Lightly, he pinched her nipple.

Her orgasm came on quickly. It harrowed her, this mixture of ecstasy, love, and sadness, gripping her tightly in its unrelenting clutches. Like a storm, it rode over her in torrential waves, pleasure upon pleasure, heightened and sharpened by the fact that this thing she and Marco shared had to pass, like any storm. And she could hope that her feelings for him would lessen over time.

Spent, she collapsed upon the bed, her breath ragged. Yet this wasn't enough.

She reached for the fastenings of his trousers. He didn't stop her, and when the fastenings were undone, he tossed his remaining clothing onto the floor.

He stretched out above her, and their gazes locked. She saw it in his eyes, too—a sorrowful hunger, a wish for something impossible.

She wanted whatever she could have. Like grabbing the ebbing tide, even as she watched the ocean slip through her fingers, called back by an unstoppable force. And when he positioned himself at her entrance, she angled her hips to meet his. His fingers interlaced with hers. They continued to hold each other's gaze. Then he slid into her.

Neither looked away as he began to move. They didn't close their eyes to lose themselves in pleasure. This was now. This moment. Her future self would face the repercussions and anguish.

He kept a steady rhythm, deliberate. Controlled. But she felt when his prized control abandoned him. His pace increased, his jaw tensed, his eyes flared. Sensation built within her again, so soon when she'd thought herself wrung out. But he called it forth from her. His palms pressed tightly against hers, almost more intimate than his flesh within her.

Neither spoke. Not a word, but their intermingled breath and enmeshed bodies spoke for them as they made love with a kind of desperation. Straining toward something. She knew it as a futile love. What he felt—she couldn't say. Only felt his body tight and hard and demanding.

Outside, all was danger. In the dusty, shabby little room behind the toy shop, everything was uncertain. Except the desire between them.

Another climax took her, bright and hard. An instant later, his followed, and he pulled out just in time to spill onto her belly.

Their fingers finally unclasped. He used a corner of the sheets to clean her, then rolled onto his back. They were apart again.

She stared up at the grimy ceiling, nude, sweat-glossed, her forearm lying across her forehead. She listened to his breathing as it eased, her own breath still heaving in and out.

They'd agreed that this thing between them could never go for very long, and never beyond the physical. And, at the time they'd made that pact, she'd believed it. She had no desire to entrap anyone with false promises.

But she'd lied not to him, but to herself. Because now she did want more. And it wasn't just the physical pleasure she craved.

No, what she wanted was *him*. In all his cunning permutations. The man capable of picking a lock in seconds. Who sought justice for those who couldn't obtain it for themselves. Who was moved to passion by her music.

She'd said that he kept himself withheld, but now she realized her mistake. All along, he'd been revealing himself to her. Perhaps without his knowledge, but he'd done it just the same. In tiny, gleaming fragments. His ethos. The tales of his family. His very opacity revealed that he was a man who felt deeply. Maybe more deeply than he knew.

In all this time, she *had* come to know him. Like an archaeologist, slowly uncovering the priceless artifact buried beneath layers of sand and history. All it took was patience.

Because there seemed to be a part of him that *wanted* to be revealed, to be known. She felt his yearning in his touch, in his dark gaze, sheltered in whispered Italian.

But she couldn't make him bridge that gap. She couldn't cling to him, trapping him with declarations of love. Unfair to expect something he wasn't willing to give. And she . . . she'd have her own life to return to, away from Nemesis and secret train rides and rooftop dangers.

As if reading her thoughts, he asked, "What will you do? Once your fortune's been returned?"

"I suppose I'll find myself someplace to live. Bloomsbury, perhaps."

"Bohemian." He stroked his fingers along her torso, and her thoughts scattered like moths.

She fought to gather herself. "More affordable than Mayfair or Bayswater. And it will be just me, so I won't need anything particularly large."

"So you'll have a home again." He sounded almost melancholy about the idea. "Then what?"

"Then . . ." She tried to picture the hazy future beyond

this moment. Since she'd learned that her fortune was gone, her life had been a series of moments strung together by fragile filaments, ready to snap. "I'd thought I'd go back to what I'd been doing. The usual society activities." Now *she* sounded melancholy. Having seen what she'd seen, done what she'd done, that old life seemed so pallid.

And a life without him . . . seemed even more wan and flat.

"No," she corrected herself. "I'll probably take a flat somewhere, like Bedford Park. Do like I said to Giovanni. Use the rest of my money to open a home for widows."

It had been all too easy for someone of her station to fall into helpless destitution. For those women already in less fortunate circumstances, they would be even more vulnerable and in need. She might never know exactly what they felt, what they experienced, but she could help where she might.

"A noble plan," he murmured.

"Selfish, actually," she corrected. "My conscience wouldn't leave me alone if I went back to picnics and dinner parties. I'd never get a decent night's sleep."

He shifted, rolling to his side and propping himself up on his elbow. His hair was in delicious disarray, a mop of black curls that begged for her fingers. More of his beard had grown in, too, giving him a raffish look, like one of the pirates that used to sail the Spanish Main, preying upon enemy ships and sending all female hearts to helpless longing.

"That's *assurdo,*" he said heatedly, "and you know it. Nothing selfish about helping others. It shows that you've got a good heart."

She smiled gently. "Is that why you do it?" She pressed her palm to the center of his chest, feeling the brush of hair, and the steady beat of his own heart.

He scowled. "Setting wrongs to right—that's why I do it. Making sense out of disorder. It's no different from solving a mathematical equation."

"Yes," she replied. "I can see why you'd risk your life again and again just because two plus two doesn't equal five."

"Bronwyn," he said warningly.

"I'm applying your logic. Action, not words, define character. If I've learned anything over the course of this mad journey, it's that." She lifted herself up, bracing herself on her elbows. "You tell me again and again that you're not a hero. And maybe you're not. What's a hero, though? Someone of pure soul and intentions? No one like that exists. But there are people like you, and Simon, and Harriet. And even Giovanni. People that do what they can with what they have. Seems fairly heroic to me—as heroic as anyone can be in the real world."

He stared at her for a moment. "I won't shake you of that belief, will I?"

"No," she answered. "Because it's *my* belief, and I'll never let it go. It's not a theory, either. It's been tested many times over the past few weeks." She smiled to herself. "Many things have been tested these past weeks."

He brushed a lock of hair back from her face. "Damn it, *fragola*. I'm going to miss you."

"I know," she replied.

Then they lay down to sleep, neither speaking of the future.

When she woke, she bathed as best she could. She used a small jug of water and ewer Marco had procured.

Despite her quick bath, though, as she and Marco approached the headquarters of the Sûreté, Paris's police, she felt distinctly unkempt. Her lone outfit showed its wear, and she'd had to dress her hair without the benefit of a mirror or maid. Marco wasn't much assistance. He, of course, looked immaculate, despite the fact that they'd both been through the same ordeals. In contrast to the way he could somehow make himself fade into near invisibility, the moment he set foot inside the building, he radiated authority and demanded respect as though it were his due.

Blue-jacketed policemen scurried out of his way as he strode to the desk sergeant, Bronwyn hurrying to keep up with him.

"Oui?" The sergeant didn't lift his head up from filling out his blotter with the latest developments in Paris's criminal activities.

Marco said nothing.

"Well?" the sergeant asked in French, still not looking up.

Yet Marco continued to remain silent.

Finally, the sergeant looked up. The moment he looked at Marco, he snapped to attention, tugging on the tunic of his uniform. "How may I help you, monsieur?"

"Captain Journet," Marco said.

"Is he expecting you?"

"No, but he'll want to see me."

The sergeant started to rise from his desk, then stopped halfway. "I'll . . . uh . . . need to tell him who you are."

"The man who can help him take a bite out of Les Grillons."

The sergeant's eyes widened, and he hurried off. After he'd gone, Bronwyn shook her head. "I doubt I'll ever get used to that," she murmured in English. "The way you can inhabit different personas."

He shrugged. "Actors do it all the time."

"Not the way you do. As if everyone has no choice but to believe you're the person you present."

"It's a useful skill."

She glanced at the hallway down which the desk sergeant had disappeared. "Clearly."

What role did he play with her? The thought lowered her already melancholy mood.

"Who shall I be?" she asked.

"A woman who rejects the word *no*."

She took the thought into herself, letting it seep into her.

Given that the police captain was likely a busy man, she expected her and Marco to be kept waiting, but within minutes, the sergeant returned. A man with a white goatee, dark suit, and sharp eyes strode behind him.

"This the man?" he asked the sergeant in French.

"Yes, sir."

"Your name?" he demanded of Marco.

Bronwyn felt as though the command couldn't be disobeyed—it was given with uncompromising authority. But Marco only shook his head.

"No names, Captain," he answered. "At least, not mine or my companion's. If we're to give you what you want, everything is done anonymously."

"My superiors won't like that."

"Then we'll say good-bye, and good luck with Les Grillons." Marco took her arm, as if to lead her out the door.

"Hold a moment," Captain Journet snapped. He thought for a moment, then motioned for Marco and Bronwyn to follow him. "Come on, then."

She'd never been inside a police station before, and the activity made her head whirl. Men in uniform and civilian clothing rushed back and forth, some carrying dossiers, others leading rough-faced men and women from one room to another. Noise buffeted her, and the eyes of many people followed her as she trailed after Marco and

Journet, but she kept her chin tilted up, her glance cool and impersonal. *I have never heard* no.

Finally, Journet waved them into an office with his name painted on the glass mounted in the door. More half windows surrounded the room, though the slats of the blinds were tilted open. As she and Marco sat in the two chairs positioned in front of a desk, Journet closed the blinds with a snap.

The captain lowered himself into his chair and laced his fingers together, resting his hands on his desk. "All right, Monsieur and Madame Nameless, I'll say this once." He pointed at a battered clock at the edge of a console. "That thing only eats time, it doesn't create it. Which means you have ten minutes before I tell Sergeant Daugier to throw you the hell out onto the street. Apologies, madame," he added in Bronwyn's direction.

"You'll make time for this, Captain," she answered.

"To wound Les Grillons?" Journet threw up his hands. "My men and I have been working for years to bring them to justice. Then you dance in here like some exile from the Moulin Rouge and tell me you've got the way to hurt that passel of bastards? Excuse me, but no, I can't believe it."

"Then believe this." Marco held up the ledger given to him by Bertrand. He tossed it across the desk at Journet, who caught it neatly and began thumbing through its pages.

"What the devil is this?" he demanded.

"Solid evidence linking two of Les Grillons' top men to the murder of Olivier Maslin," Marco replied.

Journet stood, grabbed his clock, and dropped it into the rubbish bin beside his desk. Then he sat back down.

"My time is all yours, Monsieur and Madame Nameless."

* * *

An hour later, after reviewing the evidence against Cluzet and Reynard, Bronwyn watched as Journet slowly shook his head.

"Is this Christmas?" He exhaled. "Because you've given me a gift. How'd you come by it?"

Marco only smiled. "I can't say, and you know it."

"Does it matter?" Bronwyn asked.

"Normally, yes," answered the captain. "There are practices to follow. Rules to obey. But we've been hunting Les Grillons so long, no one upstairs is going to give a damn—apologies, madame—about things like procedure and policy. We just want to throw these bastards—apologies, again—in the darkest hole in France."

"You've got your shovel right there," Marco noted, nodding toward the ledger.

"I'll need to keep this," Journet said.

"Of course."

But the captain had no idea that what he held was, in fact, a counterfeit. After they'd awakened, Marco had forged a duplicate copy of the ledger. It was a common enough notebook, found in stationer's shops all over the city. He'd purchased one, and similar ink, and then spent hours meticulously reproducing the ledger. She'd gazed in amazement as he'd duplicated the tiniest nuance of the handwriting within. But he hadn't stopped at reproducing the writing. He'd taken gritty paper and re-created the wear on the ledger, and made certain that the pages within looked as though they'd been handled many times.

Yet another of his countless skills that continued to astonish her. It was a beautiful art, in a strange way.

He'd explained that making a duplicate of the ledger gave them added insurance, in case anything should happen to the original.

The captain had no idea he held a forgery, and no one

who looked at the original and the reproduction would be able to tell the difference between the two.

"What happens now?" Bronwyn asked.

"I take this to my superiors," Journet answered, "and close the trap around Les Grillons' legs." He narrowed his eyes. "What will you gain by it, the arrest of these two men?"

"I can't tell you the particulars," Marco replied. "But suffice it to say that my parents would still be alive if it weren't for Les Grillons bleeding them dry."

He told untruths so easily. But he'd never lied to her.

"How long will it take to bring them to justice?" Marco pressed.

"Much as I want to damn the rules entirely," Journet said, "there's still paperwork to be filed, and the case assembled. But the Sûreté wants to move fast on this. I'd give it a day, and then we'll make our move. Are you on a clock, monsieur?"

"Time's always in short supply, Captain," he answered.

Did Marco want to tie everything up so he could finally be done with her and move on to the next assignment? Though he'd said he'd like to continue their relationship as lovers, once their association was over, he would soon be on his way. To the next job. The next woman.

"And we've been here too long," Marco continued. He stood. "Shall we, my dear?"

She also rose. "If our business is concluded."

"It is. For now."

"How do I get in contact with you?" the captain asked.

"I'll find you," Marco answered. He glanced at the captain's name painted on the door. "Not so hard to do."

"So says my wife," Journet answered wryly.

"Perhaps when this is done," Bronwyn suggested, "you

could take her on holiday. I'm certain your superiors would permit that, and she'd welcome the time alone with you."

"Not all married couples have the same rapport that you and Monsieur Nameless share," Journet replied. "It's a rare thing."

She stopped herself from correcting him, saying that she and Marco weren't married. What did the sharp-eyed captain see? Even Marco seemed a little startled by Journet's words.

After shaking hands with the police captain, and promising that they wouldn't disappear, she and Marco left the station. The world continued on in its rush and bustle, little knowing that another crucial step had been taken—not only in the retrieval of her fortune, but in the crippling of one of France's most notorious crime syndicates. Everything was about to change. But would anything truly change at all?

She asked this of Marco as they headed back to the toy shop.

"It's never enough," he answered. "When men like Cluzet and Reynard fall, there are always more to take their place. Like vermin. But if we hit a few of their top men, it will destabilize them enough to shake their attention from you and me."

"But if Les Grillons itself continues, why bother trying?"

He guided her around a patch of slime on the pavement. "The other option is to be complacent, and I can't be that."

"No," she murmured thoughtfully, "you can't."

At the toy shop, Bronwyn watched as Marco penned two letters. One to Reynard and one to Cluzet. She read them over his shoulder as he wrote.

Monsieur,
You have been betrayed by your own. They have
given you up to the Sûreté over the Maslin affair. I
write this to warn you. If you do not believe me,
send one of your men to police headquarters. They
will see the Sûreté ready to close in. Heed my
advice and flee Paris while you can.
—A friend

He paid a delivery boy to give the letters to second delivery boys, and those to a third set of runners. With that,
the machine was set into motion. The hope being that,
evading arrest and fearing betrayal, the Grillons bosses
would run, but not before transferring money into their
private Swiss accounts—which was, in truth, *her* account.

She and Marco had done everything they could. The
rest was out of their hands. There was no guarantee things
would work out the way they'd been arranged.

If it did . . . if the money was transferred to the new bank
account, and the arrests made, they'd return to England.
Return to their lives. Well, he'd go back to Nemesis. To
his work as an intelligence operative. Their plans were as
laid out as a cartographer's map. A new life beckoned beyond the horizon. *Here there be monsters.* The possibility
frightened and excited her. A fresh start. An existence that
had greater significance.

God, she hoped the plan worked. For so many reasons.
Including helping the widows of London. Giving back the
kindness she'd received. Perhaps even give more. Marco
had mentioned that one of their agents—who now lived
and worked for Nemesis in Manchester—was the daughter of missionaries. Since Bronwyn knew next to nothing
about how to run a charity, maybe this agent would give
her some advice. Because she was determined to make
this new way of being succeed. It had to.

Once the letters to Cluzet and Reynard went out, Marco tugged on his coat. "Come on."

She didn't question him as he led her out the door. And after taking a convoluted path through Paris, they finally arrived at what appeared to be a small, overgrown, abandoned zoo. Ivy snaked up the cages' bars, giving them the appearance of living enclosures. Weed-choked paths meandered between the cages, and the trees hung low and untrimmed. It had an eerie, neglected, and otherworldly beauty.

"Back during the siege of '70 and '71," Marco said, leading her along the paths, "Paris was being starved out by the Prussians. No food could enter the city. The *citoyens* were forced to eat horses and zoo animals to stay alive. Cleared out places like this private menagerie. The owners don't come here because they don't want to remember."

"I don't blame them." She shivered. "And I don't know why we're here."

"Look." He parted some of the ivy growing over the fence, revealing a view of Reynard's home. "A good place to keep watch over our targets. But it'll take some time for my letter to get here. We've got a few moments."

"Someone might find us."

"No one will."

She looked around and realized he was right. The former zoo was completely deserted. The menagerie itself wasn't very large, but it was large enough, and they spent a few minutes walking up and down its wild paths, studying what happened when a patch of city was left to return to nature. She read the plaques that proclaimed what animals used to live within the cages. Lions, monkeys, exotic birds.

Then she stood at the base of a tree as Marco climbed it, lightly scaling from branch to branch. He made a dark and sleek form, and she could well picture him in some jungle, hunting from above. His prey would never know they were being stalked until it was too late, and then it would be over.

What were the lives of those cats, in their secret moments away from human eyes? There was so much more than what was perceived.

She watched him climb higher, losing sight of him among the dense foliage. Strange that, for all her insistence that she didn't know him, he was more real to her than Hugh had ever been.

Poor Hugh. He'd been exactly the man he'd represented, fulfilled all the roles that society had given him. A respectable gentleman. A kind husband. And yet there wasn't much more to him than that. He liked his newspapers and having people over for dinner. Having seen his father and elder brother, she knew that, had Hugh lived, he would've kept his hair into old age. And when the time would've come for them to raise a family, he would have been attentive but reasonably distant from the children, just as his father had been with him.

He couldn't pick locks or forge documents or melt into shadows. He'd no calling higher than to simply be an example of Britain's elite.

Oh, it wasn't fair to compare one man with another. Unfair to both Hugh and to Marco.

Suddenly, Marco dropped down in front of her. Holding a very small white flower.

"One of the first of the season." He held it out to her.

She tucked the blossom into her hair. "Am I a nature spirit now?"

He stared at her a moment, something unspoken in his gaze. Then he turned abruptly away. Leaving her suspended.

"What—"

"The messenger just delivered my letter."

She peered through the ivy with him, watching the front of Reynard's home. A moment later, a man left the house, headed in the direction of the Sûreté. Many agonizing minutes passed. Would the Grillons boss get the proof he needed that he'd been betrayed, and prepare to fly from the city?

The Grillons runner returned. And left again, a short time later.

"He's heading to the bank," Marco said. "That's the only place Reynard would send him."

"This may just work, after all." She couldn't keep the optimism out of her voice, but a dark look from him quelled it.

"Assume nothing until the very last."

Just then, a police van pulled up in front of Reynard's house. So, the police were moving with special haste. The machine was in motion. But would she and Marco emerge unscathed, or be ground up in its cogs?

FIFTEEN

Marco led Bronwyn from the menagerie to watch as Journet and a dozen police officers converged on the place. The doors to the house were flung open, and several bodyguards lay on the ground, cradling their bloodied heads. The street turned into chaos, with dozens of passersby milling outside, craning their heads over the crowd to see the excitement. On this quiet, residential avenue, lined with expensive homes, something this scandalous drew a curious crowd.

Marco kept himself and Bronwyn on the far side of the street, with the throng providing a buffer between themselves and the action. He held Bronwyn's hand tightly.

His gaze moved constantly through the crowd, looking for any man with a hard, determined expression on his face, or whoever seemed to be preparing himself to move. Anyone who might be connected with Les Grillons.

A roar rose up from the crowd when a struggling Reynard was dragged out of his home, his hands manacled. The people surged forward. Despite being on the other side of the street, more pedestrians had gathered around them, so that when the rush toward Reynard's door came, it was as though a brutal wave pushed and rushed against them. Bronwyn's hand was torn from his.

Panic clutched him as he shoved forward, trying to reach her. But she wasn't there.

A litany of swearing ran through his head as he searched the crowd, elbowing people aside roughly, ignoring their curses. He couldn't even care about Reynard being led into a police van. All that mattered was finding Bronwyn.

A moment before he called her name, he spotted her. Being dragged down the street. By the same assassin who'd killed Devere.

She fought against him, but the man was too strong, and he held tight. Her screams of anger were swallowed by the sounds of the mob.

Rage and fear poured through him. With a roar, he shoved more people aside, until he broke free of the crowd. But Bronwyn and the killer had disappeared.

Furious, he searched all the streets and alleys nearby. He scanned for clues as to their whereabouts. But the damn assassin was too bloody good, and Marco found nothing. Not even a dropped hairpin.

Doubtless, word would somehow reach him that if he wanted to see Bronwyn alive again, he'd have to help Reynard escape. And even if Marco cooperated, Les Grillons wouldn't take kindly to the fact that he and Bronwyn had helped with the arrest of the two crime captains. She'd be killed anyway.

With another roar, Marco kicked apart a nearby crate. Terror unlike anything he'd ever known raced through him. And self-recrimination. Stupid bloody bastard, to lose her like this. There was no forgiveness, and he didn't want it.

He'd burn this whole damn city down to get her back.

* * *

Everything had happened in an instant. One moment, she stood beside Marco, her hand clasped securely in his, and the next, there had been an almighty shove from the crowd, and she'd found herself adrift in a sea of people, buffeted this way and that. She struggled to keep on her feet. Then someone had taken hold of her arm, and she'd naïvely believed it was a helpful citizen. But then she looked up into the face of her benefactor, and froze. She knew this man. His face had haunted her for weeks. Devere's killer.

She fought against him even as the crowd swelled around them. Frantically, she tried to twist from his hold, but it was strong as iron. When she tried to stomp on his foot or throw a knee into his groin, he evaded her strikes.

Furious, terrified, she looked for Marco, but the crowd was too thick to see him. Then suddenly, she and the Grillons assassin broke out of the throng into a patch of open street. She could just make out Marco searching for her, shouldering people aside like a battering ram, but before she could call out to him, the killer pulled her down an alley, then another, and another. She'd no idea how far they traveled, only that they were getting farther and farther from Marco.

"Easy, madame," the assassin said tonelessly. "Don't struggle and I won't hurt you."

A statement as believable as a crocodile's assurance that it wouldn't have you for dinner.

"Where the hell are you taking me?" she demanded, still fighting.

"Someplace safe." He didn't look at her as he kicked open a door to a tall, run-down building, one of many on this street, and tugged her up a dark set of stairs.

"Why do I doubt that?" she asked acidly.

"Because you're smart."

Again, not a very reassuring answer. As he pushed her in front of him, heading up the stairs, she tried to remember all the things Marco had taught her about defending herself. Those hours practicing in the freight car seemed to have slipped from her mind, and she battled to recall even the smallest maneuver.

Somewhere, at the top of these stairs, lay her ultimate fate. She had no idea what that fate was, or if she'd survive it.

Her body acted before her mind could. Instead of tugging against his hold on her arm, she leaned into it, causing his grip to loosen slightly. The moment it did, she twisted in his grasp, dug her fingers into his bicep, and pulled with all her might.

His balance was thrown off. Sensing the shift in his equilibrium, she freed her arm from his grip, then kicked him in his knee.

The assassin tumbled down, shouting, rolling down the stairs, until he made a heap at the bottom of the steps.

Two choices: either continue up the stairs to wherever they led and hope for an exit, or else go back down the steps, risking going past her kidnapper. But he seemed awfully still. Was he dead? She didn't care. She simply needed to get away. Going up meant she might corner herself.

She hurried down the stairs. Leaped over the prone form of the killer, and landed almost at the door. The bright light of freedom beckoned.

The world tilted, and the ground rushed up to meet her as the kidnapper grabbed her calf. She barely had enough time to throw out her hands to break her fall. Bronwyn thrashed as the kidnapper dragged her deeper inside the foyer. She clung to the door frame in a hope that if he didn't pull her inside, she'd somehow be safe. Or at least she could fight long enough for a passerby to see her plight and lend a hand. But no one came, and the assassin's grip was too strong. He hauled her inside, then flipped her onto her back.

As he loomed over her, his eyes cold and merciless, woman's most basic fear clawed at her. *God, please, no.* She struggled even harder, throwing punches, trying to bite whatever came near her.

But the kidnapper only looked irritated. "Didn't think you'd put up this much of a fight."

"I. Won't. Stop," she said between blows.

She remembered Marco's instructions to her in the freight car. Using her legs, she knocked him toward her. But before she could grab his ear, he drew back his hand and slapped her hard across the face. Everything faded, turned blurry. She had a vague sense of being thrown over her kidnapper's shoulder, and going back up the stairs. As her hazy mind struggled to focus, all she could think of was Marco, and whether or not he'd be the first to find her body.

Marco doubled back to Reynard's house just in time to see the police van pull away. On the van, there was a driver, a policeman beside him. Another rode on a running board mounted on the side of the wagon, guarding the prisoner within.

Wasting no time, Marco took off at a run, taking a parallel course to the van one block away. It would obviously be driving toward headquarters. And while the cumbersome vehicle would have to navigate traffic, he was on foot, and moved much faster and more nimbly.

All that mattered was reaching the van—and the man inside it.

Keeping an eye on the van as it rode the parallel avenue, Marco waited for the right opportunity to strike. As soon as the police wagon entered a narrow stretch of street, with a low wall running alongside it, he cut over and leaped up onto the wall.

The policemen on the wagon had no time to react as Marco jumped onto the roof of the moving vehicle. He stalked to the policeman sitting beside the driver, and kicked the man right in the face. Dazed, the policeman slumped, knocking into the driver.

Reaching down, Marco grabbed the driver by the lapels and hauled him onto the roof. The policeman struggled for a moment before Marco threw him off the roof and into the street.

With the driver's seat vacated, Marco dropped down into it. He snatched the ring of keys from the dazed passenger before shoving him, too, off the wagon and onto the pavement.

He pulled on the horses' reins, halting the van. Once the vehicle came to a stop, he was back onto the roof, striding toward the back of the wagon.

The third policeman had gotten down from the running board, and now guarded the back door, his truncheon drawn. Not knowing where the threat was coming from, he didn't see Marco leap down from the roof of the van, or protect himself from Marco's tackling him to the ground.

Marco and the policeman tussled over possession of the truncheon, but Marco twisted the other man's wrist, causing him to loosen his grip on the weapon. Marco immediately grabbed it, and knocked it against the copper's head—just enough to daze but not seriously injure the policeman. The guard slid to the pavement, eyes glazed.

Using the keys, Marco unlocked the back of the Black Maria. There, he found Reynard sitting on one of the benches. He was an angular, balding man, and his expensive suit had been torn in the scuffle with the police.

"Who the fuck are you?" he demanded when Marco opened the door.

"I'm the man who's going to get you out of here," he answered. He stepped into the wagon, and the crime boss stared at him in amazement.

"Do you work for me?" he asked, wide-eyed.

"I do now," Marco answered. He bent over the manacles and tried fitting different keys to the lock. "We've got the woman, and we're going to rendezvous at the spot."

"Which spot?"

Marco scowled at Reynard. "He said you'd know. Where you'd hide out until the heat cools and we can get you out of France. The safe spot in town."

"We've got them all over the city."

"What's the closest one you can rely on? And hurry, damn it, before more coppers come in here."

Reynard rubbed his forehead with the heel of his hand. "It's got to be 29 rue Vergnigaud. That's the safest place."

Marco hauled his fist back, then punched Reynard right in the face. The crime boss slumped to the floor of the van. Marco jumped down from the wagon and slammed the door shut. It was time to get his woman back.

Bronwyn's mind sharpened, and she felt her wobbly legs beneath her. She stood in the middle of an empty garret. Dormer windows lined one of the sloped walls. When she tried to turn, she couldn't. Her hands were bound around a single support post that stood in the middle of the attic. She tugged hard, but the rope around her wrists held fast.

Panic surged. She battled to keep it at bay. If she gave in to fear, she'd collapse in a terror-stricken heap, and that would serve her no purpose. The fear could come later, after she'd survived. *If* she survived.

The kidnapper stepped forward out of the shadows.

His face was carved from granite, his eyes equally emotionless.

"Tangle with Les Grillons," he said flatly, "this is what happens."

"They took *my* money," she shot back.

He only shrugged. "Can't fault us for doing our jobs. The fatal blunder was yours when you tried to strike against us. Nobody goes against Les Grillons and wins. Specially not two interlopers from England." He spat the final word.

She tugged again on her bindings. "We didn't *try* to strike," she fired back. "We *did* strike. We've hurt Les Grillons." She swallowed. "It will only get worse if you don't let me go."

"Tied up, and you threaten *me*. If your man comes for you . . ." He drew a wicked-looking knife from a sheath as he ambled toward her. "Look around. This is the last place you and he'll ever see."

Enraged, afraid, Bronwyn tried to kick him—wherever her foot could land. But he easily evaded her strike.

"Kicked me once, already," he drawled. "I've lost my taste for it."

She was about to snap a retort, but the sound of breaking glass interrupted her. She had a quick impression of a man's dark figure crashing feet first through one of the dormer windows, then landing with a nimble roll before coming to his feet.

Marco. Her heart seized.

He glanced at her quickly, assessing. A look of pure, cold rage was on his face.

From his boot he drew out a thin, mean-looking blade. "You've never made a bigger mistake, *ami,*" Marco snarled, turning to the assassin.

The killer brandished his own knife, and the two men

circled each other. "My only fault was letting you live the first time we met. Won't make that error again."

"No, you won't."

The kidnapper lunged, and Marco sidestepped the strike. He spun around and slashed with his weapon, catching the other man across the arm. Though the cut drew blood, the assassin didn't slow as he feinted, causing Marco to block a hit that didn't come. Instead, the kidnapper danced to one side, and swung his blade, cutting Marco along the cheek.

Marco didn't bother to wipe the blood dripping from his face. He sliced at the kidnapper, causing the man to edge backward—toward Bronwyn.

She'd been watching the fight with terror, helpless to do anything. But when the assassin came close enough, she kicked again, this time catching him in the back of the knee.

"There's another taste of my boot," she snapped.

The man winced from her strike. Marco leaped. He plunged his blade up and between the kidnapper's ribs. The assassin screamed, falling to his knees and dropping his own knife. Marco kicked it aside before drawing his blade out, and stabbing into the killer's chest.

Bronwyn looked on as her would-be murderer crumpled to the dusty floor, Marco's knife angling up from his heart. The assassin twitched as his lifeblood flowed onto the floorboards. Then he was still, his eyes open.

Instantly, Marco was in front of her, using the claw-shaped blade from his lapel to slice through the ropes binding her to the post.

The moment her hands were free, she wrapped her arms around him, at last letting the tremors take her. But he soothed her, whispering words in Italian, words she couldn't understand but knew their meaning.

Thank God. Thank God you're safe. But whether he said these words or she thought them, she couldn't tell. The only thing she knew was that they were both alive, and the man who'd intended to kill them both was dead. She glanced over at the corpse, and shuddered.

"Don't look at that," he commanded gently.

"I'll never stop seeing it."

"That means you survived. *Fragola mia.*" He stroked over her hair, carefully over her face, as if assuring himself that she had, indeed, made it through alive. "Did he hurt you?"

"Just the once. How did you—"

"I'll tell you everything. Later. Right now, let's get ourselves to safety."

She had no issue with that. Hand in hand, they hurried from the garret, leaving behind the body of the killer. After rushing down several flights of stairs—including the one where she'd fought with the assassin—they emerged out onto the street. It stunned her that the sun was still up, and that the day was still bright, the sky a glowing blue. Spring was nearing full bloom.

It took time to find a hotel, but they did, well away from both Reynard's and Cluzet's homes. Once in their room, she'd insisted on a long bath, as if she could wash away the lingering vestiges of fear like coal dust. After she'd finished her bath, Marco explained everything that had happened since her abduction—including his outrageous gambit with Reynard.

The arrests had created chaos for Les Grillons, and the streets were mercifully free of their spies and thugs.

"I can't believe you attacked those policemen," she said, curled up on the sofa and wrapped in a robe that Marco had mysteriously procured.

He'd also bathed and wore a silk dressing gown, though where the garment had come from, either, she'd no idea. Just another of the marvels he could perform effortlessly. *Sprezzatura.*

"I'd beat dozens of policemen if it meant keeping you safe," he said.

"How bloodthirsty," she said, "and . . . sweet."

He only shrugged.

"What's to become of Reynard?" she asked.

"He'll stand trial, but I heard from Journet and he says the case is strong, so it's a deadlock that he'll go to prison. Cluzet, though, managed to get away before the Sûreté could collar him."

She sat up, alarmed. "That means we're still in danger."

"Cluzet's on the run, without funds and powerless. It won't be long before Journet catches him. Either that, or Les Grillons will, and they won't look kindly on him trying to flee with their money."

"The threat is gone," she murmured to herself. She'd been living with it for so long that no sense of relief came at the news. Hopefully, in time, she'd feel some peace.

"I've heard from Simon," Marco continued. "The money transfers went through. Amounts worth ten thousand pounds were deposited in your account."

It took her a moment to understand what he was saying. "I'm . . . rich?"

"Far wealthier than you were before." He sat beside her. "How do you feel?"

"Numb." Literally. Her fingers and toes felt frozen, and she could barely sense the rest of her body. Not even the breath moving in and out of her lungs. "I thought I'd feel happy but . . . I can't feel anything. It's not that I'm not grateful," she added quickly. "I am. But this is what I'd wanted for so long, and now it's here, and I just feel like I'm in someone else's body, another person's life."

He nodded. "It took almost a month for the children we rescued from forced labor to smile again. Half of them believed they'd be returned to the workhouse. It takes time to understand that the ordeal is finished."

She sat back, frowning. "So it's over."

A long pause. Then, "It is."

"What happens now?"

He crossed his arms over his chest. "That's up to you. Were you serious about opening that home for widows?"

Was she? "It wouldn't be difficult to slip back into my old life," she murmured, mostly to herself. "Long as I had money, nobody would really care where it came from or what had happened to me. But . . . *I'd* care. And I can't . . . I can't return to that world. Not after everything I've seen. Everything I've done. It would all feel so . . . hollow. Oppressive."

She picked at the hem of her robe. "I've seen beyond the veil. Not just of my widowhood, but . . . everything. And if Nemesis can do so much to help others . . . opening a place for widows to take shelter is the least I can do." She glanced at him. "Is it foolish of me to think I might be able to make a difference?"

"Not foolish. Brave. And beautiful." He leaned forward and kissed her, tenderly.

She recognized the kiss for what it was. A kiss of farewell.

"We won't see each other again, will we?" she asked.

His expression darkened. "Doubtful."

They'd made plans for even a brief affair, but that wasn't to happen. She knew it was coming, yet that didn't lessen the pain. God, how was she to get through tomorrow and the day after and the next day and all the days to come without him? In the span of a few weeks, he'd become essential to her. She loved him. Yet now they'd reached the end of their time together. She'd have her work, and he had his. Nemesis. Spying. Hardly room for her in his life. And she'd never make him choose.

Still . . . "If you ever get a moment of freedom, perhaps you could come and see me."

But he shook his head. "Can't."

"I thought you said—"

The look on his face was raw, open. "I can't see you. I can't."

It felt like a slap in the face. Perhaps he was tired of her. Or perhaps he felt too much. Either way, it meant this was good-bye.

SIXTEEN

London. Three months later.

There was always a commotion. Crying children. Women squabbling over possessions. It was a struggle to get enough food, especially when there were always more and more people coming to the Home for Widows and Children. They were understaffed—especially for teachers—and at least three slept to a bed. But the home was clean and safe.

Bronwyn collapsed into bed exhausted every night, yet she rose each morning ready to meet the challenges of the day. However meager it might be, she was making a difference.

Right now, she led a roomful of children through a music lesson, some of them with tiny violins, others with wooden recorders, and whatever instruments they'd been able to buy cheaply from shops around the city. In theory, the children were performing a simple Brahms lullaby, but the unholy noise they made would never permit anyone to sleep.

Still, she praised them. "Excellent, Mary Ellen," she

said to one little girl knocking against a triangle. "Good bow work, Daniel."

The children beamed back at her. And for all her aching head, she smiled back.

After this, she'd have to go out and solicit more donations from women she once considered part of her social circle. She still wore her weeds for this purpose, lest she engender scandal. Whenever she'd go to her old friends, they'd insist she was mad for trying to actually run a home for widows on her own, rather than simply throwing money at missionaries and letting them do the work. She never answered them, not wanting to entrust this work to anyone but herself. She knew her strengths now.

At least her former friends felt enough guilt to keep the donations coming.

Yes, her days and even her nights were extremely busy. And thank God for that, because if she stopped for even a moment, memories of *him* would flood in. They left her heartbroken and melancholy. She'd thought that, over time, the pain would diminish, like a healing wound.

But it didn't. In fact, each day, it seemed to grow worse. Only the needs of the home kept her moving forward.

The music lesson finally concluded, and the children ran from the classroom, eager to go out to the yard and play. As they left, their mothers filed in, along with one of the teachers, who instructed the widows on needlework. It wouldn't be much, but it would provide the women with some means of earning a living. Some degree of freedom and security. Things that had been missing from their lives.

Bronwyn walked toward the small room that served as her office. Stacks of papers were everywhere, evidence of all her projects and investments. Knowing that she couldn't rely on the money recovered from Les

Grillons forever, and also knowing that she couldn't count on the largesse of society ladies, she'd made a few investments in sundry business ventures. They yielded a steady, though not lavish, profit. All the more to go into the home.

She took a moment to sigh and stretch her back. Soon, she'd have to put on her cloak and bonnet and venture forth to Kensington and Mayfair. But for now, she'd allow herself a brief respite.

Periodically, women showed up, having been sent by Nemesis. Bronwyn had even spoken with Harriet a few times. But, true to his word, there'd been no sign of Marco.

She supposed it was for the best. As he'd said, seeing him again would only hurt too much. So she considered it a painful blessing that he stayed away.

Though her heart ached with every thought of him. And she always thought of him.

A knock sounded on her door. "Mrs. Parrish?"

It was Vivienne, one of the young women who helped her run the home. She looked anxious.

"Sorry to disturb you, Mrs. Parrish," she continued. "But do you remember that woman we took in last week, Anna Matthews?"

The poor woman had been widowed a year earlier when her navvy husband had died when a trench collapsed on him. Since then, she'd been living with her brother, who'd been beating her.

"Is it the brother?" Bronwyn asked.

Vivienne nodded. "He demands to see her."

Bronwyn steeled herself. This wasn't going to be pleasant. With Vivienne trailing after her, she first went to Anna, cowering in the women's dormitory.

"I don't have to go with him, do I?" she asked, shaking with terror.

Rage poured through Bronwyn at the fear that louse of a brother had implanted in Anna. "Of course you don't," Bronwyn assured her. She patted the frightened woman on the shoulder. "I'll send him on his way, and make sure he never bothers you again."

"Thank you, Mrs. Parrish."

Finding Anna's brother wasn't hard to do. He stood in the entrance lobby, shouting and waving his fists. Several of the home's employees fought to hold him back. When he spotted Bronwyn, he looked at her with gin-bleary eyes that swam with hate.

"You the bitch that won't let me see my own flesh and blood?" he demanded.

"That's right," she answered.

"Let me take her home, or by God I'll—"

"Hit me, too? I wouldn't advise that."

"What you going to do? Call the damn coppers? They can't do nothing."

"They might not," she replied, "but I happen to be rather well connected to a certain section of London's East End populace. Ruthless individuals who are very effective at using their fists, too." She took a step toward the red-faced bully. "Just a word from me, or from Anna, and my East End friends will make certain you can never use your hands to hurt anyone ever again."

The brother's face went ashen.

"I think you understand me," Bronwyn continued levelly.

Anna's brother shook off the employees still clustered around him. "Who needs the whore?" he spat. "Tell her I don't ever want to see her again." With that, he trundled out the door, disappearing into the gray afternoon fog.

As soon as he was gone, Bronwyn pressed a shaking hand to her stomach. She barely heard the women around her congratulate her on her bravery.

She glanced through the open front door. A figure stood out in the street, poised to come to her aid, if she needed it.

Marco.

She stared at him for a long moment, and he stared back. Neither moved. But she felt a vicious pounding in her chest. Her heart—as if it wanted to run to him.

She turned and hurried to her office. But he followed her.

Bronwyn took a moment. Steeling herself before turning around. Yet it didn't ease the sweet, agonizing shock of seeing him again.

He appeared just as dangerous as ever, standing in her doorway, his hat in his hand. He looked a little thinner, his eyes set a little deeper, but other than that, he was the same. Sharp, handsome, and opaque.

Love flooded her, bright and wondrous and painful.

"This . . ." She swallowed hard. "This is a surprise." It took all her strength not to cross the room, go to him.

"For me, too."

His voice stroked every sense.

She frowned. "Why—"

He glanced away, his gaze alighting on small details like the painting of a flower one of the children had made for her, a half-finished embroidered pillow crafted by a widow, a stack of letters from different women who'd moved on to new lives.

"I couldn't stay away," he said, almost grudgingly. He continued to look around. "This place is doing well."

"We manage."

"And you?" He finally looked at her, and she saw now the fatigue beneath his eyes, the drawn look around his mouth. He wasn't taking care of himself. She fought to keep from leading him to their refectory and giving him a bowl of nourishing soup.

"I manage, too." But something inside her wouldn't allow her any cowardice, so she added, "Barely."

His gaze sharpened. "Do you need more money? We can get it. Are you ill? I know a doctor—"

She shook her head. Decided to be completely open. "None of that. I barely sleep. Can't eat." Her clothes hung on her, and she kept having to take them in. "But I'm not ill. Overworked, perhaps, but not sick."

"Then what—"

"You know the reason. So if you're here for a tour, I can get one of the other women to take you. Otherwise, you'd better go."

He stepped forward, stopped. "I don't want to go."

"*I* want you to."

He gazed at her. The moment stretched out with agonizing sweetness. How could she keep from touching him? Yet she had to. Or else give in to the morass of emotion engulfing her.

Instead of leaving, he reached into his coat and produced a folded letter. Tossed it lightly onto her desk. "Go on," he said softly. "Read it."

With shaking hands, she picked up the letter and did as he directed. She read it over several times. "This is . . . the resignation of Marco Galileo Black, member of the Bureau of Profit and Loss." She looked up at him. "I never knew your full name."

"My mother had astronomical ambitions," he answered.

She held up the letter. "And this means . . . ?"

"It means . . ." He took more steps toward her, coming around the desk and setting his hat upon it. "As of yesterday, I'm a pensioner. I no longer work for the British government."

She struggled to understand, even as her mind and heart shouted the truth. "You've been with them for a long time."

"Over fifteen years."

She'd been at boarding school, learning French and dancing, when he'd been roaming the globe, involved in shadowy espionage. How unalike they were. And yet, how well he knew her. Better than anyone else. And she'd wager few understood him the way she did.

"You'll miss it." She busied herself with straightening papers on her desk, though she was certain he'd recognize it for the diversionary tactic it was.

"Not especially. Had my go at the Great Game. I'm ready to stop playing. My interest lies elsewhere."

"Nemesis," she said.

"That won't ever cease, but I've spoken to Simon and Lazarus and the others. We agreed. Well, I decided. They had to agree. From now on, I'll be taking a more advisory role."

"They need you," she protested.

He gave his Italian shrug. "They do, and I'll be close. But we've got new agents coming up in the ranks." He narrowed the distance between him and her.

And she saw it. His heart was in his eyes. It ached. For her.

"Bronwyn," he said, his voice hoarse. "*Fragola mia.* I didn't think . . . I thought that I had nothing in me but my work for Nemesis and Intelligence. But then . . . but then . . . I walked into an empty house, and I met this woman. A woman who grew. Who learned how powerful she truly was. And she showed me . . . I was more than just a spy. More than an operative. I was . . . a man."

She could only stare at him, while her heart beat loudly in her ears and her breath came in fast gulps.

"She taught me something, too," he continued, words rough. "That I was capable of more than I knew. That I could . . . I could love." He looked at her directly, exposed and completely revealed. No masks. No armor.

It was the bravest thing she'd ever witnessed.

"I love you, Bronwyn," he said. "And, if you want to be my lover, be my lover. If you want to be my wife . . ." He finally glanced away, but not before she saw the need in his eyes.

For a moment, she couldn't speak. Could hardly catch her breath. If it weren't for the voices of shouting children down the hallway, and the bang of soup pots in the kitchen, she'd think herself in some opiate's throes.

Finally, she was able to find her voice. "I'm not supposed to wed yet. That's what the rules of mourning say."

A second passed, and then it dawned on him what she was saying. "I've lain in wait for days, completely still, as I watched the front of a secret Russian munitions installment. I'm very good at waiting."

She stepped close. Slowly, she brought her arms up. Then looped them around his neck. She felt a wild kind of joy, and fear at the leap she was about to take. But mostly a flood of happiness in which she'd readily drown. "I don't care if I'm being improper and wicked," she whispered. "I love you, Marco. I'll marry you, fast as you can get a license."

He held her close, an expression of profound gratitude crossing his angular face. "Fortunately, I have some connections. We could be wed by tomorrow. If that's what you want."

"I want."

They kissed, no hesitation, holding back nothing. She felt how fully he was with her, how complete he was, and she felt that same completeness in herself.

"What's Nemesis without you?" she asked, when they surfaced for air.

"A hydra. Always more of us to step in. But my head's not cut off. I won't be out in the field as much, yet that's the thing about this damned world—there's always more work to be done."

"However I can," she said, "I'll help."

"Mi amore," he said, brushing his lips over hers, "you already do. If you can teach an old spy how to love, you're capable of anything."

EPILOGUE

Two weeks later.

For all Marco's promises that the wedding could be held within a day, there were delays. Harriet insisted on an actual wedding breakfast. Via telegram, Simon demanded that Marco wait until he and Alyce could return from the Continent so he could serve as best man.

And, of course, his mother would have killed him if she hadn't been in attendance.

So on a blustery morning, Marco and Bronwyn were married. The wedding was small, held in a little London church near the widows' home. It had been an odd mix of guests—his family, Nemesis agents, a few of Marco's colleagues from Intelligence, and Bronwyn's sister—but that hadn't impeded anyone's happiness.

Least of all Marco and Bronwyn's. Joy made her glow, and she'd smiled her way through the whole ceremony. She'd even continued to smile as he'd kissed her, sealing their vows. And damn him if he didn't smile the whole time, too.

"Barely recognized you without that ice-up-your-arse look on your face," Lazarus had said.

Marco had responded by covertly flashing Lazarus one of his favorite rude hand gestures.

The women and volunteers at the home had insisted on hosting the wedding breakfast, and now they stood in the refectory, the food-laden tables all pushed to the sides, as happy chaos reigned in the echoing room—children, family, women, even a handful of musicians.

Bronwyn stood beside Marco's mother, soaking up her fussing and attention. His sisters, too, did their share of fluttering around Bronwyn.

From across the refectory, Marco watched them together. Warmth swept through him. It took him a few moments to understand fully what caused the feeling. There was his bride, looking so joyous and beautiful, being welcomed so thoroughly into a new family.

"Addictive, isn't it?" Simon asked at Marco's shoulder. He glanced over at Alyce, talking with Harriet, Desmond, Eva, and Jack. The former convict loomed hugely over the others, but with his arm draped comfortably around his wife's waist, his menace dimmed. Somewhat. "Seeing that look on their faces."

"How the hell do you stand it?" Marco wondered. "This feeling that you're nothing without them?"

"I stand it because it's the truth. If I didn't have Alyce . . ." A bleak expression crossed Simon's face. "I can't even think of it. And I see how you look at your new wife. There's no hope for you, my friend."

"I don't want hope. I just want to make sure she's safe." Bronwyn hadn't officially joined Nemesis yet, but she continued to assist them, taking in more women and children as new cases brought in those needing help. And there were always more needing help.

"With you as her protector and helpmeet," Simon noted dryly, "I doubt anything's going to happen to her."

Marco had vowed from the beginning that he'd guard

her from harm. And while she knew far more about defending herself now, he'd never lose his sense of protectiveness. This was a perilous world, and he was a ruthless man. Especially when it came to safeguarding the woman he loved.

She caught his gaze, and managed to disengage herself from his fawning family. As she crossed the refectory, Simon said in a low voice, "My well-honed senses tell me that I'm no longer needed. And it's been over ten minutes since I've stood close to *my* wife."

Marco barely noticed his friend's departure. All he saw was Bronwyn, gliding toward him in her pearl-gray lace gown.

"You're tolerating my family well," he said when she finally stood before him.

"I'm glad of their attentions," she confessed. "And they'd despaired of you ever taking a wife. They can't be blamed for their enthusiasm."

"So long as that *enthusiasm* doesn't drive you away," he growled.

"As if a doting mama could ever keep me from you," she said softly. "As if *anything* could keep me away. *Mi amore.*"

There it was again, that expansive, almost painful pleasure. But he'd rather live with it than without. How damn bleak his life had been before Bronwyn. How bloody foolish he'd been to think there was any future devoid of her.

He drew her into his embrace, ignoring the knowing smiles from the crowd. "I'm a better man with you."

She looped her arms around his neck, and shook her head. "Not better. You and I, we're like lock picks. Alone, we're capable. Together—nothing stands in our way."

He chuckled. "Thievery metaphors? Now I *know* I've corrupted you."

Her lips pursed. "The world's corrupt. But we can work to change that."

"Tomorrow," he said. "Today is just for us."

"Every day is ours." She looked wonderfully fierce. "Because we're Nemesis, damn it, and we get exactly what we want. It'll take some ruddy hard work, though."

"But it's all worth it," he said. Then, in full view of his friends, his family, and Nemesis, he kissed his bride. He loved her so bloody much. There was no disguising it. For the first time in his life, he was unafraid to show everyone who he truly was. Because of her.

Don't miss the first two novels in this
breathtaking new series by Zoë Archer

SWEET REVENGE
DANGEROUS SEDUCTION

Available from St. Martin's Paperbacks

…and don't miss Zoë Archer's e-novella

WINTER'S HEAT

www.stmartins.com